THE BLACK RECKONING

www.randomhousechildrens.co.uk

Also by
JOHN STEPHENS

THE EMERALD ATLAS
THE FIRE CHRONICLE

THE BOOKS OF BEGINNING
JOHN STEPHENS

CORGI BOOKS

THE BLACK RECKONING

A CORGI BOOK 978 0 552 56484 7

Published in Great Britain by Corgi Books,
an imprint of Random House Children's Publishers UK
A Penguin Random House Company

Penguin
Random House
UK

This edition published 2015

1 3 5 7 9 10 8 6 4 2

Penguin Random House is committed to a sustainable future for
our business, our readers and our planet. This book is made from
Forest Stewardship Council® certified paper.

MIX
Paper from
responsible sources
FSC® C018179

Set in Parango

Corgi Books are published by Random House Children's Publishers UK
61–63 Uxbridge Road, London W5 5SA

www.**randomhousechildrens**.co.uk
www.**totallyrandombooks**.co.uk
www.**randomhouse**.co.uk

Addresses for companies within The Random House Group Limited can be found at:
www.randomhouse.co.uk/offices.htm

THE RANDOM HOUSE GROUP Limited Reg. No. 954009

A CIP catalogue record for this book is available from the British Library.

Printed and bound by CPI Group (UK) Ltd, Croydon, CR0 4YY

For my sisters

CONTENTS

Emma pounded against the giant man's back. She twisted about to claw at his face and eyes. She kicked and thrashed. It did no good. Rourke had slung her over his shoulder, pinning her in place, and was walking with long, sure strides toward the flaming portal in the center of the clearing.

"Emma!"

"Emma!"

Two voices called to her out of the darkness. Emma craned her neck to try and see into the wall of trees that ringed the clearing. The first voice belonged to Michael, her brother. But the second—she had first heard it a few moments earlier, just before Rourke had dropped the glamour that had disguised him as Gabriel—the second voice belonged to Kate, her sister, whom she had thought was lost forever—

"Kate! I'm here! Kate!"

Emma twisted around to look past Rourke, to see how close they were to the portal, how much time she had. . . .

The portal was a high wooden arch wreathed in fire, and they were close enough that Emma could feel the heat from the blaze. Three more steps, and it would be too late. Just then a figure appeared, stepping forward through the flames. It was a boy; he looked to be Kate's age, or perhaps a little older. He wore a dark cloak, and his face was hidden by the shadow of the hood. All she could make out was a pair of brilliant green eyes.

Then Emma saw the boy make a gesture with his hand. . . .

CHAPTER ONE
Captive

"Let me out! Let me out!"

Emma's throat was ragged from shouting; her hands throbbed from pounding her fists against the metal door.

"Let me out!"

She had woken with a jolt several hours earlier—covered in sweat, Kate's name upon her lips—to find herself alone in a strange room. She didn't question the fact that it was no longer night, that she was no longer in the clearing. She didn't even wonder where she now was. None of that mattered. She'd been abducted, she was a prisoner, she had to escape. It was that simple.

"Let me out!"

The first thing she'd done—after trying the door and confirming that it was indeed locked—had been to inspect her cell to see if it offered any obvious means of escape. It hadn't. The walls, floor, and ceiling were made from large blocks of black stone. The three small windows, too high up for Emma to reach, showed nothing but blue sky. Besides that, there was the bed on which she'd woken—really just a mattress and a few blankets—and some food: a plate of flatbread, bowls of yogurt and yellow-brown hummus, some burned, unidentifiable meat, a clay jug of water. The food and water Emma had hurled out a window in a fit of pride and anger, an act she was now regretting as she was both hungry and very, very thirsty.

"Let—me—out!"

Emma leaned, exhausted, against the door. She felt the urge to sink to the floor, put her face in her hands, and sob. But then she thought of Kate, her older sister, and of hearing Kate's voice as Rourke had carried her across the clearing. Their sister had returned from the past only to die right in front of them. And Michael, though he was Keeper of the Book of Life, had been unable to bring her back (leading Emma to question what, then, was the point in having something called the Book of Life). But she had heard Kate's voice! That meant Michael must've succeeded! Kate was alive! And knowing Kate was out there somewhere meant there was no way, like zero-point-zero-zero-zero-zero percent chance, that Emma was just going to sit down and cry.

"LET—ME—OUT!"

Her forehead was still pressed against the cold metal of the door, and she was screaming directly into it, feeling the vibrations as she struck the door with her fists.

"LET—ME—"

Emma stopped; she held her breath. The whole time she'd been hitting the door and screaming, she'd been met with total, thundering silence. But now she heard something, footsteps. They

4

were faint and somewhere far below her, but they were growing louder. Emma backed away from the door and looked about for a weapon, cursing herself once again for throwing the clay jug out the window.

The footsteps grew even louder, a heavy, rhythmic *thud—thud—thud*. Emma decided that when the door opened, she would rush past whoever it was. Wasn't Michael always saying something about the element of surprise? If only her big toe didn't hurt so bad. She was pretty sure she'd broken it kicking the stupid door. The footsteps had stopped just outside her room, and there was the metallic rasp of a bolt being slid back. Emma tensed and got ready to spring.

Then the door opened, Rourke ducked inside, and all Emma's plans of escape vanished. The giant man filled the doorway; a fly couldn't have squeezed past.

"My, my. Aren't you making quite the racket."

He was wearing a long black coat that was lined with fur and had a high fur collar. He had on black boots that came nearly to his knees. He was smiling, showing miles of large white teeth, and his skin was smooth and unscarred, the burns the volcano had left on his face, which Emma had seen when he'd seized her in the clearing, now completely healed.

Emma felt the stone wall pressing against her back. She forced herself to look up and meet Rourke's gaze.

She said, "Gabriel's gonna kill you."

The giant laughed. Really laughed, throwing back his head like people did in movies, the sound booming off the ceiling.

"And a very good morning to you too, young lady."

"Where am I? How long have I been here?"

With Rourke standing before her, and the possibility of escape now essentially nil, Emma wanted the answers she hadn't cared about before.

"Oh, just since last night. And as to your location: you're at the far end of the world, and everything around you is shrouded in enchantments. Your friends could pass by and never know. You will not be rescued."

"Ha! Your stupid spells aren't gonna stop Dr. Pym. He'll just do *that*"—Emma snapped her fingers—"and this whole place will fall apart."

Rourke smiled at her, and Emma recognized it as the smile adults give children when they aren't taking them seriously. Had Rourke's face been anywhere remotely within reach, Emma would've punched it.

"I think, lass, that you're overestimating your wizard and underestimating my master."

"What're you talking about? The stupid Dire Magnus is dead. Dr. Pym told us."

Another of those annoying smiles. He was really asking for it.

"Was dead, child. But no more. My master is returned. You should know. You saw him yourself."

"No, I didn't—"

Emma fell silent. An image had come to her from the night before, that of the green-eyed boy stepping from the flames. And with the memory, a shadow seemed to fall over her. She struggled to throw it off, told herself it was impossible, that boy couldn't be the Dire Magnus!

Rourke said, "So you remember."

There was a tone of triumph in the Irishman's voice. But if he was expecting this small, skinny, exhausted girl to cave right then and there, to cry and crumple and give up, he was deeply mistaken. Before all other things, Emma was a fighter. She had grown up fighting, year after year, orphanage after orphanage, fighting for small things and big things, for a towel without holes, a mattress without fleas, fighting boys who were picking on Michael, fighting girls who were picking on Michael, and she knew a bully when she saw one.

She stuck out her chin and balled her fists as if she might fight him then and there.

"You're lying. He's dead."

"No, child. The Dire Magnus lives. And it is thanks to your brother."

Despite her fury, Emma sensed that Rourke was telling the truth. But it made no sense. Why would Michael have done that? Then, in a flash, she realized what must've happened: that was how Michael had brought Kate back. That was the price he'd paid. And knowing what Michael had taken on himself so that Kate might live, the blame that others would heap upon him for un-leashing the Dire Magnus on the world, Emma felt a surge of love for her brother, and it gave her strength. She stood up just a little bit straighter.

"So why isn't your stupid master here, then? Is he afraid?"

Rourke stared at her, then said, as if having made a decision, "Come with me."

He turned and strode out the door, leaving it open behind him. Emma stood there defiantly, not wanting to do anything that Rourke suggested. Then she realized that she wasn't going to ac-complish much by staying in her cell, and she hurried after him.

Directly outside her door was a staircase curving downward, and she could hear Rourke's footsteps below her, moving away. So she was in a tower. She had begun to suspect as much. She started down, and on every floor she passed an iron door similar to her own. She also passed windows at her eye level, and as she corkscrewed around the tower, she saw a sea of jagged, snowcapped mountains stretching away on all sides.

Where was she?

The staircase bottomed out in a hallway made of the same rough black rock as the tower, and Rourke turned to the right without bothering to wait. Emma, sensing an opportunity, turned left, only to find her way blocked by a pair of black-garbed, yellow-eyed *morum cadi*. Whether Rourke had placed them there or not, the creatures appeared to have been waiting for her. They stared at her, their decaying reek filling the hall, and Emma felt a terrible, shameful fear building in her chest.

"Are you coming?" Rourke's voice echoed down the hallway, mocking. "Or do you need me to hold your hand?"

Cursing herself for being weak, Emma ran after the man, biting her lip to keep from crying. She promised herself that she would be there to cheer and throw flowers when Gabriel finally chopped off Rourke's stupid, bald head.

He was waiting for her at a doorway to the outside.

"I know what you want," she said when she had come up to him. "You want me to help you find the last book. Kate's got the *Atlas*, Michael's got the *Chronicle* or whatever. I know the last one's mine."

She wasn't sure why she'd said this except that she hated having been scared by a single pair of Screechers—she'd seen hundreds before; these had just surprised her—and moreover, she wanted to prove to Rourke that she wasn't just some kid; she knew things.

Rourke looked down at her, the dome of his head outlined by a perfectly blue sky.

"And do you know what the last book is?"

"Yes."

Rourke stood there, saying nothing. An icy wind blew into the hall, but Emma stayed as she was, arms at her side. She would have died before admitting she was cold.

"It's the Book of Death. But I'm not going to help you find it. You can just forget about that."

"I will try to master my disappointment. But at least call the book by its proper name. Call it the *Reckoning*. And you're wrong about another thing: you will be finding it for us. Though not just now. The Dire Magnus has more immediate plans. You asked where he was. Come."

He headed outside and, again angry at herself for obeying, Emma followed.

They walked along the top of a stone rampart that outlined a large square courtyard extending off one side—presumably the front—of the fortress. Glancing back, Emma saw the fortress rising up black and massive, the tower where she'd been held pointing like a crooked finger at the sky. Below her, the courtyard was filled with thirty or forty Imps and *morum cadi*; nothing Dr. Pym and Gabriel couldn't handle.

But even so, Emma could feel her confidence draining away.

The fortress was built atop a rocky spire that rose up in a valley surrounded on all sides by mountains, and from the rampart walls, she could see for miles. Gabriel and the others would first have to find her, then cross all those mountains, and even then, there'd still be no approaching the fortress unseen.

Rourke had stopped where the wall turned, and he motioned her forward. She steeled herself to show no fear.

"Forty years ago," the giant man said, "Pym and others in the magical world attacked my master. They thought they bested him. Destroyed him. But he has power his enemies do not comprehend. As they will learn soon enough."

He gestured for her to look to the valley floor, and she placed her hands on the rough stone wall and leaned forward.

For a moment, she didn't understand what she was seeing. Then, despite all her promises to herself about not showing fear, she gasped. For the valley floor, which she had thought was covered in a dark forest, was alive with movement. And as her sense of what she was seeing changed, she realized she was hearing sounds, faint and far-off, of banging and pounding and shouting, of a deep, rhythmic drumbeat, and there were fires burning all over the valley, black smoke rising into the sky; what Emma had at first taken to be trees were not trees at all but figures, Imps and Screechers and who knew what else, thousands upon thousands of them.

She was looking at an army.

"The Dire Magnus," Rourke said, and his voice trembled with pure, animal excitement, "is going to war."

CHAPTER TWO
The Archipelago

"Quickly, children! There is little time."

Kate and Michael hurried with the wizard through the narrow, twisting streets. The day, which had been warm and sunny minutes before, was now blackened by clouds, and a cold wind howled through the alleys, sending small tornadoes of dust spiraling upward.

"Where're we going?" Michael demanded. He was panting, his feet pounding the cobblestones, the pouch of his bag—the one that the elf princess Wilamena had given him to replace the one he'd lost in the volcano, and that now carried the red-leather-bound *Chronicle*—slapping against his hip.

"The footbridge we crossed last night," Dr. Pym said. "My friend is creating a portal."

"A portal to where?" Kate asked.

"Somewhere safe," the wizard replied, and then added, in a voice he perhaps thought was too low to be heard, "I hope."

"But Emma—"

"We've spread the word. It is all we can do. Now hurry."

The town they were running through was a collection of gabled houses and shops nestled against the river Danube, and some miles west of Vienna. A part of the magical world, the town did not appear on any map or atlas; it was hidden away, invisible to all save a select few. Kate reckoned it was the fourteenth or fifteenth (she had lost exact count) such place that she and Michael and the wizard had visited in the three days since Emma had been abducted and they themselves had fled from the elfish forest at the bottom of the world. There'd been the village outside Mexico City where they'd talked to three blind sorcerers who'd known every word the children would utter before they spoke, there'd been the smoke-filled restaurant in Moscow where dwarves in high black boots and long, cassock-style shirts had carried around silver trays laden with steaming pots of coffee, the floating village in the South China Sea where they'd seen glowing, ghostly shapes—water spirits, the wizard had said—drifting wispily over the nighttime surface of the water, the snow-covered village in the Andes where the thin air had squeezed their lungs, the fishing outpost in Nova Scotia—it had rained and smelled like fish—the wizarding school on the sun-hammered African plain where boys and girls younger than Michael, their heads shaved and wearing bright yellow robes, had run around laughing and playing a game that involved throwing balls of blue-green fire back and forth.

And everywhere they went, they delivered the same message: the Dire Magnus has returned, you must beware.

And everywhere, they asked the same questions: Have you seen our sister? Have you seen our parents?

And everywhere, they received the same answers: No. No.

Then, the day before—or was it the same day? It was so hard to keep track when you leapfrogged across the globe and noon became deepest night in the blink of an eye—they had been in a small town on the Australian coast where waves broke in long, blue-white crescents onto a golden beach and the inhabitants seemed equally devoted to magic and surfing; they'd come to see a friend of Dr. Pym's, a lean, sun-wrinkled wizard who went everywhere barefoot and called Michael "little mate," and they'd asked him the same questions they'd asked everyone and received the same answers, when suddenly a horde of black-garbed *morum cadi* had appeared in the center of town, swords drawn, blood-chilling screams erupting from their throats. Dr. Pym had immediately opened a portal in the man's living room, a shimmering curtain of air through which he yanked the children even as they protested that they could help—

"No. Indeed, your very presence here makes it more dangerous for others."

—and a moment later, they'd been standing beside the dark blue waters of the Danube.

Exhausted and shaken, they'd gone to the house of another of the wizard's friends, a grim-faced witch with short black hair combed flat to her head, and after several cups of strong tea and the usual questions and answers (*No. No.*), Kate and Michael had been sent to wander in the woman's garden—with the warning that "some of the plants bite"—while Pym and the woman spoke.

But they hadn't been there an hour when Pym had hurried out of the house, calling their names.

"Why're we running?" Michael now asked. "Can't you open a portal anywhere?"

"No," the wizard replied. "But this is not really the time to explain."

"So why don't I use the *Atlas*?" Kate said. There was no longer any question that the magic of the *Atlas* resided within her and she could call it up at will to travel through both time and space. "I can—"

"No! Only when there is no other option. It is too dangerous!"

Kate was about to argue that their present situation seemed pretty dangerous when a Screecher's cry ripped apart the air, and she and Michael froze in their tracks. They couldn't help it. They both knew how to control the fear that gripped them when they heard the shriek of a *morum cadi*, but they needed time to prepare, to ready themselves.

This cry had taken them unawares, and was close by.

Then Kate saw the wizard turning, his hands moving in patterns, and the street behind them seemed to rise up like a wave just as two Screechers charged around a corner. The *morum cadi* were only yards away, close enough that Kate could see their glowing yellow eyes, but the stones of the street were now stacking themselves into a wall that stretched to the roofs of the houses on either side, and just when the creatures would have been upon them, Kate and Michael found themselves safe behind the wizard's wall, listening to the *clang* and *crunch* of the monsters' swords against the stones.

"Come along," Dr. Pym said, and pulled them away.

A block farther on, Kate, Michael, and the wizard burst from the warren of streets, and there was the river before them, there was the footbridge stretching across it, and there, standing at the head of the bridge, was the dark-haired witch, looking even more grim and humorless than before.

"Is it ready?" Dr. Pym asked.

"The portal is open," the witch replied. Her English was accented, and she spoke with great force, spitting out every word like a cannonball, as if determined to get it as far from her as possible. "It will take you to San Marco. You can get a boat from there."

"That's fine. And I will see you tomorrow."

"Yes."

"And don't forget—"

"To close the portal when you cross. I know. Quickly. They are almost here." Then, for a moment, the woman's eyes moved to Kate and her brother, and her face softened a very, very, very small amount. "We will find your sister and your parents. Your family is not lost. Now go."

And then Dr. Pym was pulling them up the slope of the bridge, and Kate could see the rippling in the air that was almost like the rippling of the water below, and she reached out and took her brother's hand; she had been through so many different portals in the past days, stepping through smoke that didn't choke her, through fire that didn't burn, through waterfalls, through a ray of light, but she always made sure to hold Michael's hand. She had lost so much, she was not going to lose him.

The shrieking of the Screechers was louder now, and closer, but Kate didn't turn to look; she kept her eyes on the shimmering curtain in the air; then Dr. Pym was ushering them through, and she gripped Michael's hand even more tightly, closed her eyes, and felt the familiar stomach-churning swirl, the loud, rushing, going-through-a-tunnel sound, her ears popped, and then, silence.

Or not silence exactly, for there was the gentle slap of waves on the shore, the cry of a gull overhead. Kate felt the sun on her face and opened her eyes. A blue expanse of water stretched before them, and for a moment, she thought they were back in Australia. Then she saw they were standing on a beach of smooth gray and black stones.

She looked over at Michael. "Are you all right?"

He nodded and pulled his hand from hers. "Yes."

"Any idea where we are?"

He shrugged. "I guess Dr. Pym will tell us."

But the wizard had already walked away down the beach, heading toward a pier where a dozen or so boats—small, battered-looking vessels with black nets strung over their sides—were moored. Kate studied her brother. Michael had taken off his glasses and was cleaning them on his shirt. He had been unusually silent the last few days. She understood, of course. Michael blamed himself for the Dire Magnus's return and, by extension, for Emma's abduction. Kate had tried to tell him that he had only done what he'd had to do, that what had happened was as much her fault as his.

"Yeah?" he'd said when she'd suggested this. "How's that?"

"Well, I'm the one that died."

She had died, and Michael had used the *Chronicle*, the Book of Life, to bring her back. But in order to do so, he'd first had to resurrect the Dire Magnus, who had promptly, with his servant Rourke's help, kidnapped Emma. So he'd only done what he'd done because she'd gone and gotten herself killed. That was what she'd meant.

There's enough guilt to go around, Kate had wanted to say.

But she couldn't stop thinking that there was something else. Something he wasn't telling her. What was this barrier he'd created between them?

A few minutes later, they were on a boat, the hull smacking—*thap—thap—thap*—against the small crests in the water, both sails full and straining. On all sides of them, islands studded the surface of the sea. Kate's hair kept whipping her face and she had to use both hands to hold it back. She and Michael were sitting on a bench amidships, their feet resting on the thickly folded nets. The wizard sat across from them, while the captain was in the stern, one hand casually holding the wheel. The boat smelled of dead fish and sea salt. Dr. Pym had said that their journey should not take more than an hour, and from the relative calmness of the sea and the way the boat skipped across the water, Kate suspected that the wind filling their sails was the wizard's doing.

"I want to thank you both for your patience," Dr. Pym said, lifting his voice to be heard over the rush of the wind. "I know I haven't been very forthcoming of late, but it was important that we move quickly and cover as much ground as possible. It was for that reason that I sent the others."

By "the others," he meant Gabriel and the elves. The night that Kate and Michael and Dr. Pym had left Antarctica, Gabriel and two parties of elves had also left to search for Emma and spread the word throughout the magical community that the Dire

Magnus had returned. Kate wondered if any of them had had news of Emma.

"But now," the wizard said, "it is time to begin the next phase."

"What do you mean?" Kate said. "The next phase is rescuing Emma!"

"Of course. That is our first and most important goal. But even once we rescue your sister, the return of the Dire Magnus requires action. That is part of the message I have been delivering. In the next day or so, all the members of the magical world who support our cause—elf, human, and dwarf—will send representatives here, so that we may plan our strategy."

"You mean you're going to start a war?" Michael asked.

The wizard looked suddenly very old and tired. "My boy, if recent events tell us anything, it is that the war has already begun."

"So where's here?" Kate asked. "Where're we going?"

"This"—the wizard stretched out a long arm to encompass the sea and the islands all around them—"is the Archipelago, a collection of some two-score islands that sits, unseen to the outside world, smack in the center of the Mediterranean. The islands themselves are all different: there are dwarf homelands and elf homelands, there are islands with nothing but fairies or trolls or dragons.

"But we are going there." And he pointed to a green lump in the distance. "Altre Terros, also called Loris, also called Xi 'alatn. It is our greatest city, home to the largest magical population and, in many ways, the true heart of our world. Hopefully, there we will find the answers and the help we seek."

They fell silent. Kate gave up trying to control her hair and focused on steadying herself against the motion of the boat. She also tried, as she had whenever there'd been a quiet moment in the past two days, not to think about Emma, not to wonder if she was hurt or scared, not to wonder when she would see her sister again, for to do so was to go down a rabbit hole of worry and guilt that led nowhere except to more worry and guilt.

Instead, she thought of their parents, and the message Michael had received saying that they had escaped and were hunting the last Book of Beginning. Their parents had been prisoners of the Dire Magnus for ten years. How had they escaped? Had someone helped them? If so, who? And why were they off looking for the last book instead of trying to find her and her brother and sister? Did it have something to do with their father's warning that they must not allow Dr. Pym to bring the three books together? The children had no way of knowing, because the warning had not come from their father himself, but from a ghostly projection of him contained in a glass orb that Michael had smashed, and the ghost had faded away without explaining the reason behind its warning. The children had not conveyed this part of the message to Dr. Pym, but between themselves, they had debated endlessly, and fruitlessly, about what it might mean. Kate was for asking the wizard directly, but Michael refused, saying they needed more information, and as he had been the one to receive the message, she had deferred.

Kate looked at the old wizard. He was still wearing the same fraying tweed suit, his tortoiseshell glasses were still bent and patched (their lenses now speckled with sea-foam), his white hair, always somewhat messy, was blowing wildly in the wind. Just looking at him, she felt comforted. He was Dr. Pym; he was their friend.

So why didn't she try harder to convince Michael to tell the wizard what their father had said? Was there, in fact, some part of her that doubted him?

They were nearing the island now, and Kate pulled herself from her reverie. The island, wrapped by a band of imposing white cliffs, seemed to rise up high above them. Past the cliffs, the island was covered in greenery, and at its center there was a single steep mountain, with sharp spines radiating down its sides. Kate could see no sign of a city or town.

"We are coming around the windward side," the wizard said. "Loris, the city, is on the leeward, where the cliffs reach to the water."

As he spoke, the small boat tacked, and Kate and Michael both held to the gunnels. They began seeing more boats, old fishing boats like the one they were in, small boats piloted by no-nonsense dwarfish sailors, one very fast boat painted with elaborate floral designs piloted by an elf who appeared to be singing to a school of dolphins, combing his hair, and steering all at the same time, and who waved to them airily and offered the somewhat strange greeting "*La-la-lo!*"

Kate waited for Michael to make a comment about elfish ridiculousness, but her brother remained silent.

Rounding the island, the children saw that the cliffs did indeed begin to slope down toward the water, and a harbor opened up. It was as if the island was stretching out a pair of long, rocky arms, and they entered its embrace, passing into a swath of calm blue water. Stone and wooden docks jutted into the harbor like jagged teeth, and there were dozens of boats, either docked or weaving about. The whole feeling was one of bustling commerce, as boats brought in huge catches of fish and others appeared loaded with boxes and cargo, and the air was filled with the shouts and calls of people at work.

Past the harbor, there was a narrow beach, and then high white walls that stretched up and around the city, no doubt built long ago for defense, but now the gates were wide open and the tops of the walls were festooned with explosions of flowers. The city itself climbed up the slope, a staggered collection of tightly packed, white-stone houses, but what drew Kate's attention was a single structure up at the farthest reaches of the city and backed against the cliffs. While the rest of the city was made of the same identical white stone, this building was rose-colored and massive; it loomed over the city, as if it were the refuge of giants.

Kate had no doubt that the rose-colored fortress was their destination.

By now, the enchanted wind had dropped from their sails, and they were gliding toward a stone pier where a single empty berth remained among the boats. As they drew closer, the children discerned a short, stocky figure standing on the pier and shouting at a fisherman who was attempting to dock his boat.

"Who am I?! I'm the fella that's gonna sink that rotten bathtub you call a boat if you don't shove off! This here's reserved!"

As if to press the point home, the figure pulled a gleaming ax from his belt and brandished it at the fisherman, who was now hurriedly oaring backward.

Kate, recognizing the short figure's face and voice, experienced her first real happiness in days.

At the same moment, Michael leapt up, nearly swamping the boat, shouting, "It's King Robbie! King Robbie! King Robbie!"

By then the dwarf king had seen them, and he waved his stubby arms and grinned.

"Ah, you two are a sight for sore eyes! Let me get a good look at you."

The children were standing on the pier, and Robbie McLaur, king of the dwarves near Cambridge Falls, had already hugged them tightly and given them furry, bearded kisses on both cheeks.

"You're more beautiful than ever," he said to Kate, "if such a thing were possible. And you"—he turned to Michael—"are not the same dewy-cheeked whelp I saw at Christmas! I'd bet my beard something's happened! Tell the truth now!"

"Well, Your Highness," Michael said, clearly pleased to be reunited with their old friend, "we have had quite an adventure. I had a tussle with a dragon, though it was nothing really to speak of, and there was a siege that I had some small part in—"

"You've fallen in love, haven't you? Don't lie to me, lad!" King Robbie waggled a finger in his face. "Don't try to hide it from Robbie McLaur! What's the lucky dwarf maiden's name?"

Kate watched Michael turn red and stammer, "Oh—well—I—"

The dwarf laughed and clapped him on the shoulder. "I'm only ribbing you. No shame falling for a human girl. It's not like you fell for an elf, am I right?"

Kate, who knew some of the story of Princess Wilamena and knew that Michael had a lock of hair the color of sunlight tied with a silk ribbon and tucked in his bag, watched her brother turn even redder.

"An elf," he said. "Pshaw."

The dwarf king then placed one small, strong hand on each of their shoulders, gripping them in a way that was almost painful. "I know you know this, but I'll say it all the same, for there's meaning in speaking something aloud. We will find your sister. I, Robbie McLaur, will not rest till she's free. Nor will any of my dwarves." He thought for a moment, then added, "Except Hamish. That worthless lump does nothing *but* rest. And drink and eat. Anything except work and shower. Anyway"—and he gripped their shoulders even more tightly—"we'll bring her home. You have my word."

Kate felt tears coming to her eyes, and she hugged the dwarf king fiercely.

"There, there, lass," he murmured, patting her on the back.

Dr. Pym, who'd been silent during this reunion, now spoke. "Your Majesty, we have been traveling without pause for some time, and I'm sure the children are exhausted. We should get them to their rooms."

"Right you are," the dwarf said. "This way."

The foursome walked down the pier, across the beach, past the crowds funneling through the walls, and into the town proper. The narrow streets wound up the hill, tacking back and forth in a series of long, shallow steps. Up close, the white stone that accounted for everything in the town—the houses, the streets, the garden walls, a birdbath—revealed itself to be not solid white, but speckled and veined with gray and black. They passed humans and dwarves and elves—shopping, sweeping out homes, eating in cafés—and Kate felt gaze after gaze turn toward them.

Did everyone know who they were? Kate wondered. Or did she and Michael just stand out?

"I arrived last night," King Robbie was saying. "Everything's as you asked."

"Thank you," Dr. Pym said. "Tell me, have there been reports of any attacks?"

He and King Robbie were walking a step ahead of Kate and Michael.

"Aye. Two came in today. One from South America. Another from the Horn of Africa. How'd you know?"

"We encountered our own trouble."

"It's starting, then. These are the first showers before the storm. But how the devil is he this strong? He wasn't half so bold before, waging war on the whole world!"

"Indeed, he seems to have found some new source of power. I tremble to think what it might be. Have you had word from Gabriel or the others?"

"No."

King Robbie and the wizard went on talking, but Kate stopped listening. She'd heard what she wanted to know. Emma was still lost.

They came around a corner, and at the end of the street, Kate saw the rose-colored building that she'd first noticed from the boat. What was most striking—apart from its enormous size and the vibrant rose hue of the stone—was how wildly thrown together it looked. The façade jerked up and down at odd intervals; the roof was studded with a series of domes and pergolas and towers, all of different sizes and shapes; there were dozens of balconies and colonnades and arches scattered about; it was a giant mishmash. And yet there was a strange, almost perfect beauty to it all, like the natural, complex growth of a flower.

And there was more: the building was home to something powerful. Kate had felt a vibration in her chest when she'd seen it from the boat, and now, up close, she knew for sure. The rose-colored building was built to protect something. But what?

They walked through an archway where two armed guards (one human and one dwarf) saluted, and found themselves in a passageway under the building.

The wizard stopped. "This is the Rose Citadel. When we of the magical world have gatherings, this is where we meet. This building holds the greatest magical library in existence, as well as being home to innumerable treasures and mysteries. It is part museum, part university, part council chamber. And on its upper floors, there are some very comfortable guest rooms. I've reserved a pair for you."

"What's that way?" Kate asked, pointing down the passageway to where she could see a swath of green.

"The Garden," the wizard said. "The Citadel is built around it. I will take you through it later."

It's in there, Kate thought. Whatever it is I'm feeling, it's in there.

They said goodbye to King Robbie, who promised he would see them at dinner, and Dr. Pym led them through a doorway and up a hopeless zigzag of stairs and hallways till, finally, he brought them into a large, cool, dimly lit room. Kate could make out a bed, a chair, a table; then the wizard pushed open a pair of heavy wooden shutters, light poured in, and the blue sea appeared, far below them. He pointed to a door.

"That leads to a second bedroom. Take some time to rest, gather yourselves. I'll come to get you for dinner. And do know, you are safer here than you are anywhere else in the world."

Then he turned and walked out.

As if her exhaustion had been there waiting for her, Kate felt a heaviness settle on her shoulders. She sat down on the bed. Another moment, and she might have fallen over.

"Well," Michael said, "guess I'll take the other room."

"Michael . . ."

He turned back at the door.

"I wanted to ask—"

"Yes, I know, I didn't tell King Robbie about Wilamena. But—"

"It's not that." And while she had meant to ask if he too had sensed the presence of some great power in the Citadel, instead, looking at her brother's face and feeling more than ever the new, awful distance between them, she asked, "Is something wrong?"

"What do you mean?"

"Are you angry at me?"

"What? No! Of course not."

Kate said nothing. The silence stretched out. Michael stared at the floor, and when he spoke again, his voice was different. It was his voice this time, his real one.

"When I use the *Chronicle*, I live another person's whole life. All their memories and feelings, for a few seconds, they're mine. I should've told you before. I don't want it to happen; it just does. Most of it I can't remember afterward. It's like trying to remember a dream."

"But some things you do remember."

"Yes."

"And when you brought me back . . ."

Michael looked up, and the instant he met her eyes, Kate knew what he would say.

"That boy in the bell tower, the one who became the Dire Magnus . . ."

Kate's throat was as dry as paper. "Rafe."

"You love him."

Kate didn't know what threw her more, that Michael had said this or that he had said it so simply and directly. The old Michael, the one she'd left in Baltimore a week before, would have danced around and basically done all he could to avoid mentioning the subject of feelings, his own or anyone else's.

"You love him," he went on. "I mean, you know he's the Dire Magnus. You know he's the enemy. But you still love him."

"No, I don't . . ." Kate was gripping the edge of the bed with both hands. "I don't . . . love the Dire Magnus."

"I mean you love him, Rafe. And he is the Dire Magnus. They're the same person."

"Why are you saying this? What's—"

"You can't save him. You have to know that."

Now it was Kate's turn to stare at the floor. For as shocked as she'd been by Michael's declaration that she loved Rafe, the boy she had met a hundred years in the past, who had saved her life and in so doing had become the Dire Magnus, no part of her denied the truth of it. How often in the past days—despite jumping around the world, despite being hounded by Screechers, despite Emma being gone—had she closed her eyes and pictured Rafe's face before her, or remembered riding with him on the top of the elevated train as the wind bit into her cheeks or sitting in the warm, smoky comfort of the Chinese restaurant as he'd taught her to eat noodles or dancing with him in the snow and feeling the beat of his heart? How many times had she told herself to stop thinking of him, to forget him, only to be drawn back by the simple memory of her hand folded inside his?

She said, "Have you told Dr. Pym?"

"No. And I won't. But you've got to choose. Emma or him. You can't save both. You have to choose."

Then he turned and walked out of the room, leaving her alone.

CHAPTER THREE
The Crushed Leaf

"So, you can imagine life here?"

Gabriel stood in a village on the Rijkinka Fjord, a long sliver of water that curved deep into the dense forests of western Norway. The village was small, only thirty or so homes nestled between the trees and the glasslike surface of the fjord. At his side was a thin old woman with white hair and large blue eyes. One hand held a cane, the other rested on Gabriel's arm. She was waiting for an answer, and so Gabriel looked again at the stillness of the water, listened to the silence of the trees.

"It is beautiful. Peaceful."

"Yes," the old woman said. And she sighed, "It was."

All about them, villagers were moving among the ruins of smoking and blackened houses, sorting through their possessions for anything that could be saved. A smudge of dark smoke hung in the sky. Gabriel and the woman started down the muddy street, her cane feeling the way through the ash and debris.

"Of course, Miriam and I set up defenses, the standard wards to protect against vampires and werewolves and the like. But that was decades ago. I suppose we'd become forgetful. Not that it would've done much good. There were hundreds of them. *Morum cadi.* Imps. Even a troll."

"Was he here?"

"No. Rourke led them."

"Did he say anything?"

The old witch gave a short, dry snort. "Oh yes. He sought us out. Told us, 'You once stood against my master. That's why this is happening. Defy him again and he will not be so merciful.' He said that Pym would not defend us this time."

Gabriel said nothing.

The old witch stopped. Her bony hand gripped Gabriel's arm. "He's more powerful than before. I could feel it."

"We do not believe he yet has the *Reckoning.*"

"But he has the Keeper, doesn't he? He has the Keeper of the *Reckoning*?"

"Yes."

The woman's grip slackened, as if some strength had gone out of her. "Then it is only a matter of time until he finds it. After that, he will be unstoppable."

"That will not happen."

The old woman patted him on the arm.

"Tell Pym we're with him. We may not be what we once were, but we're with him to the end." She paused. "I mean to say, I'm with him."

"I am sorry about your sister."

She nodded her thanks, and pointed with her cane toward the line of trees. "They came from there." Then she tottered off down the street, her cane making little *pat-pat* noises in the mud. Gabriel watched her go.

It did not take him long to find where Rourke and his army had materialized. The trees had been felled in a large ring, and the ground was scorched black. But where had they appeared from? Gabriel knew that once a portal closed, there was no way of following it back to its source. At least no magical means. But his advantage was that he was not a wizard. He was simply a man. A man who knew about trees and plants and the land, and he crouched now and lifted a small crushed leaf out of the soil. The leaf had been trampled by many boots, and he gently smoothed it across his palm.

Gabriel didn't recognize the leaf, but he knew that whatever it was, it would never grow in this forest. That meant it must have come through on the boot of one of the attackers. But from where? Gabriel sensed that if he found the plant, he would find the Dire Magnus; and if he found the Dire Magnus, he would find Emma.

But to do that, he needed help.

Two hours later, and five thousand miles southwest, Gabriel was walking along a steep, rocky trail as the sun fell behind the mountains and the trees threw long shadows across his path. The approaching darkness didn't trouble him—he could've found his way blindfolded—and soon enough, he reached the crest of the ridge and stood gazing down at the small village that lay in the fold of the mountain.

In the fifteen years since Stanislaus Pym had recruited him to the cause of defeating the Dire Magnus and saving the children, Gabriel had returned here only a handful of times. And each time, it had felt less and less like home.

He knew it would be fully dark by the time he reached the village, and he would've gotten there earlier, but the golden key the wizard had given him, the one that allowed him to move swiftly around the world, required a keyhole or a lock to work, and his village had none. He had had to come through the mansion in Cambridge Falls, in the process terrifying half to death the old caretaker, Abraham. Once he'd recovered, the old man had pressed him for news of the children, and Gabriel had told him, while the sour-faced housekeeper, Miss Sallow, had eavesdropped from the kitchen. When he'd reached the part about Emma's abduction, Miss Sallow had come out and taken Abraham's hand.

"You have to save her," the old woman had said, her voice tight with emotion. "You have to."

He had left soon after.

The village was silent and dark; no one was about, and Gabriel felt like a ghost moving through the shadows.

He came to a ramshackle hut at the base of the village and raised his hand to knock. Before he could, a voice called from inside, "Come in, come in."

Gabriel pushed open the door and peered into the smoky interior of the hut. He could see a single cookfire in the center of the room and the large, messy outline of a woman bending over a pot. For a moment, he didn't move. The sight of the old woman at her fire and the smell of her hut—the smoke, the scents of burning pine, of wild onions and carrots, of boiling potatoes and thyme—

loosened a knot in the center of his chest, and he was a boy again; he was home.

"I put on a stew when I knew you were coming," Granny Peet said. "Though I don't stand by the potatoes. Bad lot this year."

Pulled back to the present, Gabriel stepped inside and shut the door behind him. "I won't ask how you knew I was coming."

"Good. You wouldn't understand anyway. Sit."

Gabriel took one of the low stools by the fire as Granny Peet continued to stir the pot, the charms and vials dangling from her necklaces clinking softly as they knocked together. Gabriel still felt the tug of home, but already the tension was returning to his chest. It would be there, he knew, until Emma was safe.

"You've been gone too long," the old woman muttered, the fire multiplying the wrinkles of her face. "This is your home. It nourishes you."

"Things have happened."

"I know. I hear whispers. What have you brought me?"

Gabriel reached into his bag and pulled out a folded square of cloth. He opened it, displaying the limp, black leaf. It seemed an impossibly small thing to pin his hopes on, but it was all he had. "A village in Norway was attacked. I found this."

Granny Peet had dirty, swollen fingers and thick, yellow nails, but she lifted the leaf delicately, turning it about in the light of the fire, then finally bringing it to one large nostril to sniff. "Hmph."

She carried the leaf to a table behind Gabriel where a pot of soil sat among a clutter of roots and branches. She poked a hole in the soil, placed the leaf inside, and covered it over. Then she ladled in what to Gabriel looked like ordinary water. She shuffled back to the fire.

"We'll see if it has anything to say. Now, you eat, then you'll tell me what else is bothering you." And she pushed a brimming, steaming bowl of stew into his hands.

Gabriel was about to say he had come only about the leaf when he realized that wasn't so. There was something else. Something that had been gnawing at his thoughts for days. But he also knew that Granny Peet wouldn't listen to anything till his bowl was clean, so he picked up a spoon and ate. The stew was too hot and burned his mouth, but with each bite he was taken back to the hours he used to sit at the wise woman's fire and listen to her stories about the world outside their village, how he'd nod when she'd tell him that he would be called to serve in a great cause. "Much will be asked of you," she used to say. "A terrible sacrifice."

He had been a small boy, smaller than others his age, his parents dead in a landslide when he was younger than Emma (did that explain his bond to the children?), and he had been raised by the entire village, and by Granny Peet in particular. She had fed him, schooled him, and he had grown quickly, and while yet a boy, he had towered over the men in the village. He'd often wondered if Granny Peet had put something in his food. But when he'd asked her about it, she'd scoffed, saying, "Don't question your strength. Be thankful. You'll need every bit of it when the time comes."

When Gabriel finished the stew, he felt more rested than he had in days, and he sat there, the empty bowl in his hands. The old woman squatted on the stool beside him, smoking a short, gnarled pipe, her eyes two dark pits among the folds of her face.

He began to speak: "For fifteen years, I have been helping Pym search for the missing Books. He told me that finding them was the only way to keep the children safe." Gabriel did not say how often his own life had been in peril, how many new scars he bore, how much he himself had given up; the old woman knew. "But recently, I fought a man, a servant of the Dire Magnus." Gabriel didn't notice, but his hands tightened on the bowl as he recalled his battle with Rourke in the volcano. "He told me that if the children succeed in finding all three Books of Beginning and bringing them together, they will die. And he said that Pym knows this."

For a time, Granny Peet did not respond, but sat there, drawing on her pipe and letting smoke curl from her mouth. Gabriel could hear the trees creaking outside, the whisper of the branches rubbing against one another.

Finally she said, "It is possible."

It seemed to Gabriel that he could feel the world moving beneath him, and he gripped the wooden bowl as if it were an anchor that would hold him in place. "So it is true, they will die if they bring the Books together?"

"Yes. Most likely."

"And Pym knows?"

"I have no doubt."

"And how have you known this and not told me? All this time I have been searching for the Books, I have been speeding the children to their doom."

Gabriel could hear the anger in his voice and he didn't care. The old woman looked at him, motionless, her dark eyes unreadable. She seemed to be letting Gabriel's anger subside, like waiting for a wave to crash and return to the sea.

"The Books must be found," she said at last. "They must be found, and the children are the only ones who can do it."

"But why must they be found? Because the Dire Magnus also

seeks them? That cannot be the only means of defeating him. If necessary, I will kill him and each and every one of his followers. I do not—"

"No," the old woman said. And suddenly there was nothing shambling or messy or indefinite about her. She was hard and precise. "The Dire Magnus has grown in power. For all your strength and heart, for all Pym's knowledge, for all the will and power of all good people in our world, it is not enough. Only the Books can defeat him now. And the children alone can find them."

Gabriel fell silent and stared at the fire. He saw how he'd been gripping the bowl and slowly unclenched his fingers and set it down.

"But there is another reason," the old woman said. "Something has come loose in the fabric of the world. It began long ago, but recently, the unraveling has quickened. If it is not fixed, and soon, there will be a cataclysm none can contain. The Books alone can prevent this disaster. All of Pym's thoughts bend toward this one point."

Gabriel looked at her, and the scar that ran down the side of his face throbbed. "So the children are to be sacrificed."

"Perhaps," the old woman said. "And perhaps not. Prophecies are tricky things."

"You mean there may be a way to save them?"

"I do not know. But I choose to believe there is." She placed a warm hand on his arm. "You care for all the children, but the youngest, she is the daughter you never had. You would do anything for her."

At the old woman's words, Gabriel found himself thinking of Emma, and the morning, years before, after he'd saved the three of them from the Countess's wolves, how she had followed him into the woods and watched as he'd stalked and killed a deer. The way she had mastered her fear. It had moved him, and a desire to protect her, a love, had entered his heart and never gone away.

He nodded, but said nothing.

"You must speak to Pym," the old woman said. "Do not give up on him. He too cares for the children. Now, let us look at your leaf."

She rose and shuffled past him to the table. When she returned, she was carrying the pot, only now a foot-tall plant was sprouting from the soil. It had a narrow, spiny stalk and long, jagged leaves. Granny Peet placed it beside the fire, then knelt down, cupping its branches, lowering her face to the leaves, and inhaling deeply.

"Clear, high air. Mountains. Iron and sulfur. Mars in the spring sky. The urine of blue sheep. Bones of a tyrannosaurus. Anger. Hatred. Death." She broke one of the leaves and rubbed the moisture between her fingers. "Search eastward. Look for a place where three rivers meet and there are fields of mint. You remember how to detect an enchantment?"

Gabriel nodded and began to rise, but the old woman clucked her tongue.

"Tomorrow, boy. Even you must sleep."

"Not while she is held prisoner."

He'd gotten as far as the door when the old woman said his name. Gabriel turned to see her sorting through a jumble of objects in one corner of the hut. She pulled something free and came toward him. The object was three feet long and wrapped in a soiled, dark cloth. She held it out in both hands.

"At least take this. I know you need a weapon. And this one you will not lose."

Again, Gabriel didn't ask how the old woman knew what she did, but it was true: the razor-edge falchion he had carried through countless battles, that had felt like an extension of his own arm, was now in a volcano in Antarctica. He took the object from her and undid the wrapping at one end, exposing a hilt of worn leather and bone. He slid out four inches of steel, and the metal seemed to gather the meager light from the fire and reflect it back tenfold. He returned the blade to the sheath and nodded his thanks.

The old woman placed both hands on his arms.

"She is the daughter you never had, and you are the child of my heart. Go well."

She turned away before he could respond. For a long moment, Gabriel looked at her, standing beside the fire in the same pose as when he'd entered; then he walked out and through the village, leaving as quietly as he had come.

CHAPTER FOUR
Chocolate Cake

Emma heard the thud of footsteps ascending the tower stairs, recognized who they belonged to, and sat up. The sky through the windows was dark, and the drumming and shrieking from the army in the valley had reached its nightly fever pitch.

She was standing when Rourke, holding a torch, opened the door.

"Come with me."

"Why?"

"He wants to see you."

He didn't bother explaining who "he" was. Emma thought of refusing but knew that if she did, Rourke would just lift her and throw her over his shoulder.

She had been a prisoner for four days. Nothing particularly bad had happened; if anything, her days and nights had an almost tedious sameness. Every morning, a pair of pinch-faced gnomes would bring her breakfast, which she ate dutifully, telling herself she would need her strength when she was rescued (she'd tried several times to dart past the gnomes and each time she'd been pinned to the ground and her arms and fingers were twisted about painfully; the little creatures were much stronger than they looked, and utterly vicious). At some point, an hour, two hours, three hours later, Rourke would come and take her for a walk on the ramparts, blathering on about how great his master was and how, very soon, Emma would help them find the *Reckoning*. Then, in the evening, two more gnomes would bring her dinner (she had just as much luck getting past them); and as darkness fell, the drumming and shrieking coming from the army would rise up, and Emma would sit there with her hands pressed to her ears, telling herself that Kate and Michael were safe, that Dr. Pym would protect them, that Gabriel would rescue her, that everything would be okay. And just as the sky was growing light and the noise was abating, Emma would fall asleep.

Rourke was silent as he led her down the twisting stairs of the tower. The air was cold, and there were more torches burning in the iron brackets on the wall. When they reached the main corridor, rather than turning right, they went down another set of stairs, and soon Rourke was leading her through the courtyard and out a gate, leaving the fortress behind.

"You see the fires?"

She and Rourke were walking along a steep, wide path that wound down to the valley floor. Below them, hundreds of fires lit the darkness, but it was clear which ones he meant, a few of them being many times larger than the others.

"Those are portals. Our army uses them to jump around the

world. We appear without warning, sow death and terror. Then vanish."

"Like a bunch of cowards."

Rourke smiled but said nothing.

All the time they'd been descending the path, the drumming had grown louder. Now, Emma could feel the vibrations in her chest, and it was making her whole body thrum with fear. But she forced herself to keep pace with Rourke.

Then they reached the valley floor and were swallowed up by the army.

Strangely, what struck her first was the stench. It wasn't just the *morum cadi*; over the past four days, Emma had become almost used to their constant, moldering reek. But the press of thousands of the half-dead creatures along with the smell of heated metal and sweat and blood and burning meat created an almost tangible fug, and every breath—she took as few as she could—brought the rot inside her.

And then there was the sheer loudness, for the drumming and shrieking was now joined with snarls and growls and oaths and the constant clamor of shouting and fighting, and Emma fought the urge to press her hands to her ears.

There was no order that she could see. Small fires burned on all sides of them, and around each fire would be a group of *morum cadi* or Imps or, now and then, trolls. The creatures were eating, drinking, sharpening weapons, fighting—sometimes all at once. Emma saw one twelve-foot troll roasting an entire cow on a spit and licking his lips with an enormous purple tongue. They passed blacksmiths pounding away, the *clink-clink-clink* of their hammers as steady as the beating of the drums. And there were humans too, which shocked Emma, men and women, black-garbed and thuggish, crowded about fires and speaking in harsh languages that Emma had never heard.

And then, finally, there were the red-robed figures. In some ways, they were the most frightening of all. She and Rourke passed close by a trio that was huddled around a smoking, bubbling pot like witches in a fairy tale. Hoods covered their faces, but they seemed to be human, and Emma noticed how even the Screechers and the Imps gave them a wide berth. One of the figures turned to look at Emma as she passed; he was a very old man with a long, twisted nose and stringy gray hair. He was leaning on a staff, and one of his eyes was completely white.

"Who're they?" she asked quietly.

"The *necromati*. Mages and wizards who serve the master. Most come to him eager for power, which he gives in exchange for their loyalty. Others are former enemies he has broken and bent to his will. They serve as reminders to all who would stand against him."

Emma couldn't stop staring at the old man and his creepy white eye, and she was peering back over her shoulder when she collided with something hard and was knocked to the ground.

"Ohh!"

Emma found herself looking up into the face—if you could call it that—of an equally surprised Imp. The creature held a half-eaten drumstick in one hand.

"What—" the Imp began. And then Rourke stuck a knife in its throat and shoved the body casually beside.

He yanked Emma to her feet. "Watch where you're going."

He dragged her onward through the camp, then abruptly pulled her into the doorway of a large tent. Once inside, Emma found herself in a hushed, almost sweet-smelling space, as if the clamor and stench of the camp couldn't penetrate the canvas walls. Lanterns strung from chains illuminated a wooden table, on which were strewn a jumbled collection of books, maps, and half-rolled parchments. There was a small camp bed against one wall. Otherwise, the tent was bare, and its sole occupant appeared to be a cloaked figure kneeling in the center of the floor.

And the figure was on fire.

Or perhaps not on fire, as he did not appear to be burning. Yet Emma could feel the heat against her own skin; the flames were real.

"Wait," Rourke said, placing a heavy hand on her shoulder.

The cloaked figure remained motionless, his head hooded and bowed, as the flames traveled over his body. It seemed to Emma that she could see shapes moving in the flames, but though she tried, she couldn't make the shapes resolve into anything specific.

And then, quite suddenly, the flames died away and the figure stood. He moved toward the back of the tent, gesturing with his hand.

"Walk." Rourke pushed her forward.

Emma moved deeper into the tent, passing over the spot where the fire had wreathed the figure, noting that the floor, covered with overlapping rugs, was unharmed. Emma could feel her heart beating all through her body, pulsing down to the tips of her fingers. The cloaked figure stood before a shallow silver bowl that was supported, waist-high, on three iron legs.

He turned as Emma approached.

"Hello."

Emma had been prepared; she'd told herself she was prepared, but still she was taken aback. Standing there, staring at her, was a boy. But *boy* was the wrong word. He was in that place when he was no longer a boy, and yet not quite a man. She guessed he was perhaps a year older than Kate, maybe sixteen. He had unkempt dark hair, wide-set cheekbones, a nose that was slightly bent, and he was grinning, as if this was all somehow enjoyable. There was something wild about him, and his grin was like that of the wolf in a fairy tale.

His eyes were the most brilliant emerald green imaginable.

"I'm Rafe," he said, and put out his hand.

Emma just looked at it. "You're the Dire Magnus, aren't you?"

He shrugged and took his hand back, not seeming offended. "If you like. But it's kind of a mouthful. *Rafe*'s easier. I've wanted to meet you for a long time."

Emma tried to make sense of what was happening. This was the Dire Magnus; she was certain. He was the same boy—she couldn't stop using the word even while admitting it wasn't totally accurate—who'd stepped from the flaming portal in Antarctica. But he was hardly older than she was! How could he be the Dire Magnus? And why was he acting, so . . . normal?

"C'mere. I want to show you something."

Emma felt her legs move her forward, and she came to a stop on the other side of the iron stand, so that the wide silver bowl was between them. She kept her arms at her sides, resisting the urge to cross them over her chest, knowing that would make her appear defensive and fearful.

She realized that he was still staring at her, and still grinning.

"What?" she demanded.

"Nothing, just, it's funny."

She waited for him to go on.

"At first, I thought you didn't look like her at all. I couldn't even see how you were sisters. But now that I see you closer, there's something there. It's interesting."

He reached across as if to touch her face, but Emma pulled back, her body rigid with alarm.

"What're you talking about?"

"What do you think I'm talking about?" He said it in the same mildly sarcastic way any boy his age might have said it. "How much you look like Kate. Or don't. Depending on how you see it."

"How . . . do you know my sister?"

Emma had been preparing herself for threats. For him to try to scare her. She'd even tried to imagine him torturing her. She had been prepared for anything but this seemingly normal, almost friendly boy. She felt utterly at sea.

He pushed back his hood, and he smiled in a knowing way that made Emma furious. "It's kind of a long story. Better for another time."

"You're lying."

"If that's what you want to think."

"I'm not stupid."

"I never said you were."

"You're trying to trick me somehow. So I'll help you find the book."

He seemed to consider what Emma was saying, and he gave a shrugging nod. "Maybe. I certainly do want your help. But I'm not lying to you. Kate and I . . ." He trailed off and seemed for a moment to be somewhere else. Then he looked back at her. "Like I said, it's a long story. One she and I will have to work out ourselves. But I brought you here for another reason. Look."

He moved his hand over the dish—Emma had realized by now that it was a scrying bowl, like the one that she and Michael had used in Antarctica; it allowed you to see things that were far away—and as she looked into it, an image appeared in the half-inch of water in the bottom. Emma leaned closer, craning her neck to bring the image right-side up. She gasped, grabbing the sides of the dish so that a tremor rippled through the water.

"Miss Crumley! That's Miss Crumley!"

It was indeed Miss Crumley, the woman who, as head of the Edgar Allan Poe Home for Hopeless and Incorrigible Orphans, had done as much as anyone to make Emma's and her brother's and sister's lives miserable. Selfish, greedy, short-tempered, and small-minded, she'd seemed to actively dislike children, and Emma and her siblings in particular. Just looking at the woman, Emma felt her anger and resentment rise up, and she gripped the dish so hard that her knuckles turned white.

The woman was sitting at her desk, apparently working through an entire chocolate cake all by herself. Leaning closer, Emma saw that written on the cake were the words *Happy Birthday, Neil*. She didn't know who Neil was, but it was no surprise that Miss Crumley had stolen his birthday cake. She hoped the woman choked on it.

"Is that what you want?"

Emma looked up sharply. "What?"

"To have her choke. Sorry, I wasn't trying to read your mind, but some thoughts are so loud you might as well shout them. So, should we?"

"What're you talking about?"

For the first time, the boy looked annoyed. "You said you're not stupid, so don't act like you are. You know what I mean: Should we make her pay for all she's done to you, to your brother and sister, and to every other child who had the bad luck to cross her path? She deserves it."

He was serious, Emma realized, and she glanced back down at Miss Crumley, who from the way she was shoveling in chocolate cake was most likely going to choke with no help from anyone else. It was true, Emma had dreamed of revenge. When Miss Crumley had made them take cold showers in the winter while her office hummed like a sauna. When they ate the same soggy beans and gray meat day after day while she had elaborate meals in her private dining room, waited on by children who were punished if they stole so much as a single piece of bread. If anyone deserved it, she did.

Emma could feel the boy waiting, watching her. Her hands trembled as she lifted them from the dish.

"No."

The boy said nothing. Emma forced herself to meet his eyes.

"I said no."

He sighed. "Rourke tells me you're a fighter. But there's one fight you'll never win."

Emma tensed, expecting him to say that she and Gabriel and Kate and Michael and Dr. Pym would never defeat him. But again, he surprised her.

"The one against your own nature. Trust me, I've gone down that road, and it's a dead end. You've got anger inside you. Let it out. Deny it, and you just deny yourself." He looked into the bowl. "And the fact is, there are those who deserve to be punished."

He moved his hand, and Miss Crumley dropped her fork and grabbed at her throat.

"What're you doing? I said no!"

Miss Crumley tried to rise up, lurching about this way and that. Her face was quickly turning purple.

"Stop it! You said—"

"I didn't promise anything." His eyes burned bright green. "I gave you a chance to do some actual good. You didn't take it. I did."

Frantic, Emma looked down at the awful, silent scene before her. She knew she had to do something, but what? In the end, she just stood there, watching as Miss Crumley pitched forward onto her desk and lay still, facedown in the smashed remains of the cake.

"I didn't . . . ," Emma said quietly. "I didn't want that."

"Yes, you did. The sooner you accept that, the better." He gestured to Rourke, saying to Emma, "And next time, call me Rafe. I want us to be friends."

Later, after leading Emma back to her cell, Rourke returned to the tent. He stood quietly, letting the boy speak first.

"You think I'm wasting time with her."

"My lord, I do not question—"

"But you do."

Rourke took a breath, as if he were treading somewhere very

dangerous and knew he had to be careful. "It is simply that the sooner we perform the Bonding, the sooner we will have the *Reckoning*. And forgive me, but I've had more opportunity to observe her. She is fiercely loyal to her friends and family. She will not betray them."

"That is just what I'm counting on." The boy moved, allowing Rourke to see into the bowl. There was Emma, sitting in her cell, her back against the stone wall. Her head was down and her shoulders shook as if she were crying. "Anger is a dangerous thing. It can burn a person up, and hers burns very hot indeed. When she learns that Pym has planned the deaths of her and her brother and sister, when she feels the depths of that betrayal, it will burn even hotter."

Rourke looked confused. "And you think she will help us?"

"Yes. Whether she knows it or not."

"So, you do not show her mercy because of the other girl, her sister—"

The boy turned. Despite the apparent difference in ages, the difference in their sizes, the look in the boy's eyes caused the giant man to take a step back, staggering, as if from a blow. The bald man bowed his head.

"Forgive me."

"Go," the boy said, and turned back to the bowl.

CHAPTER FIVE
The Council

Kate didn't know how much more of this she could take. Why didn't Dr. Pym just ask if anyone had any information about Emma and be done with it?

"War is upon us," Dr. Pym was saying. "Since last night, refugees have been arriving at our port by the hundred, and every hour brings word of some town or village that has been attacked and destroyed. So far, Loris and the other islands of the Archipelago have been spared. But for how long? The enemy is coming. Yet we still have no idea where his army is based or how great a force he actually commands—we must work together or we will all perish.

"So please," he said, "stop squabbling and behave."

They were sitting at a round table on an open terrace high up in the Rose Citadel. There were twelve of them in all: Kate; Michael; Dr. Pym; King Robbie; a red-bearded dwarf named

Har-something; Wilamena; her father; a beautiful silver-haired elf lady; a bald-headed, white-bearded man named Captain Stefano who was apparently in command of the city guard; the stern witch from Vienna whose name turned out to be Magda von Klappen; a plump, green-robed wizard from China; and finally, a stocky, wild-haired man who, Michael had whispered, was named Hugo Algernon and was a friend of their parents and "a little crazy."

From where she sat, Kate could see the white rooftops of the town terracing down to the port, which was clogged, as Dr. Pym had said, with boats carrying refugees. Beyond that stretched the wide blue sweep of the sea. The sun hung at midday, and the air was hot and still and tinged with salt. Things had gotten off to a poor start when, half an hour after the meeting was scheduled to begin, there had still been no sign of the elves. By the time Wilamena; her father, King Bernard; and Lady Gwendolyn, the silver-haired elf, had finally stepped out onto the terrace, tempers were beginning to fray.

"Nice of you to make the time," Robbie McLaur had growled.

"Yes, it is, isn't it?" King Bernard had said, not looking the least bit apologetic. He was tall and slim, had the same golden hair as his daughter, and his eyes—Kate had gotten a look at them when the elf king had taken her hand and bowed—were the dark blue that precedes the dawn. "Our boat only just arrived."

"And I wager you had to stop and get your hair done too," Haraald, the red-bearded dwarf, had snickered. Together, he and King Robbie made up the dwarfish delegation.

"Why yes!" Wilamena had said, and spun so that her hair flowed about in a shimmering golden arc. "Do you like it?"

"Well, um, it's, uh, very nice," the dwarf had stammered, turning as red as his beard, before catching himself and snorting in annoyance. "Elfish piffle."

As Dr. Pym had welcomed everyone, Kate had glanced at Michael and seen that all the color had drained from his face. Clearly, Wilamena's being there was a surprise. For Wilamena's part, as soon as she'd taken her seat, she'd begun trying to catch Michael's attention with a series of winks, waves, the sort of tongue clucks you might use to call a horse, and flamboyantly blown kisses.

Michael had kept his focus steadfastly on the wizard.

Dr. Pym had started by discussing the newest reports from around the globe, and Kate had found herself again thinking of Emma, wondering if she was scared, if she was cold or hungry, feeling again the dull, empty ache in her chest. How could she have failed her sister so badly? And how was it possible that she, who commanded the power of the *Atlas*, who could stop time, who could jump a thousand years into the past as quick as thought, was unable to find her? It didn't seem right.

She'd been called back to the conversation by the sounds of an argument.

"Lady Gwendolyn," Dr. Pym had said, "be reasonable—"

"But a dwarf? Oh no, no, Doctor, I think not."

"Please understand," King Bernard had said, gesturing about with a large peacock feather (where had that come from?). "We think dwarves are marvelous at certain things—pounding bits of metal with other bits of metal, getting insensibly drunk. But large-scale strategic thinking is not really a dwarf's forte. Or small-scale strategic thinking, for that matter. Or, well, thinking—full stop."

Kate had leaned toward Michael. "What's going on?"

"Dr. Pym told them that he's putting King Robbie in charge of the defense of Loris and the Archipelago, and the elves don't like it. Typical." Then he'd added, "Did you notice how Wilamena's hair seems to have its own private breeze?"

Kate had ignored this last, noting that it wasn't just the elves who objected to King Robbie being in charge. Captain Stefano was purple-faced with fury, and Magda von Klappen, the Viennese witch, was leaning forward and rapping her knuckles on the table.

"Pym, Captain Stefano has led the city guard for forty years! He should command the defense. And honestly, you can't expect a witch or wizard to take orders from a dwarf!"

"Exactly," King Bernard had said. "Now, if he were giving counsel on belching—"

"Listen here, blondie." The dwarf king's eyes were dark with anger. "I've been patient this far—"

"ENOUGH!"

And that was when Dr. Pym had admonished them for fighting, warning them what would happen if they didn't band together, and Kate had begun to wonder how much longer they would bicker and dither before discussing the real reason they were all here: rescuing Emma.

"Captain Stefano has put in great service over the years," the wizard went on, "and we will need his help and expertise. But he has never actually fought a war; King Robbie has. Not to mention, I shall be working closely with King Robbie on all details of the defense. Does that satisfy everyone?"

There was a general, if grudging, nodding.

"In any case," Dr. Pym said, "all this talk of war is mere preamble. It is my suspicion that these attacks, perhaps the Dire

Magnus's entire war, represent little more than an attempt to occupy us while he pursues his true purpose, namely, the recovery of the *Reckoning*."

A deep silence fell on the gathering. Kate could hear distant voices drifting upward from the town.

Finally, she thought.

"However," Dr. Pym said, "I would first like to acknowledge the debt we owe to two of our company. Without their courage and sacrifice and steadfastness, the *Chronicle* and the *Atlas* would already be in the enemy's hands and our cause lost. We owe them our most profound thanks."

Kate saw the whole Council, dwarves, elves, witches, and wizards, giving her and her brother small, deferential bows as Michael nodded and made "it's no big deal" gestures.

"But our greatest challenge lies before us," Dr. Pym said. "Five days ago, Katherine and Michael's younger sister, Emma, who is destined to be the Keeper of the *Reckoning*, was kidnapped by the Dire Magnus. The *Reckoning*, as you all well know, is the Book of Death. Should it fall into the enemy's hands, all our lives, indeed, the life of every being in both the magical and nonmagical worlds, is forfeit. It cannot—it must not happen."

"And how close to finding the *Reckoning* is Mr. Dark and Terrible?" asked Hugo Algernon. "Must be close or you wouldn't have dragged me here to listen to you palaver and play referee to these dunderheads." And he gestured to include pretty much everyone present.

"I fear our enemy is very close. In fact—"

"But perhaps you panic a bit too much, Doctor," interrupted

the plump Chinese wizard, stroking his long white beard as he spoke. "The *Reckoning* has not been seen in thousands of years, yes? What truly are the chances?"

"Master Chu is right," said Magda von Klappen. "The *Reckoning* has been missing since the fall of Rhakotis. I think it very unlikely the Dire Magnus will find it anytime soon. Even if he does possess the girl."

Dr. Pym shook his head. "Magda, you of all people should know that things have changed. The *Atlas* and the *Chronicle* have both been recovered. The *Reckoning* will sense this. It will attempt to reach out to its Keeper. Every moment she is in the Dire Magnus's control, his chances of finding the book increase. And as you all must have noticed, he is not the same being we faced before. His power seems to have increased tenfold. He may have means of finding the book we cannot even imagine."

"Ha!" Hugo Algernon barked. "That shut you up, von Klapper. Congrats, Pym, that's the least stupid thing you've said this century."

The dark-haired witch and Dr. Pym both ignored this, and Dr. Pym went on.

"I know you've all had meetings with your various clans and subcouncils, and I am hoping that you are here to tell us that you have a lead on where the child is being held, that we have some clue that might help us forestall this catastrophe."

This was it. Kate held her breath and looked about the table.

No one spoke.

Then Haraald exploded, "Well, it's not like they'd tell us if they did know!"

He was glaring across at the elfish delegation.

"And what precisely is that supposed to mean?" asked King Bernard.

"Oh, so you're saying that if the elves knew where this wee lass was being held, you wouldn't try to get her and the *Reckoning* for yourselves? You could be sitting here now just to throw us off while your elf commandos or whatever are out grabbing her! Maybe that's why you were late! Off making your secret plans!"

"Now, brother," King Robbie said, "there's no proof of that." But he was looking at the elves suspiciously.

"Preposterous," King Bernard sniffed. "It is well known that we care very little about such things. The same way dwarves care little about personal grooming or bodily cleanliness."

"If there's anyone who'd like the *Reckoning* for themselves," Hugo Algernon said, "she's sitting right there." And he jabbed a stubby finger at Magda von Klappen. "But she'll be disappointed, 'cause last I heard, there's no recipes for apple strudel in the Book of Death."

"Oh be quiet, you hairy fool," the witch snapped. "You're embarrassing yourself."

"Von Klapper, you've been obsessed with the *Reckoning* for decades, and everyone knows it."

"Of course I have. It must be found before it falls into the wrong hands."

"And I suppose that yours would be the right hands, would they? Ha!"

"Tell me"—King Bernard leaned toward Robbie McLaur—"have you heard of this invention called shampoo?"

"That's it!" Robbie McLaur jumped up, pulling his ax from his belt. "I'll part that pretty hair a' yours right now!"

"STOP IT! WHAT IS WRONG WITH YOU ALL?!"

In the silence that followed this outburst, Kate just had time to realize that she was standing, that everyone was staring at her, and that it was she who had spoken. But by then, more words were pouring out of her.

"Didn't you hear Dr. Pym?! If you don't work together, you're going to die! And you know what, go ahead! Let the Dire Magnus kill you, I could care less! I'm here for my sister! She's only twelve years old and he has her! And all I want to know is, can any of you tell me anything about where she is? Can you?! Can any of you help?"

Wilamena was the first to speak. Her voice was gentle and surprisingly unsilly.

"We just heard from the last of our scouts, the ones who left the night your sister was taken. They have found nothing."

"Nor have any of our colonies around the world detected any hint of her," King Bernard said. "I am sorry."

"But someone"—Kate's voice was cracking, and she could feel tears burning the corners of her eyes—"someone must've found something!"

She looked at Robbie McLaur, but the dwarf king shook his head. "Haraald and I have just come from the dwarfish Council. Not a whisper."

Kate turned to Magda von Klappen and Master Chu. The witch shook her head, and Master Chu murmured, "Regrettable. Very regrettable," and for a moment, he gave off stroking his beard.

"Katherine—" Dr. Pym said.

But Kate had heard enough. She turned and ran from the terrace.

She ended up in the Garden. She had not planned on going there. She had run from the Council blindly, knowing only that she had to get away, rushing down hallways and staircases as if she could somehow outrun the despair that was threatening to crush her.

Then she charged out a door and came to a sudden halt.

The day before, she'd seen only a small piece of greenery through the end of the tunnel. Now, up close, she was struck by the Garden's size; it appeared to be more forest than garden, albeit one enclosed by the rose-colored walls of the Citadel. A path lay open before her, and Kate, still with no distinct plan in mind, began walking forward.

Unlike the vegetation on the rest of the island, which was dry and Mediterranean, the Garden was lush, the trees and plants seemed to hum with life, and, strangely, Kate found that the farther she walked and the more the Garden closed in about her, the better and calmer she felt.

Kate's hand had found its way to the golden locket that hung from her neck, the one her mother had given her the night, more than ten years earlier, when their family had been separated. All her life, it had comforted Kate to worry the locket between her thumb and forefinger and recall memories of their parents and tell herself that if she just held on, if she kept Michael and Emma safe just a little bit longer, their family would be together once again.

But as she delved farther into the Garden, Kate found herself thinking not of her parents, but of Rafe; in particular, of a dream she'd had the night before. In the dream, she'd been dancing with Rafe in the snow in New York. The thing was, it wasn't just a dream. She and Rafe had danced in the snow, on New Year's Eve, more than a hundred years in the past. Even now, she could recall the chill of the night air, she could feel Rafe's arms around her, the warmth of his body, she could hear the thud of his heart as she lay her head against his chest. All of that had been in her dream. But there had been more: in the dream, Rafe had leaned down and whispered in her ear:

I'll never leave you.

That hadn't happened in real life. So why had her mind added it?

And she was still wondering about that as she stepped out into a clearing.

Before her stood a giant tree. The trunk was enormous, wide, and deeply ridged, a gray-brown contour of gullies and crevices, and as the tree climbed upward, it split again and again, sending out thick, knobby branches in all directions. Kate had seen bigger trees, just days before, in Antarctica; but this one was different. Those trees had just been trees; this one felt almost like a person. It had a presence. And the tree seemed to be spreading its arms not just over the clearing but over the entire Garden, and beyond.

Nor was that all; before the tree was a small, still, very dark pool. Kate tried to peer into it but could see nothing, as if the water itself were black.

She realized then that all the time she'd been walking in the Garden, something had been drawing her forward; it had been the power she'd sensed the day before, and this place, the tree and pool, was the source. But how was that possible?

Kate placed her hand against the ridged bark, closed her eyes, and felt the power humming through her. She suddenly had the thought that if she opened her eyes, she would see Rafe standing beside her, and she couldn't tell if she was more scared that he would be there, or more scared that he wouldn't be.

"Katherine."

Kate opened her eyes and turned. Dr. Pym was stepping into the clearing. Rafe was nowhere to be seen.

"I thought I might find you here."

The old wizard came and sat on a large, flat stone near the base of the tree. He took out his pipe and began to pack it full of tobacco. "I want to apologize. That must have been disheartening. Remember, we're dealing with centuries of suspicion, distrust, and prejudice between the magical races. Sometimes I fear that the Separation, in isolating them further, has only made matters worse."

"It's okay. I'm sorry I yelled."

"On the contrary, I'm glad you did. It shocked them into acting like adults." He had his pipe going and he blew out a cloud of bluish smoke. "But the reason I followed you was that we have not yet spoken of what happened in New York."

Dr. Pym gestured to a stone beside his. There were perhaps a dozen of them, spaced in a circle beneath the tree's branches. Hesitating just a moment, Kate took a seat.

"Of course, I know much of the story. I've had a hundred years to research it. I know of the children whose lives you saved; many of them grew up to be fine witches and wizards of my acquaintance. I know you met Henrietta Burke, such a fierce, proud woman. I'm glad you got to know her. I know too that you met the boy who became the Dire Magnus. But some details I have never been able to uncover. I would very much like to hear your side; also, I think speaking of it would do you good."

He fell silent. Kate could hear insects buzzing and whirring among the trees. She knew she had to get this out. Holding in the story—and the guilt—had been killing her. Still, she resisted.

"Dr. Pym, I don't—"

"Just begin at the beginning. Please."

And so that was what she did. She started with the attack on the orphanage in Baltimore, when she had used the *Atlas* to take the Screecher into the past, how she had ended up stranded in New York in 1899, a day before the Separation, and how she'd fallen among a tribe of magical street urchins led by the one-armed witch, Henrietta Burke, and the boy, Rafe. Focused as she was on telling the story, Kate didn't hear how her voice tightened when she spoke of Rafe, or see how her cheeks turned red, but the wizard heard, and saw. She told about being captured by Rourke and taken before the ancient, dying Dire Magnus. She told the wizard how Rafe's mother had been killed by humans, about the anger she'd felt in him, she told about the church where the children lived being burned by the mob, how she and Rafe had gotten the children out, how Henrietta Burke had died in the blaze, but not before first commanding Kate to "love him." Then she was at the part that made her feel like a traitor to her brother and sister, but she kept going, knowing she had to get it out, and she recounted to the wizard how she had stopped time when the bell had been about to crush Rafe, how she'd been shot by one of the mob, and how Rafe had gone to the old Dire Magnus and traded his own life, agreeing to become the new Dire Magnus, in order to save Kate.

"Michael keeps thinking that this is all his fault, that Emma would never have been kidnapped if he hadn't brought the Dire Magnus back to life," Kate said, "but really, it's my fault. Rafe became the Dire Magnus to save me!"

"My dear, if you'll forgive me"—the wizard knocked his pipe against the stone and ground out the embers with his heel—"it is pointless to think that way."

"But don't you see? Of all the possible times the *Atlas* could've sent me to in the past, it sent me there! It wanted me there for a reason! It wanted me to keep Rafe from becoming the Dire Magnus, and I didn't do it. If anything, I made it worse!"

"And I'm saying, you don't know that."

"Yes, I do! I—"

"No, you assume that the *Atlas* intended you to keep him from becoming the Dire Magnus, but you can't know that for certain. None of us do. Indeed, you may have fulfilled your role exactly as the *Atlas* intended."

"But I didn't change anything!"

The wizard chuckled. "Oh, Katherine, excuse me, you changed quite a bit. Consider: in a world in which you did not go into the past, Rafe became the Dire Magnus—"

"That's what I'm saying—"

"Let me finish. He became the Dire Magnus. But that was a Dire Magnus who did not know you. Who had not loved you or been loved in return."

Kate felt the heat in her cheeks. "You don't know that he . . . loved me."

Dr. Pym's voice softened. "He gave himself up for you. His actions speak for themselves. And I know you love him because I have eyes and ears, and I have been alive a very, very long time. So you say you changed nothing, but because of you, the Rafe who became the Dire Magnus knows love. And in the end, that may make all the difference."

"How?"

"Honestly?" He shrugged. "I don't know."

Kate was silent for a long moment. Just say it, she told herself. "Sometimes . . . I think I should have let him die."

She didn't dare look at him, but simply waited, staring at the ground.

He sighed. "I understand why you think that. But mercy is a quality never to be regretted. And who knows but that the Dire Magnus has some role to play in all this. I know it is hard to see, but what is happening now goes beyond even him.

"Now tell me, my dear, is there something else bothering you?"

Kate thought again of their father's message, that they must not allow Dr. Pym to bring the three Books together, and again, part of her wanted to tell him. But she would not break Michael's trust. She shook her head.

"No."

"Very well. Then I must say this: when we find Emma—and we will—I cannot allow you to come with us to rescue her."

"But—"

"To rescue Emma, wherever she is being held, we shall have to be fast and silent. If the enemy knows we are coming, he will move or threaten her. And the fact is, you and the Dire Magnus are somehow tied together. If you are with us, he will know immediately. I'm sorry. You must remain here."

Kate wanted to argue, but she also knew the wizard was right.

"I just want her back."

Dr. Pym squeezed her hand. "Katherine, I have been alive for thousands of years, but little, in all that time, gives me the pride I feel in you. You have become the person I knew you would be. Whatever happens, the world is in good hands."

Kate looked at him. She had the strangest feeling that the old wizard was saying goodbye.

He stood. "Come. Let us find your brother. I suspect he's hiding from the Princess."

Together, the two of them walked out of the Garden. Kate, her mind swimming, forgot to ask about the power she felt in this place. They found Michael in her room, and the three of them ate lunch on the balcony, where they could see the ships of refugees continuing to stream into port.

Soon afterward, word reached them that Gabriel had returned. He was waiting in the wizard's quarters, exhausted and ashen-faced. He told them that Emma was being held prisoner in the Altai Mountains of Mongolia, in a fortress surrounded by an army of ten thousand Imps and Screechers and the Dire Magnus himself.

CHAPTER SIX
The Bonding

"I apologize we could not come through closer to the valley," Dr. Pym said. "But there are wards that prevent my opening a portal there."

Michael, Wilamena, Dr. Pym, and Wallace, the sturdy-legged, black-bearded dwarf who was a veteran of the children's adventure in Cambridge Falls, were huddled in the shadow of a crag on the side of a mountain. They were waiting for the return of Gabriel and Captain Anton, the elf warrior, the pair of whom had gone ahead to ensure that the passage into the valley was safe and unguarded. Michael and the others had come through the portal perhaps a mile from their present location and then hiked to where they were over steep, rocky terrain, Michael's lungs gasping in the thin air.

"I'm fine," Michael said, though his chest was still heaving. "Really."

It was deep night, and there was no moon, but a thick blanket of stars gave light enough to see, and as they'd hiked and Michael had adjusted to the altitude, he'd been able to take in the soaring, snowcapped peaks, almost glowing in the starlight; he'd run his hands over the jagged-leafed plants that grew along the slope, which he'd assumed were the same as the one Gabriel had discovered and taken to Granny Peet; he'd even appreciated how clean and cold the air was, shockingly thin though it might be. The landscape was harsh and spare and yet, he'd reflected, had much to recommend it.

Except for the yaks. When they'd first stepped through the portal, Michael had heard something (definitely not human) bellowing close by, and he'd whipped about to see a group of large creatures above them on the slope.

"Watch out!" he'd cried. "There're—"

"Yaks," Gabriel had said. "Harmless."

"Never fear, Rabbit," Wilamena had said, sweeping up his hand in both of hers. "I won't let those nasty things eat you."

And as the elf princess had pressed herself to him (part of Michael's brain registering that she smelled of honey and dewdrops and, somehow, the hope of youth), he'd glanced over to see Wallace staring at him, his mouth agape.

Oh yes, he could've done without the yaks.

Luckily, their band had immediately begun walking, and the path had been narrow enough that they'd had to go single file, which meant that Wilamena had been unable to walk beside him and hold his "little rabbit paw-paw." Finally, they'd arrived at what seemed a dead end, an impassable rock wall rising up between two peaks, and Dr. Pym had led Michael, Wilamena, and Wallace to the cover of an outcropping while the elf captain and Gabriel went ahead to secure the passage.

"Dr. Pym," he said, "what's the plan?"

"My boy, I'm afraid that we must first get there and reconnoiter the situation."

"Okay, but once we rescue Emma, we'll still have to escape somehow, right? Are we just going to fight our way out?"

"If we must. But the wards around the valley seem to function only in one direction, to stop intrusion from the outside. I suspect that once we find your sister, we will be able to open a portal and escape. Indeed, I'm counting on it."

They were taking care to keep their voices low, as every sound echoed across the rocky slope. Michael was also inching to his left as Wilamena, crouched beside him, kept trying to wiggle her hand under his elbow. Of course, every time he moved, so did she. Fortunately, Wallace had stepped a few paces out onto the slope to stand watch.

As they waited, Michael found himself thinking about his conversation with Kate before they'd left, when they'd all been gathered on the terrace, only a few hours after Gabriel's return.

"I'm not coming," she had said. "Dr. Pym doesn't think I should, and he's right. Be safe, okay? Don't do anything stupid."

"You mean, like going right into the enemy's stronghold?"

"Yeah, like that."

Then she'd taken his hand and looked into his eyes. "Michael, you know I'd never choose anyone over you and Emma. You do know that, don't you?"

Michael had nodded, and now, sitting in the shadow of the outcropping, he felt ashamed for having ever suggested otherwise.

Kate had hugged him, and he'd found himself hugging her just as fiercely, promising, "I'll bring her back."

The moment had then taken a slightly weird turn when Kate and Michael had become aware that someone else was hugging them, the elf princess having wrapped her arms around the both of them, murmuring, "Our sweet family."

"Rabbit." Wilamena had finally wormed her hand through the crook of his arm and was holding it in a python-like grip. "Did you not see me motioning to you during the Council this morning? It felt almost as if you were ignoring me."

Michael glanced out at Wallace's short, blocky shape standing watch on the slope and hoped the dwarf was too far away to hear.

"Oh? You were? Sorry. I was just really focused on Dr. Pym."

"Of course, concern for your poor sister. Anywaaaay—I was thinking, when we return to Loris, we should announce our engagement publicly."

"Our what?"

"Our wedding engagement, silly. Are you feeling ill? You don't look at all well."

Michael was spared from replying by a loud crack of thunder. He stepped out onto the slope. The wizard stood looking up at the still-clear sky.

"What is it?" Michael asked. "Is there a storm coming?"

"Shhhh."

Dr. Pym had his eyes closed as if he was listening to the wind. And then it seemed to Michael that he felt a tremor in the air, and his hand went down to his bag, feeling for the bulk of the *Chronicle*. Something was wrong.

"No," the wizard whispered, "he can't be . . ."

"What?" Michael demanded. "What's happening?"

"The Dire Magnus. He's attempting a Bonding."

Emma heard the thunder boom and she gazed up through the windows of her cell, wondering how long till the storm was above her.

I'm gonna get drenched, she thought.

She had scarcely slept in two days. Every time she closed her eyes, she saw Miss Crumley facedown in the ruined chocolate cake. She told herself that it wasn't her fault, but it did no good. She felt like a murderer.

Rourke had come again the night before, leading her down out of the fortress and to the tent in the middle of the army where the Dire Magnus—she wouldn't even think of him as Rafe—had waited beside the silver scrying bowl.

"Right," he'd said. "We have a lot to do, ten years of orphanage directors to get through."

But Emma had refused to so much as look in the bowl.

"I could make you look." His voice had been even, almost friendly.

She had held her ground, and in the end, he had just spoken to her, which had been almost as bad, telling her that if she continued to fight her nature, to deny the anger that lived inside her, she would only destroy herself.

Except it wasn't true! That wasn't who she was; she wasn't a murderer!

But wasn't she? Wouldn't she kill him if given the chance? And Rourke? Hadn't she spent long hours in her cell imagining all different ways that she could massacre them both? But they deserved it! Killing someone who deserved it didn't make you a murderer! You were doing the world a favor.

Still, she knew it was not good for her to fantasize about killing the Dire Magnus and Rourke. It just happened so naturally; she would be thinking of Kate and Michael and Gabriel, wondering where they were, why they weren't coming for her; she'd grow more and more nervous and fearful; her fear would turn to anger—which she of course directed toward the Dire Magnus and Rourke—and then her anger would just keep building, making her more and more panicked and desperate, so that when she was least prepared to deal with it, there would be Miss Crumley's face, purple and gasping, accusing her of being a murderer.

Emma sat up. There were footsteps on the stairs. Then the door opened, and Rourke stood in her doorway, holding aloft a torch and flanked by a pair of *morum cadi*.

"I'm not going down to his stupid tent," she said. "You'll have to carry me."

Rourke smiled, a gloating, triumphant smile. "Oh, there'll be no looking in bowls tonight, child."

Emma heard a new sound then, or rather became aware of it, a steady *thock-thock-thock* growing louder on the stairs. Then Rourke stepped aside, and a red-robed figure shuffled into the room. It was the old man she had seen when she'd first gone among the army, two nights before. He stood there, leaning on his staff and staring at her with one dark gray eye and his eerie, blind, all-white one.

"Remember I told you," Rourke said, "that some of the *necromati* were former enemies of the Dire Magnus? This fellow here was one of those who helped Pym kill my master forty years ago.

He and Pym were bosom chums. Now he's my master's faithful servant. Aren't you?"

The old man said nothing, but continued staring at Emma.

"Of course, he doesn't remember," Rourke went on. "He couldn't even tell you his own name. He only knows that he loves our master and lives to serve him. And tonight that means something very special for you."

Then the old man stepped forward, his staff striking the stone floor, one hand raised and reaching toward her, and Emma couldn't help herself; she screamed.

"A Bonding," Dr. Pym said. "I always knew it was a possibility, but I did not believe that he would risk it. The more foolish I, for underestimating him."

"So what is it?" Michael wasn't even trying to keep his voice down. With the thunder and the wind, there seemed no point. Wilamena and Wallace had stepped up beside him. They were still waiting for the return of Gabriel and the elf captain.

The wizard looked at him.

"You and Katherine each are bound to your Books as Keepers. Those bonds developed naturally, as they should. But there is a ritual—I should say, *in theory*, as it has never actually been performed—that would force the bond between Emma and the *Reckoning*."

"And it's dangerous? This ritual thing?"

"Yes. It is dangerous." Dr. Pym placed a hand on Michael's shoulder. "There is a part of you that is neither mind nor body: call it the spirit, the soul, the *anima*. It is where the magic in you is to be found."

"You mean the *Chronicle*?"

"No, I mean the magic you were born with."

"But—"

"Let me finish. The Dire Magnus talks about the divide between the magical and the nonmagical, but he knows this is a fallacy. All living beings have magic in them, even if it lies dormant all their lives. Indeed, it may be that your spirit is in its very nature magic. This is a mystery I have never fully plumbed. What you must understand is that when you became Keeper, the *Chronicle* bound itself to your spirit. Just as the *Atlas* did with Katherine. And now the Dire Magnus is attempting to split Emma's spirit off from her body and send it out to find the *Reckoning*."

"And then she could lead him to where it's hidden?" Michael asked.

"Yes, that is one possibility."

And what are the other possibilities? Michael wondered.

The old wizard gripped his shoulder. "We must get there before the ritual is complete. And you must use the *Chronicle* to draw her spirit back."

Michael gave a jerky, nervous nod. He told himself that this would allow him to atone for bringing the Dire Magnus back to life; this was his chance.

Just then Gabriel returned. "The passage is open. Captain Anton stands guard. Come."

They started off and, very quickly, arrived at the base of the rock wall. It rose up before them, massive and unbroken, but Gabriel paused only to glance back and make sure they were all there; then he walked into the mountain and disappeared.

Michael let out a small gasp.

"An illusion," Dr. Pym said. "Let us hurry. Princess?"

Wilamena kissed Michael on the cheek and stepped through the rock face. Dr. Pym went next, vanishing as well, and then it was just Michael and Wallace.

Michael glanced awkwardly at the dwarf, the spot on his cheek where Wilamena had kissed him still burning.

"Elves," he muttered, not knowing what else to say.

Wallace tucked his thumbs into his belt and shook his head. "Never fear, lad. Wallace the dwarf knows how to keep a secret. Always said, a fella's private life is private." Then he added, "Even when it's deeply, deeply strange."

It turned out to be difficult not to flinch when advancing directly toward a rock wall, but Michael simply closed his eyes, and when he opened them a moment later, he was walking along a narrow gap between two peaks. And he could now hear drumming and shrieking in the distance, and there was light up ahead that wasn't starlight.

The others were waiting on a slope that tumbled down into a wide valley, and as he joined them, Michael saw, stretching away in both directions, a vast, dark, teeming mass, marked everywhere by orange-red plumes of fire. Michael knew he was looking at an army, and the sheer size of it made his legs tremble. He heard Wallace step up beside him and mutter, "Blimey but that's a big bloody army."

"There," Gabriel said, pointing.

Michael looked and saw the fortress perched on a rocky spire in the center of the valley. It was lit by torches, and Michael could make out the tower rising crookedly into the sky. Was Emma there, or had she been moved for the ritual? If she had been moved, how would they find her?

Michael was thinking this when, from the corner of his eye, he saw lightning snake across the sky. At the same moment, there was another crack, and he saw, on the opposite horizon, more lightning and a massing of dark clouds. It was a storm such as Michael had never seen, for it seemed to be coming from all directions at once and converging on the valley at incredible speed.

"Princess," the wizard said, "are you ready?"

Wilamena nodded and pulled something from a pocket at her waist. Michael recognized the golden bracelet that had once turned her into a dragon.

"But that was cut off! After she rescued us and brought us to the elves!"

"True," Dr. Pym said. "But I had a feeling that having a dragon on our side might come in handy. I reworked the enchantment and had a dwarfish smith forge a clasp so that the Princess could don and remove it at will. You might want to back up."

And Wilamena, who had snapped the bracelet over her wrist, was already transforming into the huge, golden-scaled dragon that Michael had met in Antarctica. Her back stretched wide and long; her fingers grew into talons; great, batlike wings fanned outward from her sides; she fell to all fours as a tail whipped into existence; and as the dragon's head swiveled toward him, Michael saw that the princess's liquid blue eyes had turned blood-red.

"Hello, Rabbit," the dragon said in a deep, purring rumble.

The lightning was now rippling at the edges of the valley. The wind slammed into Michael, nearly knocking him off his feet.

"My friends!" the wizard shouted. "The Dire Magnus will have committed much of his power to completing the Bonding. He is vulnerable. But there is little time! We must be speed itself!"

Michael was hoisted up by Gabriel, and an instant later they were all seated on the dragon's back, and Wilamena, with one powerful leap, sprang into the air.

The old white-eyed wizard touched Emma's forehead with one gnarled finger, muttering under his breath, and she felt a tremor pass through her body, as if everything in her was being shaken loose. Then he turned, nodded to Rourke, and one of the Screechers stepped forward and hoisted her onto its shoulder. Emma tried to struggle, but the touch of the creature's cold, half-decayed hands made her nauseous, sapping all her strength. And really, what was she going to do? Escape? Rourke led them down the tower stairs and down more stairs and then out into the courtyard, the *thock-thock* of the old man's staff steady and constant behind them.

In the center of the courtyard was a large fire, its flames whipping about wildly in the wind. Two more of the red-robed figures circled the fire, chanting and tossing in what looked like handfuls of sand or dust that caused the flames to rage even higher, and the white-eyed wizard moved to join them. Imps and Screechers lined the courtyard walls. A wooden chair was brought forward, and Emma was placed facing the fire, close enough that she could feel the heat against her skin. Her arms and legs were bound to the chair with leather straps.

From every corner of the sky, lightning arced toward the fortress.

The Dire Magnus was nowhere to be seen.

"Never fear, child," said Rourke, as if reading her thoughts. "My master's power is all around us."

Emma said nothing. Up until the moment she had been placed in the chair, she had been certain, absolutely, one hundred percent, willing-to-bet-her-life certain that she would be rescued, that Kate, Michael, Gabriel, Dr. Pym, all of them, any of them, would come and take her away. But as she saw the flames leaping above her, she realized, finally, that no one was coming. She was alone.

The robed figures were chanting more and more loudly, but the wind took their voices. She looked at Rourke and it was on her tongue to plead with him to stop, words that, days before, it would have killed her to utter. But she was too terrified to speak. She could only bite her lips and whimper.

She wanted her sister. It wasn't even about being rescued now. She wanted Kate there to hold her; she wanted to feel her sister's arms around her, hear her voice saying that it would all be okay. But Kate hadn't come; no one had come.

She would not cry; that was the one thing she wouldn't give them.

Don't be scared.

Emma jerked her head round; it was his voice. But where was he?

I'm helping you fulfill your destiny. And mine too.

What're—and she realized, with a start, that she was thinking her response, not speaking it—what're you doing to me?

I'm sending you out to find the Reckoning. *That is, I'm sending part of you.*

And before she could ask what he meant, something began to happen.

It was almost as if the air around Emma was thickening. She felt it pushing against her eyes, her eardrums, the palms of her hands, even the balls of her feet. And then it was inside her, squeezing her bones, her organs, her heart, and she began to feel that something was being pressed out of her, out of every fiber and cell of her body, as if she were a piece of fruit that was being wrung dry. And the thing that was being taken from her was both insubstantial and yet somehow vital. She tried to hold on to it, whatever it was, but she couldn't. She felt the thing leave her body, and then, for a single strange, awful moment, she saw it in the air before her, shimmering, and then, with one wrenching yank, it was pulled into the fire, and Emma fell back against the chair, empty.

CHAPTER SEVEN
The Wizard Pays His Debt

The wind knocked into them, throwing them about the sky. A lightning bolt shuddered past, close enough for Michael to feel the electricity tearing apart the air. Seated just behind the dragon's head, Michael found he had nowhere to grip, and he had to use his thighs to squeeze the scaly, barrel-like body. But he would have tumbled off for sure had not Gabriel, sitting behind him, kept one arm wrapped around his middle.

Once they were over the fortress, Wilamena banked into a tight circle so that they were looking down into the courtyard, a single bright patch in the darkness below.

"I see her," the dragon said. "She is tied to a chair. I count forty *morum cadi* and Imps. Rourke is there as well."

"I will deal with Rourke," Gabriel said.

"There are also three *necromati*," the dragon continued. "But I do not see the Dark One."

"He is there." Dr. Pym's voice came from behind Gabriel, and he was shouting to be heard over the rush of wind. "We must be fast. Gabriel will hold off Rourke. Wallace, Captain Anton, and Princess Wilamena will deal with the Imps and *morum cadi*. Leave the *necromati* to me. Michael, you must free your sister."

"Okay!" Michael's hand went to his side; the dwarfish blade was still there.

"I could just lift her away," the dragon said. "We could be gone in an instant."

"No," the wizard shouted. "The ritual has begun! Her spirit must be returned. Now—dive!"

And Michael felt Gabriel tighten his grip as the dragon banked even more sharply and, with a few beats of her wings, plunged into a steep, spiraling dive. The icy air whipped past him, and Michael threw up a hand to keep his glasses from flying away. The *Chronicle*, in the pouch of his bag, flapped about behind him as figures in the courtyard rushed into view. His eyes watered, but Michael could still make out the lines of *morum cadi* and Imps, he could see the red-robed figures around the fire, he could see Rourke, his bald head reflecting back the flames.

And then he saw Emma, her head bowed, looking so small and vulnerable.

I'm here, he thought. I'm coming.

Then, when they were still a hundred feet above the courtyard, Rourke looked up.

Michael didn't hear the giant man's shout—the wind rushing past was deafening, but the effect on the assembled Imps and *morum cadi* was instantaneous. Blades appeared all over the courtyard, and Michael saw Rourke move a step closer to Emma and pull a pair of long, curved knives from under his coat.

Then Wilamena was swooping twenty feet over the courtyard, and Michael felt Gabriel's arm pull away, and he glanced back to see Gabriel leap off the dragon's back, flying through the air to smash feet-first into Rourke's chest, carrying with him all the force of their dive and knocking the man to the ground; then Michael whipped his head back around as Wilamena unleashed a torrent of flame that consumed an entire third of the courtyard along with a dozen Screechers and Imps, and she was beating her wings, slowing to land, but before her claws had even touched the stones, Wallace and Captain Anton, ax and sword out and ready, had already leapt off her back.

"Go!" Dr. Pym yelled, pulling Michael off the dragon and pushing him toward Emma, who now sat unguarded beside the fire. "Go!"

As Michael ran toward his sister, he heard Wilamena unleashing another jet of flame and he saw Rourke starting to rise while Gabriel battled Imps and *morum cadi* on all sides, and Captain Anton and Wallace were running beside Michael, flanking him, and just before he reached Emma, Michael looked over to see Dr. Pym advancing toward the three red-robed figures, two of whom had stepped forward, while the third—an old, gray-haired man who was leaning on a staff and who had something wrong with one of his eyes—hung back, and Dr. Pym's hands burned with blue fire—

And then Michael was kneeling before Emma and he forgot everything else.

Her arms and legs had been tied to the chair with leather

straps. Her head had fallen forward so that her chin rested on her chest. Michael couldn't see any injuries, there were no cuts or bruises, but her hands and face were filthy, and she was wearing the same clothes she'd been abducted in days before.

"Emma!"

He cut her bonds; her hands fell into her lap, but her head stayed lolled forward, her eyes closed.

"Quickly!" Dr. Pym's voice carried over the din of battle. "The *Chronicle*!"

Turning slightly, Michael saw that two of the red-robed figures had become pillars of fire, burning where they stood, and the old wizard was facing off against the gray-haired man, who now struck the courtyard with his staff so that a crack opened in the stones, splintering across to Dr. Pym, forcing the wizard to leap away from the widening gulf, and Michael heard, or thought he heard, Dr. Pym say, "I'm sorry, old friend," as he waved his hand and flames erupted about the man. Michael turned his back on the scene, reached into his bag, and pulled out the *Chronicle*. The heavy red-leather book seemed to hum in anticipation, and there was a similar stirring in Michael, knowing that he would soon be in touch with its power. Then, just as he'd begun to open it, he felt something behind him and spun about—

Kate had been given no inkling about when the rescuers might return, but she'd assumed it would be several hours at least, and perhaps much longer. She told herself this so that she would not worry as the night crept on; but she knew that she would worry even so, every second till Michael and the others returned with Emma.

They had left at dusk from the open terrace where the Council had been held, vanishing into a portal created by Dr. Pym. Afterward, Kate had stood there alone, watching the sun sink into the sea and hugging herself against the gathering chill.

By now, it was fully dark and the lights of the approaching boats were strung out like jewels flung across the black table of the sea. She turned away, intending to go down to the port where King Robbie was overseeing the work to fortify the harbor. But ten minutes later, through no conscious decision, she found herself again in the Garden, under the arms of the great tree, sitting beside the black pool.

In the gloom, the tree seemed even more massive and primeval, the pool darker and more still, and she closed her eyes and felt the power radiating outward, through the roots under her feet, through the branches above her, through the air. And as before, she felt calmed. She sat down on one of the flat, white rocks that were arranged in the clearing. Time seemed to slow. Her anxiety about Emma and Michael ebbed.

She found herself thinking about an exchange between Gabriel and Dr. Pym that had taken place just before the group had departed. She'd only heard some of what was said, but the tenor of the conversation had made a deep impression. In the past, Gabriel had always been very deferential to the wizard. But his attitude as the two of them had spoken on the terrace had been challenging and wary. Then there was the snippet that Kate had overheard, the wizard saying, "I understand your feelings. I only ask that you trust me a little further. The prophecy is the key. . . ."

What had they been talking about? Why would Dr. Pym have to ask Gabriel to trust him? Did this have something to do with the warning their father had given Michael about not allowing Dr. Pym to bring the three Books together? And what did he mean about the prophecy? Kate decided that when Michael returned, she would convince him that they had to speak to Dr. Pym. Enough with the secrets and the not knowing.

She was not sure exactly when she was aware that someone was behind her. She didn't hear anyone approach. There was no snapped twig. No one coughed or said her name. She just suddenly knew that she was not alone.

She turned, and the world stopped.

He was standing six feet away. She would've said that he was in shadow, but the whole clearing was in shadow, only speckled here and there with slivers and flecks of starlight. He was wearing the same clothes she had last seen him in, more than a hundred years before. His dark hair was messy, his eyes almost black in the gloom.

He wasn't real; he couldn't be. And she told herself to shut her eyes, count to ten, and he would be gone.

She had gotten as far as three when he said her name.

When she opened her eyes, Rafe had not moved.

He said, "It's a trap; he knows they're coming."

Michael watched as the boy emerged untouched from the fire. Michael was less surprised than Emma had been by his apparent youth. After all, Michael had encountered him once before, in the ghostly church in the Fold, the crossover point between the worlds of the living and the dead. So it was not his age that momentarily froze Michael, but rather his perfect calmness and self-possession in the midst of the chaos. The last of the red-robed figures, the old white-eyed man, was engulfed in flames and quickly turning to ash, but the boy didn't even look over. In fact, he was smiling.

"Pym"—he laced the name with contempt—"I have so looked forward to this moment." Michael felt the boy's eyes move from Dr. Pym to him. "And you even brought me Michael."

Pym's response was to mumble a few words that Michael couldn't quite hear and flick his right hand outward. The courtyard wall behind the boy was covered in thick vines, and they whipped out and wrapped around him, encircling his arms and legs and body and dragging him to the ground.

"Princess!" the wizard shouted, and Michael saw the golden dragon leap across the courtyard to hover over the struggling body and unleash a blue-white blast of flame. Michael turned his head away, but the heat prickled the hair on the back of his head. When the roar of the flame stopped, he heard another noise, a grinding and crunching, and he saw Dr. Pym swing his arms forward, and the fortress's tower teetered in the sky above them. Michael threw his body across Emma just before the crash jolted them sideways and shards of rock peppered his back and arms, and when it was finally silent—an eerie silence, the only noise the storm still gathering overhead—he turned with the dust stinging his eyes and saw the mountain of broken black stones where the boy, the Dire Magnus, had stood.

Then Dr. Pym swiveled on him, shouting:

"For mercy's sake! He won't stay trapped long! Bring her back! Now!"

And Michael turned to his sister, opened the *Chronicle*, and was stopped.

Emma was looking right at him, and there was such emptiness and desolation in her eyes that it stabbed Michael in the heart.

She said, "You're too late."

Gabriel heard the wizard shouting, but he didn't look over. Rourke was bearing down on him, his knives (which in a normal man's hands would've been swords) moving so fast that Gabriel was blocking on instinct and guesswork.

It was astonishing that Rourke was even up and fighting, considering the force with which Gabriel had struck him after leaping from the dragon's back. But nothing about Rourke was normal, and Gabriel now had cuts on both arms and a gash across his ribs, while Rourke was bleeding from a deep cut on his shoulder and a blow to his forehead that Gabriel had delivered with the butt of his sword.

Gabriel had seen the toppling of the tower and knew Rourke had noted it as well, but if the giant was at all discouraged by his master being subdued, he gave no sign.

"I'm surprised at you, lad"—the tip of one of Rourke's knives sliced through the air an inch from Gabriel's eye—"still helping the old wizard. Weren't you listening when I told you that he's leading the children to their doom?"

Gabriel landed a kick in the man's middle, which felt like kicking stone.

"But your little Emma is quite the wonder," the giant went on, unfazed. "My master sees in her an anger that could tear apart the world."

Gabriel blocked one of Rourke's knives, but felt the other draw a hot, bloody line across his forearm.

"Wouldn't that be a magnificent end to the story? The child you work so hard to save destroys us all and herself in the bargain. Could it be your wizard has the same idea? Perhaps we should be allies after all."

With a cry, Gabriel brought down his sword with all his strength. Rourke caught the blade in the V of his raised knives.

"I think, lad, you must be your own particular kind of fool."

He wrenched the sword out of Gabriel's hands and flung it across the courtyard. He moved in, and Gabriel spoke for the first time.

"There are many types of fool," he said, and ducked.

Rourke turned just in time to see the dragon's great mailed tail as it swung about and knocked him through the wall of the fortress. Gabriel had seen the dragon over Rourke's shoulder and read her intention, and now he watched as Rourke tumbled down the escarpment and out of sight. He turned to the golden dragon.

"Thank you."

The dragon rumbled an acknowledgment, then spun around to roast a troop of Screechers behind her. Gabriel looked for his sword and, with some surprise, found it at his feet. He seized it, then took quick stock of the situation in the courtyard. Only a handful of the enemy remained, but it would not be long till reinforcements arrived from the valley. Or the Dire Magnus broke free from his makeshift prison. The time to leave was now.

But, unable to help himself, Gabriel looked at Emma's small form slumped in the chair and his mind went to what Rourke had said:

An anger that could tear apart the world.

What were they doing to her?

* * *

It was gone. Whatever the thing was that had been taken from her had been drawn into the fire. And then to where? All she knew was that it was somewhere else, somewhere impossibly far away. And perhaps *gone* was the wrong word, as she could still feel it. Like she was flying a kite on a very, very, very long string.

But the farther away the thing had drifted, the fainter the connection had become, the thinner the cord bonding her to it, and now the slightest movement or jarring threatened to sever the bond completely.

What was it that had been taken from her? She still didn't know. She felt so cold and empty, as if she were a glass shell that might shatter at the slightest touch.

Michael was kneeling beside her, that red book of his open on his thighs. Flames appeared over the surface of the book, and there was a sharp *snap* on the cord that connected her to that lost and distant part of herself, and she could feel Michael trying to reel it back in. Only it didn't want to come.

She heard him shouting to Dr. Pym that it wasn't working, that he needed help.

Suddenly Gabriel was beside her, his face bloody and urgent, and at the sight of him, Emma's heart swelled in her chest, telling her that she wasn't hollow after all. If she hadn't felt so weak, she would've leapt into his arms.

"We must leave now!" he said to the wizard. "While we can."

But Michael was arguing, saying that he still hadn't brought back her spirit. Her spirit? Was that what had been taken from her?

Then Dr. Pym opened his mouth to speak, but the explosion cut him off.

Emma scarcely felt it, for she had realized that that missing part of her hadn't just drifted away; there was something out there, pulling it on.

And she knew what that something was.

She felt the world around her falling away, and then, following some instinct—or was it her spirit, sending her a message down the cord that still connected them?—she closed her eyes.

For a few moments, all Michael could hear was a ringing in his head.

When the smoke and dust had cleared, he looked up.

He saw the golden dragon flying toward the figure of the Dire Magnus, who was emerging, seemingly unscathed, from the smoke and fire—

He saw the boy sorcerer wave his hand and the dragon turn upon Wallace—

He saw the blast of white flame that engulfed the dwarf—

He saw Captain Anton leap away from the jet of flame aimed at him.

Michael closed his eyes, choking on the dust, and when he looked again, the elf was astride the dragon with a rope lashed about her neck, the dragon bucking and twisting in the air, trying to dislodge her rider—

He saw Wallace's ax on the ground, black and smoking—

He saw Dr. Pym nod at Gabriel and walk out to meet the Dire Magnus—

It was then that Michael's hearing began to return, and the first thing he heard was his own voice, shouting the wizard's name, but the wizard did not turn back.

A wind that had nothing to do with the storm overhead had sprung up in the courtyard. It swirled about, dispelling the mustard-colored smoke from the dissolving bodies of the *morum cadi*, lashing Michael's cheek with small sticks and bits of stone, and creating a cyclone around Dr. Pym and the dark-haired boy.

"What's he doing?!" Michael shouted.

But Gabriel was standing still as a statue and said nothing, and Michael watched as the old wizard and the dark-haired boy came face to face, the tornado tightening around them, and Michael lost sight of them in the whirl of dust and debris, though it seemed to him that they were lifted up into the air. He saw the golden dragon and her rider caught by the cyclone, spun about and thrown away, cartwheeling into the night. In the corner of his vision, Michael saw the courtyard doors burst open as Rourke charged in at the head of a horde of Screechers, then stopped, held in check by the tornado. Suddenly, anything that was not stone was lifted into the air, and Michael closed his eyes as Gabriel threw his body over him and Emma, anchoring them to the ground.

Then a voice was shouting his name, and Michael knew that something was wrong with his hearing, for he couldn't actually be hearing the voice.

"Michael!"

He opened his eyes into the swirling wind and saw Kate standing there, gripping his hand. Gabriel held Emma in his arms, and Kate was reaching toward him.

"We have to leave! Now!"

"No!"

"Yes! We—"

"No! Wait!"

He had to try, once more, to call back Emma's spirit, and he opened the book, placed his hand on the page—

But then the wind stopped, all was still, and Michael, unable not to, turned and saw the Dire Magnus standing in the center of the courtyard, his hand resting on the shoulder of Dr. Pym, who was slumped forward, head down, on his knees.

"If you leave," he said, "the wizard dies."

It was like being in a dream.

Emma knew that her body was back in the courtyard, with Michael and Gabriel at her side. But her spirit was here, wherever *here* was, and she was seeing what it saw. She was flying over a land of smoke and fire, being pulled onward by the same inexorable force as before.

She felt a shiver of terror: Was this what happened after you died? Had she died? What if she couldn't get back?

Then she was soaring up the face of an enormous cliff, moving faster and faster, and the question was forgotten.

She saw a creature, perched on the cliff, turning to look at her; the creature had the body of a man, but the face and head of a great black bird, and then she was past it, moving through darkness, picking up even more speed. It was here, the thing that was calling her, pulling her on—the book.

She reached out with ghostly fingers. She was so close—

And then the cord tying her to her body, now worlds away, snapped taut—

The courtyard was still.

Rafe stood with his hand on the wizard's shoulder, smiling.

"Kate, it's really you—"

"Don't!" Kate could feel tears burning her eyes. "Don't do that!"

Don't act like you're you, she wanted to say. But she couldn't, for he was Rafe, exactly Rafe, exactly as she remembered, exactly as she'd seen him only moments before. And seeing him, hearing him, her heart twisted painfully in her chest. She told herself that if only she'd had more time to prepare, she could've been ready for this. But one second she'd been standing in the Garden, calling on the magic of the *Atlas*, and the next she was here, amid the chaos, Emma slumped beside her, Michael frantic, Wallace and Wilamena and Captain Anton nowhere to be seen, Dr. Pym on his knees, Rafe standing there, looking at her—

And truthfully, no amount of time could've prepared her.

"Kate!" Michael's face was covered in sweat; his voice and body trembled. He slammed shut the red book; its fire went out. "I did it! I brought her spirit back!"

What was he talking about? Brought her spirit back from where?

"We can go," Michael hissed. "Now!"

"Kate." Rafe's voice pulled at her. "The wizard is your enemy. Not me. Did he promise that if you find the Books, you'll defeat me and be reunited with your parents? It's not true. The prophecy says that the Keepers will find the Books and bring them together, but it also says that the Keepers will die. Pym knows this; he's always known it. To destroy me, he's willing to sacrifice you and your brother and sister."

Kate's eyes whipped again to Michael. Was this what their father had meant when he'd warned Michael not to let Dr. Pym bring all three Books together? She felt a nauseous lurch in her stomach. But it couldn't be true! Dr. Pym wouldn't have lied to them! Not about that!

"I can promise you what the wizard never could. Life. Kate, help me—"

"Lies . . ."

Dr. Pym had raised his head. His face was ravaged with pain, the whites of his eyes shot through with blood, his voice weak and hurried.

"Yes, the prophecy foretells the deaths of the Keepers, but there is a way that you and your brother and sister can survive. You must—"

He groaned and pitched forward.

Rafe shook his head. "See? He even admits lying. Trust me, Kate! Please!"

Kate's breath was coming fast and shallow, and she felt like the earth had shifted under her feet. She knew she should just take her brother and sister and Gabriel and escape.

"Kate . . ."

Emma had struggled back to consciousness.

"I can find it, Kate. I can find the book. I can feel it."

Kate grabbed her sister's hand and tried to calm herself, to think. If she left, Dr. Pym was as good as dead. However much the boy looked like Rafe, he was the Dire Magnus, and he would kill the wizard.

But if she stayed, she would be dooming them all. And there was no reason to stay! Dr. Pym had lied to them; he'd said so himself! She owed him nothing!

Then she looked across at the wizard, his thin shoulders and white hair, the ripped tweed suit; she saw his glasses on the stones before him, one lens now shattered; and she knew if not what to do, then the one thing she couldn't do. For whatever Dr. Pym might've lied about or hidden from them, Kate knew what love felt like, and she knew the wizard loved her and her brother and sister. She couldn't leave him here to die.

She gripped Emma's hand and took a deep breath.

"Let Dr. Pym go."

The dark-haired boy shook his head. "You have to choose who you believe." The courtyard became even more still and quiet, and it seemed that everyone else faded away, and there was only her and Rafe. "I've been waiting for you such a long time."

And he was Rafe, she saw that now; he was not the Dire Magnus, not her enemy; he was the boy she'd danced with on the street in New York, who'd held her hand, who'd saved her life. . . .

She took a step forward.

"No."

The wizard's voice broke the spell. Kate saw that Dr. Pym's hands, his arms—his whole body—was beginning to shimmer.

"Go," he said, looking up to meet her gaze. "Find the last book. It is the only hope for defeating him. I swear to you, there is a way to survive. The prophecy is incomplete. There is more to it than you know. More than even I know." He gripped Rafe's arm as the light coming from him grew brighter. It was as if every atom of the wizard's body was turning into an atom of light, streaming away behind him, and Rafe was caught in its wake.

"I'm sorry I cannot guide you. But know that I will always be with you."

Kate felt dread building in her chest; something terrible was about to happen, but she didn't know what, or how to stop it.

"I won't leave you!"

"I know," the wizard said. "That is what he is counting on."

Kate could see a black cloud pulsing about Rafe; the darkness seemed to be pressing back against the light pouring from the wizard, fighting it.

"Foolish old man," Rafe's voice was tense with effort. "Destroying yourself will accomplish nothing."

Dr. Pym paid him no mind, but kept his eyes fixed on Kate.

"And I have owed the universe a death for many years. It is past time I paid my debt. Now go."

Kate's scream was cut off as time snapped forward, and the light streaming from the wizard gathered itself and exploded backward, blasting the boy out into the night, and the entire half of the courtyard, the fortress, gave way, tumbling into the valley in a great, crashing roar.

Kate stared in disbelief. In the moment before the explosion, the wizard's body had changed entirely into light and energy. He was gone.

Then Rourke rushed forward, the horde at his heels, and Kate gripped her brother's and sister's hands, closed her eyes, and felt the ground vanish beneath her feet. A second later, she dropped to her knees on the soft, wet earth. The night around them was silent and still, and a sob of pain broke from her throat.

CHAPTER EIGHT
The New World

Kate opened her eyes feeling as if she had not slept at all, though she knew she must've, for it was now light, just barely light, just the gray beginnings of morning. The ground she was lying on was damp, as were her clothes, the early-morning mist having gathered and thickened while she slept.

She saw that she was alone and stepped out of the hollowed-out nook in the hillside where she and Michael and Emma had slept. She saw a country of rugged, treeless hills that fell down to narrow silver-blue lakes. She could see no town or city or houses. There were no roads or train tracks. No columns of smoke telling of hidden chimneys. The land was deserted.

Standing there, Kate allowed herself to think back to the night before. Not to what had happened in the fortress, but afterward, when they'd arrived here, wherever *here* was. There had been tears and embraces, Emma clinging to Kate, Kate clinging to Emma,

Emma seizing Michael around the neck and wrenching him into a three-way embrace, Emma saying how she'd heard Kate calling to her just before she'd been kidnapped and had known she wasn't dead, known that sooner or later her sister would rescue her, telling them she wasn't hurt, she was fine, really—

Kate stopped herself. She could feel the black cloud of the night before yearning to envelop her. She had to focus on the here and now.

Michael was sitting a few yards away. He had his journal propped up against his knees and was writing quickly, his face close to the page. As she walked over, Michael capped his pen and slid it and his notebook into his bag. He didn't seem surprised when Kate hugged him.

"Hi," he said.

"Hi."

They were keeping their voices low, as if not wanting to disturb the stillness of the morning. Michael gestured to a flat rock beside him.

"I'm afraid this is all I had with me."

On the rock were four small, neat piles of nuts and dried fruits. Kate recognized the "emergency rations" that he kept in his bag, and she felt herself smile. Despite how much he had changed, Michael was still the person he always had been: prepared, organized, meticulous, and unashamed of it, certain that those qualities would pay off in the end, as they always did.

She picked up a few almonds and ate them. They were hard and crunchy, and she swallowed dryly, wishing she had water.

"Where're Emma and Gabriel?"

"They went to try and figure out where we are. Maybe find some food."

"You could have woken me."

"Gabriel said not to. He said you needed the rest."

The night before, after their first moments of reunion had passed, they'd discussed returning immediately to Loris and the Rose Citadel—escaping from the Dire Magnus's fortress, Kate had, in fact, told the *Atlas* to take them to Loris, only somehow they'd ended up instead in this strange, lonely place—but the days of Emma's abduction and the confrontation in the fortress had taxed all of them to the limit, and Kate had felt her confidence in her power to command the *Atlas* shaken, so eventually, they'd decided to spend the night here, on this empty hillside.

"Anyway," Michael said, "this place isn't quite as deserted as we thought. I saw some sheep over there. And there was this weird shaking or rumbling a while ago. At first, I thought it was a train, only it didn't really feel like a train. Gabriel and Emma will find out what it is."

"How'd she seem to you?"

Michael shrugged. "Okay. Kind of like always."

"But . . ."

"It's just . . . the Dire Magnus forced her spirit out of her body. I could feel it out there. And when I tried to pull it back, something pulled against me. I think it was the book. Her book. There's no way all that didn't affect her."

"We'll just have to ask her when she gets back."

"And if she keeps saying she's okay?"

Kate shrugged.

"If Dr. Pym were here," Michael said, "we could ask him."

They had spoken a little about the wizard the night before. As Emma had been in and out of consciousness during their last moments in the fortress, Kate and Michael had had to tell her how Dr. Pym had sacrificed himself so that they could escape. They'd said nothing of the terrible truth the wizard had kept from them, how the prophecy foretold they would find the Books, bring them together, and then die. That revelation, she and Michael had agreed, could keep till they were all better rested.

In any case, the news that Dr. Pym was gone, that he was gone beyond any ability of Michael's and the *Chronicle*'s to bring him back, had shaken Emma in a profound way. "No," she'd kept saying. "No! You must've seen it wrong! You gotta be wrong! He can't be dead! He can't be!" In fact, the purity and keenness of Emma's distress had allowed Michael and Kate to forget, momentarily, their own recent, conflicted feelings about Dr. Pym and mourn the loss of someone they'd considered a dear, devoted friend.

Now Michael said, "I still can't believe he lied to us."

"I know."

In the end, that was the hardest to swallow. Their entire lives, growing up in orphanage after orphanage, Kate and her brother and sister had learned one lesson by heart: trust no one but each other. Anyone else, adults especially, would lie to them. But Dr. Pym had gotten inside; he'd won their trust. Now it turned out that he too had deceived them.

Kate still believed he'd cared for her and Michael and Emma; the certainty she'd felt the night before, looking at him across the courtyard, hadn't gone away. But that didn't mean she trusted him.

And she could feel herself building up, once more, the protective wall around her heart.

"You wouldn't leave him," Michael said. "Even after the Dire Magnus told you how Dr. Pym had lied, you wouldn't leave him there."

"I just couldn't."

Michael nodded, then said, quietly, "I hope Wilamena's okay."

"You said that she and Captain Anton got tossed away by the tornado. I doubt she was still possessed or controlled by then. She must've escaped."

"I don't mean that."

Kate understood. He meant that Wilamena, under the control of the Dire Magnus, had been forced to kill Wallace. How would she deal with that guilt?

"Do you think he was telling the truth about the prophecy?" Michael asked, changing the subject. "That there's more to it?"

"You mean that there's some way we won't all be killed? I don't know."

"So what do we do about the *Reckoning*? Should we try to find it? Or . . ."

He trailed off, but Kate knew what he meant; it was the same question that was swirling around her own mind. Did they believe Dr. Pym, who had by his own admission been lying to them, that finding the *Reckoning* was the only way to kill the Dire Magnus and that there was some secret wrinkle in the prophecy that would allow them to survive? Did his having sacrificed himself mean they now *had* to believe him? Or did they believe the Dire Magnus, whom they'd been struggling against for so long, and who said that bringing the Books together would lead only to her and Michael's and Emma's deaths?

It was all so confusing, and without Dr. Pym, there was no one to tell them what to do.

"I don't know."

Before Michael could ask anything else, she stood and looked down at the shrouds of mist that clung to the bottom of the valley, half obscuring the lakes.

"I'm thirsty; there must be water below. As soon as Emma and Gabriel are back, I'll take us to Loris. King Robbie will know what to do next. And hopefully we'll get some word of Wilamena and Captain Anton."

"Kate"—Michael was looking up at her—"why did you come to the fortress? How did you know we were in trouble? Or where to go?"

She didn't respond right away. She knew her brother. She knew he would already have come up with his own theories and hypotheses. She wondered if he'd guessed the truth. Maybe. But it would only be a guess. He couldn't know for sure.

She shrugged. "I just had a feeling. And then I told the Atlas to take me there."

He nodded. "Kate . . ."

"Uh-huh?"

"How was it . . . seeing him?"

She knew what he meant: How was it seeing Rafe, the boy she loved, their enemy?

She said, "It wasn't him."

Michael nodded again, then went back to rearranging his piles of rations. "Well, be careful. Don't go too far."

Kate started down into the valley. The ground was soft, and as she descended, she dug her heels into the spongy covering of heather. Soon, the mist had swallowed her, and when she glanced back, she could no longer see her brother on the slope above her. She came to a stop near the bottom of the hill where a small stream trickled past. She didn't drink at first, but sat down on a large rock and let herself sob, biting her hand to stifle the sound.

Why had she lied to Michael? Why hadn't she just told him the truth? How were they going to get through this if they didn't trust each other completely? A small voice in her head asked whether Dr. Pym hadn't faced a similar dilemma as he'd struggled with how much to tell her and her brother and sister. It wasn't fair, to want only the best for those around you, while at the same time knowing there were things they wouldn't understand. For what could she tell Michael? That Rafe, or the ghost of Rafe, had appeared and warned her that Michael and the others were walking into a trap? Even now, if she closed her eyes, she could see him, standing in the shadows of the tree.

"I know this is a lot to take in," he'd said. "Like how can I even be here? And aren't I your enemy? All I can tell you is that you have to trust me." He'd been so close that despite the darkness she'd been able to see the deep emerald green of his eyes, and she'd known that this was Rafe, her Rafe. She'd even imagined that he'd smelled the way he had the night the church had burned, of smoke and sweat. She'd wanted to ask him how it was possible that he was there with her, but she'd been speechless, his presence filling her with a terrible, guilty joy.

"I'm not a ghost, and I'm not your enemy."

He'd reached out, his fingertips seeming to touch her forehead, though she'd felt no pressure, just a sort of tingling, and she'd gasped aloud, for she'd seen an image in her mind: a fortress in a wide valley, surrounded by mountains.

"Only you can save them." He'd leaned in, and she'd thought he was going to kiss her, but instead he'd put his lips to her ear and whispered, "Trust me."

Then she'd been alone.

And she had been right to trust him. She had saved Michael and Emma.

But what were they to do now? Kate felt the pressures of leadership descending on her, and for the millionth time she wished her parents were there, that they could make the decisions so that she didn't have to.

Kate knelt down, holding back her hair with one hand, and with the other bringing up handful after handful of water. It was clean and very cold, and she drank till her teeth ached, then sat back on her heels and wiped her mouth.

This time, when she felt the presence, she knew what it was.

"You're there, aren't you?"

And she turned and saw Rafe on the large stone beside the stream.

"Nothing," Emma said. "Just sheep. Sheep sheep sheep sheep."

She and Gabriel stood peering through the early-morning mist at the cluster of whitish blobs in the distance.

"But this place can't be totally deserted. There's gotta be, like . . ." Emma searched for and failed to find the word, finally settling on "some sheep guy."

Gabriel merely nodded and gestured that they should move

on. They were making a wide circle around the camp, and so far they had seen nothing to give any sign about where the *Atlas* had brought them.

Emma had woken in the dark, trembling and gasping for air. It had taken her noticing Kate on the ground beside her to remember where she was and all that had happened. For some moments, she'd just sat there, letting her breathing slow, letting the dream and the voices fade.

Out on the hillside, she'd found Gabriel keeping watch and had hugged him.

"What has happened?"

But she'd only shaken her head, wiping away the tears still clinging to her eyes.

Gabriel had understood and not pressed her.

"Have you figured out where we are?" she'd asked.

"I am waiting for your brother or sister to wake. Then I will search the area more fully."

Hearing this, Emma had gone and shaken Michael.

"Emma?" Michael had rubbed his eyes groggily. "What's wrong?"

"Nothing. Will you watch Kate while Gabriel and I look around?"

"Huh?"

"Great. Oh, thanks again for rescuing me."

And she'd kissed him on the cheek, then padded off with Gabriel into the predawn gray.

Emma had never been one for sitting still and working through a problem. That was Michael's way, and a pretty boring way, in her opinion. She had always found that if something was bothering her and she tried *not* to think about it, if she kept moving and doing other things, then sooner or later the answer would present itself.

Or she'd just forget about it, which was almost as good.

In this case, not thinking about it was proving difficult because every time her mind strayed, she would again have the sense of part of herself drifting away, of that force out there, pulling her on; she would see the land on fire, the cliff, the bird-headed creature; she'd remember touching the book—

"Are you warm enough?"

Emma glanced up and saw that Gabriel was looking down at her.

"What? Oh. I'm fine. Why'd we stop?"

"We did not stop. You stopped. And you are shivering."

"Oh. I thought I saw something. Over there." She pointed at a random hillside, and Gabriel obligingly turned to look.

"I see nothing."

"Huh. It must've moved— *Shepherd!* That's the word! There's gotta be a shepherd here, right?"

"Possibly."

"Well, where is he? He shouldn't just let his sheep run all over! We should steal some of 'em just to teach him a lesson!"

Gabriel knelt, bringing his eyes level with hers, and took her small, cold hands in his large, callused ones. She saw the wounds that he'd dressed on his arms and side, the bandages now dark and stiff with dried blood.

"There is something you must know."

Then he told her what the wizard had hidden from them.

For several moments, Emma couldn't speak.

"He—he lied to us?!" she finally sputtered. "Dr. Pym lied to us?! And—and we're just gonna die?! After all this we're just gonna die?!"

"It may be," Gabriel said slowly, "that the prophecy does foretell your deaths. But I think the wizard was sincere, and that he truly believed there was a way you could survive. He and I spoke only yesterday, and he told me there was more to the prophecy than any of us knew, and that when fully revealed, it would explain how the Keepers might unite the Books and live. He spoke of this again just before he died."

"Then he should've told us that! He shouldn't have lied!"

"I agree. But we must deal with what is, not what we would wish could be."

"I'm glad he's dead!"

Gabriel said nothing.

"I mean it! He deserved it! He—"

She had been crying and shouting, and she realized that in her fury she had been hitting Gabriel's wounded arm and making it bleed, while Gabriel simply let her vent her anger. Emma threw her arms around his neck and sobbed.

"He should not have done what he did," Gabriel said quietly. "But do not doubt that he loved you. That was not a lie."

Emma pulled back. She could feel the tears running down her cheeks, but she made no move to wipe them; her hands stayed clenched into fists.

"It's the Dire Magnus! We just gotta kill him! We gotta find the book and kill him! I'll do it! I'll—"

Gabriel said, "What happened last night?"

"Nothing. He tried to make me find the book for him. And it

almost worked! Then Michael brought my spirit or whatever back. I feel fine!" But even as she said it, Emma knew it wasn't true.

The sky was now fully light. There was the bleating of sheep in the distance.

Gabriel was still watching her, waiting. She kicked at the earth with her toe.

"I think I felt it, the book, out there somewhere. Or my spirit felt it."

"And you had a dream this morning?"

"How'd you know?"

"You were upset when you woke."

Emma nodded. "But . . . I don't know if it was a dream or I was just remembering from last night. Wherever he sent my spirit, I was flying over this place, and it was all on fire, the land, I mean. Then there was this cliff and a kind of a monster; it looked like a man but had the head of a bird. Really, really creepy. Then it was all dark, like I was in a cave or something, and I . . . I knew the book was close, but I couldn't get to it 'cause there were these shadows crowding me; they were begging and shouting. I couldn't hear myself think." She looked at him, pleading. "What's it all mean?"

Gabriel shook his head. "I am not sure. We must return to Loris. Someone there can perhaps explain."

Emma nodded and dug her toe deeper into the dirt.

"What is it?" he asked.

"Just . . . I know we need to find the *Reckoning*, to beat the Dire Magnus and all. I just—I don't think it's like Michael's and Kate's books. I think it might be, I don't know, bad. Evil somehow." Then she added, "Not that I'm scared."

Gabriel gripped her hands. "Whatever it is, I will be with you. Come. Your sister will be awake."

But as they started walking, the earth shook, and Emma, off balance, teetered and slipped down the hillside, tumbling into a shallow depression. Gabriel was there in an instant, reaching for her.

"What was that?" she asked, taking his hand.

"I do not know—"

He stopped; he was looking, Emma saw, at the hole she had fallen in.

"We must find your brother and sister," he hissed. "Now!"

"So do you trust me now?"

Kate was sitting beside Rafe on the large stone next to the creek. In the early-morning light, he looked somehow even more real and solid than he had in the Garden the night before.

"Because if helping you save your brother and sister doesn't make you trust me, then I might be in trouble."

His tone was light, but he was staring at her, as if trying to read every emotion and thought that flitted across her face. Kate held his gaze for as long as she could, then looked down, her heart feeling like a piece of paper that might blow away.

"I think," she said, "you were trying to help."

Rafe nodded. "I'll take it." Then he said, "So you saw him."

It was a statement, but also a question.

"Yes."

"And?"

How to answer that question? She'd told Michael that the Dire Magnus was not Rafe, but that was a lie. He'd looked like Rafe, talked like him, and though she had steeled herself beforehand, had told herself she knew where her loyalties and affections lay—with Michael and Emma, entirely and always—she had felt herself pulled toward him.

"He's you."

"But?"

That was the thing. There had to be a but, some way the Dire Magnus was not Rafe. Only what was it?

"I don't know. I guess he's the dark version of you."

"Dark Rafe. I kind of like it."

"It's not funny."

Because if that was the only difference, then there was no difference, for all the darkness and anger she'd sensed in the Dire Magnus the night before had been there in the boy a hundred years ago.

But how could that be? Dr. Pym had said that because Rafe had known love, the Dire Magnus would be different. So where was the Rafe she'd loved? Who'd loved her? Was any of him in the Dire Magnus? Or was he only this apparition now beside her?

"None of this makes any sense. Even your being here—how is it you can appear wherever I am?"

"I'm not sure I can explain it myself. It's just that . . . we're connected. We have been ever since that moment in New York, when I sent you back." He paused and corrected himself. "When he sent you back."

"How can you talk about the Dire Magnus as *him*?" Kate was keeping her voice low. She didn't want Michael hearing her arguing. But would he hear Rafe? If he came down here, would he see him? "The Rafe I knew became the Dire Magnus! He did it—you did it—to save me! So who are you? Or are you just a figment of my imagination?"

She was angry now, and angrier still that Rafe seemed so calm.

"I'm sorry I haven't explained it better. You're right: I am him. You have to understand, when you become the Dire Magnus, you don't just take on the powers, you take on the memories and experiences of each Dire Magnus that came before, going back thousands of years. All those lives were laid into and built on top of the Rafe you knew. I'm in him, but he's not me! I don't have all those other memories! I'm just me!"

Kate shook her head. "You can say all that but I still don't understand—who you are—why you're helping us—any of it!"

He looked at her, and it was unnerving to see the same green eyes she had stared at across the courtyard the night before.

"I'm the part you loved. The part you changed. The night I became the Dire Magnus, I built a wall around it, and then I hid."

"Hid where?"

He shrugged. "Where else? Inside of him. And all this time, I've been waiting for you."

There was a long moment in which neither spoke, and the only sound was the trickling of water in the stream. Kate could feel the last of her resistance crumbling. She wanted so badly to believe that what he said was true.

"And I've been able to stay hidden because I've never contacted you. Now that I have, he knows."

"Knows what? What do you mean?"

Rafe gave a sardonic half smile. "Knows I'm alive. That I held something back."

"So what's going to happen?"

"He'll start looking for me. He already has."

"Will he find you?"

"Yes."

"And then what?"

"I'll die. The last part of me that's still me, the part you helped keep alive, he'll kill it. It'll become part of him." Rafe dropped his gaze. "But the thing is, at first, you won't even know. If he doesn't have the Books yet, he'll keep appearing to you as me, making you do what he wants." Rafe gave a short, empty laugh. "Maybe he already has. Maybe he's doing it right now."

"No," Kate said fiercely, her doubts of a moment before forgotten. "I would know."

"Would you? He's me, remember? Could you really tell us apart?"

"Yes. I would always know you."

And she reached out her hand, but it passed through his as if he were made of smoke. She had wanted to try it ever since she'd seen him the night before.

"Sorry," Rafe said.

She looked away, feeling stupid. "It doesn't matter."

"Kate . . ."

She wiped at her eyes with the back of her hand. "What?"

"Look at me."

She turned toward him, her eyes glistening.

"You asked why I'm helping you, but you know, don't you? You have to know."

He seemed so urgent, so desperate that she should understand. Kate nodded; and this time she didn't wipe away her tears.

"Yes. Yes, I know."

She saw the relief in his face, and she was about to speak—to tell him that he was wrong, that it wasn't just a part of him she loved—but he looked away sharply, staring up the hill.

"You need to go. Your brother and sister are in danger."

She didn't say goodbye. She just turned and ran. As she sprinted uphill, she could hear Michael and Emma screaming. Then, abruptly, they were silent. A few moments later, she came out of the mist to the place where they had spent the night. It was deserted, Michael's emergency rations still in neat piles on the rock.

"Michael! Emma!"

"Kate!"

It was Emma's voice. She was close by, but farther along the hill. Kate set off running; the hill curved and, after fifty or so yards, stopped, turning into a cliff that dropped thirty feet. Kate found herself staring out over the rough, hilly landscape. Her brother and sister were nowhere to be seen.

"Michael! Emma—"

"GOTCHA!"

The voice was a deep, mountainous rumble, and Kate was seized before she could react. It took her a second to realize that what had grabbed her was a hand as large as her entire body. She was lifted up into the air, and she found herself looking at . . . a face? There were two eyes, a gigantic nose, a low, lumpy forehead, and a mouth full of snaggly teeth. The creature's boulder-like head was attached to an enormous neck, which was attached to enormous shoulders and an enormous body.

"Kate!"

Kate saw her brother and sister in the giant's other fist. Then the giant spoke, blasting her with a wave of warm, wet, sour breath.

"MORE TINY PEOPLE!"

CHAPTER NINE
Willy

Racing up the hill, Emma had been some yards behind Gabriel and gotten a clear view of the giant leaping out from behind the cliff and snatching up Gabriel with a gleeful laugh. Even in the moment, as part of her brain had shouted *Giant! That's a giant! I need a camera!* another part had been amazed that something that large could hide that well; but the giant looked so much like the earth itself, all rough and craggy and dirty and mucky, that it was little wonder he'd blended in perfectly with the landscape. Gabriel had managed to pull his sword, and as he was lifted into the air, he'd jabbed it into the giant's hand, causing the monster to give a strangely high-pitched shriek. The giant had yanked out the sword and thrown it spinning away into the distance; then, with his thumb and forefinger, he'd flicked Gabriel in the side of the head and dropped his limp body into a leather pouch at his side.

All this had taken no more than a few seconds, and by the time Emma had overcome her shock, she herself had been snatched up. Michael had appeared a minute later, having heard Emma's scream, and he'd been seized as well, and, with a child in each hand, the giant had brought them up close to his face so that they were only feet from his great, mossy, snaggletoothed grin. Then he'd begun literally jumping up and down with glee, making the whole hillside tremble.

"TINY PEOPLE! TINY PEOPLE!"

"Let go of us!" Emma had shouted. "Put us down!"

But the giant had sniffed the air and pressed himself back against the cliff face, while also transferring Michael to the same hand as Emma and crushing them both in his moist, filthy, eggy-smelling fist. Emma was wondering what he was doing when she heard Kate calling her name and tried to claw her way up out of the giant's fist to warn her sister, but it had been too late.

And then they were all caught.

Clearly feeling that he'd done a good morning's work, the giant walked along humming gaily, carrying Emma and Michael in one hand and Kate in the other. Emma had managed to worm her head out of the giant's fist, but Michael was stuck down deep in the pit of the massive palm, and she could see him slowly turning green as he breathed in the rank, funky air.

As the giant lumbered along, swinging them forward and back, forward and back, in long sweeping arcs, Emma and Kate tried calling to each other in the moment or two the other was visible during passes over the enormous bulge of the giant's belly.

"Are you okay?!" Kate yelled.

"We're okay!" She looked down at Michael. "Are you okay?"

Michael nodded, though he looked more and more like he might be sick.

"We're okay!" Emma shouted, and then shouted it again. The first time she had mistimed it and shouted as Kate was disappearing behind the giant's back. Kate asked about Gabriel, and—again it took a few tries to get the message across—Emma told her that he'd been knocked unconscious and stuck in the giant's pouch.

Kate and Emma both screamed at the giant to put them down, pounding their fists ineffectually against his hands. Emma even bit the skin of the giant's thumb to try and get his attention, which was far and away the grossest thing she'd ever done, and it turned out to be pointless anyway because the giant didn't seem to notice but went trundling along, singing a made-up-sounding song, the few words of which Emma picked out were *pie* and *yum-yum*.

Emma knew that the *Atlas* was their best chance of escape, but for that to work, they would have to be touching each other and not touching the giant. For now, all they could do was wait.

And hope Michael didn't suffocate.

They were moving quickly, as you do when the legs of the person carrying you are fifteen feet long. The giant's booming footfalls left deep craters in the earth, and Emma realized that it was one of his footprints she'd fallen into, and what had first caught Gabriel's attention.

The giant kept mostly to the valleys and had no compunction about wading through the center of a lake so that Emma and Michael (and Kate in the opposite hand) were repeatedly dunked as his hands swung in and out of the icy water. Emma wondered that the cold water didn't wake Gabriel, but there was no movement in the leather pouch, and she began to worry that her friend was more gravely wounded than she'd thought.

By now, Emma had been able to really look at the giant. Obviously, the most immediately impressive fact was that he was forty feet tall. But he wasn't just tall, he was also wide. And thick. So much so, his proportions seemed off. His face too wide, his eyes too big, his hands and fingers too cumbersome and massive. If anything, Emma reflected, he should've been taller and more stretched out.

He had shaggy brown hair that looked as if it had been cut with some sort of tree-trimming tool, his eyebrows—or rather *eyebrow*, as it was one continuous line—was a dense brown shrub that curved around the corners of his eyes. His features were heavy to the point of being grotesque, but there was also a certain goofiness to him, which would've been more pronounced, Emma reflected, if he hadn't been planning to eat them. That he was going to eat them, Emma had no doubt. She'd also made the mistake—only once—of looking up while directly below the giant so that she'd seen into his nostrils, where something (she wasn't sure what, that it was brown and furry was all she could be sure of) was moving about.

His clothes all looked decidedly homemade—which made sense, as where would a giant go to buy clothes?—and his pants, shirt, and vest were stitched together from various sources (all of them in the tan-to-dark-brown spectrum), giving him a hodge-podge, village-idiot sort of look.

They went on like this for perhaps twenty minutes, the giant humming and singing all the while. Kate would periodically call over to make sure they were okay, and Emma would say they were, or that Michael had thrown up again, but yes, otherwise, they were okay. When she could, Emma would glance toward the leather pouch for some sign of Gabriel stirring (still none), and several times, she caught sight of other figures in the distance, massive heads and shoulders bobbing along the tops of hills. Once, the giant crouched down behind a large rock outcropping, again effortlessly becoming part of the landscape, to let another giant, a great, fat, shambling mountain of arms and legs and stomach, pass by, the earth shaking as he went.

"It was another giant," Emma told Michael, who couldn't see anything from inside their giant's fist. His face was now a green, sluggy color. "Our giant's hiding."

"He probably doesn't want to share his dinner," Michael said flatly.

Emma reflected that this was probably true.

"Did you know giants were real?" she asked.

Nauseated as he was, this was the kind of question that Michael loved, and he rallied himself to answer. "I never . . . considered the existence of giants as such, but it stands to reason that if dwarves and dragons and—"

"Never mind," Emma said, already regretting she'd asked.

Once the fat giant (or really, the *fatter* giant) had moved off, the children's captor rose and continued on. He seemed to be heading toward a line of higher hills in the distance, and, again thanks to the length of his stride, it was not long before they were being carried down a steep-sided valley with the hills rising up directly before them.

"Look!"

It was Kate, shouting to them from the giant's other fist and pointing. Farther along the valley stood an enormous, ramshackle wooden house. It looked exactly like the sort of house that someone forty feet tall and not overly concerned with cleanliness and appearance might choose to live in. It was probably twice the size of the mansion in Cambridge Falls, but while the mansion had been imposing and grand, this house, for all its size, was more shacklike and thrown together. Parts of the roof appeared to have caved in, walls were buttressed with tree trunks, filthy canvas flaps covered the glassless windows, and the whole thing was listing dangerously to one side. A crooked, gray-stone chimney rose from the roof, dark smoke climbing into the sky.

The giant stopped, turned, and crouched down so that his back blocked them from view of the house. He placed his fists on top of a large boulder and brought his face down close to the children. When he spoke, it was obvious he was trying to keep his voice low, but the effect was still deafening.

"Now listen, tiny little people, when we get inside, not a peep!"

"My brother can't hear you!" Emma shouted. "And he's suffocating inside your stupid, smelly hand!"

The giant frowned as if he hadn't heard, then turned his head so that one ear faced Emma, causing Emma to exclaim:

"Oh! That is so, so gross!"

For the giant's ear was clogged with clumpy mounds of blackened dirt and wax, some of which hung from the ceiling of his ear canal like rotted-yellow stalactites, and there was a wall of wax at the back of his ear so thick-looking that Emma wondered how he heard anything at all. Still, she was about to shout again when she and Michael were lifted in the air. They were both then upside down and screaming as he stuck out a massive pinky finger—causing Michael's legs to kick furiously in the air—and screwed his pinky back and forth in his ear, making loud *squeak-squeak* noises and no doubt packing the wax in tighter, as if he were loading a huge, fleshy blunderbuss.

Then he placed his fist, and the extremely dizzy Michael and Emma, back on the rock, turned his ear toward them, and said:

"Whazzat? Didn't hear ya!"

Emma cupped her hands around her mouth and shouted, "My brother can't breathe!"

"Oh." The giant opened his fist so that Michael and Emma both tumbled out onto the boulder. Michael immediately fell to his knees, gasping. Emma glanced over at Kate, but she was still held tight in the giant's other fist.

"Like I was saying, no talking when we get inside or it's right straight into the pie."

"Put my sister down too!" Emma demanded. "And let Gabriel go!"

"Huh?"

"You are so annoying! I said—" She cupped her hands around her mouth and was about to yell when there was a noise from the house, a clatter like a dropped pan, followed by the sound of someone cursing.

"Oh no," the giant said, and he snatched up Michael, who still looked extremely woozy, dropped him into one of his vest pockets, and then, before Emma could protest, snatched her up as well and placed her in another pocket. She landed facedown in a pile of dirt and twigs and small rocks, bits of hard cheese, and what felt very much like bones.

She was just getting to her knees when something landed hard on her back.

"Oww!"

"Sorry!"

It was Kate. The sisters embraced in the dank darkness of the giant's pocket, and Kate asked if she was hurt.

"I'm fine."

"And Michael?"

"Just sick."

"Did you say Gabriel's in the giant's pouch?"

"Uh-huh. That smelly creep knocked him out and stuck him in there. I'm worried. I don't think he's moved."

Kate reached out and gave her hand a comforting squeeze. "As soon as we're all together, I'll use the *Atlas*. Are you really okay?"

There was light coming in from the top of the pocket and more through a small rip near their heads, but it was still dim, and they were both trying to keep their balance, as the giant had risen and begun lumbering, presumably, toward the house.

But Emma could see Kate studying her closely.

"I'm fine. Really." And to change the subject, she said, "There're bones in here."

"I think they're sheep. At least, I hope."

"Yeah."

Through the rip in the pocket, they could see the house getting closer. As they neared the front door, the giant (sort of) whispered, **"Remember—quiet!"** then pushed on the door, and they entered a large, smoky, poorly lit room. There was a heavy, slightly sour odor made up of bubbling fat and fermenting beer and body odor. Despite there being no glass in the windows, the room smelled like it had not been aired out in years. Emma and Kate caught glimpses of an enormous wooden table and chairs, collections of jars and cups, various roots and leaves and dried meats hanging from the ceiling, a goodly amount of trash, and, against one wall and throwing an orange-red glow across the room, a large gray-stone fireplace at which a woman (a giant woman, obviously) with long, dirty blond hair and a dress of washed-out gray was leaning over an iron pot, stirring a concoction with a wooden spoon that looked to have been carved from the trunk of an entire tree. The sleeves of her dress had been pushed up, revealing massive, muscled forearms.

"Finally!" She hawked a large, brown glob of spit into the pot. "You been gone all mornin'! What'd you bring, then?"

"Nothin', Sall. Sorry."

"Nothin'?!" The blond giantess turned toward them, and Kate and Emma instinctively pulled back deeper into the giant's pocket. But the woman's attention was on the giant's face. As she spoke, she waved about her spoon, sending globby droplets of stew this way and that. "You been out all mornin' wanderin' around like a simpleton, probably starin' at clouds and rocks, and you come back and tell me you got nothin' for the stew?! Oh, but you're still expectin' to be fed, ain't ya? Old Sall, she can just make a stew outta nothin', can't she? Well, it's a big pot of nothin' you'll be eatin' for supper, you half-wit!"

"Said I'm sorry, Sall."

"Sorry?!" She laughed sourly. "Don't you go apologizin' to me! It's gonna be Big Rog's Thumb you'll have to be apologizin' to, sayin' you're sorry as he's gouging out your eye!"

"Ah now, Sall. Don't be tellin' the Thumb, right?"

"'Don't be tellin' the Thumb,' is it? I will be tellin' the Thumb!" The giantess had come over so that she was right in the other giant's face, and she poked him as she spoke, her finger like a battering ram and coming awfully near Kate and Emma. "I'll be tellin' the Thumb the minute he walks in the door, and then it'll be half-wit-eyeball soup we'll be havin'! Oh indeed! *Num, num, num!*" And she made loud slurping sounds and rubbed a massive hand over her massive belly.

"I'm goin' to me room," the giant muttered, and he started to turn, but the giantess caught his arm.

"You wouldn't be holdin' out on me now, would you, Willy? Not holdin' out on your own only sister? 'Cause not findin' nothing, maybe—*maybe*—we could forgive that, you bein' the half-wit moron dunderhead boogers-for-brains you are. But holdin' out on us? Well, that's malicious and unforgivable, ain't it? And then the Thumb'll be down on you for sure!"

"I ain't holdin' out nothin'!" And he yanked his arm away.

Emma looked at Kate and mouthed, "He doesn't want to share. He wants to eat us all by himself." And she made her eyes wide to put three exclamation points after it.

Just then there was a yelp from the giant's other pocket. The giant froze. The blond giantess froze. Emma and Kate froze. They knew their brother's voice.

The blond giantess let out a cry and sprang forward. The children's giant tried to run, but he was too slow. Kate and Emma screamed, but their screams were drowned out by the sounds of the giants grappling, banging into the walls, the table, knocking pitchers and pots on the floor; it was obvious that the blond giantess was trying to dig into the giant's pocket and the giant was trying to protect it, and Emma was sure that they were going to be crushed—

"Do something!" she shouted to Kate.

"Okay! I'll stop time—"

"You'll what?!" This was the first Emma had heard about this power.

"I'll stop time! Just—"

But before she could, there was a squeal of triumph, and the blond giantess leapt back, and the giant who'd captured them scrambled to his feet. As soon as Kate and Emma had regained their balance, they pressed their eyes to the hole in his pocket, expecting to see Michael in the giantess's hand. But she was holding aloft a plump, fluffy, frantically bleating sheep, which she now brandished in the other giant's face.

"Found nothin', did ya? Just gonna keep this secret, were ya? Ha!"

"Ah, Sall, I forgot it was there. Don't tell Big Rog."

"'Forgot it was there,' my foot! You mean you forgot it was there till you got hungry back in your room and had yourself a private little sheepy snack. And I will be tellin' Big Rog, and you'll be talkin' to the Thumb soon enough, believe you me! Now get outta my kitchen 'fore I put you in the pot!"

Emma and Kate, both now utterly confused, watched the room spin as the giant turned and walked down a long (though no doubt short to the giant) hallway and through a door, which he shut and bolted behind him with a wooden bar.

They heard a great sigh, then a creaking of wood as the giant settled into a chair. Two mammoth fingers probed down into the pocket, scooped Emma and Kate up and out, and set them on a table. It took them a moment to get their bearings, and Emma looked about the room as the giant reached into his other pocket and pulled out Michael.

It was a much smaller room than Emma would have expected, for even though the giant was seated, his head nearly brushed the ceiling. As for furniture, there was a table, the stool or chair on which the giant sat, and that was it. A narrow window covered by a loose piece of canvas let in light, and a pile of old, tattered furs against one wall seemed to serve as a bed. The place looked more like a closet than a bedroom, and a small and shabby one at that.

Yet for all that, it was chock-full of stuff. Teacups, teapots, plates, thimbles, scissors, candleholders, shards of colored glass— red, green, blue, yellow—decorative pins, pieces of cracked enamel, what looked like a doll whose face had been worn off, an array of different-sized knives, a clock that was missing its back, a cobbler's hob—and everything, obviously, giant-sized.

There was something altogether odd about the collection, but Emma couldn't put her finger on exactly what that something was.

Kate, meanwhile, the moment Michael had been placed on the table, had grabbed him into a hug. Michael was still green-faced and dazed-looking and, in addition, was now covered with sheep fuzz.

"That was a close one," the giant said. **"What'd you go squawking for? Lucky I had a sheep in there."**

"It bit me," Michael said, displaying a red mark on his arm.

"Emma," Kate said, holding Michael's hand in one of hers while reaching out to Emma, "take my hand."

"Now, Sall's gonna tell Big Rog I was hidin' that sheep and he's gonna come in here with the Thumb. Nothin' ever goes right for me."

"Emma!" Kate hissed.

"Hold on." And Emma actually moved a step farther away from her sister.

She knew Kate wanted to transport them away. But Emma wasn't going anywhere without Gabriel. And there was something else too. Over the years, as Emma and her siblings had been bounced from orphanage to orphanage, plunged into the midst of one group of strangers after another, she had developed the skill of discerning, in an instant, which children or adults were threats and which were not. It had never steered her wrong, and right now, it was telling her that the forty-foot-tall creature before them, each of whose teeth was the size of her head, meant them no harm.

"And can you believe that was me own sister? If me da' were still alive, you think he'd stand for how they treat me? Getting abused on a daily basis? And this was supposed to be my house when Da' died! Look where they got me living! In a closet! Ain't right, no no, ain't right at all!" The giant seemed to grow wistful. "Ah, me da' were a wonderful man, he was. I'm named after him, you know—Willy. 'Old Willy,' they called him. A gentle soul. And a marvelous whistler. Why—"

"Hey, you're not gonna eat us, are you?"

The giant looked at Emma, then dug a finger in his ear, dislodging several pounds of grayish muck.

"Huh?"

"Emma!" Kate reached for her again, but Emma moved even farther away.

"I said—YOU'RE NOT GOING TO EAT US, ARE YOU?"

"Shhh!" The giant showered them with warm spittle. **"Not so loud! Sall hears you, she'll stick you in a pie for Big Rog's dinner and that'll be that! 'Course I ain't gonna eat you! Who put an idea like that in your head?"**

"You did! You said to be quiet or it was straight in the pie."

"I was talkin' about Sall. I'd never eat the three a' you!" And he actually managed to look offended.

Emma glanced at Kate and Michael. They were both staring up at the giant, and Kate seemed to have relaxed a bit and was no longer reaching for Emma's hand.

"What'd you say your name was?" Emma asked.

"Willy."

"Uh-huh. Well, I'm Dorothy. This is my sister, Evelina. And this is my brother, Toadlip."

"Nice to meet you."

"You too. Would you excuse us? I need to talk to them for a second."

Emma stepped over to Kate and Michael and turned her back on the giant.

"Why'd you say my name was Toadlip?" Michael hissed.

"Because," Emma hissed back, "we don't want to use our real names. What if the Dire Magnus is looking for us? Duh!"

"Yeah, but you two got normal names. Toadlip?"

"Michael," Kate said, "let it go." She looked at Emma. "What're you doing? Do you really believe he's not going to eat us?"

"Yeah. If he was, he would've done it by now. And I just know, okay? You've gotta trust me. Anyway, I've been thinking, what if the *Atlas* brought us here for a reason? It doesn't make sense to leave before we figure out what that is. And he lives here. He can help."

"As long as he doesn't eat us," Michael said.

"Well, he might eat you," Emma snapped. "Which would be a huge tragedy, obviously."

"Hey—"

"Please, Kate," Emma said, turning back to her sister, "I can't explain it more. I just know we're supposed to be here is all. Please."

Kate didn't respond right away, and Emma—who knew that Kate's first and last thought was always to protect them—considered saying that sometimes you had to do things that were dangerous in order to be safe later; sometimes, you had to take chances. But she kept silent. And standing there, waiting, she felt her position as the youngest as she never had before, the fact that she was always having to ask, to convince, to plead. It was never up to her to choose the path; that was Kate's job, and now Michael's a little too. She supposed it had always been this way, so why did it rankle? Was it just that this was her book they were going after, or was it something else?

"Fine," Kate said. "But stay close. If he tries anything, I can use the *Atlas*."

Emma turned back to the giant, who was blowing his nose on a handkerchief the size of a bedsheet, dislodging half a dozen startled brown bats that flopped about on the table and then took awkward flight. Her first concern now was to get Gabriel released.

"Listen, Willy—"

"Uh-oh." The giant seemed to have had the same idea, for he was twisted about and peering into his leather sack. **"He's gone."**

"Wait—you mean Gabriel?"

"Is that his name? Your friend who tried to murder my hand with that toothpick a' his? He ruined my best bag, he did. Look."

Willy held up the pouch, and the children saw a long slice in the bottom of it. Evidently, Gabriel had woken at some point during their journey and cut his way out. Seeing the hole, Emma was relieved.

"He escaped is all. He's probably coming here now to kill you for kidnapping us. Don't worry. We won't let him."

"Oh. Thanks, I guess."

"Sure. So, Willy—"

"Shhhhh." He twisted his head toward the door, listening. After a moment, he nodded. **"Sorry. Thought I heard the Thumb."**

Emma had been intending to ask him where exactly they were, what the land was called, and if he knew anything about the *Reckoning* (posing the question subtly, like, "Soooooo . . . you know where the *Reckoning* is?"), but her curiosity got the better of her. "What's this whole Thumb business?"

"You mean Big Rog?"

"I guess."

"Well, Big Rog is Sall's husband. And his thumb, well, it's the terror a' the land, it is. You see this thumb here?" He held up his right thumb, which was the size of Emma herself. **"This is a respectable thumb. No man need be ashamed of a thumb like that. But Big Rog's thumb? Why if he wanted to, he could reach up with it and rub out the sun. He holds it over his head in the**

rain and he don't get wet. He's used it to dam rivers so they run backward. A thumb like that's a thing a' Fate, with a capital F." He thought, then added, **"And a capital T for Thumb."**

"So he's got a big thumb," Michael asked. "So what?"

"Well, Toadlip—"

"My name—"

"Is Toadlip," Emma finished. "Go on, Willy."

"Everyone knows that a fella's whole power is in his thumb, don't they? It's what separates us from the animals. Opposable thumbs!"

"That and you being forty feet tall," Emma said.

"True. There's that too. Anyway, he's the reason I don't have no friends. Everyone's too afraid a' that thumb a' his. But no more!" And he smiled his huge snaggly smile. **"Not when people know that I'm the one that found you three! Ah, if only me da' could've been here. He would've been proud, he would. He's the one who told me about you."**

The giant leaned down and waggled a massive finger at them while putting on a deep, rumbling voice that was apparently an imitation of his father, **" 'Now, Willy, you be on the lookout! Ever you see three little wee children, you snatch them up right quick and don't let no one put 'em in a pie! Remember the prophecy! Remember the prophecy!' "**

Emma looked at her brother and sister and saw they had the same surprised expression she did. She'd thought the giant would be helpful, but she never would've imagined that he would know about the prophecy, especially since he didn't seem like the sharpest tool in the shed.

Michael said as much: "You know about the prophecy?"

Willy the Giant made a *pshaw* face. **"Do I know about the prophecy?! Didn't me da'**—he really was the kindest of giants, even let seagulls nest in his hair, not every giant will do that, the poop, you know, can be a bit overwhelming—**didn't he tell me about it when I was only yea high?"** He held his hand about ten feet off the floor.

"See"—Emma turned to her brother and sister—"I told you he could help us!"

She knew you shouldn't say *I told you so*, but sometimes you just had to.

"So," Kate said, "you know where the last book is?"

"Hmm?"

"I said, do you know where the last book is?"

"What book?"

"The last Book of Beginning."

"The what of the what?"

"You know," Emma said. "The last Book of Beginning! The *Reckoning!*"

"Oh." The giant thought for a moment, then shook his head, smiling innocently. **"Nope. Never heard of it."**

"Wait," Emma said, getting annoyed and now very consciously not looking at her brother and sister. "What prophecy are you talking about?"

The giant looked confused. **"The dark stranger's prophecy, the last words he spoke before he took the city. *'Three children will come, and they will take death from the land.'* And you're the first children, you're the first anybody, to come here in thousands of years. And there's three a' you. You gotta be them! What prophecy are *you* talking about?"**

"Oh," Emma said, "that one. I just got confused for a second. Excuse us again."

The children all turned to each other, speaking in quiet (really, their normal) voices that the giant couldn't hear.

"Are you guys thinking what I'm thinking?" Emma asked.

"'Take death from the land,'" Michael said. "That's gotta be the Book of Death, don't you think? Weird, though, that there's another prophecy about us."

"Whatever," Emma said. "The book's here. The *Atlas* brought us to the right place!" And then, because she couldn't resist, she added, "I told you so!"

Kate smiled at her. "You were right."

Having Kate smile at her filled Emma with such joy and pride that she felt bad for having said *I told you so*. But, she reasoned, maybe if Kate and Michael treated her less like a little kid and listened to her ideas, she wouldn't have to say *I told you so*. That made her feel better.

Kate said, "But are we even sure we should be finding the book? Emma, there's something you don't know—"

"Yeah, yeah, we'll all die if we bring them together! Gabriel told me! But we don't know that for certain! Dr. Pym was a big fat liar, but maybe he was telling the truth and there really is some part of the prophecy no one knows, like, blah, blah, blah, Michael and Kate and Emma are gonna die unless they blah, blah, blah."

"I'm sure that's what the prophecy says," Michael muttered.

"I'm just saying, we don't know that the Books are gonna kill us, but we do know the Dire Magnus will! So we've gotta kill him first! And the only way we can do that is by getting the last book!"

"I agree," Michael said. "Whether Dr. Pym was telling the

truth or not, if we don't try to find the *Reckoning*, we're just giving up."

"See?" Emma said, seizing her sister's arm. "Please, Kate!"

Kate's eyes moved from her brother to her sister, and as Emma watched her sister take a breath, sigh, and nod, she felt a deep sense of relief. She hadn't realized till then how much she wanted to find the book, how much she needed to, and Emma was about to tell her it would all be okay, and maybe—she might as well plant the idea—Kate and Michael should learn to trust her a little more, when she let out a cry and tumbled forward, senseless, onto the table.

At the same moment, there was a shattering *crack* as the door to Willy's room crashed open, and an enormous, black-bearded giant burst in upon them. He saw the children on the table—Kate holding the now-unconscious Emma—and with a roar swung a massive fist into the side of Willy's head, knocking him to the floor. With his other hand, which did indeed have a thumb the size of a small locomotive, he swept up the children.

"I knew I smelled something funny in here!"

The giant brought them close to his great, grinning mouth as if he would eat them raw, then and there, and growled:

"Oh aye! Big Rog will be having a feast tonight!"

CHAPTER TEN
Big Rog's Feast

The children were placed in three separate wooden cages, almost like giant birdcages, which were hung from the branches of a tree in the open area in front of the house. Then Big Rog had Willy, whose nose was bloody and whose eyes were beginning to swell from Big Rog's clobbering, build up a large fire and carry out several of Sall's pots and pans, as well as plates, chairs, stools, and tankards.

"**Go spread the word, dum-dum,**" Big Rog told Willy after the fire was roaring and an enormous cauldron of water had been brought to a boil. "**It's going to be little-people pie at the Thumb's tonight! A delicacy not seen or tasted in thousands a' years! But make sure they know to bring their own beer. Big Rog ain't running a charity! Now, get on with ya!**" And he aimed a kick at Willy that sent him scurrying away down the valley.

As her cage turned in the heat fumes rising from the fire, Kate fought to stay calm. Emma was still unconscious; she had not moved or stirred since she'd collapsed in Willy's room. The three of them were separated, so using the *Atlas* was not an option. They were on the menu for dinner. So, yes, all that was bad. But on the plus side, they were still alive, Michael still had the *Chronicle*, Gabriel was still at large and might yet appear and effect a rescue, and, if all else failed, sooner or later they would have to be taken out of the cages to be cooked. Awful as that prospect sounded, chances were that she and Emma and Michael would be then close enough to touch and she could use the *Atlas* to take them away.

She just had to remain calm.

And keep Michael calm.

"It's the *Reckoning*," he was saying, gripping the bars of his own cage and staring at Emma's unconscious form. "I knew the Dire Magnus's ritual did something!"

"She'll be fine."

"How do you know that?"

"Because I know."

"No offense, Kate, but that's not really an answer."

"We just have to wait. As soon as he takes us out of the cages, I'll use the *Atlas*."

"But we still have to get the *Reckoning*!"

"I know."

"And we haven't heard the rest of that prophecy!"

"I know."

"And what 'dark stranger' was Willy talking about? That's what he said, a 'dark stranger' predicted we would come. Who was that . . ."

And on and on. She knew it was part of Michael's personality that he could never stop turning over and examining the same facts and questions, but sometimes it was exhausting. She didn't know what had happened to Emma, didn't really know if she'd be okay, didn't know what the rest of this other prophecy held, didn't know where the *Reckoning* was hidden or how they'd find it (which she was still not completely on board with, despite having given in to Michael and Emma), but none of that actually mattered, for she had already willed herself to believe that they would, somehow, survive and be okay.

This was when they needed Dr. Pym, and Kate found herself wishing that Rafe would appear, even if it meant Michael seeing him. She needed to talk to someone.

"It'll be fine," she repeated, rubbing her mother's locket between her thumb and forefinger. "It'll all be fine."

"They're coming," Michael said.

Kate heard it too, a far-off *thud*, *thud*, *thud*, *thud* growing steadily louder, and the ground began to shake, the tree trembled, and the branch from which their cages hung quivered so that Kate and Michael had to hold the cages' bars for balance. Whether by chance or intention, the giants were approaching as a group, and the effect was like watching a mountain range sprout legs and march toward you. As they came closer, Kate could pick out individual giants, fatter ones, taller ones, bearded ones, bald ones, a few women; there were perhaps fifteen in all, moving at a jog, driven on by excitement, curiosity, and (Kate feared) hunger.

"That's right!" Big Rog roared. "Come and look at 'em! Come see what the Thumb's found!"

The giants amassed around the children's cages, jostling and elbowing and punching one another to get a better look. The cages were almost exactly at the giants' eye level, and for a moment, Kate thought that she and Michael and Emma were going to be crushed, as humongous eyes and noses and mouths pushed in, *ooohing* and *aaahing*. A few of the giants were licking their lips. Kate felt like an animal in a zoo, though in this case, a zoo where the animals got eaten.

Up close, the giants were stomach-churningly gross. It wasn't just that they were so generally unclean and mucky, that they had families of rodents living in their hair, that they were so extravagantly warted, that the breath of any one of them could have knocked over a cow; it was their sheer size that tipped the scales of repulsiveness. Kate could see deep into the pores of their faces, dark, greasy pits she could've placed a whole finger inside; she could see the crusty yellow-brown tartar that covered their teeth, the mossy green-black patches on their tongues, the mushroomy yellow goo in the corners of their eyes. She found herself wondering if this was what everyone looked like close up. Was everyone this revolting?

The giants were all talking at once:

"Look at 'em! Look at 'em—"

"Tiny little wee folks, sure enough—"

"Bet they taste good fried—"

"Everything tastes good fried—"

"Serve 'em with 'tatoes, I would—"

"Hardly a mouthful, any of them—"

"This one's all skin and bone! No meat at all—"

"Me uncle Nathan ate tiny people once. Said they taste like chicken—"

"All right, get back the lot a' you!" Big Rog came through pushing and shoving, moving the giants away from the cages. Kate glanced over and saw Michael, one hand on the bag that held the *Chronicle*, looking very pale.

"Michael?"

"It'll be okay, right? You said it'll be okay?"

She nodded firmly. "It'll be okay."

Big Rog was now addressing the assembled giants. The sun had begun to set behind the hill, and shadows stretched across the valley. Strangely, Kate found that she was starving. Was it weird to be hungry when you yourself might soon be dinner?

"Now listen up!" Big Rog was saying. **"Sall's gonna put together a nice pie with 'tatoes and onions and leeks and carrots and"**—he paused for effect—**"TINY LITTLE WEE FOLK!"**

There was a cheer among the giants.

"You all seen there ain't a lot a' meat on their bones. They're more a delicacy than a main course. But you'll each get a slice a' tiny-people pie that you can tell your grandnippers about, you have the Thumb's word on that, and Sall's also cooking up her sheep stew, there'll be sheep kebabs, a few sheep dumplings, and even a sheep custard for dessert! Now crack that cask! The Thumb's thirsty!"

There was more roaring and cheering, and a pair of giants pulled the lid off an enormous cask, and flagons were dunked into the frothy dark brown brew, which the giants proceeded to chug with no concern about how much streamed down their fronts.

"Maybe they'll get too drunk and forget to cook us," Michael said.

"Yeah," Kate said. "Maybe."

The next hour or so passed with drinking; singing (mostly drinking songs); a kind of dancing that looked a lot like stomping and made the branch holding them shake so badly that Kate and Michael were forced to lie flat on the floors of their cages; a flatulence contest won by a giant named, appropriately, Stinky Bill, though really Kate thought it was a draw between him and half a dozen other giants; and a great deal of fighting, which Big Rog always seemed to be in the center of, executing his favored move of jumping on an opponent's back and jamming his thumb into the other's ear or using it to fishhook a giant's cheek till he cried for mercy.

All the while, Kate watched Sall cooking her various sheep dishes while also carefully preparing a huge round tin with giant-sized leeks, carrots, onions, and potatoes.

That's for us, Kate thought.

Part of her was glad that Emma was unconscious and not seeing all this.

She didn't hear Willy till he was right behind them.

"I'm real, real sorry."

The giant was cowering in the shadows under the tree, out of light of the fire where the other giants were drinking and singing and carrying on.

"Can't you do something?" Michael demanded. "Get us out of here?"

"Well, now," Willy said cautiously, **"I could, technically, yes, but I think that might make the Thumb awful mad."**

"What about the prophecy?" Kate said. "We're supposed to take death away? Don't they all know that?"

"Well, now, I sort of doubt they do. We live in a degraded time. The old stories aren't given the same respect they once were. People forget."

"But you remember!" Michael insisted.

"Well, now, true, true. But it won't do me much good if you take death away and the Thumb's already killed me. Bit of a dilemma, that."

Part of Kate wanted to call him a coward, as she knew Emma would if Emma had been awake, but she also knew that wouldn't get them anywhere. She took another tack.

"What would your dad say if he knew you were letting them make us into pie?"

"That's right!" Michael said. "I bet he'd be ashamed."

"Ah now," the giant said, hanging his enormous head, **"don't be bringing me old da' into it."**

"You have a chance," Kate said. "You could make him proud of you."

"Instead of him being glad he's dead," Michael said, "so he doesn't have to watch you be such a big chicken."

Kate thought this was a bit much and was going to signal to Michael to lay it on more mildly when Big Rog's voice boomed across the clearing.

"What're you talking about I can't eat them? They're my little wee folk! You're lucky I'm sharing 'em at all, ya ungrateful slob!"

Kate and Michael both turned to see Big Rog, his black beard glistening with pearls of beer, talking to a jowly, round-bodied giant. Big Rog kept jabbing the other giant in the gut with his thumb as he spluttered in his face.

"You're trying to spoil my feast!"

The other giant held up his hands in surrender. **"It's just an old story, is all! I don't even know the whole of it! Just thought I'd mention."**

"Just thought you'd mention," sneered Big Rog. "Well, I never heard of it!"

"IT'S TRUE!" Kate shouted. "YOU CAN'T EAT US! ASK WILLY! HE KNOWS! MAKE HIM TELL YOU ABOUT THE PROPHECY!"

With the attention of the other giants on him, Willy tried to shrink back into the shadows, but Big Rog seized him by the collar and dragged him out into the firelight.

"What's this she's talking about? What prophecy?"

Willy was waving his hands before his face. "I don't know! I don't know what she's talking about!"

"He's lying!" Kate and Michael both shouted. "Tell him! Your father told you the story!"

Big Rog laughed. "Oh, so that's what it is, is it? More of that old fool's stories! I always was sorry he fell off that ridge and cracked open his stupid head. Meant we didn't get to hear more of his nonsense! Ha!"

It was in that moment that Kate saw the change come over Willy. His enormous eyes narrowed (very slightly), his shoulders drew back, and he even stood up a little straighter, another three feet or so.

"They weren't just stories. Me da' knew things about the old world. Things everyone else has forgot. That's a lie, saying they're stories."

Big Rog snorted. "Oh is that right? Like how I'm not supposed to eat these little people?"

"For one. Yeah."

Big Rog stared at him, and for a second Kate thought he was

going to slaughter Willy then and there. But Big Rog turned to face the other giants.

"Right! Everyone, listen up! We got a treat. While Sall finishes up her sheep stew and puts together the fixing for the pie, Willy here is gonna tell us one of his dear old da's stories. Now make sure no one laughs or sniggers, 'cause it's one hundred percent true! Every word! And not a bunch of made-up gibberish! Ha!"

Willy glanced over at the children, and Kate nodded and tried to give him strength with her eyes. Then he turned back to the group of sneering, hooting, and really pretty sloshed giants and waited for them to quiet down.

Michael looked over at Kate. "At least it bought us some time. And we'll get to hear the whole story."

Kate said nothing. She was watching Sall cutting onions into the pie. It would be ready for them soon.

"This wasn't always the way things were."

It was very nearly fully night, and Willy stood in the slashing glare of the firelight, facing the half ring of giants. To Kate's surprise, the other giants had all taken seats—some on rocks, some on the ground—and now appeared to be giving Willy their whole attention, the only noise being the gulping of beer and an occasional ear-splitting belch.

Emma still had yet to stir.

"We didn't always live as we do now. As little better than animals. Drunken. Filthy. Scrabbling for food. Giants used to be a respected race. We lived in the High City—"

He said this, Kate noticed, with capital letters, and the other giants nodded, as if the High City was something they had all heard of. And she noticed too that Willy was speaking differently than he normally did, and it occurred to her that he must be telling the story as his father had told it to him, in his father's own words and tone.

"We all know where the High City is. North. Through the forest. Past the wide river, which no giant has crossed and returned from in a thousand years. But that was where we once lived. And it was a golden time. We giants had culture and music and literature. There were tailors who made the most exquisite clothes, not these stitched-together rags we wear now. There were smiths who made the finest tools and weapons. The shops were filled with goods. And the most delicious sheep-liver Danishes anywhere in the world!"

There was a gasp of awed appreciation among the giants.

"And we had a king in those days too. King Davey the Extremely Tall. It was said that he'd go out for a walk and come back with the clouds wreathed about his hair like a crown from heaven.

"A golden time . . ."

Willy paused—somewhat melodramatically, in Kate's opinion—but the giants were all listening with rapt attention. She tried to imagine a time when these giants had been all that Willy described, cultured, with fine clothes and tools, living in a great city. Was it true? Or was it merely a story that had been created to make them feel better about themselves?

"Then one day, a troubling report reached the king. An entire community of giants, out at the edge of the kingdom, had perished suddenly. It was said the buzzards circled about so thick that noon was like the deepest night. King Davey sent two scouts to find out what had happened, but the scouts never returned.

"Next, he sent a platoon of soldiers. Twelve giants, girded for battle. A week passed. One soldier returned. He told the king that death had entered the land. That it had been brought by a stranger. That the stranger had let him live so that he could bring a message to the king.

"'What message?' King Davey asked.

"'That the stranger is coming to take possession of your throne and your city. And anyone still within the walls in two days' time will die.'

"Well, the first thing King Davey did was to lop off the soldier's head, since it was a long-standing tradition to kill the bearer of bad news."

Kate was shocked by this, but she saw that all the giants were nodding, and one raised his hand and asked, **"Did he eat it?"** but was quickly shushed by the others.

Willy went on: **"Now, there was a great field before the city, and exactly two days later, the sentries saw the stranger approaching from the distance. A tiny little dark speck. King Davey marched out with fifty of his warriors, all armed to the teeth. They say you could feel the ground shake a thousand miles away, that waves the size of mountains flooded cities on the far side of the world.**

"King Davey led his soldiers forward, intending to crush the stranger underfoot and grind his bones into the earth."

Willy paused again. He was not afraid, Kate saw, of abusing the dramatic pause. But again, it worked. The giants, even Big Rog, were hanging on his words.

"The stranger killed them. Faster than you can blink, King Davey and all his warriors were dead on the field. And this is the truth, passed down from those that watched it happen from the city walls. They had been expecting to see the stranger stomped to bits, but instead their king and all their soldiers were lying dead and the stranger was walking toward the city.

"So they ran. They abandoned their homes, left pots boiling, sheep half-cooked, laundry half-clean, and when the stranger entered the city, the gates closed, and no giant has set foot in the High City ever since. And in the years that followed, we fell into the sad state we find ourselves in now. As little more than animals."

Michael had whispered, "What about the prophecy—" when Willy spoke again.

"But the giants who fled heard the stranger's last words. Just before entering the city, he said, 'I will abide in here till three children come who will take death from this land.'" Willy gestured to the cages. "Now they have. The first humans seen here since the stranger's time, more than two thousand years ago, and three children at that. We can't eat them. This is our last chance, you see, to return to what we once were."

He stopped talking, and Kate waited, holding her breath. Would this be enough to save them?

"He must've had the Book of Death," Michael whispered. "The stranger, I mean. That's the only way he could've killed all those giants. Emma was right: the book is here."

Kate couldn't argue. But she also found herself wondering, as Michael had earlier, who the stranger was. It couldn't have been the Dire Magnus, because the Dire Magnus was searching for the book. So who was it?

"Well, that's a fine old story, Willy-boy." Big Rog stood up. "But if you think it means that I'm not eating these tiny wee children, then you're even loonier than your loony father was. And be reminding me to give you a good clout later for trying to ruin my feast. Now, Sall, how's that piecrust coming?"

"You're going to die soon."

The voice that spoke was not a voice that had yet been heard and it was not loud, but it was loud enough for Big Rog and Willy and the other giants, and especially for Kate and Michael, who were closer and knew the voice well, to hear it and turn.

Emma was standing up and gripping the bars of her cage.

"You're going to die soon," Emma repeated.

Emma heard Kate say her name, but she didn't look over. She was staring at Big Rog, who had stepped past Willy and come up to her cage.

"Ah, so you're feeling better. That's fine. I wouldn't want to eat you when you were sick. Might give me a bellyache."

"You won't die tonight," Emma said, as if the giant had not spoken. "But soon." Then she pointed at the jowly giant who was refilling his tankard in the cask. "Him, the fat one, he's gonna die tonight."

"And how do you know that?" Big Rog sneered.

"I just do. Same way I know that you killed Willy's dad."

A tight, deadly silence descended on the clearing. Big Rog leaned in till the bulbous tip of his nose was almost touching the bars of Emma's cage.

"Don't be telling stories that're gonna get you into even

more trouble, girl. I'm gonna eat you, sure. But humane-like. In a pie. Get me angry and I might just eat you raw, limb by limb."

But Emma couldn't have stopped talking if she had tried. It felt as if she was on a path, clear and definite, and there was no way but forward.

"You came up behind him and bashed him in the head with a rock. Then you pushed his body down the hill and told everyone he had fallen." Emma looked at Sall, who had frozen next to the pie tin. "It was your idea. You talked him into it so you could get that cruddy house. You knew your dad was going to give it to Willy."

Emma could feel Kate and Michael staring at her, but she kept her eyes on Big Rog.

Then Big Rog did exactly what Emma was hoping.

He turned and roared at the other giants.

"So what? He was old and useless and ate too much and who was gonna stop me, eh? Ha! That's right—"

That was all he got out before Willy barreled into him. The other giants were on their feet in a moment and forming a ring. As high up in the tree as they were, the children had a good view of the proceedings.

Willy had rammed his head directly into Big Rog's stomach and momentarily winded him. Then he got his brother-in-law on the ground and was pounding him left and right, left and right. But it was clear from the start that besides being smaller than Big Rog, Willy was by far the less seasoned fighter, and his punches were doing no real harm. And Big Rog, as soon as he had his breath back, delivered a blow to Willy's ear that knocked him sideways.

Big Rog lurched to his feet and kicked Willy hard in the stomach.

"You want this, boy? That's fine! I'll give you what I gave your dad!"

He kicked him again and again. He was red-faced and grinning, spit flying from his mouth. He looked like some great, savage animal. Then, while Willy lay gasping, Big Rog stalked over to a tree at the edge of the clearing, wrapped his arms about it, and yanked it this way and that, and then with a heave, ripped it out of the ground. Willy was just getting to his feet when Big Rog swung the tree and clobbered him over the head. Big Rog went on pounding Willy with the tree while Sall ran around and laughed, sneaking in now and then to kick her moaning brother.

Emma felt a surge of panic. This wasn't right! Willy wasn't supposed to die now! She hadn't seen it; she would've seen it if he was going to die! Wouldn't she?

Emma's cage shook, and she looked up and for a moment couldn't comprehend what she was seeing. How was Gabriel on top of her cage? Then it all clicked into place. Gabriel was here to rescue them. He must've tracked them here, then climbed up the tree and out onto the limb. And that wasn't all; Michael and Kate were up on the limb above him. He had already rescued them. Emma had been so focused on the giants' fight that she hadn't noticed.

With his knife, Gabriel slashed once, twice, and ripped open the door at the top of her cage. He reached down, hissing, "Come! Take my hand!"

Emma knew that Kate would use the *Atlas* to take them to safety. And there was nothing stopping them now. They knew the rest of the prophecy; they knew about King Davey and the stranger. They could find the High City themselves; they didn't need Willy.

She glanced toward the fire as Big Rog continued to kick and pound Willy.

Then she looked up to where Michael and Kate, on the branch above Gabriel, were waving their arms for her to hurry. She said, "I can't leave Willy!"

"We cannot help him," Gabriel said.

Emma knew that, but she had made this fight happen by telling the story about Willy's dad; she was responsible.

"I know! But I can't leave him."

Gabriel, whose scar was throbbing with the blood rushing to his face, stared at her for a moment while the thumps and thuds of Big Rog's blows and Sall's laughter mixed with Willy's grunts of pain.

"Very well. But come with me, in case . . ."

He did not say in case of what, but Emma knew: in case Big Rog killed Willy and they had to escape quickly. Just then a roar made her turn, and she saw that Big Rog had tossed away the tree and jumped astride Willy's moaning form.

"Right, boy! Let's see what happens when I shove my thumb through your eyeball and give your brain a tickle!"

And he raised his hand high in the air, his great thumb extended—

Emma screamed—

Big Rog drove his thumb down—and Willy caught it. Emma couldn't see what happened next, her view blocked by Big Rog's body, but she heard Big Rog shrieking and trying to get away, but

Willy seemed to be holding on to him. Finally, Big Rog fell backward and there was blood shooting out the side of his hand and Emma saw that where his thumb had been was now a stump.

"Me thumb! Me beautiful thumb!"

Then Willy stood and spat something onto the ground as he bent to pick up the tree that Big Rog had dropped.

"You bit off me thumb!"

"Aye," Willy said. And he swung the tree, there was a *clud*, and Big Rog went down hard. Willy looked at Sall, who ran into the house and slammed the door.

There was an astonished silence among the giants.

Then one said, **"He's dead."**

"He ain't dead." Willy prodded Big Rog with his toe. **"Unfortunately."**

"No. Jasper's dead." The giant who had spoken pointed to the jowly, round-bodied giant, who lay sprawled upon the ground. **"Rog hit him accident-like with the tree, and Jasper fell and bashed his head on a rock. The little girl knew. She said so."**

It was then the giants turned, en masse, toward the cages. Emma felt like she could see what they must be seeing, two of the cages empty, a new, strange human atop her own cage, their dinner escaping. For an instant, Emma regretted having stayed.

Then Willy walked calmly across the clearing and held out his hand.

"Well, little wee folk, will you come with me to the High City?"

He still had blood all over his mouth from biting off Big Rog's thumb, but Emma thought he looked noble.

"Yes," she said, answering for them all, and she finally let Gabriel pull her out of the cage. Willy settled Michael and Kate on his left shoulder, then extended a hand for Gabriel and Emma.

"I'm glad to see you're not dead," he said to Gabriel. "Sorry about plucking you in the noddle before."

Gabriel said nothing, but sheathed his knife.

Then, having placed Gabriel and Emma on his right shoulder, Willy turned to face the giants.

"I'm taking the wee folk to the High City and we're going to find out if that stranger's still there and they're going to fulfill this prophecy. Anyone got a problem with that?"

None of the giants spoke.

"Right, then." And Willy strode off into the darkness.

Emma felt Gabriel's arm around her, and she let out a trembling breath.

"I am sorry it took me so long to catch up with you," Gabriel said.

"It's okay. You're here."

"How did you know that giant was going to die?"

"I saw death hanging over him. Like a shadow. Same as over Big Rog. Gabriel?"

"Yes?"

"Can we not talk about it right now?"

He nodded, and they moved on in silence. Emma kept her eyes straight ahead, not daring to look at Gabriel, or at her brother and sister on the giant's other shoulder, fearing that she would see again, as she had beside the fire, the shadows that hung over each of them.

CHAPTER ELEVEN
The High City

Willy carried the children and Gabriel through the darkness. Finally, some hours after riding on the rolling swell of the giant's shoulders—Kate and Michael on one shoulder, Gabriel and Emma on the other—they came to a stop at the edge of the river. They could see past the dark stretch of water to more hills, and what looked like a forest, on the other side. The river was perhaps a quarter of a mile across.

"No giant's been over this river in a thousand years," Willy said. "We'd best camp here and cross when it's light. I imagine you tiny wee folk could do with a rest. As could I; besting the biggest giant in the land takes something out of a fella; it does at that."

He set them down and went off to collect wood for the fire. Soon, he had what he called "a small little mite of a fire going," which to the children seemed like a raging inferno, and he passed out hunks of sheep kebab that he'd stuffed in his pockets during Big Rog's feast. Once the children had cleaned off the dirt and sheep fuzz, they found the kebab to be quite delicious.

"Oh aye," the giant said, "Sall may be an evil, father-murdering hag, but she knows her way around a sheep, she does that."

The children were exhausted but ravenous, and while they ate, Willy practiced with his sword. He'd gone back to retrieve it from his room shortly after they'd left Big Rog and the others, saying it might come in handy where they were headed. The sword was a fearsome instrument, the blade alone perhaps twenty feet long, but it was most notable for the obvious artistry with which it had been made. "It's a relic from the old world. Me da' gave it to me," Willy said, adding, somewhat unnecessarily, "before he was murdered." But it was clear that Willy's dad had never taught him to use it, and as the children and Gabriel sat by the fire and ate their kebabs, the giant leapt around, jabbing into the darkness and shouting, "Ahhh-YAAA!" and "GOTCHA!" as if his intention were not so much to wound his opponents as to surprise them to death.

It was then that Gabriel told the children how he had used his knife to cut his way through Willy's pouch soon after being captured and had dropped to the ground.

"Did you go looking for your sword?" Emma said. The weapon lay on the ground beside him. "'Cause Willy threw it, like, miles and miles away. I remember."

"No. When I escaped, I merely thought of the sword, and there it was in my hand. A similar thing happened in the Dire Magnus's fortress. Rourke disarmed me, but when I needed my sword, I suddenly had it again."

"You mean it's enchanted?" Michael said, a little awestruck, reaching out to touch the smooth bone of the handle.

Gabriel told them how Granny Peet had given him the sword to replace the falchion he'd lost in the volcano, how she'd told him that this one he would not lose. "I gave it no thought at the time, but there is more to it than meets the eye."

"That's Granny Peet for you," Emma said approvingly. "She's a good one."

Gabriel said how he had then spent the rest of the day following the crater-sized footprints to the giant's home and had arrived just after the feast had gotten under way.

"Well, I'm glad you caught up with us," Michael said. "Though I was never really worried. I still had a few moves I hadn't tried."

"That is very reassuring," Gabriel said.

"Are you sure you're okay?" Kate asked Emma for the ninth time since they'd escaped from Big Rog.

"Yes, I'm fine."

Emma didn't glance at her sister as she said this, for she knew if she looked at her, or at Michael, or at Gabriel, she would see again the shadows hanging over them. Not as fearsome and dark and close as the shadow she'd seen hanging over the obese giant Jasper, who'd died after smashing his head on a rock, or even the shadow over Big Rog, but the shadows were there nonetheless, and she knew it meant that death was coming for each of them. What she didn't know was how much time she had to save them. A day? Two days? Whatever it was, it wasn't long. And she sensed, on some bone-deep level, that her only hope for saving them lay in finding the *Reckoning* and killing the Dire Magnus.

"How was it you knew that giant was going to die?" Michael said as he gnawed on a caveman-sized hunk of meat.

"I just knew," Emma said, hoping to end the discussion.

"But what about Willy's dad? How'd you know what Big Rog did?"

"That was different. I could see it in my head. Guess I'm psychic now too."

"Odd," Michael said. "But it seems obvious this ability of yours is related to the *Reckoning*. You foresee people's deaths and you're the Keeper of the Book of Death? You must be somehow connected to the book. Logic would say that's due to the Bonding ritual the Dire Magnus performed."

"But I feel fine!" Emma insisted. "Totally, totally fine! Better than normal!"

This was not exactly true, but it made the point.

"So why did you pass out in Willy's room, then?" Michael asked.

"In Cambridge Falls," Kate said, "even after we lost the *Atlas*, it kept sending me visions and dreams. That was because some of the magic had passed into me. Michael's right; some of the *Reckoning*'s power must be in you too."

Emma considered the idea that a portion of the *Reckoning*'s magic was now a part of her. The thought made her uneasy.

"It is rather curious," Michael said, "that here we are going to all these lengths to get the book, but we don't really know anything about it."

"Sure we do," Emma said. "It kills people."

"But why's it called the *Reckoning*? That has to mean something, right?"

Emma groaned, sensing that Michael was in one of his let's-analyze-stuff-so-I-can-show-how-smart-I-am moods and not to be stopped.

"Think about it. A *reckoning* can mean a debt or a bill. Maybe that's important. Or—this is interesting—it can also mean a judgment. Maybe you're supposed to judge who should live and who should die."

"As long as it kills the Dire Magnus," Emma said, "who cares?"

She saw Michael throw a look at Kate, and it was a look Emma knew well. It said that Emma was just a kid and they couldn't expect her to take adult things seriously. She was about to remind him that it had been her, and not him or Kate, that had saved them from Sall's pie by goading Willy into fighting Big Rog, but she was tired, and anyway Michael was already moving into plan-making mode.

He said they needed to know all they could before they entered the giant's city the next day. He brought up the subject of Willy's dad's story.

"It has to be that this dark stranger, whoever he was, had the *Reckoning*. How else could he have killed all those giants?"

(They had to pause for a moment to bring Emma up to speed; she'd only heard the end of the story.)

Michael went on: "So the question I come back to is, Just who *is* this stranger? It can't be the Dire Magnus; he's still looking for the book. It could be one of the Guardians. Bert thought that only a few of them escaped Rhakotis, but maybe he was wrong.

"If we step back a moment"—Michael had his notebook out and was tapping his pen on the open page—"there were three Books. They were held in the wizard's tower in Rhakotis. They all disappeared when Alexander the Great, with the help of the then

Dire Magnus, sacked the city. We know that Dr. Pym took the *Atlas* to the dwarves of Cambridge Falls. Bert took the *Chronicle* to Antarctica. The *Reckoning* simply disappeared. Willy says that the stranger arrived more than two thousand years ago, which suggests that he was also the one who took the book from Rhakotis during the siege. So it could've been one of the Guardians. It could also have been one of the wizards of Dr. Pym's Council."

"Or it could be someone else entirely," Gabriel said. "Someone we don't know about."

"Exactly," Michael said. "An unknown. An X factor."

Emma could see that he took pleasure in saying X *factor*. He even repeated it:

"Yep. A real X factor."

"Whoever the stranger is," Kate said, "do we think they're still alive? Dr. Pym lived for thousands of years, remember. And this Bert you met was alive."

"That was because of the *Chronicle*," Michael said. "The *Reckoning* is the Book of Death."

"But if it is one of the wizards," Gabriel said, "he could have been exposed to the Book of Life the same as Dr. Pym. He might have been in this city all this time, waiting."

"That's a good point, Gabriel," Michael admitted, in a somewhat patronizing tone. "But how did he know about the three of us? The actual prophecy about us finding the Books wasn't made till a thousand years after the fall of Rhakotis."

"How do you remember all that?" Emma asked.

Michael held up his notebook. "I made a timeline."

Emma groaned. And for a moment, she forgot about the shadows looming over her brother and sister and friend, about what it meant that the book was called the *Reckoning* or how it worked, and allowed herself to think about what a colossal nerd Michael could be. It made her feel significantly better.

"Willy," Kate called up, "do you know if the stranger is still in the city? Still alive, I mean?"

Willy settled himself down cross-legged by the fire. He was breathing hard and sweating from his practice with the sword. Emma reflected that for all his size, the giant wasn't in the best shape.

"Well, Evelina"—Emma saw Gabriel throw her a look and she whispered, "We gave him fake names. My idea"—**"that's a difficult question, as no one's been inside the city in thousands a' years. Few giants have even come this far—"**

"But . . ." Emma could always tell when someone was winding up for a *but*.

"But there've been stories, haven't there?"

"What kind of stories?" Michael asked.

"Stories there's something alive in the city. Could be the stranger. Could be something the stranger brought with 'im. Or could be something else. Dark magic draws other dark creatures, you know."

"So there are stories of something alive there," Kate said.

"Used to be. Not so much in recent years. The short answer is—maybe."

He said this with some satisfaction, as if he'd actually answered their question, rather than simply raise more questions.

"We should get some sleep," Gabriel said. "Tomorrow will be a long day."

"I'll stand guard. Or sit guard, if you don't mind, me legs are

kinda tired. It's dreadful hard work, all this ridding death from the land."

The children lay down beside the fire. Michael put his head on his bag, and Kate, without Emma asking her to, wrapped both arms around her. Gabriel settled in a few yards away, drawing his sword and laying it beside him so it would be ready if the need arose. Emma was relieved they were done talking. She was exhausted, and she told herself that whatever was waiting for them, they would deal with it tomorrow.

Kate woke and found that the fire had burned down from bonfire-sized to something more human in scale. The sky showed the first gray softenings of dawn. Emma and Michael were both still asleep, though Emma's hands were clenched into fists and now and then she would jerk and whimper. Gabriel—whom Kate realized she'd never seen in any state other than awake and vigilant—was asleep with his right hand upon the handle of his sword. She knew that Gabriel had been searching for Emma nonstop since her abduction, and she was glad he had finally allowed himself to rest. She was not so glad to see Willy asleep. The giant was on his side and snoring loudly, drool from the corner of his mouth turning the ground below into mud.

So much for our sentry, she thought.

Kate carefully lifted her arm from Emma and stood. She walked out of the circle of light, stopping a dozen or so yards into the gloom of the surrounding trees. She was still able to see her brother and sister and Gabriel asleep beside the fire.

She turned and looked into the darkness.

"Come out."

There was a moment of silence. Then a voice said: "How'd you know?"

Rafe, or Rafe's ghost—she still wasn't sure how to think of him—stepped from behind a tree, shadows obscuring his features.

"I just felt it."

This was not exactly true. She'd only hoped he would be there, but hoped it so fervently that she had felt it had to be so.

Kate said, "Aren't you supposed to tell me it's really you?"

He shrugged. "What's the point? If the Dire Magnus was pretending to be me, wouldn't he say the same thing?"

"I guess."

Rafe stepped closer. Gray light filtering through the trees fell across his face.

"Well?"

Kate studied him for a long moment. "It's you."

"You're sure?"

Kate was about to answer when she realized she couldn't. All she knew was that she wanted to believe; and right then, she knew she was lost.

But she pushed the thought away and said what had been turning through her mind all night.

"We're going to the old giant city. We think whoever took the *Reckoning* from Rhakotis brought it there. He may still be there too. We don't know what's waiting for us. And with Dr. Pym gone, there's no one to ask. Can you help?"

Rafe shook his head. "The Dire Magnus doesn't know who took the *Reckoning*. If he did, it would've made finding it easier."

Kate nodded, having half expected that answer. She said, "Emma can see people's deaths."

"What?"

"She can see people's deaths. She said this one giant was going to die and then he did. Does it—"

"It means the Bonding worked. At least partly. She's connected to the *Reckoning*. As she gets closer, she'll be able to feel the book itself. It'll call to her."

They were both silent then for a few moments. Kate could hear the background rumbling of the giant's snores, and in the pauses between them, the crackle of the fire and the soft passage of the river, so close by. The first shock of seeing Rafe, the wild, heart-pounding strangeness of being able to talk to him again, had passed, and Kate was filled instead with an appreciation of what this interaction really was. The Rafe she knew, the boy she had danced with, who'd protected her, who had held her in his arms, was gone forever. She was talking to a ghost. And sometime very soon, she would lose even that.

She sensed too that Rafe knew what she was thinking and didn't begrudge it, that he understood her reserve and that was why he wasn't pressing her for more than she could give. It occurred to her that that was how she knew it was really him.

"There's something else. I can't explain it, but ever since we rescued Emma, I've felt . . ."

Kate found to her frustration that she really couldn't explain it. For how could she describe the vague sense of unease she felt, the disturbing undercurrent that told her some unnamed and unseen trouble, some danger she had not yet encountered, was stirring?

Rafe said, "It's the Books."

"What?"

"What you're feeling. It's the Books."

"What're you talking about?"

Rafe took a moment before responding, but when he spoke, Kate felt that she had asked the thing he'd been waiting for her to ask.

"You have to understand, the wizards who created the Books, your friend Pym among them, drew the magic out of the very heart of the world. But the Books are still connected to everything around us. Imagine them at the center of an enormous web, and each time you use the *Atlas* or your brother uses the *Chronicle*, the whole web trembles."

"But what does that really mean?"

"You and your brother think what you're doing doesn't have larger effects, but it does. You stop one moment in time; he brings one person back to life; the power radiates outward, shaking everything. That's what you're feeling. And it's going to get worse."

"So we shouldn't use the Books anymore? We have to!"

"I'm just saying: the bonds that hold the universe together can only bear so much. Soon, they'll begin to snap."

Kate turned away. She didn't want to hear any more. She needed the *Atlas* to take them all back to Loris. She had to use it!

"What you asked before," Rafe said, "about what's waiting in the city, there is one thing I can tell you. Whoever brought the *Reckoning* here didn't do it by accident. There're a thousand other places it could've been hidden, dragon lairs, caves at the bottom of the ocean. Something about this place is special."

"Willy hasn't said anything—"

"He wouldn't know. I have the feeling it was a secret. Be careful."

The sky was getting lighter. In another time, another place, they would've just been two teenagers standing alone in the shadows.

Kate said quietly, "I had a dream last night. We were in the church. In New York. It was snowing." She turned and looked at him. "Rafe, the next time, if I know it's not you . . ."

She was breathing hard now, her heart thudding against her chest, and the words caught in her throat.

He nodded. "I know. Me too."

After a quick breakfast of mutton (another word for sheep, it turned out), the small group crossed the river, the children and Gabriel riding on Willy's shoulders as he waded through the thick brown water. When they reached the other shore, they found themselves entering a forest. But the forest was strangely, eerily silent. There were no birds calling to one another and announcing the dawn, no squirrels skittering along branches; everything was quiet and still, and the children, feeling this, grew quiet as well.

Emma had woken before Gabriel and Michael and seen that Kate was not with them. She'd lain there without moving, till she'd heard Kate's footsteps.

"Where'd you go?"

Kate had seemed surprised to be caught sneaking back, and Emma had watched her forming the lie.

"Oh. I thought I heard a noise. It was nothing."

Emma hadn't pressed her. In the morning light, the shadow hanging over her sister had been darker than ever.

Gabriel had woken at the sound of the girls' voices; they had then woken Michael, and the four of them had worked together to wake the giant. Shouts, pinches, kicks to his stomach—none of it had had any effect. Finally, Emma had snatched a burning branch from the fire and stuck it up his nose.

The giant had let out a bellow that blew them off their feet, and he'd leapt up, dancing around and swatting at his face, crying, "Oh! Oh! Oh!" Kate had scolded Emma, and Emma had apologized to the giant, but really, she'd thought, he'd fallen asleep on guard duty; in some armies, he would've been shot.

The forest was thick, but Willy was tall enough that the children and Gabriel could ride on his shoulders and not be clawed and swatted by passing branches. Willy seemed to pay the trees no mind, and Emma, looking back, could track the giant's passage by the broken branches and trampled saplings in their wake. If anyone had a mind to follow them, the path could hardly have been clearer.

It was midmorning when they came to the top of a rise, and Willy raised his arm and pointed into the distance. **"There! That's it!"**

"You mean behind those hills?" Michael asked.

"Those're no hills, Toadlip. That's the city."

"My name—"

"Is Toadlip," Emma said automatically.

She heard Michael mutter something unintelligible.

Standing on the hill, they could see down to where the trees stopped and a broad plain opened up. Past the plain was what Michael had taken for a knot of gray hills. But it was now apparent they were looking not at hills but at an immense gray-black wall and, above that, the studded tops of buildings, clustering upward. Emma could see one building rising higher than the others, its roof gleaming as it caught the morning sun.

"If only me da' could see what I'm seeing now," Willy murmured. "The High City of King Davey. Amazing what you find when you leave the house. Amazing."

"Emma," said Kate, who was sitting beside her sister, "do you feel anything?"

"What do you mean?"

"She means do you feel the *Reckoning*," Michael called from Willy's other shoulder, where he and Gabriel sat. "Both of us, when we got close to our Books, felt them. Almost like something's pulling on your chest."

Emma stared at the city in the distance and waited, hardly breathing. But she felt no tug or pull, just a vague nausea from eating too much sheep and then riding for hours on a giant's shoulder.

"I don't feel anything."

"It doesn't mean it's not there!" Michael shouted. "We might just have to get closer!"

Emma said nothing, and Willy thudded down the slope, eager to reach the city, and soon they came out of the forest onto the open plain. Willy was moving more and more quickly, and the children and Gabriel had to hold on tightly. But then, halfway across the plain, they came upon a stand of unusual-looking trees, and the giant slowed. The trees appeared to be all trunk, no branches at all, and were encased in moss and curving up out of the earth at strange angles. The trees were also surrounded by odd-shaped moss-and-grass-covered boulders.

"They're bones," Michael said when they were right up next to them. "The bones of the giants that were killed."

It was indeed an enormous boneyard; the trees were the ribs of the giants, the moss-covered boulders the skulls, hands, knees, and legs. Willy and Gabriel and the children moved past the skeletons in silence.

Finally, Kate said, "It's really true. The story about King Davey and his giants going out to fight the stranger; it happened."

They passed one set of bones that was separate from the others, and when they reached the skull, for the giant appeared to have fallen backward when he died, they could see the ridges of the moss-covered crown that still encircled his brow.

"It's him," Willy said in the nearest thing he could manage to a whisper. **"It's King Davey. Lookit his bones! He must've been fifty feet tall! Taller even than Big Rog!"**

For a moment, Emma was silent. She didn't want to say it, but seeing the bones of the dead giants had filled her with a wild, almost giddy excitement. If the *Reckoning* had done this, then it could certainly kill the Dire Magnus.

"Come on!" she said. "What're we waiting for? Let's go!"

"You mean . . . go to the city, then?"

Willy's voice had none of the eagerness he'd displayed all morning, and Emma could see that even Kate was looking stunned and wary.

"Yes, the city! Where else?!" And to Kate, she said, "The *Reckoning*'s the only way we're gonna kill the Dire Magnus! You know it!"

Kate nodded and told Willy that yes, they should go on.

With clear reluctance, Willy resumed walking toward the city, throwing occasional glances back at the remains of King Davey and his soldiers and murmuring things like **"I wonder, did I leave the kettle on back at the house?"** Still, he kept on. And the nearer they got to the city, the larger it grew, the walls stretching both outward and upward, half a mile to the other side and hundreds of feet high. By the time Willy stopped before the city gates, he himself was dwarfed by the scale of the city.

"Wow," he said, looking up, "it's . . . really big."

The walls were made of heavy blocks of gray-black stone that had been fitted together with great craftsmanship and precision. Indeed, the very fact that the walls were still standing so many centuries after the city had been abandoned—though they were covered by a thick lattice of weeds and vines, and there were large holes where chunks of stone had sheared away—testified to the skill of the city's masons.

The gates were as high as the walls and made of wood and, no doubt thanks to whatever their makers had treated them with, appeared whole and solid. Somewhat gingerly, Willy placed one palm against the wood and pushed. The gate opened a few feet, then stopped. He pushed harder, and the gate gave a little more. Finally, he set the children and Gabriel on the ground, took two steps back, charged forward, and rammed his shoulder against the gate. The children heard ripping and snapping, Emma saw strange, silvery-gray bands on the inside breaking free, and the gate flew open.

Picking himself up from the ground, Willy lifted the children and Gabriel to his shoulders and stepped through the gate, along a portico, and out into a large square. A wide boulevard of flattened stone led away from them, down through the center of the city, while two other streets split off to either side. The buildings before them were both impossibly massive and impossibly tall. It was hard for the children even to process what they were seeing; it was almost as if the city were normal-sized and they had shrunk to the size of insects.

But what was most notable, what had the children's hearts beating in their throats, was not the sheer enormity of the city. It was that everything—the streets, the buildings, the walls, even the giant streetlamps—was covered by the same silvery-gray bands that had barred the door. It was almost a kind of netting or even—

"They're spiderwebs!" Emma said.

"But that's—that's not possible!" Michael exclaimed. He had a long history of arachnophobia (he even yelped at the harmless daddy longlegs Emma routinely put in his bed as "therapy"). "They'd have to be—"

"Giant," Willy said. **"Giant spiders. Yep."**

"You knew about this?" Kate asked.

"Well, I didn't know that they'd taken over the city. But back in King Davey's time, there was giant everything, giant sheep and giant cows and giant chickens. The royal magicians did that, made everything up to scale, so to speak—only way you could hope to feed a city full of big folk. Problem was, in the casting of the spell, wasn't just chickens and sheep that got big. Other things got big too."

"Like spiders," Emma said.

"Most a' the giant creatures died out or were eaten up long ago, and we don't have magicians now to do the spell; that's why we spend all our time scrounging for food. But looks like the spiders might've survived."

For a moment, they just stared at the mummified city. Here and there, strands of webbing had broken free and wafted in the breeze.

"So where are they?" Emma said.

For besides the drifting webs, nothing moved. Nor were there any bodies of spiders lying about.

"Perhaps they are dead," Gabriel said. "Or have abandoned the city. Those webs look old."

The children had to agree. The webbing was dried out and fraying, like ancient lace.

"So what do we do now?" Michael said, and it sounded as if he would've been quite happy if someone had said, "We turn around and forget all about this."

"We go on," Emma said, and, unable to resist, she added, "even if there are giant, hairy spiders waiting to eat us!"

Kate gave her a look.

After a short discussion, they decided to proceed straight down the boulevard, into the heart of the city. Willy had drawn his sword, and he used it to clear the way, though he had to pause regularly and clean off the webs that stuck to the blade. His steps were quieter than normal, and when Emma glanced down, she saw that webs were clinging to the giant's feet, so that it looked like he was wearing a pair of fluffy white shoes.

As they moved forward, the children stared up at the buildings on either side, and the hugeness of the city began to strike home. Indeed, peering down side streets—which were crisscrossed with gray webs like streamers for a parade—the children found that the town houses and buildings in the distance seemed like far-off mountain ranges.

Still they saw no spiders, living or dead.

"It's actually a nice city," Michael said, after they'd been walking for a while and were passing a park surrounded by shops and cafés.

Even Willy seemed to have overcome his nerves.

"It's just as Da' always said. Beautiful."

Then they entered an enormous square and stopped. Before them stood a massive building from which a tower rose five hundred feet into the air, far above anything else in the city. It was capped by a silver dome, and Emma realized that this was the tower and dome she'd seen from the forest.

"It's the palace of King Davey," Willy said, with dumbfounded reverence. **"He had it built 'cause he kept banging his head on the doorways of the old palace."**

"We have to go inside," Emma said.

"Is it in there?" Kate asked. "Do you feel something?"

Emma shook her head. "I just know."

Willy needed no more encouragement, and with the children and Gabriel holding on as best they could, he hurried across the square, ran up half a dozen stone steps to an open colonnade, and then used his sword to hack through the thick webbing that swathed a set of giant ceremonial doors.

The inside of the palace was free of webs, and the group made fast progress through a series of vestibules and waiting rooms. The air was musty and stale, and though it was the middle of the day, only a faint grayish light penetrated the webbing that covered the windows from the outside, giving the palace a gloomy, tomblike air. A thick layer of dust carpeted the floor, and Willy left a cloudy trail behind them. After passing through the sixth or seventh antechamber, Willy pushed open a pair of intricately wrought metal doors, they entered a large circular room, and Willy stopped dead.

"King Davey's throne room. Has to be."

The room was built directly beneath the tower, allowing Willy and Gabriel and the children to look straight up nearly five hundred feet. Light filtering down showed a chamber that seemed oddly plain and unadorned, as if everything had been stripped away to focus all attention on the round dais in the center.

"That was where he sat, dispensing wisdom to his people. But what happened to his throne?"

For an immense stone chair, one that clearly was intended to sit on top of the dais, lay upturned on the floor, giving the impression that it had been thrown roughly aside.

"Willy," Kate said, "put us down."

The giant knelt at the edge of the dais, and Gabriel and the children leapt down. They peered through the gloom.

"There is something there," Gabriel said. "I will—"

But Emma was already hurrying forward. The others were just behind her, and they all gathered about the object in the center of the dais. It lay beneath a shroud of black linen and was surrounded by a ring of rose petals and half-burned candles.

"It's almost like a shrine or something," Michael said.

"Someone has been here recently," Gabriel said, staring at the shadows in the corners of the chamber. "The last day or so."

Emma reached out and began to pull back the shroud.

"Emma," Kate said, "wait—"

There was a collective gasp, and Emma jerked her hand away. Beneath the shroud lay a figure, arms crossed neatly over its chest. That the figure was dead, there was no doubt. But it was not a skeleton, nor was it the fresh body of a corpse. It seemed to be something in between. It was as if all the liquid had been sucked out of the body so that the skin was drawn back hard and dark against its bones. Its mouth was stretched open, displaying small, yellow-black teeth. Rotten bandages were wrapped around its body.

"It's almost like a mummy," Michael said.

"Is that the stranger, then?" Willy asked. **"'E's so small."**

"There's something in his hand," Emma said, and she carefully pulled the object from the corpse's fingers. It was an ancient, dry, time-darkened piece of parchment. "It's a message."

"You won't be able to read it," Michael said. "I imagine it's written in some old, forgotten language. Better give it here."

"No, I can read it."

"That doesn't make sense," Michael argued. "English wasn't even invented two thousand or whatever years ago."

"What's it say?" Kate asked.

"It says"—Emma's voice echoed in the throne room—"'If you want the *Reckoning,* you will have to bring me back.'"

There was a long moment in which the only sound was Willy's thick breathing overhead.

Then Gabriel said: "This is a trap."

"Yes," Kate said. "Obviously."

"So what?" Emma said, angry that once again she was having to explain herself, that the others, and Kate especially, didn't just trust her. "Getting the book is our only hope! And we've already been here for two days! Who knows what the Dire Magnus is doing! But I doubt he's been, like, taking a vacation! And you can get us out of here if something happens! We don't—"

"Emma's right," Michael said, cutting her off. "We don't have a choice."

And without waiting for Kate to agree, Michael pulled the

red-leather *Chronicle* from his bag and knelt on the stone dais beside the linen-wrapped figure. He opened to a seemingly random place in the middle, then reached out with his right hand and took hold of the figure's blackened, shriveled hand. His other hand he placed on the book.

Emma glanced at Kate, but their older sister seemed, at least for now, willing to go along. Then Michael closed his eyes, and flames erupted over the surface of the book. Emma couldn't help but note that this was the second time in two days that Michael had supported her in an argument with Kate. Yesterday in Willy's room, and now here. She knew Michael still thought of her as a little kid—she'd seen the look he'd given Kate last night beside the fire—so then why did he keep taking her side? It confused her and annoyed her and pleased her all at once.

Suddenly, Michael gasped, his eyes snapped open, and the book fell from his lap. The flames died, and the room became darker. Emma dropped down beside him.

"Michael?! What is it? What happened?"

He was covered in sweat and shaking, gasping. "It's . . . it's . . ."

"Oh no. . . ."

Emma saw Kate staring down at the figure, and there was a look of both recognition and horror on her face. Emma turned back; the figure's dry, blackened skin was filling out and growing lighter. She could hear a cracking and looked to see the skeletal hand flexing its fingers as the wrappings holding it in place began to disintegrate.

"Michael!" Kate's voice was frantic. "You have to stop it! You—"

"I can't! It's too late!"

The tattered bandages were flaking and falling away as the figure began to stir. There was a snapping as its jaw moved.

"What's going on?" Emma demanded. "Who—"

The figure was identifiable now as a woman, though a very old one. Then it—or rather she—coughed, a dry, hacking cough, as if clearing her throat of centuries of dust and congealed phlegm.

"We have to go," Kate said. "Take my hand!"

"No!" Emma said, pulling away. "Tell me who it is!"

The figure slowly sat up, using her shriveled, clawlike hand to tear away more of the wrappings. She may have been alive, Emma reflected, but she didn't look that much better than when she'd been dead. Her skin was sagging and mottled. Her hair was gray and stringy, her teeth yellowed and cracked.

Then she spoke, and the voice, though hoarse and shaking, was familiar.

"Yes, tell her who I am, my dear. I'm hurt she doesn't recognize her old friend."

The figure blinked, and Emma saw a pair of violet eyes and knew, finally, whom they had brought back to life.

"Shall I tell you?" The Countess pushed herself up to standing. "I'm the only person in the world who knows where the *Reckoning* is hidden. More than two thousand years I've waited for you. I want what was taken from me! My youth! My beauty! The *Chronicle* has that power. Restore me to what I was, and I will give you not just the *Reckoning*, but something you desire even more! Our journey together is not yet ended! You thought your Countess was dead! You were wrong! I live! I live, and I will have my revenge! I will—"

And that was all she got out before Willy stomped on her.

CHAPTER TWELVE
The Nest

Willy was grinding his foot left and right, left and right, as if intent on turning whatever remained of the Countess into powder, then periodically raising his foot for another stomp, which simply sent more Countess splatter shooting toward the children.

"And that's for killing King Davey!" Stomp! **"And that's for destroying my entire civilization!"** Stomp! **"And that's for Big Rog always clouting me on the head!"** Stomp! **"And that's—"**

Finally, the screams of the children stopped him.

"What?" he asked innocently. **"What's wrong?"**

"What's wrong?" Emma shrieked. "You *stomped* her!"

"'Course I stomped her! You saw what she did to King Davey!"

"But we needed her! And you—you smooshed her!"

"We don't need her," Michael said quietly.

"What're you talking about?" Emma whirled toward him.

"She knew where the *Reckoning* was! Now she's just goop! We'll never—"

"I know where the *Reckoning* is. When I use the *Chronicle*, I live the other person's whole life, remember? I know where she hid it."

Emma stared at her brother. He had picked up the *Chronicle*, which he'd dropped when the Countess had come back to life, and now held it tight against his chest. Beads of sweat stood out on his face and forehead.

"You really know where it is?" Kate asked.

Michael nodded. "And I know how she got it, and why she brought it here, and what we have to do to get it."

"Oh," Emma said, "that's okay, then."

The children sat down on the edge of the dais, while Gabriel remained standing. Emma was impatient for Michael to tell them where the *Reckoning* was, but he was clearly shaken and needed to recover.

"Take your time," Kate said.

"Yeah," Emma said. "But not, you know, too much time."

Behind them, Willy was using a soiled handkerchief the size of a bedsheet to clean Countess off the bottom of his foot. Emma tried not to watch. She told herself the Countess had deserved it, but even so, she had to admit that getting stomped on was not the nicest way to go.

"After everything happened in Cambridge Falls and we saved the kids, the Countess waited around for fifteen years to try to surprise Kate, remember? When we were down at the Christmas party, she cornered her with a knife."

"Yeah," Emma said, "and Kate took her into the past and dumped her."

Kate said nothing; she was looking at Michael with a tense, worried expression, as if scared of what he might say next. But why? Emma wondered. She hadn't done anything wrong.

"Kate left the Countess on top of a house in Rhakotis," Michael went on. He was speaking softly, but his voice seemed loud in the empty chamber. "This was twenty-five hundred years ago. The city was under attack from Alexander the Great and the Dire Magnus. The sky was thick with dragons. Buildings crumbled as sand trolls tunneled up from below. There was screaming. Fire. The city was doomed. She was doomed."

Emma heard Willy walk across the chamber and start up the stairs that led to the tower. Michael had slid the *Chronicle* into his bag, and he was clenching his hands to stop, or at least hide, their trembling.

"But it was then, standing on the roof, that she realized that far from killing her, Kate had given her the chance for her ultimate revenge."

"Oh no . . . ," Kate whispered.

"'Oh no' what?" Emma said. "'Oh no' what?"

"Let your brother speak," Gabriel said softly.

"I am!" Emma protested, then murmured, "Sorry. Go on."

"After the siege of Rhakotis," Michael said, "the Books were lost for more than two thousand years. What Kate did was to take the Countess to the last moment that all three were gathered together in the same place. It was exactly what she wanted."

Kate shook her head, muttering, "How could I have been so stupid?"

Dust was drifting down on the children's heads as Willy tromped up the stairs of the tower, but none of them noticed, intent as they were on Michael describing how the Countess had made her way through the city, how when she'd arrived at the tower of the magicians, she'd seen a group of small figures at the very top, how she'd known they were the wizards, using all their art and power to defend the city, how she'd been knocked backward by an explosion, and how when the dust had cleared, the top of the tower, and the wizards, were gone.

"That was her chance. The tower's defenses were down, and she made herself invisible and slipped inside."

Then it had been simple. The Countess had come upon two from the Order of the Guardians, and she'd followed them as they went to a hidden staircase and then down, deep into the earth. They unknowingly guided her past dozens of traps and defenses. Finally, they'd come to the door of a vault.

"She'd hoped for the *Chronicle*," Michael told his sisters. "She wanted to be young again. Beautiful. But when the door opened and she saw the *Reckoning*, she knew this was better. The *Reckoning* was the book the Dire Magnus wanted most of all, the one most necessary to his plans, and also the only one that could kill him." Michael looked up at Kate. "As much as she hated you—hated all of us—she hated him more. He'd stolen her youth, made her old and ugly. She would never forgive him.

"She slit both the Guardians' throats and took the book for herself."

None of them spoke. More dust showered down.

"And why didn't she simply kill the Dire Magnus then?" Gabriel said. "She had the book."

"She couldn't. She still wanted to come back to life. And if she'd killed the Dire Magnus, he'd never have been there to find her when she was a teenager in Russia. She couldn't mess with the future. She had to hide the book and hope we would come and find her. So that's what she did. She came here, hid it, then lay down and died."

"So where is it?" Kate asked.

Michael rose and walked to the center of the dais, where there was still an ugly, dark, Countess-y smear. He pulled out his knife and cut a thin red line across his palm, letting three drops of blood fall onto the stone. For a moment, nothing happened. Then the stone seemed to absorb the blood, there was a rumbling and scraping, and the dais began to separate down the middle. Emma was pulled back by Gabriel as two staircases were revealed, one giant-sized and another human-sized, side by side, corkscrewing down into the darkness.

"She knew the book had to stay hidden for thousands of years," Michael said. "But where could she hide it so that no one, not even the Dire Magnus, would find it? Then she remembered that the king of the giants had guarded a great secret."

Emma peered over the edge into the darkness. A rank odor rose up, assaulting her nostrils. She still didn't feel anything. No pull at her chest. Nothing.

"Did I ever tell you"—Michael too was peering down into the darkness—"what drew the elves to that valley in Antarctica? There was a portal there, between the worlds of the living and the dead. Turns out, it's not the only one."

"Wait," Kate said. "You mean—"

"She hid the book in the world of the dead."

* * *

Gabriel prepared a pair of torches, while Michael pulled two small flashlights from his bag and gave one to Emma. Kate took a torch. Just then, thundering footsteps boomed from above, and they looked up through the dust-choked air to see Willy racing down the tower stairs, shouting, **"Big Rog . . . Big Rog . . . Big Rog . . ."** He was taking the stairs two and three at a time, and in a few moments he was beside them, bent over and panting: **"Big Rog—Sall—couple others! They're out there! Heading this way!"**

"You'd better come with us," Kate told the giant.

But Willy straightened—with some difficulty, as he was still panting—and laid his hand on the hilt of his sword. **"No. It's time I stood up to him for good. And where better than the throne room a' King Davey?"**

"But there're four of them!" Emma said.

"I'll challenge Big Rog to single combat," Willy said stoutly. **"He'll have to honor that. Also, you need someone to slide the dais back so he don't follow you."**

Emma doubted that Big Rog would honor the traditions of single combat, since he didn't even honor the traditions of basic hygiene, but Willy seemed determined, and they had no more time. The children and Gabriel started down the staircase, and Willy began to close the dais behind them. They had only gone a little way when they looked up to see the last sliver of light disappear.

Then all was silent and dark.

"This way," Michael said.

The passage they were descending was appropriately enormous, and it went on and on, deeper and deeper underground.

And the deeper they went, the colder the air grew, and the stronger the foul, rotting smell became.

"What I don't understand," Emma said, "is that the Countess only got the *Reckoning* because Kate took her back in time. And that only just happened. Who had the *Reckoning* before that?"

"Probably those other two Guardians," Michael said. "They were on their way to get it when she killed them."

"Which all got changed because of me," Kate said. "And it's my fault too that they're dead."

"You had no way of knowing," Gabriel said.

"Yeah," Emma said. "It's not like the stupid *Atlas* came with instructions."

They kept on walking. After a few minutes, they heard a muffled cry from above, followed by sounds of thudding and crashing. No one spoke; they knew that Willy was probably being ganged up on by Big Rog and Sall and the others, but there was nothing they could do. They simply kept moving downward, and the sounds faded.

Finally, the carved stairs ended, and the passage below them opened up into a deeper, vaster cavern. Michael was in the lead, but before he could take another step, Gabriel reached forward and seized his shoulder, stopping him.

"What is it?" Michael said. "We're getting close—"

"Look." Gabriel raised his torch, gesturing into the darkness. Emma and Michael both lifted the beams of their flashlights.

"*Gaahghh!*" Michael fell backward into Emma, nearly knocking them both over. Directly in front of them, a few feet above their heads and perched on a swath of webbing that stretched across the passage, was a spider the size of a hippopotamus. Its jointed legs were curled up under its body, and the light from their flashlights and torches refracted off the creature's eyes in dozens of directions. Its fangs were the length of Emma's forearm.

"Is it . . . dead?" Kate said.

For though it seemed to be staring right at them, the spider had yet to move.

"Perhaps," Gabriel said. "I am no expert in spiders. But none of them appear to be moving."

"'Them'?!" Michael blurted. "What do you mean '*them*'?"

Again, Gabriel pointed, and Michael and Emma turned their flashlights outward and down, illuminating the thick webbing that crisscrossed the entire stadium-sized cavern below them. Even then it took Emma a moment to understand what she was seeing, what the large, heavy shapes hanging here and there—hanging everywhere—actually were.

They had found the missing spiders.

The smallest were the size of pigs, while the largest, with their massive rounded bodies, were elephantine. And everywhere Michael and Emma moved their flashlights they saw more pairs of glittering eyes. There must've been fifty or sixty spiders spread about the cavern, their jaws bristling with enormous fangs.

Emma could hear Michael beginning to hyperventilate.

"They're not moving," Kate said. "Are they dead?"

"That or sleeping," Gabriel said. "Having devoured everything in the city, they may have gone into hibernation."

"You mean they could just . . . wake up?" Michael whispered.

"We must avoid the webbing," Gabriel said. "That is how they sense the presence of a threat."

"Or food," Emma muttered.

Michael's eyes seemed to have doubled in size, and his voice shook. "None of this was in the Countess's memories."

"No," Gabriel said. "They would have come after. Where do we go?"

Michael didn't respond, so Emma took his hand and stepped in front of him, forcing him to look at her. "Michael, we can't stay here. Where do we go?"

Michael took a deep breath, then pointed his flashlight at the base of the cavern, the trembling beam illuminating the mouth of a large tunnel that wormed its way deeper into the black rock. "There."

"Good," Emma said. "Now come on. I'll hold your hand."

And the two of them led Gabriel and Kate down a rough pathway that snaked along the wall to the bottom of the cavern. It was slow going avoiding the webs, and once Michael's foot caught on a strand and it twanged like piano wire, setting the entire structure humming and the spiders' bodies quivering and shaking. The children and Gabriel, his sword out and ready, all froze, hardly breathing, watching. . . .

But the quivering finally ceased, and the spiders did not stir.

Shortly afterward, they reached the base of the cavern. The spiders were now all above them, their shadows wavering in the torchlight.

"Don't look at them," Emma whispered to her brother.

Michael held her hand even more tightly and nodded at the mouth of the tunnel. "The portal's just down at the end. Not far."

There was more webbing in the tunnel, but no more spiders. The children and Gabriel moved slowly, careful to avoid the strands, now getting down on their hands and knees to crawl under a web, now having to step over a cable. The floor of the tunnel was littered with old bones, mostly, the children hoped, of sheep. Here and there they saw the mouths of other tunnels, all of them latticed with webs, but Michael kept them going straight.

Emma waited to feel that pull in her chest that Michael and Kate had spoken of, but still she felt nothing.

The tunnel doglegged to the left, and as they rounded the corner, Michael said, "We're almost there. I have to tell you something—"

But then, for the second time, Gabriel stopped them.

"Do not move."

The end of the tunnel was perhaps twenty yards farther on, and as Emma looked up, she finally did feel something in her chest. Only it was not the pull of the missing book. It was panic, utter and complete panic. Covering the end of the tunnel was a web, and in the middle of the web was by far the biggest spider they had yet encountered. Its body was made of two enormous segmented pods. Its legs were spread out like the buttresses of a cathedral. It had not one set of fangs but three, each tusk at least a yard long.

"But that's"—Michael's voice rose to the point of hysteria—"where the opening to the portal is!"

Gabriel grunted, as if to say, "Of course."

"You mean," Kate said, "we have to go through that . . . thing to get to the portal?"

"Not 'we' . . . ," Michael said, turning to face his sisters. "That's what I was going to tell you. Emma, you have to go. Alone."

"*What*?!" Kate's voice echoed off the tunnel walls.

Michael spoke hurriedly. "It's like Wilamena told me. The living can't pass into the world of the dead. But the Keeper of the

Book of Death can. The Countess knew that. That's how she knew she was hiding the book somewhere only Emma could get to it, how she knew it'd be safe!" He looked at Emma and his eyes were filled with regret. "I'm so sorry. I wish there was some other way. I wish we could all go, or that I could go! I would! You have to believe me!"

Emma said nothing. From the moment Michael had said that she would have to go into the world of the dead alone, she'd felt the strongest sense of déjà vu, as if she had been here before, had known this was going to happen. She wasn't even upset.

Not surprisingly, it was Kate who objected.

"No! That doesn't make any sense!"

"Kate," Michael said, glancing nervously at the spider, "could you maybe keep your voice down. . . ."

"How did the Countess hide the book in the world of the dead if she couldn't take it there herself? Explain that."

"She went as far as she could," Michael said, "to the edge of the portal, and summoned a spirit from that world. She gave it the book, then went back to the throne room, lay down, and died."

"Why didn't she get the book back after she died?" Emma asked.

"I don't know," Michael said. "I only have her memories from when she was alive."

"It doesn't matter," Kate said, and Emma could see she was becoming more and more set and determined. "It's obvious the Countess is trying to split us up. Emma's not going anywhere alone. How can you even suggest it?"

"Honestly?" Michael said, growing agitated himself. "How can you be against it? I was in the Countess's memories. I've seen what the *Reckoning* can do! You've seen it too. The Dire Magnus showed you on the boat in Cambridge Falls. He showed you the world on fire! That's what he'll do if he gets the book! We have to stop him!"

"That doesn't—"

"I don't want Emma to go any more than you do! I wish I could go in her place! But this is the only way!"

"No. I made a promise to Mom to protect you both. I can't let her go."

Then Michael said, "Really, Kate, it's not up to you, is it?"

Kate opened her mouth to respond, but nothing came out. It was a strange moment to happen in that place, but Emma had been noticing how much older Michael had seemed, how the balance of power between him and Kate had become more equal in the past days. It had been a subtle, gradual change. Now he was saying definitely that Kate no longer had to, or got to, make all the decisions. At the same time, Emma understood that she was not yet a part of their club of adulthood, that Michael was simply supporting her in this one thing. He was stepping up beside Kate, while Emma remained where she was.

Still, it mattered that he believed she could do this.

Michael pulled his dwarfish knife from his belt and handed it to her. "You might need this."

"Thank you." As she took it, she looked directly at him, not worrying about the tears she could feel gathering in her eyes, letting him know what his words had meant.

He nodded, and Emma turned to her sister.

"I'm sorry, Kate. Michael's right; I have to go."

"Emma . . ." Kate reached for her hand. "There has to be another way. Give us some time to think. Please."

Emma shook her head. "It's too late. Some of the *Reckoning* is already in me. I have to see this through."

Before Kate could say anything more, there was a sound, something between a shout and a roar echoing down the tunnel. All four of them turned.

"What . . . was that?" Michael said.

"Quiet," Gabriel said.

Then they heard it, faint but steadily building, a clicking and snapping and hissing, and they looked up and saw the silvery-gray webbing that stretched above them vibrating furiously. The children and Gabriel turned back, following the trembling to the end of the tunnel. They turned almost slowly, as if knowing what they would see but wanting to delay the moment of seeing it as long as possible. The great spider's head was raised, and it was staring down at them with huge, glittering eyes. Three sets of fangs opened wide.

Gabriel shouted, "Run!"

They bolted toward the main cavern, making no attempt now to avoid the webs, the old strands ripping from the walls, clinging to their arms and legs. They ran toward the cries and yells and clicking and hissing, while behind them, the giant spider charged forward, its approach heralded by the pounding of its legs on the rock, the snapping of its jaws. Kate shouted that she could use the *Atlas*, she could take them away—and knowing what that would mean, Emma realized what she had to do.

* * *

Gabriel had charged ahead, cutting a path through the webs with his sword, perhaps not hearing Kate's cry about the *Atlas*. "This way!" he shouted. "Quickly!" And he led them down smaller, twisting side tunnels, clearly hoping the great spider would be unable to follow. Then, with no warning, they emerged from a tunnel and found themselves at the edge of the main cavern. They were covered in strands and wisps of old webbing, so that they looked like ghouls that had escaped from their graves, but they paid that no mind. They simply stopped and stared.

In the middle of the cavern, screaming and flailing about and tangled up in webs, were three giants. The children recognized Sall, Willy's sister, waving about a torch—which was not so much a torch as an entire uprooted tree, the branches of which had been lit on fire—and vainly trying to stomp on and kill the dozen or so spiders that were crawling all over her. And there were two other giants as well, both of whom Kate recognized from Big Rog's feast, a red-faced, googly-eyed giant and a squat, bald giant. They too had burning trees, but they also had clubs and were using both trees and clubs to swat at the spiders as they were attacked and swarmed, all the time screaming at the tops of their lungs.

Just then, an enormous spider landed on top of the bald giant's head, and the giant shrieked, **"Get it off! Get it off!"** and the other, somewhat goofy-looking giant lifted his club and smashed the spider, and the other giant's head in the process. The bald giant dropped senseless to the floor and was immediately covered by spiders, who began wrapping him in webs even as the other giant went on clubbing both the spiders and the body of his friend.

Then Michael said, "It's not following us."

"What?" Kate said.

"The big spider, it's not following us anymore."

He was shining his light down the tunnel, and Kate looked back the way they had come and saw that the tunnel was empty.

"Wait—" Kate said, suddenly frantic. "Where's Emma?"

For Emma, it was now apparent, was not with them.

"She must have dropped back," Gabriel said. "I did not see."

But before Kate could do or say anything else, Michael was lifted into the air. Gabriel leapt for him, but Michael was already too high, raised aloft by the forelegs of a gigantic spider. Michael screamed, and Kate was reaching into herself for the magic to stop time, when something smashed down on the spider from above, crushing it into a wet glob. Released, Michael fell to the ground. Kate ran to him; he was shaking with fear and shock.

"Michael!"

"I'm . . . I'm . . ." was all he could get out.

A voice boomed, **"You two all right, then?"**

Willy stood above them, holding a flaming tree in one hand and what looked like a mace in the other. He had blood on the side of his head, but looked otherwise unharmed.

"Where's the wee-est one?"

"Down . . . the tunnel," Kate said. "She . . ."

Behind Willy, a dozen giants carrying torches and clubs were thundering into the cavern, leaping down to crush the spiders as they landed, rescuing Sall and the red-faced giant, both of whom were almost completely covered in a scrambling mass of legs and fangs. And the spiders seemed to sense the danger and made to flee, but the giants were after them, hitting them—and frequently hitting each other—with enormous blows from their clubs.

"Seems Big Rog don't hold to the traditions of single

combat," Willy said. "**All four of 'em ganged up on me and whacked me on the head. And they must've seen me moving the dais back 'cause when I came to, I seen they'd scuttered down here. Sorry about that.**"

"But—who're all these other giants?" Michael said.

"**Oh yeah. Turned out that hearing how Big Rog was coming to beat my brains in, everyone else had one a' them epiphany things. Decided it was time to get back to some a' what we giants used to be. Reclaim our lost dignity. They found me on the floor a' the throne room. Now we're clearing these spiders out of our city, ain't we?**"

As he said this, he swung his mace and obliterated a spider that was escaping along the cavern wall.

Kate didn't wait to hear any more. Without saying anything to Michael, she turned and ran back down the tunnel, following the path Gabriel had cleared, while behind her Willy said:

"**Where's Big Rog, then? I owe him a lump.**"

Michael's knife sliced easily through the web at the back of the cave, but Emma found that the web gummed the edge and she had to keep stopping to pull off the gooey, prickly strands.

In truth, she was amazed she was still alive.

When she and her brother and sister and Gabriel had rounded the corner, she'd thrown herself onto the ground, turned off her flashlight, and covered her head. As the footsteps of the others had sped away, every part of her body had screamed for her to get up, but then it was already too late. She'd heard the spider coming closer, and she pressed herself into the rock, her face in a pool of dank, foul-smelling water, and closed her eyes. It had been a terrifying few moments, lying there as the great spider had passed over her, its metallic legs striking the rock floor only inches from her head. But then she'd looked up to see its silhouette disappear around the bend, and she'd risen and raced back the other way.

Now, little by little, she cut away the webbing, revealing a smaller, person-sized tunnel going back into the rock wall. She shone the flashlight into it, but the beam couldn't penetrate the darkness. She had the oddest sense that the tunnel had been waiting for her. That the entire reason it had come into being was so she could pass through. She took a step forward and gasped.

It was that sudden: one step and there it was, just as Michael had said, a hook in her chest, pulling her forward. Any doubts she'd had that this was the right course, the only course, vanished. But she hesitated. She sensed that she was on the cusp of something irrevocable, that if she took just one step farther, she would be leaving behind not just her brother and sister, not just the world of the living, but in some fundamental way, she would be leaving behind her own self, that if she managed to get the book and make it back to the other side, she would be different than she now was.

That, as much as anything else, scared her.

"Well, well, well. Look what we have here!"

Emma turned. Big Rog stood behind her, holding a burning tree in a thumbless hand that was wrapped in a dirty, bloody bandage. His other hand held an iron-studded club. His eyes were wild and murderous.

"Knew I'd catch you. No one gets away from Big Rog! Least

of all 'is dinner. So what's so special down here? What's it you're all looking for? Gold? Treasure? What?"

"Nothing like that." Emma heard her own voice, calm, even cold. "There's a portal here. It takes you to the world of the dead."

"How very NOT interesting! But the only place you're going is in me mouth! And we'll see if you can go predicting a fella's death then, eh?!"

"I don't have to predict your death."

"And why's that?"

"'Cause you're gonna die right now."

"Oh, and who's gonna kill me? You?"

"No." And Emma pointed over the giant's shoulder. "She is."

Big Rog turned, and when he did, the great spider, which had been clinging to the ceiling just behind him, landed full on the giant's face. Big Rog fell over backward, screaming, dropping his torch and club, scrabbling to pull off the spider as it plunged its fangs into his throat again and again. Emma thought the creature's fangs must've been coated in poison, for she could see the giant growing weaker by the second as the spider's legs locked fast around his face.

When he was still, the spider neatly lifted Big Rog up off the floor and spun her silk around and around him, encasing him in silvery-gray thread. In a moment, Big Rog was wrapped up neatly in a cocoon, and the spider dragged him off down a side tunnel.

Emma watched it all without moving. Then, as she began to turn:

"Emma!"

Kate appeared around the corner, Michael just behind her, her torch and his flashlight bobbing in the darkness.

"Stop!"

But Emma had to go—she had to find the book. And she could feel it still, pulling her onward. She wanted to tell Kate and Michael that she loved them, that she would see them again, but there was no time. She took three steps into the tunnel and stopped. She looked back. The cavern, Kate, and her brother were gone. There was only a rock wall. The portal had done what it had been built for. The Keeper had passed through. "Okay," Emma said quietly. And she turned back around, to where the tunnel still stretched away into darkness, and walked on, into the world of the dead.

CHAPTER THIRTEEN
Refugees

"Come," Gabriel said, and led them close to the wall of the throne room.

The thick layer of dust that had blanketed the floor had been stirred up by the stomping of the giants, but Gabriel pointed to a set of human-sized footprints that proceeded through an untouched section.

"Those belong to the Secretary. I would know his tread anywhere."

Kate looked at the footprints and thought of the sniveling, scraggly-haired, utterly ruthless, deeply unhygienic servant of the Countess. Kate had done her best not to think about the man at all in the past year—even his memory was unpleasant—but she forced herself to do so now, though all she really wanted was to go back into the cavern, past the giants who were chasing down the last of the spiders, and to the tunnel where Emma had walked into the world of the dead. But she knew that she would find only a solid rock wall.

Emma was gone.

"No doubt it was he who placed the rose petals and candles around the body of the Countess," Gabriel went on. "I believe he was here in the past forty-eight hours."

Willy had sent several giants out to clear the cobwebs from the palace windows, and sunlight now streamed into the throne room, transforming the gloom and revealing the stark, awesome beauty of the chamber.

Kate saw none of it.

"So where did he go?" Michael asked.

"Here." Gabriel stepped over to the wall where there was, of all things, a human-sized door. He turned the ornate metal handle, revealing a corridor that stretched back into the palace.

"It's normal size," Michael said.

"In times past," Gabriel said, "the king of the giants would have received emissaries and dignitaries from the human world; he would have had a suitable place for them to stay. But here is what is of note. The footprints begin on this side of the door but do not extend past it. The Secretary used it as a portal. I always assumed he had some magical ability. It was how he avoided me for so many years—"

"Stop it!" Kate couldn't take any more. "Am I the only one who realizes what just happened? We rescued Emma, and now we've lost her—again! We have to do something!"

"But the portal closed after her," Michael said, with a calmness that Kate found infuriating. "And even if it was open, we couldn't go through."

"So? There are other portals, right? Like the one in Antarctica! She has to come through somewhere! There must be something we can do!"

"I agree," Gabriel said.

"You do?"

"Your sister has gone into the world of the dead. We cannot follow. As you say, our only hope is to find out where she is likely to emerge and be there when she does. But none of us are experts in such matters. You must use the *Atlas* to return to Loris and confer with the Council. They will have answers and guidance." He shut the door. "But I will not be coming with you."

"What? Why not?"

"Before the giant crushed the witch, she said she had something you wanted even more than the *Reckoning*. It may be that this is the answer Pym spoke of, the means of saving your lives; I must find out. The Secretary will know."

Michael nodded. "If that's true, she must've learned about it in the world of the dead; otherwise, I'd have gotten the memory. How will you find him?"

Gabriel knelt and took a pinch of yellow-brown dirt from one of the footprints and rubbed it between his fingers. "I have seen this color before. I know where it comes from." He rose and pulled a golden key from his pocket.

Michael murmured, "That's Dr. Pym's."

"Go to Loris," Gabriel said. "Tell King Robbie all that has happened. Find out where your sister will emerge." Gabriel inserted the key into the lock, the mustard-colored dirt rubbing off his fingers as he turned the key this way and that. Then there was a snapping sound, and Gabriel was holding the end of the key in his hand.

"It broke!" Michael exclaimed. "Were you turning it too hard? You shouldn't force things."

"I thought it might happen," Gabriel said. "With Pym gone, his magic is fading." But he opened the door, and the hallway beyond had been replaced by a vision of pine trees and a darkening sky. Kate and Michael smelled cool, clean air from somewhere else in the world, and heard the high buzzing of an engine. "Still, it has served us one last time. I will come as soon as I can."

Then he stepped through, shut the door, and was gone.

"Where was that?" Michael said. "Where'd he go?"

"I don't know." There was no time to ponder, and anyway, Kate felt calmed by Gabriel's words; they had a plan now, a direction. "Let's say goodbye to Willy."

The giant seemed genuinely sad to see them go, and he made them promise to return, saying they would find the city restored to its former glory. **"And no one'll try and put you in a pie! If they do, they'll have me to answer to!"**

They thanked him again; then Kate took Michael's hand and, glancing about one last time, summoned the power of the *Atlas* and felt the ground vanish beneath her feet.

She knew instantly that something was wrong.

A second later, she was on her knees in her room in the Rose Citadel. The stone floor was cool and solid. Michael was pulling on her arm and shouting her name. There was a roaring in her ears, and she was gasping for breath.

"I'm . . . I'm okay."

She struggled to understand what had happened. As she'd called up the magic of the *Atlas*, she'd felt a ripping, as if the air itself was being torn apart. But she'd kept going—indeed, at that point, she couldn't have stopped if she'd wanted to. Only then it wasn't just the air that was being torn apart, it was something inside of her.

This is what Rafe warned you about, she thought.

"Kate—"

"I'm okay." She forced herself to stand and look around. It had been midafternoon in the city of the giants, but it was night here. At least the *Atlas* had taken them where they'd wanted to go. She could see Michael in the darkness, silhouetted by an orange-red glow outside the shuttered windows.

Then she realized that the roaring was not in her ears.

"Do you—"

"Yeah, that's what I've been trying to tell you."

Together, she and Michael pushed open the shutters and stepped out onto the balcony. Fires burned all over the city. A vast armada pressed against the harbor and extended far out to sea. Swarms of figures were rushing up through the streets. Dark shapes flew across the sky. The screams of *morum cadi* tore apart the night.

The island was under attack.

They had to find King Robbie. That was the thought driving them forward. But as they raced through the darkened hallways, down staircases, and along twisting corridors, hearing the shouts and clamor from the city below, they found not a single soul. The Rose Citadel seemed to have been deserted.

But there was still fighting going on; they could hear it.

Then Kate and Michael burst through a door on the ground floor, almost falling over each other, and found themselves in the tunnel that led from the Garden to the front courtyard, where they saw a small group of dwarves battling a tide of Screechers and Imps swarming in through the Citadel gate.

Kate grabbed Michael's hand. She had to use the *Atlas*; there was no other option. But where could they go? Where would it take them? Suddenly, the idea of using the magic scared her more than anything else.

Then one of the figures in the courtyard—it was too dark to see if it was friend or foe—broke away from the fighting and rushed toward them. Before Kate could decide what to do, the figure was on them.

"Bloody— It's the children!"

And Kate and Michael found themselves looking at the smoke- and sweat- and blood-smeared face of Haraald, the red-bearded dwarf from Pym's Council. He was wearing armor and held an ax in one mailed hand.

"What's happening?" Kate was half-frantic. "Where's—"

"No time! The city's lost! We're the last ones out! That's if we make it! Now! Run!"

Haraald seized Kate's hand, and she just had time to grab Michael's as she was yanked away; but the dwarf was pulling her *toward* the fight in the courtyard, toward the Screechers and the Imps, and every part of Kate was thinking *no no no no*, but as soon as they reached the courtyard, Haraald pulled them to the right while shouting an order, and half a dozen dwarves broke off to follow. Kate and Michael and the dwarves ran around the side of the courtyard, away from the clanging of swords and axes and the shrieking of the Screechers, and then they were at the side wall, and there was a door, small and barred, and Haraald was shooting back the bolts, yanking the door open—

"Where're we going?!" Kate shouted. "Where're you taking us?"

"The boats! The city's lost, I said! The Dire Magnus himself is in the harbor! We have to go! Now!"

And, shouting for the door to be barred behind them, he dragged her through, with Michael still a step behind—

Then they were on a narrow, dark, steep path that wound down and away from the Rose Citadel and the city, and Haraald was pulling her at a run and Kate couldn't see where she was stepping and she was terrified she would lose her footing and fall, for she could feel the emptiness to her side, and then her brother's hand slipped from hers—

"Michael!"

"I'm okay! I'm here!"

His voice came from just behind her, and by then she saw the water below them, close now, and she saw too a pale beach and the dark shapes of boats drawn up on the shore, and then her feet were sinking among the small smooth stones of the beach, making *cush-cush-cush* sounds as she ran toward the water, and Haraald turned and she felt herself lifted up and other hands taking her and she was passed into one of the boats, and a moment later, Michael tumbled in beside her, and the boat was already pushing away, and she heard Haraald's voice shouting, "Go! Get them to the King! Go!" She raised herself up to look at the rapidly receding shoreline and saw Haraald sprinting back up the beach to where the dwarves who'd followed them were battling a stream of Screechers and Imps that were pouring down the path. Then the boat passed out of the cove, around the side of the cliff, the scene vanished, and they were moving swiftly away across the dark water.

* * *

Kate lost track of how long they were on the water, but it was several hours at least. As soon as they had gotten clear of the cove, the dwarves on board—there were three of them, none of whom introduced themselves—had raised a set of black sails, which had immediately caught a stiff breeze and yanked the boat forward, across the water.

The island of Loris had disappeared quickly, but for a long time afterward, Kate could see the red-orange glow in the darkness, telling her where the island lay and that the fires still burned.

As Kate sat in the prow, listening to the keel cutting smoothly through the water, Michael went and spoke to the dwarves. He came back a while later, moving in a low crouch, his hand on the gunnel to steady himself.

"They're taking us to meet up with King Robbie and the others."

"The others?" Kate asked.

"The other refugees. The ones that got away from Loris."

He said it as if there were those who hadn't gotten away, and the thought chilled her. How had this happened? How had the city fallen so quickly?

"They wouldn't tell me much," Michael went on, "but I guess the attack started last night. They say it was clear from the beginning that the city couldn't be saved and King Robbie ordered people to evacuate, but he kept fighting till almost everyone was out and safe."

"What about the other dwarf? The one who helped us?"

"Haraald?" Michael looked back toward the island. "I think we just have to hope he got away."

They were silent for a time. Kate could feel Michael watching her.

He asked, "How do you feel?"

"Fine."

"Something's wrong, isn't it?"

"No, I feel fine, really—"

"Kate." And Michael's tone stopped her.

She gave in. "It's like I can't control the *Atlas* anymore. And . . ."

She found she couldn't actually explain how it felt, but her frustration and confusion were apparent.

Michael nodded. "I didn't say it before, but when I used the *Chronicle* to bring back the Countess, I felt like I was forcing something. There was this . . . ripping. I felt it with Emma too, in the fortress, only not as bad. It's getting worse."

"It's the Books."

"What do you mean?"

Kate thought of how to explain, and then how to explain how she knew what she knew without giving away that she had learned it from Rafe.

For a moment, she thought about telling him the truth.

But she said, "I don't know. Dr. Pym just warned me it might happen."

"Are we going to die?"

"No! Of course not—"

"Kate."

Again it was that serious tone, and it was like the moment beneath the giants' city when he'd challenged her authority, and she realized, *He doesn't need me to protect him anymore, he can pro-*

tect himself, and that realization made her both happy and sad, for her little brother had grown up, and he had grown up well, he was strong and capable; and she thought that maybe she had done her job, done what she had promised her mother so many years before; and yet she was sad too, because he didn't need her as much, and in that moment, part of Kate's self fell away.

She said, "I don't know."

Michael nodded, and he sat down beside her and took her hand, and Kate felt something new beginning in the place of the thing that had just ended: she would not protect him anymore; they would protect each other.

They sailed on in silence, the trio of dwarves working the boat with quiet, grim efficiency. Islands slid by on either side, some of them just dark masses against the horizon, blotting out the stars, others close enough that the children could see individual features along their coasts. One island they passed glowed with an eerie green light, while another followed them for a while, like a dog herding a stranger off its land, before finally turning aside.

Time slipped away, and Kate was drifting off to sleep when she heard the dwarves giving and relaying orders in their low, gruff voices, and the boat tacked hard. She glanced over the prow to see where they were going, but the sea stretched on flat and empty. Then one of the dwarves came forward and tied a sprig from an olive tree onto the bow ring. Kate looked at Michael, but he only shrugged.

There was a shimmer in the air, the night seemed to part like a curtain, and where before had been open water there was now an island, dead ahead. It was hard to see much in the darkness, but Kate's impression was that this was not the picturesque island that Loris was, with its olive trees and mountain and romantically soaring cliffs, but a brutal, rocky crag jutting up out of the water.

The dwarves had steered them toward a large natural harbor, and as they drew closer, Kate and Michael could see dozens of ships, from small fishing vessels to warships that could hold a hundred soldiers, anchored in the waters of the marina. Sounds were now reaching the children, of voices shouting, of the hammering of metal, the hulls of ships rocking against the water. And the children could see small fires all up and down the slope of the island, and figures, hundreds of them, moving about.

The sails were lowered; two of the dwarves grasped the oars and began pulling for shore while the third came forward and picked up a coiled rope attached to the bow.

He said simply, "We're here."

The boat glided between the ships at anchor, and as they neared the beach, a figure standing in shadow called out, "Who comes?"

"From Loris," returned the dwarf in the bow, and he flung the rope to the figure, who caught it and began pulling the boat in. "We were with Haraald."

"Who do you have with you?"

Kate saw Michael sit up straighter, as if he had recognized the voice of the speaker.

"Two of the children. We're to bring them to the King."

The figure hauled the boat up onto the rocky shore, and Kate and Michael felt it crunch to a stop; then they saw the speaker clearly for the first time.

"Captain Anton!" Michael said. "You're alive!"

It was indeed the dark-haired elf captain, and not only was he alive, but he also looked to be, despite all that must've happened, as perfectly groomed as ever.

"I am. It is good to see you both well. The Princess especially will be pleased."

He helped Kate down onto the beach. Michael leapt over the side himself and sort of sprawled on the rocks, but he was quickly up again, saying, "I'm okay, I'm okay."

The elf captain looked back at the dwarf in the boat. "What of Haraald? The King has been eager for his arrival."

"We left him fighting on the beach. He sent us on with the children. You'll see them to the King?"

Captain Anton nodded. Kate, watching this exchange, had the sense that something significant was happening, but she wasn't sure what.

Then the elf handed the rope back to the dwarf, took hold of the prow, and pushed the boat back into the water.

"Thank you!" Kate called.

"Yes. Thank you!" Michael said, but there was no answer from the boat; the dwarves were already moving out of the harbor.

"Where are they going?" Kate asked.

"To see if they can find Haraald," Captain Anton said. "They won't. Come."

He led them up the beach and through what was, the children saw, a vast encampment. All along the shore to a hundred yards inland, groups of men and dwarves were massed around fires. Many of them were busy ferrying supplies from the boats, and then carrying them farther up the island. There were wounded everywhere, and those who were not themselves wounded, or tending to the wounded, or cooking or eating food, were sharpening and polishing weapons and armor.

"Where is your sister?" Captain Anton asked.

"That's . . . kind of a long story," Kate said.

"But she is alive? Safe?"

Kate glanced at Michael, wondering how to answer that question.

"Yes," she said finally, because she herself had to believe it. "She is."

"Captain," Michael said, his voice betraying his nervousness, "you mentioned Princess Wilamena. Is she okay?"

"She is well. After being thrown by the cyclone, she was released from the Dark One's hold. We saw you had escaped and therefore fled ourselves. Once we were clear of the valley, we passed through the portal that Pym had set up for our retreat. His death was a grave blow. You know that Wallace fell?"

"Yes," Michael said. "I remember."

"He was our friend," Kate said. "We'll miss him."

"It is a dark moment in which we find ourselves," Captain Anton said. "We must stand by one another. That is the only hope any of us has."

Kate glanced at her brother, to see if he too had picked up some deeper meaning in the elf captain's words, but Michael was staring straight ahead, his face unreadable.

They had been walking steadily uphill since leaving the beach, and Kate saw that they had come to a kind of division, and that while the fires and encampments continued on, the makeup of the camp had changed, as if in the lower camp, the one by the water, was the army, and in the upper, the civilian refugees, the shop owners and fishermen and families that lived on Loris and had been driven away.

Where the two camps met was a large green tent. There were torches on either side of the entrance, and several dwarfish guards stood out front. As they approached, the children could hear voices from inside, talking loudly over one another. And then figures began to emerge. Kate and Michael saw Wilamena's father and Lady Gwendolyn, the silver-haired elf, appear and stalk off—gracefully, of course. They saw Magda von Klappen and Hugo Algernon and Captain Stefano and Master Chu, the Chinese wizard, emerge whispering and hissing to one another, and they saw three or four other dwarves and humans and elves whom they did not recognize all come out and head off to different parts of the camp.

"I would venture," Captain Anton said, "that the Council did not go well."

A solitary figure stepped out after the others and stood there, his face lit by the flare of the torches. It was King Robbie, and Kate's first thought was how old and tired and gray-faced he looked. Then he turned and saw the children—there was a moment of shock—and his expression regained, for a moment, some of its former life.

"Why, bless me. . . ."

And he was hugging both of them at once, pressing them against the metal studs of his tunic.

"We had no word of you!" He held them back to look at them, though only for a moment. Then he peered past them into the darkness. "But where's wee Emma?"

"That's what we have to talk to you about," Kate said. "She's okay. We think. But—"

"You can tell me as you eat. And I have much to tell you as well." He glanced up at the elf. "Thank you, Captain."

"I only escorted them from the beach. It was Haraald and his dwarves who got them out of Loris."

"And Haraald is back safe?"

The elf captain shook his head.

"I see. Thank you all the same."

Then he put his arms around the children and guided them into the tent.

The dwarf king sat them at the end of a table in the middle of his tent around which there were many chairs, most of them looking as if they had been roughly pushed back. It was there, Kate surmised, that the meeting had just taken place.

The tent itself was simply furnished, with half a dozen candles and lanterns illuminating the interior. There was the council table, which was strewn with various maps and papers and dirty glasses, and there was a smaller, square table on which stood various platters of food and jugs and bottles. King Robbie gathered the children's dinner: fish, potatoes, olives, a kind of rice. A simple desk and chair faced one canvas wall. A suit of armor and a great ax stood at the back of the tent, as if waiting patiently for their master. There was nowhere to sleep, and Kate wondered if the dwarf king even planned on sleeping or had put that off for some other, more peaceful time.

"Eat. You both look famished. That's a danger in wartime. You keep going and going, not realizing how run-down you are, and then, when you need your strength most, you have none." He nodded at two dwarf servants who were taking away the last of the glasses and plates. "Thank you, lads. You be sure and get some sleep now." He turned back to the children. "We just had a Council meeting. I'm worried, I don't mind telling you. I don't know that any of us ever really appreciated how much Pym did. I don't mean his magic. I mean him, as a person. Elves, dwarves, humans—historically, there's a lot a' mistrust and bad blood. And I'm not saying the dwarves are innocent; we're as guilty as any of 'em. But Pym helped us forget all that and work together. With him gone, well, I try, but . . ." He shrugged, and his hands fell open. "Aye, it's a grave blow, losing Stanislaus Pym, a grave blow."

And Kate thought again that he looked very old and tired.

"But, Your Majesty," Michael said, "what happened? We only left Loris a couple of days ago. How could it have been captured?"

Robbie McLaur gave a short, humorless laugh. "Ah, lad, I don't know that we ever had much of a chance. Those who might be our natural allies—I'm talking humans, dwarves, elves, merfolk, fairies, some gnomes and giants—they're scattered across a hundred miles a' sea, and even farther afield, on the other side of the world. Getting them to abandon their homes and send their forces to Loris so we could concentrate our strength and perhaps have some hope of defeating the Dire Magnus? Well, they wouldn't, would they?

"So the Dark One took the city with no more trouble than if we'd wrapped it up and given it to him. I take no joy in the fact that I predicted how it would go, but predict it I did. That's why one a' the first things I did when Pym put me in charge was to arrange a fallback point if we had to abandon Loris. A hidden place where we could keep a resistance alive. And so far, we've done that.

"But where to go from here, that's the question."

He sighed again and rubbed his face, and Kate stole a glance at Michael, seeing in his expression the same concern and worry she was feeling.

The dwarf king waved his hand. "Enough a' that. The last I heard of you two was from Princess Wilamena and Captain Anton. They said that you"—he looked at Kate—"appeared in the Dire Magnus's fortress and took your brother and sister and Gabriel and vanished. So where the devil, excuse my language, have you been these past days? Where's your sister? I do hope wherever she is, she's with Gabriel. Tell me that at least."

And so Kate and Michael told him about the *Atlas* taking them to the land of the giants, how they'd almost been put into a pie, about going to the ancient city that had been taken over by monster spiders, how they had found the remains of the person who'd stolen the *Reckoning* from Rhakotis long ago and it had turned out to be the Countess—

"Not the same witch from Cambridge Falls!" King Robbie exclaimed, slapping the table with his fist. "She's not back, is she?"

"No," Kate said. "Well, she was for a second. Michael brought her back with the *Chronicle*, but then a giant stepped on her."

Robbie McLaur chuckled. "Is that so? That would've been worth seeing. But did you find out where the *Reckoning* is hidden?"

Kate said they had, and she told how they had gone into the cavern below the giant city and found the sleeping spiders, and how it turned out that there was a portal to the world of the dead, and that that was where the Countess had hidden the *Reckoning* all those years before—

"You don't say," the dwarf king murmured. "Fiendishly clever, I'll give her that, fiendishly clever."

But then, they said, the spiders had woken up—

"They didn't!"

If nothing else, the dwarf king was an excellent audience.

The children were both speaking, hurrying to get to the end, and they told how only Emma, the Keeper of the *Reckoning*, was able to go into the world of the dead, and after she had passed through, the portal had closed, and now they didn't know where she would come out or when or even if.

"You don't mean she's gone there alone?" Robbie McLaur exclaimed. "What about Gabriel?"

"He went off to look for the Secretary."

"Hmm. And you say the portal closed?"

"Yes. Which is why we have to find the other portals to the world of the dead. We know one's in Antarctica, in the elfish forest, but there must be more. And then we have to figure out which one Emma will come through."

Just saying all this stoked Kate's panic anew. In the rush of events since leaving the giants' city—the pain she'd felt when using the *Atlas*, Michael's admission that he'd felt the same disturbance when he'd used the *Chronicle*—she'd allowed herself to forget just how distant Emma was, how great the obstacles were that separated them. But now it was all before her again, and she felt small and weak and hopeless.

The dwarf king stood, refilled his glass with wine, drank it off, refilled it again, and then returned to the table.

"Aye, there is one portal in the land of the lad's Princess Wilamena—"

"She's not my Princess Wilamena," Michael said quickly. "I don't know why you'd think that—"

"Michael—" Kate warned.

"And at least one more, on an island off the coast of Scotland."

"That's it?" Michael said. "Just those two?"

"Well, now, no," the King said, looking down at his glass. "There's one more that I know of."

"Still, that's only three!" Michael said. "We'll just send a team to each of them, and sooner or later Emma will come through and she'll have the *Reckoning* and we'll use it to kill the Dire Magnus and that will be that!"

"I've no doubt she will have the *Reckoning*," Robbie McLaur said. "You are a formidable family, and that little one's a born fighter."

Kate could see there was something the dwarf king didn't want to tell them.

She forced herself to ask, "Then what's the problem?"

"The problem"—Robbie McLaur looked up, and he seemed to be asking forgiveness even as he said it—"is that the last portal to the world of the dead is in the Garden of the Rose Citadel. Which means if your sister comes through, she'll be delivering the *Reckoning*—and herself—smack into the hands of the Dire Magnus."

Kate felt as if the dwarf king's words had turned her to stone; she couldn't move.

It must've been the same for Michael, for just then there was a squeal, a flash of gold, and the elf princess flew in and threw herself on him, crying, "You're alive, you're alive! My beloved Rabbit!" and Michael didn't even protest.

CHAPTER FOURTEEN
The Ferryman

At more or less the same time that Kate and Michael were listen-ing to Robbie McLaur tell them about the portal in the Garden of the Rose Citadel, Emma was trying to convince herself to just go down and join the line of stupid ghosts.

It's not like they can hurt you, she told herself.

Or could they? She wasn't some ghost expert. She didn't know what ghosts could and couldn't do. And were they ghosts? They didn't really look like ghosts. They just looked like people. She could just imagine how if Michael had been there, he would've been pushing his glasses up the bridge of his nose and reeling off some long, boring speech about ghosts and their ghost habits until someone (probably her) flicked him in the head. But he wasn't here; no one was; she was alone.

At first, walking away from Kate and Michael and Gabriel through the dark tunnel that led from the spider's nest, with

Michael's dinky flashlight doing almost nothing to show her where she was going, she'd been full of energy and high purpose. She was going to find the *Reckoning*, save everyone, and pretty much be the total hero. But after walking for what had felt like hours—but had really been more like twenty minutes—she had begun to consider how little she actually knew about where she was going. How big was the world of the dead? What if the book was thousands of miles away? What if it took her years to find it? Was the world of the dead cold? Should she have brought a sweater? What if it rained? Where would she get food? How would she find her way back out?

While thinking all this, she'd noticed a grayness in front of her, and she'd passed from the blackness of the tunnel into a thick, wet mist, at the same moment becoming aware that she was walking on dirt instead of rock.

She'd known then that she had crossed over.

Soon, the mist had begun to thin, and she'd found herself on a hillside of skeletal trees. She'd let her feet carry her down the slope, the mist still pearling on her clothes and hair, till she had arrived at last at a wide road of packed dirt; and it was there that she'd found the procession of the dead.

For a second, she'd thought the walkers were transparent, they were so gray and fuzzy, but as she hid behind a tree to watch them pass, she saw that the grayness and fuzziness was just the mist, and the dead—for they had to be dead, didn't they?—were not see-through at all. Did that mean they were solid? She could hear the soft shuffling of their feet in the dirt, so maybe they were. Only, how was that possible? Hadn't they left their bodies in the world of the living?

A memory came back to Emma, of being in school the year before, and reading all these Viking myths—which as far as school readings went had been pretty great, as they'd been mostly about chopping the heads off giants and trolls—and she remembered how Viking heaven was a place where the dead Vikings sat around eating and drinking all the time. It stood to reason they couldn't very well have done that without bodies. Maybe that meant you got two bodies, one in the world of the living, and another one down here. How exactly that happened, Emma had no idea, but she felt better knowing that there was at least some kind of precedent.

The figures were all moving in the same direction, at the same steady, hypnotic pace, as if obeying some silent call. They did not speak. There were men and women, old and young, there were children, there were babies being carried. There was no uniformity to the clothes. It was almost as if each person was wearing whatever they'd had on when they died. Did that mean if you had a heart attack while wearing some ratty old bathrobe, you had to wear that till the end of time? Though even that would be better than being naked. Emma made a mental note to be sure to be wearing clothes when she died.

Emma would've just gone around them, only the walkers were going the same direction she was. For her part, she had no choice in the matter. Since that first moment under the spider's web when she'd stared into the portal, the *Reckoning* had been pulling her onward.

So finally, not knowing what else to do, she stepped from behind the tree and, with her chin thrust out and her hands in fists at her sides, she walked firmly and directly down to join the parade of the dead.

A few of the walkers glanced over; otherwise, her arrival occasioned no reaction.

Emma made a point of sticking to the edge of the road, but after a few moments, she began to relax and look around her. She had fallen in beside a woman who was wearing a gray business suit. She looked very old, Emma thought, like forty.

"Hi."

The woman turned her head slowly. Her gaze had the fuzziness of a person who's just woken from a deep sleep.

"Why're you all going this way?"

The woman stared down the road. "I . . . I don't know. I just . . . have to."

"Where're you from?"

"I'm from . . ." Again the woman seemed lost. "I don't know actually. I can't remember."

"Well, how'd you die?" Emma hoped this wasn't a rude question, but really, the woman was dead; there was no getting around that.

"I . . . I don't remember that either."

As they walked on, Emma asked several others where they were from and how they'd died. None could remember. They couldn't even recall their own names; their memories had been wiped clean. Nor could any of them say what was drawing them down the road. But as the walkers didn't seem dangerous, she continued on with them. It made her deeply sad that none of the dead could remember their lives. To forget where they'd lived or what jobs they'd had was one thing. But to forget everything about who they'd been—that meant forgetting their families and friends, everyone they'd ever loved. And that was awful. Emma had never been scared of dying. But what was the point of living if she was just going to die and forget about Kate and Michael and Gabriel? If she was going to lose all those memories that made her her?

Before long, the road curved and came to its end, spilling out onto a wide, rocky beach that gave way to a body of eerily calm, gray-black water. Whether it was a river or a sea or an ocean was impossible to tell, because the same mist that clung to the land also clung to the water. A fleet of small boats—they looked to be little more than rowboats, piloted by figures wearing dark, hooded cloaks—was making its way to the shore, loading up the dead, and then heading back out into the mist.

There was also a concrete jetty jutting out into the water, but the dark-garbed boatmen were avoiding it, pulling their boats right up onto the rocky shoals of the beach.

Emma looked out past the beach and the boats, willing the mist to clear so that she could see across the water. The book was out there somewhere, calling her onward.

Go on, she thought. You know you have to.

The beach was made of rough black rocks, and after the silence of the march, everything felt loud, the scraping and crunch of her footsteps, the slap of the boatmen's oars, the sound of the keels striking the rocks. There was no shoving or pushing among the dead. They were slowly and calmly climbing into the boats, and then the boatmen would push off from the shore, swing their small crafts around, and vanish back into the mist.

As if by appointment, Emma walked directly to a boat that had beached itself so its prow rose high out of the water. Had she taken more time, she might've noticed that the dead were avoiding that particular boat. Emma felt a strange, inexplicable fear; her heart pounded in her chest, and every part of her wanted to turn back. But back to where? The way was forward. She could feel cold water lapping around her ankles and soaking her shoes. The cowl of the boatman's hood covered his face.

"Where do these boats go?" she asked.

"The world of the dead."

"I thought *this* was the world of the dead."

"This is just the road thereto."

Emma stopped; there was something about the voice that was strangely, deeply familiar. She stepped forward, grabbed his hood, and ripped it back.

"I knew it! I knew it was you!"

She was looking at the face of the old wizard, Stanislaus Pym. Only, he had changed. The ratty tweed suit and mangled tie were gone, as were the broken and patched eyeglasses. He now wore a hooded robe of dark gray. His perpetually messy white hair had been tamed and, somehow, gotten longer. He'd even found time since dying to grow a rather substantial beard. In many ways, he looked more like a wizard than he ever had, though the expression on his face was calm, and oddly vacant.

"What're you doing here?!"

"I'm a ferryman."

"Stop that! You're trying to trick me again."

He looked genuinely confused. "Trick you? I ferry the dead—"

"You know what I mean!" She was shouting now. "You lied to us! You betrayed us! You were planning on getting us all killed!"

He shook his head. "I'm sorry. Did we know each other when I was alive?"

Emma felt her fury gathering. Of course, it made sense that he would have no more memory of his life than any of the other dead, but somehow the fact of it made her even more furious, as if he had forgotten what he'd done only to spite her.

"You pretended to be our friend!" She could feel tears burning her eyes. "Me and my brother and sister. And the whole time you knew we were probably going to die and you didn't care. You're a liar! And I'm glad you're dead!"

Then she had to turn away because she was crying, her shoulders heaving, and she didn't want him to see. The wizard thankfully said nothing, and she took deep breaths, trying to get herself under control. She wiped her eyes and turned back around.

"Fine, whatever, you don't remember who you are, I don't care. How were you waiting here for me? I know you were! How'd you know I'd be coming?"

He shrugged. "I just came."

"But you were waiting for me!"

"Yes."

"And how could you be waiting for me and not remember me?!"

"I don't know."

Enough. Emma decided she was going to walk off without another word. Whatever or whoever had brought the wizard here, however innocent he might act, she wasn't going with him; she would find another boat. But just as she started to turn, a horn blasted across the beach, and Emma whipped about to see a ship, an enormous one built to carry cargo, emerging from the mist. It was made of metal, and tiger-striped with rust. Emma could hear the whining of its engine, the propeller churning the water; she could smell burning oil. The horn sounded again; the ship was working hard to slow itself, and Emma watched as it bumped and crunched heavily against the concrete pier. There were figures on board—men and women dressed in black—who were looping ropes around pylons, stopping the ship in place. With a metallic screech, a wide panel hinged open on the side of the ship and crashed onto the jetty, creating an impromptu gangplank, and the men and women poured out. They were a savage-looking lot and carried whips that cracked dully in the misty air as they ran down the pier, screaming.

"What's going on?!" Emma cried. "What're they doing?"

The old wizard didn't answer, and anyway, she could already see the answer, for they were herding the dead together, forcing them down the dock and onto the boat.

Then a figure stepped from the hold of the ship. Amid the grayness of the beach and the water and the sky, the blood-red hue of the man's robe stood out, and Emma felt her heart clench, for the man was dressed the same as the red-robed sorcerers she'd seen among the Dire Magnus's camp only days before. They had a special name, these wizards who served the Dire Magnus, Rourke had told her, but the name wouldn't come to her now.

Then the figure shouted, his voice carrying across the beach, "Forget the others! Find the girl! She is here!"

Emma knew he was speaking about her.

"Get in."

Emma whirled around. Dr. Pym had spoken. She opened her mouth to tell him she wasn't going anywhere with him, that she hated him, but there was now a commotion behind her, the thick snapping of whips, the sounds of boots on the rocks, and a hoarse roar that told her she'd been spotted.

He repeated, "Get in the boat."

The men from the metal ship were nearly to them, and Emma took hold of the rowboat and heaved herself up, telling herself she would kick the wizard if he tried to touch her. And then she was in the boat, sitting on one of the benches.

The mob of whip-wielding men and women had stopped at the edge of the water, panting like dogs brought up short in a hunt. They were only a step away; they could easily have yanked her out of the boat, but they stayed where they were, moving aside only when the red-robed figure stepped between them. Though he was dressed like the sorcerers from the Dire Magnus's army, Emma had not seen this particular man before. He had lank black hair and a narrow, ratlike face. His bony hands were balled into fists.

"You cannot protect her forever," the man hissed. "She belongs to the master."

Dr. Pym merely said, "She is in the boat."

The rat-faced man looked about to spit he was so angry; then a voice said, "Enough. Take her," and the crowd parted a second time, revealing a figure who stood leaning on a staff of gnarled black wood. Emma gasped. It was the old, red-robed sorcerer she had seen at the Dire Magnus's fortress. He had the same stringy gray hair, the same long, twisted nose, the same clouded-over eye. He'd been there when the Dire Magnus had tried to bond her to the *Reckoning*, and Dr. Pym himself—Emma had a vague memory of this—had killed him. She recalled, too, Rourke telling her that he had once been a friend of Dr. Pym's, that he'd fought against the Dire Magnus and the Dire Magnus had broken him and bent him to his will. Even here, the man was forced to serve his enemy.

He said, "We will find her on the far shore."

Behind her, Dr. Pym lifted his oars, set his feet against one of the wooden seats, and began to pull away from the beach.

Emma still half expected the throng of men to plunge into the water and seize hold of the boat, but they didn't move, and the pounding of her heart began to lessen as the wizard took them farther and farther away. She heard the old, white-eyed man say, "Collect as many of the others as you can," and the whip-wielding men and women turned to drive the dead aboard the metal ship. Then the fog hid the beach from view.

Emma looked at the wizard. There was no way she was saying thank you.

"Where're you taking me?"

"I told you, to the world of the dead."

He really doesn't remember me, she thought.

She stared into the gray nothing of the mist. She could feel the book out there, calling to her. And with each pull of the boat's oars, she was getting closer.

"You should sleep," the wizard said.

"Oh, shut up," she muttered.

But whether it was magic or she was simply so tired that she could no longer fight it, Emma found herself lying down in the hollow space between the benches, curling herself into as small a ball as possible, and, with one final thought that maybe, just maybe, she would see Michael and Kate and Gabriel again, falling fast asleep.

CHAPTER FIFTEEN
The Witch's Secret

"Listen, please—"

"She's dead! Dead! Dead! Dead! Dead!"

"You don't have to do this—"

The man inched his chair forward, straining against the ropes, trying as best he could to place his body between the sweating, wild-eyed, knife-wielding figure and his wife, who was tied to a chair beside him. The man's name was Richard Wibberly. His wife's name was Clare. On this night, neither had seen their children in more than ten years.

"Killing us does nothing—"

"Nothing?! It does nothing?!" The wild-eyed man lurched forward, pressing the knife against his prisoner's face. "It makes you dead, is what it does! And hurts them! That is enough!"

The blade flashed, and a long, bloody line appeared on Richard's cheek.

Clare screamed and unleashed a string of curses and threats.

The couple's captor pushed Richard roughly to the floor and stepped toward the woman.

Only he never made it, for just then the door burst in and an enormous man, one of the largest men either Richard or his wife had ever seen, stepped into the room. He wore an old cloak, and the handle of a sword jabbed upward from a sheath on his back. He had long black hair and a vicious scar running down the side of his face. Everything about him spoke of purpose, power, and a fearsome violence.

The fury coming off him charged the air all around.

The couple's captor shrieked and swung the knife, but the intruder knocked it away, lifted the man into the air, and threw him out the window. There was a shattering crash, a half breath of silence, and then the thud of a body striking the ground twenty feet below, followed by the dull tinkling of broken glass.

The enormous man stood there a moment; then his shoulders dropped, his body relaxed, and he gave off the impression of someone who had put down a burden that he had been carrying for a long, long time.

He righted Richard's chair, took the discarded knife, and cut his bonds.

"Who are you?" Richard asked, rubbing the grooves the cord had dug into his wrists, watching as the man cut his wife's bonds.

"My name is Gabriel. I am a friend of your children."

It had taken Gabriel less than three hours after leaving Kate and Michael in the giants' city to find the Secretary, but in some ways it was the culmination of a fifteen-year search.

A decade and a half earlier, after the events in Cambridge Falls, the Countess's Secretary had disappeared, and Dr. Pym had tasked Gabriel with finding the man. "He knows much. He has been a party to the Dire Magnus's most secret plans. The enemy will hunt him, to punish him for the witch's betrayal. We must find him before they do."

And so, for years, Gabriel had trekked all over the globe, following whatever clues, whispers, or desperate hintings he could uncover, combing through the dredges of the magical and non-magical worlds, arriving always a day, an hour, a moment too late. He had found traces of the man among the voodoo priests and cut-throats of New Orleans; he just missed him in a remote village in the Andes; once—and only once—he had been face to face with his quarry, having come upon the Secretary on a street in Paris as the man tried to catch a pigeon with his hands, presumably for lunch. A sightseeing group had moved between them, and by the time Gabriel had reached the far side of the street, the Secretary had vanished. After that, Dr. Pym had told him to give up the chase; there were other, more pressing matters: the enemy was on the move; war was at hand.

But in the end, the effort had paid off, for in the course of his search, Gabriel had visited a town nestled in a tiny wedge of the magical world along the coast of the Adriatic, where the Secretary had lived for some months in an abandoned dye factory. And it was the chalky yellow dye, still fresh on the floor of the giant king's throne room, that had told Gabriel where his quarry was hiding.

Gabriel had not risked appearing in the factory itself, having learned from his past failures that if the Secretary was there, he would have devised wards against any sort of magical intrusion, or at the very least, an alarm to give him time to flee. So Gabriel had used Dr. Pym's golden key (in its last service before snapping) to appear at the airfield outside of town, where he was remembered by the wrinkled owner (and the town's sole pilot) from his visit a decade and a half before.

"The factory is still there, still empty for all I know," the pilot had said. "But be you careful. There been *morum cadi* and Imps 'round of late. A storm is coming."

Night had been falling when Gabriel crossed a small footbridge and entered the town. He'd seen only a few people on the streets, and all of those were hurrying home to beat the darkness. Like much of the magical world, the town gave the impression of being trapped in the past and had changed little since Gabriel's last visit.

But the fear and wariness on the faces of those he passed was new, and Gabriel had kept the hood of his cloak up and stuck to side streets till he'd arrived at the factory. Once there, he'd seen a light flickering in a second-floor window and slipped inside, completing his fifteen-year quest just in time.

The woman looked so like her older daughter that Gabriel almost felt he was looking not at the children's mother, but at Kate herself, seen through the prism of time. There was the same dark blond hair, the same hazel eyes flecked with gold; the contours and angles of her face were exactly like her daughter's. But as he looked again, he saw the difference: it wasn't just the lines of fatigue and age at the corners of the woman's eyes, or the slight hollowness to her cheeks; what set them apart was a certain unflinching directness in the woman's gaze that Gabriel associated not with Kate, but with Emma.

Their father, obviously, looked most like Michael. They wore the same type of wire-rim spectacles, both had the same chestnut hair and dark eyes (which Emma also shared), but it was yet deeper than that. There was about the man, as there was about Michael, an air of professorial deliberation, a sense that his first reaction to any problem would be to think it through and, if possible, make a list.

The man and woman were both thin and exhausted, but besides the wound on the man's face, which the woman cleaned and dressed with alcohol and bandages that Gabriel had produced from his cloak, they were essentially unharmed.

A breeze drifted in, bringing cool, fresh air into the stale atmosphere of the factory. The room was a simple concrete box with only the one door and the one window, both now broken.

The Wibberlys had already thanked Gabriel, multiple times.

"For rescuing us, obviously," Richard said. "But also for what you've done for our children. We know who you are. Pym told us years ago, after everything that happened in Cambridge Falls. Back before the children were even born."

"How long have you been here?"

"A few weeks. We were somewhere else before. I don't know where. Much colder. Then he got scared and moved us. He rescued us, you know. At least we thought he did. We'd been in that mansion in New York for—"

"Ten years," his wife said.

"That's right. Ten years. Ever since Rourke captured us. You know Rourke?"

"Yes."

"Then five, maybe six weeks ago, he appears, Cavendish, that was his name. Just stepped through a solid wall into our room. At that point, we didn't know who he was, but honestly, after ten years of being prisoners, we'd have followed a singing mouse if it promised a way out."

The man was speaking quickly, as if a decade's worth of talk had built up inside him, like water behind a dam, and now was all coming out.

"He said he could help us find the *Reckoning*, that he wanted to prove to Pym he had changed his ways; he made us send a message to the children. I don't know if they got it—"

"They did."

"Well, it was right after that that he brought us here, and it was clear he'd lied, that we'd just traded one prison for another." He looked at his wife. "It was my fault. I should never have believed him."

She took his hand. "It was both our faults. And what choice did we have?"

"He planned to hold you as hostages," Gabriel said, "on behalf of the Countess. She wanted Michael to use the *Chronicle* to make her young again."

"Michael has the *Chronicle*?" Richard stepped forward, suddenly sharp. "What about the *Reckoning*? They don't have that yet, do they?"

"No."

"Where are the children?" Clare asked. "Will you take us to them?"

Gabriel said, "Can you both walk?"

* * *

The town was silent, the streets dark and empty, and Gabriel and the couple moved through them as quickly and quietly as they could. But the man and woman were shaky-limbed with exhaustion, and he could only push them so much.

As they made their way, Gabriel told them in a whisper about Michael becoming master of the *Chronicle*; how Michael had received his father's message; about Emma's abduction; how he, Gabriel, and others had raided the Dire Magnus's fortress and attempted to free her; how Kate had finally spirited them away to the land of the giants; how he and the children had discovered the location of the *Reckoning*—

"Wait." Richard stopped them in a narrow alley, along a row of shuttered shop windows. "You know where the *Reckoning* is? You said you didn't have it."

"And we do not, not as yet."

"So where is it?" Clare asked.

Gabriel wanted nothing more than to get out of this town and back to Loris. He had been uncomfortable every moment he'd been separated from the children, and now that he had discovered the "secret" the Countess had been hiding, there was no more reason to tarry.

But some things would not keep.

"It is in the world of the dead."

The man and woman both stared at him.

Then Clare's face became stony. "Where are our children?"

"I sent Michael and Kate to Loris. Robbie McLaur, the king of the dwarves near Cambridge Falls, is there and will watch over them. It is where we are going now."

He started off, but Clare held his arm, her grip surprisingly strong. "And where's Emma?"

Gabriel looked down at the woman; she was a good foot shorter than he, and again, despite how much she looked like Kate—her eyes, her hair, the bones of her face—the fierceness in her was entirely Emma's.

"She is in the world of the dead."

It was as if he had cut off her legs. Gabriel and her husband reached for her, but she caught herself, holding up a hand in a sign that neither were to touch her.

She said, thickly, "Alone? She went there alone?"

"Only the Keeper of the *Reckoning* could pass into that world. I could not accompany her."

The man was shaking his head. "How could Pym allow that?"

"Pym is dead."

This stopped them both.

"What?" Richard said. "When?"

"When we rescued Emma from the enemy. He sacrificed himself so that the children and I might escape."

Gabriel knew that the man and woman had been friends with the old wizard—indeed, they had entrusted him with the lives of their children. Recently, however, they had sent the children a message warning them not to allow Pym to bring the three Books together. Why? Did they know that the prophecy foretold that the Books' coming together—which was Pym's whole plan for defeating the Dire Magnus—would result in Kate and Michael and Emma's deaths? Would they now consider Pym an enemy? But Gabriel watched the looks they gave each other and saw no joy or satisfaction; if anything, the opposite.

"I'm sorry to hear that," Richard said finally. "He was a friend of ours. I'll be honest, if you'd told us this a few months ago, we might've had a different reaction. You see, we found out—"

"That if the children bring the Books together, they will die. I just learned of it myself."

"Then you understand how it made us question everything! Who Pym really was. Did he intend to sacrifice our children for some greater good? We just didn't know."

"He did care for them," Clare said firmly. "However much we talked about it, we always came back to that. We told ourselves that he must know something we didn't, some way of saving their lives."

"Only, that wasn't a chance we were willing to take on faith. That was the point of the message we sent the children. But if Pym is dead . . ."

Though they had been speaking in hushed tones, their voices were the only sounds in the streets, and Gabriel felt how exposed they were; they had to move.

"You are right," he whispered. "Pym cared for your children, and he believed there was a way they could use the Books and not be destroyed themselves."

"But how?" Richard demanded. "What did he tell you exactly?"

"Very little. Just that he had come to believe that the answer was in the prophecy itself, that there was more to it than even he knew. When I learned the Countess guarded a secret, I thought she might have the knowledge we sought. That is why I tracked the Secretary. Finding you was mere chance."

"So Pym didn't tell you," Clare said, "how to find out the rest of the prophecy?"

"No."

Then Gabriel turned to glance around the corner of the alley, to ensure that the way was still clear, and so he missed the look that passed between the man and woman.

"Come," he said.

They hurried on through the streets, stopping a few minutes later at the edge of a square, in the center of which was a statue of a man on a horse. Both man and horse had strangely gigantic heads, the man's topped by an even more gigantic plumed hat. Gabriel peered into the shadows of the shuttered shops and cafés. All was still.

"I don't hear anything," Clare said.

"No," Gabriel said. "That is what worries me."

He pointed at a small street on the opposite side of the square.

"If something happens, keep running—straight on. You will come to a bridge; cross it and go up the hill. Keep going and you will find an airfield." He gave them the name of the pilot. "Tell him you are my friends and to take you to San Marco. Once there, he will direct you to a ship that will take you to Loris."

"But you're coming too," the woman said.

"I intend to," Gabriel said. "But do not wait for me."

He pulled Granny Peet's sword from its sheath while also drawing a long knife from a scabbard at his waist.

"Now."

They had gotten as far as the man on the horse when the first Imp leapt from behind the statue's pedestal. Gabriel didn't break stride, but swung his sword with such force that the jagged-edged sword the Imp raised to block the blow was driven downward, clubbing its owner in the face. Then, with a backhand swipe, Gabriel separated the creature's head from its body. He saw three more Imps rushing out from the side streets.

"Go!" he shouted. "Do not stop!"

The couple ran on; he heard their footsteps disappearing down the alley behind him as the first two Imps drew near. He had fought Imps many times before and knew their ways. They were a magical crossbreed between boars and men, and they had retained much of their bestial heritage. Part of that was an inclination to fight in packs. And Gabriel knew that the two Imps attacking him from the front were a diversion from the one circling behind, and after he used his sword to block the first blow, he immediately ducked and heard the creature's blade slice through the air above him. In the same motion, Gabriel was spinning, and he felt his sword cut through the creature's legs. Gabriel didn't pause—he knew the other two Imps would already be closing—and from his crouch, he exploded upward, his sword parrying the downward blow of the third Imp as he drove his long knife through the creature's chest, twisted it, then pushed the creature away. Before he could turn, he was knocked sideways by a blow from the first Imp's mace—a glancing blow, fortunately, as a direct one would have shattered his shoulder. He staggered and caught himself on the pillar supporting the stone rider. The Imp's next blow was aimed at Gabriel's head, but he ducked and twisted as the creature's mace tore a hunk of stone from the pedestal. Gabriel continued his twisting movement, and in his mind, he already saw how his sword would swing upward, entering the Imp's lower left side and exiting just below the creature's right arm. But as he spun, his foot slipped on a slick patch on the cobblestones and then he was on his back, the Imp above him, raising his mace to crush him—

Then everything stopped. The point of a sword was protruding from the Imp's chest, and the creature slid forward and crumpled on the stones, revealing the children's father standing there. Behind him, the Imp Gabriel had stabbed with his knife was trying to rise, an action that was abruptly stopped when the children's mother brought down a mace on the creature's head.

The children's father reached out his hand, and Gabriel took it.

"I will say this." Gabriel sheathed his sword, wincing as pain blossomed in his shoulder. "You follow directions as well as your children."

"Listen," Richard said, "there's something we need tell you."

"Not now—"

"The prophecy, we might know how to find out the rest of it. Where to look, I mean."

Gabriel said nothing for a moment, but merely stared at them.

"So we can't go with you to Loris," Clare said. "We want to. You don't know how much we want to see the children. But if what you say is true, that discovering the rest of the prophecy is the key to saving the children, then we have to— Wait, what're you doing?!"

Gabriel had taken both their arms and started walking quickly toward the alley.

"There is no time to lose."

Richard said, "You mean—"

"Yes, I am coming with you."

CHAPTER SIXTEEN
The Carriadin

Emma woke once during their journey to find that darkness had fallen and the wizard had hung a lantern from an iron spike in the front of the boat. They were still moving at the same steady pace, and, raising herself up, Emma could see other lights, presumably of other rowboats, strung across the water and fuzzy in the misty darkness.

She listened for the sound of the metal ship's engine, but heard nothing.

Emma felt woolly-headed and heavy-limbed, as if she were somehow still asleep, or dreaming, and she lay down again and fell fast asleep.

She woke once more—it must've been hours later—and saw cliffs ahead in the darkness, a shoreline, and there was a break in the cliffs, the mouth of a river, and it seemed they were heading toward it. She felt anxious and tense, and was sweating, though the night was cool.

"What is troubling you?" the wizard asked.

"Nothing."

"I don't think you're being completely honest with me."

"Fine. What do you know about the book?"

"The what?"

"That's great. You're real helpful. Row the boat."

In truth, she hadn't expected much. And what, really, did she need to know, besides that they were getting closer? And they were; the tugging at her chest was stronger and more insistent with each stroke of the wizard's oars. So why did she feel so unsettled? She let her mind wander, and soon found herself thinking of something Michael had said the night before, when they'd all been gathered around the fire. He'd said it almost in passing, while talking about the *Reckoning*, what it did, why it was called the *Reckoning*. He'd said there were two meanings to the word. One was something you owed. The other meaning was judgment.

Emma had no problem with the idea that the book could kill someone—in this case, the someone being the Dire Magnus. But the idea that she'd have to judge a person (and judge them for what, on the basis of what, she had no idea) made her deeply uneasy. Killing someone felt fast and full of fury; it was over in a moment. Judging someone, you had to think about stuff; there'd be things that weren't clear. She didn't want that responsibility. That kind of thing was more for Kate. Or even Michael.

But didn't she want to be their equal?

Yeah, but not like that. There had to be some, well, easier way.

And was that even really it? For as she sat there, swaying with the movement of the boat, Emma found herself remembering the dream she'd had that first night in the land of the giants. In the dream, she had come upon the book only to be attacked by thousands of shadowy figures. Then, as now, she had woken trembling and sweating. Why? What was it about the book that scared her so?

"You should try to sleep," the wizard said.

"Oh, be quiet," she muttered, then lay back down and was asleep in an instant.

When she woke again, there was a hand on her shoulder, the boat wasn't moving, and it was light. The wizard was leaning over her. She pushed his hand away and sat up.

The boat was moored at a wooden dock at the edge of a brown-green river. There were a few other boats tied up nearby, but they looked neglected. She could see a path going up the bank and, in the distance, sloped roofs and the gray stone walls of houses. It was very quiet, and the light was oddly muted. Emma didn't see anyone else around. The wizard climbed onto the dock and she followed, adjusting Michael's dwarfish knife so that it was tucked snugly into her belt.

"What is this place?"

He shrugged. "It's very curious. I'm not sure where this is, or why we're here, I only know that I am taking you where you have to go. And we are not there yet. Come, my dear."

In so many ways—how he tilted his head slightly to the side when he was thinking, how he called her "my dear," how he seemed to feel no need to explain anything and just assumed she would follow along, which, of course, she did—he was Dr. Pym. And yet without his memories, he wasn't. It confused her and made her uncertain about how to approach him.

Emma let herself feel the pull of the book; he had indeed brought her closer. Then she coughed, and realized that her eyes and throat were burning and that what she'd taken for cloud cover was actually a low, thick ceiling of smoke.

"What's burning?"

The wizard said he didn't know; he began walking up the pier.

"Where're you going?" Emma asked.

"You must be hungry. We will get you something to eat. Then I will take you the rest of the way. That is my charge."

Somewhat grudgingly, Emma followed him down the dock and into the village. It looked like she was stuck with him for a while, and though she never would have admitted it, part of her was glad.

"Where is everybody?" Emma said. "What happened to this place?"

They were walking through the center of what could have been a charming village. There were stone houses, people had kept gardens, trees lined the streets. But the houses were empty, the gardens brown, the trees leafless or burned and broken at the trunk, and there were small fires burning seemingly everywhere. It was like the aftermath of some war or devastation.

"I do not know," the wizard said. "Something terrible."

"Yeah," Emma said. "Duh."

She said nothing more, but she felt an uneasiness, a sense of following a path that had been laid out for her long before, of walking into a trap.

They came to a square lined with dark-windowed shops.

"Come on," she said, taking command, and led him to a small grocery.

A bell tinkled as she stepped through the door, and Emma

waited but no one emerged from the back. There were loaves of bread (stale, she tried to break one on the counter and failed), several kinds of nuts, some sawdust-tasting chocolate, fruit—apples and what looked like plums, all wrinkled and sour—and though none of it was that fresh or good, it helped quell the gnawing in her stomach.

"I don't get it," she said, through a mouthful of mealy apple. "There're apples and bread and nuts. How can they grow all this stuff here? Do they have farms?"

"And what did you imagine the world of the dead would be?" the wizard asked. "A featureless desert where spirits float about, moaning for all eternity? This world is as solid and complete as the one above. There is water here; you have seen it. The air nourishes you with each breath. The land is fertile. If you can live here, then why not a tree? Or—" He looked away sharply. "We should go. Now."

He was already heading to the door. Emma followed, shoving more apples in her pockets. A few minutes later, they were outside the village, striding down a dirt road. The wizard took her arm.

"We must leave the road. Which way do we go?"

She realized he was asking her. She allowed herself to grow quiet, to feel the pull of the book, then pointed off through the burned-out forest that stood close by. Soon, they were out of sight of the road, and soon after that, they heard voices and the stamp of feet. They froze, listening, until the sounds had faded away.

"They're looking for me, aren't they?"

"Yes."

"It's the Dire Magnus."

"I do not know who that is. But there is a great evil in this place."

"Yeah," Emma said, fear giving an angry edge to her voice. "It's the world of the dead! 'Course it's evil! Look around!"

The wizard shook his head. "The world of the dead is not evil. Indeed, it could be a paradise. Imagine that village we passed through, full of noise and people. Imagine this forest green."

"You've gotta be kidding."

"You do not believe me. But the fact remains that those who hunt you brought their evil with them. This world itself is blameless. It exists only as the place where the dead wait."

"What're you talking about? Wait for what?"

"To be reborn." He spoke in the same automatic way he had in the shop, like someone who'd been taught a thing by rote. "The universe has been created and destroyed, over and over. It's happened before and will happen again. The spirits of the dead bide here until the time of rebirth. It could be a thousand years or a day. To the dead, it is all the same. They exist in an eternal present."

Emma thought she understood what the wizard was saying, that the dead just hung around here till the universe started over. But she couldn't get past the idea that when you died, you forgot everything you had built up in your life, including the people you were closest to. No wonder all those people walking on the road had looked like zombies. Everything that had mattered to them had been stripped away.

"But why do they have to forget who they were? It's not fair!"

The wizard shrugged again. "That's death, child."

With her eyes watering from the smoke, Emma gazed out at the burned and blackened forest. The wizard could say what he wanted about its being a paradise; as far as she was concerned, this place was hell.

"Let's just find the book so I can get out of here."

The farther they walked, the more difficult it became to breathe. When they reached a stream, the wizard wet a cloth, which Emma tied around her mouth and nose. The smoke grew so thick that she even let Dr. Pym take her hand so she could walk with her eyes shut, relying on him to warn her of roots and rocks.

Finally, she felt him stop.

"Open your eyes."

They had come out of the woods, and Emma looked, half knowing what she would see.

"I've been here before."

The wizard actually seemed surprised. "How is that possible?"

"The Dire Magnus pulled my spirit out of my body and sent it to look for the book. I saw things. This place, the fires. And I saw this."

They were standing before a nearly vertical rock wall that rose thousands of feet into the air. A winding, twisting staircase was carved into the rock. High up, Emma could see dark clusters that she took to be birds.

"He sent my spirit into the world of the dead. I guess I should've known. I never really thought about it; I didn't want to."

Just then there was an explosion above, accompanied by a furious, collective cawing, and a black cloud swirled down toward them. Emma's instinct was to duck, but Dr. Pym gripped her arm, silently commanding her to be still, and the swarm of birds swept over her head, once, twice, and then flew back up the cliff.

All except one. Emma saw that the bird—her mind supplied the word *raven*—had landed at the bottom stair. And then it was not a raven at all. The creature now before them had the body of a human, with a human's legs and arms, but a raven's head, with a great, shiny black beak. It was wearing a dark cloak with a hood.

It was the same one she had seen in her vision.

"A *carriadin*," the wizard said. "A guardian of this world. It will guide you the rest of the way."

"What?! You're leaving me with that?!"

"My charge is ended. I can go no farther. And it will not harm you."

Emma looked at the bird-creature, then up at the cliff. She could feel the book close by. The old wizard knelt, placing a hand on her arm.

"I do not remember you. Or your brother and sister. Or any of my life before this. But if I injured or betrayed you while I was alive, I can only ask for your forgiveness."

Emma stared at him. She didn't want to forgive him. She was still hurt and angry. But she found herself, against her will, thinking of all the things he had done for them, all the times he had been kind or patient or understanding, moments that had felt real, not planned or manipulative.

"Maybe . . . you thought you were doing the right thing or . . . you had some idea how to save us. I don't know. But you weren't always terrible."

"Thank you."

And before she could stop him, the wizard hugged her, and before she could stop herself, she hugged him back.

"Goodbye," he said, then stood and turned away into the trees.

Wiping the tears from her eyes, Emma looked at the bird-creature, and though its beak did not open, she heard the words in her head:

Come, Emma Wibberly.

It began walking up the stairs, and Emma had no choice but to follow.

The creature's cloak was ragged at the bottom, almost like the feathers of a very old bird, and its bare feet were blackened and callused.

They climbed, winding back and forth over the face of the cliff, the steps so steep that sometimes Emma had to go on all fours, and as they climbed, the other ravens flew about, as if daring her to step out into the air.

Finally, she stopped. "I have to rest."

She sat on one of the steps and looked down, trying to see if she could spot Dr. Pym, but either she was too high or the smoke was too thick or the birds circling through the air blocked her view. Then she looked farther out. Perhaps a mile or so distant, past a steep, rocky ridge, rose a column of black smoke thicker and wider than any other, and she felt a tension and nervousness in her breast. What was happening there?

Unconsciously, she inched forward, as if to gain a better view; her foot slipped, and then she was sliding, falling, nothing below her, nothing to stop her—

A hand grabbed her shoulder, roughly pulling her back. She was shaken, trembling. She looked at the creature on the step above her.

"Thank . . . thank you."

Again, she heard its voice in her head. *"Come."*

They kept climbing, up into the thickest part of the smoke. Emma's vision was blurry with tears, and she was hacking almost constantly when they finally stopped on a small ledge. Before them was a cave, tunneling back into the rock wall. Emma stared into the darkness. The pull of the book was like a second heart straining against her chest.

The creature began to turn away.

"Wait!"

Its black eyes stared at her, inhuman and unreadable.

"It was you, wasn't it? Or someone like you, that the Countess gave the book to? Michael said she gave it to a spirit or something. It was you."

The *carriadin* said nothing.

"And you sent Dr. Pym to get me, didn't you? You made him bring me here. He said you're a guardian of this world. You think me taking the book away will help fix things."

Emma didn't know how she knew this, but it was all suddenly so clear. She could feel the intelligence thrumming within her, stirred by her proximity to the book.

Then she heard the voice in her head:

Goodbye, Emma Wibberly.

And she gasped as the creature launched itself out into the air and, while still keeping the shape of a man, giant black wings opened from its back, and the *carriadin* soared down and out of sight.

"If he could do that," Emma muttered, "why didn't he just fly me up here?"

Then she turned and walked, alone, into the cave.

* * *

The air in the cave was cleaner, more breathable, and Emma's eyes stopped watering and she coughed less. She had switched on Michael's flashlight, and she felt a kind of giddiness and was soon hurrying forward, almost recklessly, as the tunnel curved deeper into the rock, and then, abruptly, she was at the end, and there, resting on a ledge carved into the back wall of the tunnel, was the book.

For a moment, Emma stood there, her chest heaving, as if unable to believe what she was seeing. She had actually done it. She had come into the world of the dead all alone—she didn't count Dr. Pym, she hadn't asked him to come, and really, a monkey could've rowed the boat—and she had done it. She felt a deep stirring of pride that she, the youngest, the one who everyone thought was only good for punching and kicking people, that she had done something no one else could have. And here was the hard proof that would put her on the same standing as her brother and sister in one leap.

All she had to do was reach out and pick it up.

But still, she hesitated.

For being the Book of Death, Emma thought the *Reckoning* could've been a little more impressive. Granted, its corners were rimmed with dark metal, but the book was both smaller and slimmer than either the *Atlas* or the *Chronicle*. It almost looked like a diary. Had it really sat here for two thousand years? Had it been waiting for her all this time?

Yes, Emma thought, without knowing how she knew, it had been.

"So pick it up, then," she whispered, and her voice echoed

back, urging her on. Her hand trembled as it came into the beam of light, and she lifted the book off the rock shelf.

It felt no different from any other book, the metal corners cold and slightly sharp at the tips, and she ran her fingers over the pebbled black leather of the cover. Her heart was beating fast. She set Michael's flashlight on the ledge so its light shone out into the cave, and, taking a deep breath, she opened the book.

It was blank, but she had expected that; the *Atlas* and the *Chronicle* had also been blank. Despite the coolness of the cave air, Emma could feel herself beginning to sweat. She knew she didn't have to go any farther. She had the book now; she could just take it and find her way back home; she'd already accomplished what she'd come here to do.

She laid her hand, palm down, on the open page.

It felt like the top of her head was ripped open.

She cried out and staggered backward, the book tumbling to the ground. She stood there, gasping, trying to process what had just happened. The book had fallen closed upon the floor. For a long time, she didn't move.

She must've done something wrong, or triggered some kind of alarm or trap set to scare people off. She just had to try again.

She thought she could hear something in the cave, whispers, circling about, growing closer; she ignored them.

Quickly, before she could change her mind, Emma reached out and placed her palm on the page.

It was the same as before, but worse because she kept her hand pressed down. A million voices, shouting, crying, desperate to be heard, clamored inside her head; she could feel her own self being trampled on and torn apart.

She fell backward again, her head ringing, her heart shuddering in her chest.

Whose voices were they? What did they want? What were they doing in the book?

A memory came to her, of her dream that first night in the land of the giants. In the dream, shadowy figures had crowded around her, pleading, shouting.

She took a deep breath and tried to pull herself together. She just had to get help. She would take the book back to the world of the living and get someone to show her how to shut off the voices so she could use the book to kill the Dire Magnus.

Then she looked up, and froze. Words were appearing on the open page:

Release them. . . .

Emma raced down the rocky stairs, two steps at a time, hardly seeing where she was going. She held the book clutched to her chest. She had to find Dr. Pym! Or that bird-creature. They would know where to find the portal to the world of the living.

Then she was at the bottom of the cliff.

"Dr. Pym! Dr. Pym!"

No answer; her throat burned horribly.

She shut her eyes. She could still hear the voices, whispering, nipping at the edges of her mind.

"Hello." A man with a hairy gut sticking out of his black leather tunic stepped from the trees. "Who're you, then?"

Emma turned to run and collided with another man, who shoved her to the ground, took the dwarfish knife from her belt, and quickly and expertly tied a cord around her wrists. She struggled, but he knelt on her, patient, as if he had done this many times before. Then the first one returned with a line of men and women, their wrists bound like Emma's, and the tall man pulled her to her feet and tied her to the others.

"What's this?" said the fat man, picking up the black book from where Emma had dropped it. "Little bit of light reading? Mine now."

He shoved the book into the top of his pants.

"Don't," Emma said. "That's my—"

The other man struck her hard across the mouth.

"Shut it." Then to his companion, "We're late. Come on."

And Emma, tasting blood, was pulled away.

CHAPTER SEVENTEEN
The Thing on the Beach

Kate woke, rubbed her eyes, and looked about, trying to remember where she was. . . .

She was in a narrow, canvas tent. Sunlight streamed through a gap in the front flap. She had slept in her clothes, not even bothering to remove her boots, and she could feel how her body was covered with a grimy film of sweat. Michael lay with his back to her, on a cot a few feet away. From outside, she could hear voices, footsteps, hammering, the clinking and scraping of metal; and she could smell breakfast, eggs and bacon and coffee and what she would've sworn were pancakes, and suddenly her stomach felt like a great hollow pit inside her. She couldn't go back to sleep.

And by then too she had remembered the night before, the meeting with King Robbie, and what he had told them about Emma and the portal.

"Hello?"

There was a voice outside the tent. It belonged to a dwarf.

"Yes?"

"Ah, you're awake? The King would like you both to come to a Council. Not a moment to lose. Though I've brought you something to nibble on. Nothing fancy. Just a dozen or so scrambled eggs, poached eggs, fried eggs, four or five rashers of bacon, pancakes, toast, marmalade, currant scones, blueberry scones, this little frittata I whipped up . . ."

After Kate had woken Michael, told him about the Council, and the two of them had crammed in as much food as they could as quickly as they could, they followed their escort—an old dwarf with a wispy gray beard and very large, floppy ears—across the camp to King Robbie's tent.

In the daylight, Kate perceived that the island was in the shape of a large, stretched-out horseshoe, the whole thing set on an incline. Downhill lay the various tents and encampments, and Kate could see hundreds, perhaps thousands, of men and dwarves moving about, making their breakfasts, checking their weapons, while beyond them lay the beach and blue water of the marina, where she and Michael had arrived the night before, and where the small fleet still sat at anchor.

Looking directly ahead, past the green tent of the dwarf king, was what looked like a field of enormous wildflowers. In fact, they were brightly colored tents and pavilions, blues and greens and pinks and yellows; and moving among them, Kate could see hundreds of elves. Some of them must've been playing music, and the tune seemed to Kate to somehow be a part of the morning sunlight, to echo the distant sound of sea, the movement of the breeze, and it calmed her. She could see a few elves polishing swords and making arrows, but most of them were simply combing their hair or, it appeared, giving advice to others about combing their hair, demonstrating technique and so on.

"They're keeping away from each other," Michael said.

"What?"

"The three camps. The dwarves, humans, elves. None of them are having anything to do with each other."

He was right; each of the camps had clearly marked its own territory, and none of them—humans, dwarves, or elves—were to be seen among the others.

This did not, Kate thought, bode well.

Kate then briefly turned her gaze uphill, toward the camp of the refugees. These were the families who had lived on Loris—she could see them, husbands and wives, old people, children. The Dire Magnus is hunting us, she thought. We're responsible for what happens to them.

As they approached the entrance to Robbie McLaur's tent, Kate and her brother could hear raised voices, all talking, or rather shouting, at once.

"Our goose is cooked, we might as well admit it—"

"Perhaps if we hadn't given up Loris—"

"We had no choice, you know that—"

"An assault on the Dire Magnus now would be suicide—"

"It's suicide if he gets his hands on the *Reckoning*—"

"Perhaps if a few of those elves at home doing their nails were to come help us—"

"They won't follow a dwarf. I've said that. Perhaps if you cleaned your ears. Or any part of your body—"

The old dwarf pulled back the flap and said quietly, "Good luck," and Kate and Michael walked inside.

"Oh, yes, well, it's good to see you too, lass."

Haraald patted Kate on the back as she continued to hug him tightly.

Haraald was alive; that had been the first and best surprise to greet the children when they'd entered the tent, and Kate had raced over to throw her arms around him. In truth, her joy at finding the red-bearded dwarf alive surprised even her, as she didn't really know him all that well. But when it felt like they were losing people left and right, having Haraald come back against impossible odds meant there was hope for all of them, hope for Emma. The dwarf's face was still streaked with smoke and blood and dirt, and his right hand was wrapped in a clean bandage, but he was here, he was alive.

"When did you get back?" Kate asked, finally letting him go.

"Just before dawn." He coughed. "Captain . . . um . . . Captain . . . well, you see . . ."

"Captain Anton went back and rescued him," King Robbie said. "Found him swimming along, a mile or so from Loris. For which we are indebted to our allies . . ." And he nodded at the elf king, who waved his hand breezily.

"That's the size of it," Haraald said. "Though I could've swum here if I'd had to."

"Really?" the elf king said. "Thirty miles of open ocean?"

"You've never seen me swim!" the dwarf all but roared. "I'm a veritable guppy!"

"Well," Kate said, "thank you again. You saved our lives."

"Nothing to it, lass." And the dwarf's weathered face softened to something like an actual smile.

Kate and Michael were given chairs on the right side of King Robbie, and in many ways the Council was a reprise of the one they'd attended in the Rose Citadel a few days before. Around the table were Magda von Klappen, the stern Austrian witch; Master Chu, the plump Chinese wizard; Hugo Algernon; Captain Stefano, the bald commander of the Guard of Loris; the silver-haired Lady Gwendolyn; King Bernard, Wilamena's father; and Haraald and King Robbie. The differences were that this time there was no Dr. Pym, several of the Council members displayed wounds (Captain Stefano had a bandage around his head and one arm in a sling), and from the glares being passed around, any pretense of civility was gone. Kate suspected it was all Robbie McLaur could do to keep them from attacking each other.

When the children were seated, the dwarf king addressed himself to Kate and Michael. "So then, I've told the Council what happened to you all, where your sister has gone to get the *Reckoning,* and where she might appear. We've been discussing what we can do about it."

"Find a well-stocked bar and wait for the roof to cave in," grumbled Hugo Algernon.

"Dr. Algernon," the dwarf king warned, "I told you, none of that."

"Before we go further, I have some distressing news," King

Bernard said. "I've spoken with our colony back in Antarctica, and they inform me that the gateway to the world of the dead has inexplicably closed itself off."

Kate said nothing, but she could feel panic beginning to stir inside her.

"Right," King Robbie said grimly. "Then that leaves the portal on the Hebrides—"

"I'm afraid," Magda von Klappen said, "that I just received word that that portal has sealed itself off as well."

There was a long, heavy moment of silence. Kate reached out and took Michael's hand even as he was reaching for hers.

"I see," the dwarf king said. "And any idea why?"

"The Books," Hugo Algernon growled. "You need another answer? And what's it matter? It is what it is. There's only one portal left and we all knew it would come to that, didn't we?"

"But could that one . . ."—Kate's voice trembled—"close too?"

"Doubtful," said Master Chu, in his calm murmur. "It is the oldest of the gateways, and the strongest. It forms part of the axis between our world and the world of the dead. Were it to close, then the entire universe would most likely come to an end."

"Well," King Robbie said, after no one else had spoken, "I suppose that's reassuring."

But in fact, Kate was reassured, and she felt Michael squeeze her hand.

"I'll ask a stupid question," Haraald said.

"By all means," King Bernard said magnanimously, "that is your right as a dwarf."

Kate saw Haraald, his face flaming as red as his beard, whirl toward the elf king, but Robbie McLaur put a hand on his arm.

"Go on, Haraald."

"It's just that, say this child comes through the portal with the *Reckoning*, why don't she just kill the Dire Magnus right then and there? End this whole thing. Ain't that what this is all about, getting this fancy book so we can kill him?"

"I think that's an excellent question," Kate said, and she looked hard at the elf king (but only for a moment, for the elf king looked at her with eyes of such unparalleled blue and with such sweetness of expression that she found herself having the odd thought *I bet he's a wonderful dancer*. And the elf king even gave a tiny nod as if to say, *I am, I'm a wonderful dancer*).

"Unfortunately, it is not so simple." Magda von Klappen's stern, clipped voice spoke from across the table. "The fact is, these Books are fantastically complex magical instruments. They require time and skill to master. Correct me if I'm wrong, but it was some time before either of you could fully use your Books, was it not?"

"Yes," Michael said. "That's true."

And Kate found herself nodding as well.

"So the wee lass might come through with the book, having endured who knows what horrors in the world of the dead"—the dwarf king paused and looked apologetically at Kate and Michael—"though probably nothing too, too bad."

"Oh, it will be horrible," Magda von Klappen said. "Count on that."

"But as I was saying, she won't even be able to use its power to kill the fiend. She'll need help from you lot." Robbie McLaur nodded at the wizarding contingent.

"Exactly so," Magda von Klappen said.

"Ha!" barked Hugo Algernon.

"You've something you want to say, Doctor?" the dwarf king asked wearily.

"Yes, I have something to say. First off, Magda von Klappen here wears old-lady underwear. I know because I saw her washing it this morning—"

"This is ridic—"

"I thought she was washing a bedsheet or maybe a tablecloth, but they were her knickers all right. Second, even if the girl could use the *Reckoning*, haven't any of you realized that she probably won't get the chance?"

This silenced everyone, even Magda von Klappen, and Hugo Algernon glared around triumphantly.

"Yes," Michael said quietly.

The entire Council turned to look at him, even Kate, who wondered what Michael knew that he hadn't shared.

"What do you mean, lad?" the dwarf king asked. "What's he getting at?"

"Well," Michael said, adjusting his glasses, "you have to question the coincidence of the Dire Magnus attacking Loris and taking control of the portal right before Emma is going to come through it with the *Reckoning*."

"You mean," Robbie McLaur said, "he knows she's in the world of the dead?"

"Possibly. If so, he'll be waiting for her. So even if she could use the book, like Dr. Algernon says, he wouldn't give her the chance. He'll have some trap set up."

"But how would he know?" King Bernard said. "You think he has spies here?"

"Maybe," Michael said. "Though there is one other explanation."

Hugo Algernon was nodding. "At least two people at this table aren't total morons. Bright lad. Like his dad in that. 'Course I taught his dad, so I get most of the credit."

"What do you mean?" Kate asked. "What other explanation?"

Michael looked at her. "That the Dire Magnus planned it all. Our escaping from his fortress, discovering the Countess's remains, bringing her back to life, finding out where the *Reckoning* is hidden. Think about it, if he knew where the book was, then he would've also known that only the Keeper of the *Reckoning* could pass into the world of the dead, so he would've made us think we were doing everything ourselves, and all the while he knew Emma would be bringing the book right to him."

"But how," Kate said, her throat so thick she could scarcely speak, "how could he have done that?"

Michael shook his head. "I haven't figured that out. He would've had to 've been pushing us along somehow."

Michael was still staring at her, and for an instant Kate thought, He knows, he knows Rafe has been appearing to me. . . .

But even if Michael did suspect, what did it matter? He was wrong about at least one thing; it had been Rafe, and not the Dire Magnus, appearing to her!

And yet, a voice inside her asked, could she say that for certain? When it came down to it, what did she have that she could point to, besides her own belief, that it had been Rafe, and not their enemy, who'd come to her on Loris, and then again in the land of the giants? And did she truly believe it, or, as she'd wondered before, did she just want to believe it? Wasn't the very fact that she had avoided saying anything to her brother and sister proof that she had her doubts?

She felt her heart beginning to race and gripped the arms of her chair to steady herself. For if it had been the Dire Magnus manipulating her all this time, that meant she had done the one thing she'd never thought possible: she had chosen someone else over Michael and Emma; and in the process, she had doomed them all.

She could see Michael looking at her, trying to read in her face what was happening, and when Lady Gwendolyn, the silver-haired elf, began speaking, it was with immense relief that Kate turned from him and looked across the table.

"If we may speak of practical matters," Lady Gwendolyn said, "we cannot open a portal into the Garden of the Citadel. We all know there are wards to prevent such a thing. But what of the *Atlas*? Its power could override any such defense. It could take a band in to rescue the girl and bring her back here, where we could instruct her in using the book."

"Maybe. It's just . . . something's happening with the *Atlas*." Kate had had to swallow before she'd been able to speak, and her voice was far from steady. She hoped the others—mostly Michael—would hear it as nervousness about using the *Atlas*. "I can't control it the way I used to. Leaving the Dire Magnus's fortress, I tried to take us to Loris and we ended up in the giants' land. Then last night . . ." And she thought again of the pain she'd felt when she'd used the magic. "I mean . . . I'll do whatever you think best. I just don't know if we should count on it."

"I'm guessing you've felt the same thing, haven't you, boy?"

Hugo Algernon was almost glaring at Michael from beneath his bushy eyebrows. "When you used the *Chronicle*?"

Michael nodded. "Yes. I've felt it."

"Well, that's that," the man grunted, and crossed his arms, as if he'd definitively proven some point that only he understood.

"So," Robbie McLaur said, in the tone of someone trying to keep things on track, "what we've got is that the Dire Magnus might or might not have planned this whole thing—I vote for he has, though I've no idea how he managed it—might or might not be waiting for the lass—again, I go with he is—and we've no way of simply magicking ourselves into the Garden. Fine. But still, we have to get in there and get the girl and the book before he does or our collective goose is bloody well cooked! Is that about the size of it?"

"There is also the very tricky issue of timing," King Bernard said—the elf had, Kate reflected, the longest eyelashes she'd ever seen. "When will the girl come through? Tonight? Tomorrow? She could be appearing right this very moment while we sit here bathed in dwarfish body odor—"

"Hey now!" Haraald started to rise, but King Robbie's hand on his shoulder forced him back down.

"And before anyone raises the prospect of a small band sneaking into the Garden to rescue the girl, consider, they would have to remain there, undiscovered, until such time as the girl appeared. A proposition, I think, with little hope of success. The fact is, the only sure way for us to protect the child and keep the enemy from gaining control of the *Reckoning* is to retake Loris and the Rose Citadel and hold it ourselves till she comes through. But seeing as we just abandoned Loris—"

"Unnecessarily," muttered Captain Stefano, the first words he'd yet spoken.

"—and our forces are weaker now than they were then, that would seem an impossibility. What are we, therefore, to do?"

"I told you," Hugo Algernon said. "Make our way to a well-stocked bar. I know a couple if anyone's interested."

"Everything King Bernard says is correct," Robbie McLaur said, anger burning in his eyes, "except in regard to retaking Loris. It ain't impossible. All's we need is a bigger bloody army. And we've got one, just waiting to be snatched up!" He jabbed a stubby finger at the elf king. "How many elf clans are there spread around the world? Dozens. How many a' those elves, not counting the ones you brought yourself, have shown up to help us? Zero!" He whirled on Captain Stefano. "And you, Captain, despite all your grumbling about abandoning Loris, you've yet to call in the oaths from the other humans in the magical world! As I recall, each one of them is sworn to protect the island and the Citadel. But we've not seen hide nor hair of any of them! So don't tell me it's impossible, because it's not!"

"The other elf clans will not come to fight under a dwarf," King Bernard said crossly. "Even though I've told them that for a dwarf you are almost completely unobjectionable and rather clean."

"And I have tried contacting the other fiefs," Captain Stefano said. "No one will be the first to move. They say they pledged their oath to the city of Loris. Not to a dwarf king—"

"So I'll step aside!" King Robbie cried, slapping the table. "You can be the bloody general! Or you! I don't care!"

Haraald shook his head. "Your Majesty, you know well that

the dwarf battalions who've answered your call wouldn't follow an elf—"

"And I," Captain Stefano said wearily, raising his wounded arm, "am in no state for the job."

Michael pushed his chair back and stood. The action was abrupt enough that it silenced the table.

"What is it, lad?" King Robbie said. "You have something to say?"

"What? Oh, no. Just . . ." His face was red, but Kate saw that it was not anger; he was blushing. "The princess is here."

Kate and the rest of the table shifted about and looked toward the entrance of the tent. Wilamena stood there, wearing a dress the color of the desert sky. Her hair shone as brightly as if she'd been dipped in the sun.

Perhaps having been embarrassed by Michael, Robbie McLaur, Haraald, Master Chu, and even Hugo Algernon all stood.

"Welcome, Princess," King Robbie said. "There's a chair next to your father—"

"She can sit here," Michael said, indicating a chair beside him. "I mean, if she wants to."

"Thank you," Wilamena said.

The dwarves and the two wizards remained standing while Wilamena floated around the table to the chair Michael was holding. Then, after pushing it in and asking if she wanted anything to drink (she didn't), Michael glanced around, saw everyone staring at him, and turned even redder. It was as if he'd forgotten they all were there. But then Kate saw a change come over her brother; it was as if he had said to himself, "Well, so what?" and he stood up a little straighter, and when he spoke, his voice was clear and strong.

"There's something I'd like to say: while you sit here arguing, my sister has gone into the world of the dead alone, something no one else has ever done. She's risking her life to save all of us, not just me and my sister, but all of us. And she's twelve years old. So, no disrespect, but you need to grow up."

He sat down and, as Kate and the others watched, the elf princess, her eyes shining with pride, took his hand, and Michael, though he blushed even redder, did not pull it away.

The first person to speak was King Robbie.

"Hold now, hold now." A smile was creeping at the corners of his mouth. "I believe I'm getting an idea. . . ."

But they were not to hear what it was, for right then, Captain Anton rushed in to say the island was under attack.

"Where?" King Robbie roared.

They were in the sunlight outside the tent. There were screams, people running around, pandemonium. King Robbie was holding an ax, as was Haraald, and Kate saw that King Bernard and Lady Gwendolyn both had their gleaming swords out and by their sides.

"On the northern shore. It looks to be a single raiding vessel, perhaps a scout. They came up over the cliffs."

"The northern shore? Bloody— Princess?"

"I left my bracelet in my tent." And then Wilamena was gone, a flash of gold streaking away.

King Robbie looked at Kate and Michael. "You two stay back." Then he shouted for the others to follow, turned, and began running up the island's hill.

Kate threw one glance at Michael, and they both took off after King Robbie, Captain Anton, and the others.

As the island sloped gently uphill, it meant that Kate and Michael had a clear view of what was happening. They could see, perhaps half a mile away, the dark shapes streaming over the edge of the cliff and toward the families and children from Loris.

But Kate and Michael had run only a short way when both were roughly grabbed by the backs of their collars. "Right. Hold it. You heard the king."

It was Hugo Algernon.

"What're you doing?" Kate demanded. "We can help."

"You can help more by not being dead. Oh, hello—"

Throngs of people were pouring toward them, running away from the attackers, while from behind rushed a wave of their own soldiers.

"We're gonna get sandwiched," Hugo Algernon said, and he lifted them in his arms and turned sharply to the left. After a minute of huffing and rough shaking, he'd reached the edge of the island and set them down atop a small cliff.

"There," he said. "Safe enough."

"But how did they find us?" Michael said. "I thought this island was invisible."

"The Dire Magnus has dozens of ships out looking for us. Get close enough, it's not hard to see the enchantment. Now you two be good kiddies and wait here, and maybe I'll buy you an ice cream later. Stay here! I mean that!"

Then he turned and ran toward the battle that was now going on at the upper end of the island. The air was thick with cries of fear, the clanging and crashing of metal, and the shrieks of *morum cadi*.

"This isn't right," Michael said. "We should be allowed to help and—"

He was cut off by a scream, a child's scream, and both he and Kate turned. Thirty yards below them was a rocky beach. A pair of children, a boy and a girl, perhaps seven and eight years old, stood on the beach as a creature—an Imp, Kate saw—climbed out of the water toward them, a black mace in one hand.

"Kate!"

The Imp grabbed the boy, lifting him up in the air. There was no one else around, no one to help. As the creature lifted the mace, Kate seized Michael's hand, reached inside herself for the magic, and stopped time.

"Kate—"

Michael's voice was strangely flat and toneless, and yet it was the only sound in the world. Kate tried to speak, but she felt a great, crushing pressure on her chest.

"You stopped time, didn't you? You—are you all right?"

"We—have to—get down there. I can't—hold it long."

There was a narrow path winding down the cliff, and Michael took the lead. Kate followed, every muscle in her body shaking with effort. She felt that every second she kept time suspended, she was doing terrible damage, to the world and to herself.

When they reached the beach, Michael ran forward and yanked the boy from the Imp's grasp. He bent to pick up the girl as well, but he couldn't carry both.

"Kate, we have to— What're you doing?"

Kate had rushed past Michael and stopped a foot from the

Imp. She was too weak to carry the girl, and if she restarted time, the Imp would catch them. She pulled a short, ugly sword from the creature's scabbard.

She heard Michael say her name again.

Bracing the sword with both hands—her vision seemed to be clouding over—she held the blade, trembling, tip out toward the Imp.

"You have to run," she shouted. "I'll hold it here as long as I can. Get help!"

"Kate! No!"

She let time restart.

And she had just said, "Don't move—" when the Imp rushed forward, impaling itself on its own sword and knocking Kate to the ground.

The last thing she remembered was the back of her head hitting a rock.

CHAPTER EIGHTEEN
The Lost Tribe

The boy who'd given them a ride from the village stopped his truck and told them he could go no farther.

"Okay," Clare said, speaking, as the boy had, in Arabic. "We'll get out." And she called out the window to Gabriel and her husband, who had ridden in the truck's bed. "This is as far as he'll go."

It had been a four-hour trip, and the truck, a rusted-out, loosely bolted scavenge job of three or four different trucks, had seemed at the point of rattling apart with every bump and pothole; indeed, Gabriel was surprised they'd made it this far. Now, lifting his pack and sword, he climbed out, the whole truck tilting sharply as he swung himself over the side. The children's father climbed out next. Like Gabriel, he was covered in red-brown dust, and he unwrapped the scarf from his head, took a sip of water from his canteen, swirled it around in his mouth, and spat to clear the grit. He gave his wife and Gabriel a smile.

"So, that was awful."

The boy had maneuvered the truck around and was already headed back the way they had come. Alone, the group turned and looked about. Gabriel had been to many places in the world, but never anywhere quite like this. Narrow, stony mountains lurched upward all around them, tilting this way and that at odd, almost impossible angles. Richard had explained that thousands of years before, the land here had been lush, and rivers had carved strange formations in the rock. But now there was no water, and the landscape was all burnt-red and brown. Even the sky, thick with dust, was lit red by the setting sun, as if the air itself was on fire. The sound of the truck had already faded, and the silence was complete.

The rutted path they had been following snaked upward over the rocks.

"He said there's nothing up here," Clare said. "Just more mountains."

"Well," Richard said, "let's find out."

And the trio began walking uphill.

It had been almost a day since they had left the small town on the Adriatic in the plane flown by Gabriel's friend, hopscotching their way across the Mediterranean, landing on splinters and shards of the magical world, first in Greece, then Cyprus, and lastly in Lebanon, refueling each time, before flying out over the endless desert of the Arabian Peninsula. The pilot had landed at the base of the mountains on the southern coast, next to a village of mud and concrete houses. It was there that they'd found the boy with the truck.

Gabriel's shoulder was stiff from the blow he'd received the night before, and he adjusted the strap of his pack, which carried food and water for him and the couple. The man and woman were still weak, but they were tough and kept on, uncomplaining. Gabriel gauged that they had three hours till nightfall, and then the temperature would drop quickly.

"It is time," Gabriel said, keeping a steady, tireless stride, pausing only now and then so he did not overtake the couple, "for you to tell me what we are doing here, and how you hope to uncover the rest of the prophecy."

He had not pressed them during the previous legs of their journey, the noise of the airplane and the rattling of the truck having rendered conversation impossible, and during their brief breaks, the couple had needed all the rest they could get.

"Of course," Richard said, breathing hard. "Tell me, though, how much do you know about the prophecy and the prophet? What did Pym tell you?"

Gabriel confessed that, in truth, he knew very little about the ancient prophecy that had so ruled his and the children's lives— only its essence: that the children would find the Books, unite them, and then perish.

"That's not surprising," Richard said. "Most people, if they know about the prophecy at all, don't know more than that."

But the couple explained how, years before, when Dr. Pym had told them who their children were destined to be, they had devoted themselves to learning everything they could about the Books and their history, and this had included the prophecy.

"We didn't learn everything, obviously," Richard said. "We only found out about the predictions of the children's deaths when Rourke told us a few months ago."

"But we still know quite a bit," Clare said.

"Right. So more than a thousand years ago, there was a famous seer among one of the nomadic tribes of the Sahara. He made hundreds of predictions, about wars, famines, plagues, disasters both natural and magical. And they weren't your usual vague, mumbly sorts of prophecies that could be yanked to fit almost any situation. They were specific. Like 'Everyone in this particular village should get out by this date because there's going to be a plague of killer bees.'"

"And he was right," Clare said. "Again and again."

"And the last prediction he made," Richard said, "was about the children and the Books. Then he vanished."

"You mean he died?"

"No, vanished. Along with his whole tribe. Just disappeared out of the desert. There're plenty of mentions in contemporary accounts. He was famous, after all; people noticed he was gone. Maybe he got tired of people always hunting him down and asking him to predict the future. Or maybe he was in some kind of danger, so he disappeared and took his people with him. No one knows."

"Only the tribe didn't really vanish," Clare said. "It wasn't long before reports began popping up, of people seeing the tribe in the South American jungle. In Papua New Guinea. On the Russian steppes. The Faeroe Islands."

"And this is one of the places," Gabriel said, "these mountains?"

"Yes," Richard said. "We found an account in the memoirs of a fourteenth-century spice trader who stumbled onto the tribe. That village where we left the plane, that was an old trading post. The trader went east from there, into the mountains, same as we are, and that's where he found them."

"And are you simply hoping this tribe is still here?" Gabriel said, suddenly afraid he had been mistaken in trusting the couple's judgment.

"No, no, of course not," Clare said. "We studied this. We went through all the accounts we could find, plotting out the places they'd been seen, and eventually a pattern emerged. It turned out the tribe was still nomadic. Only instead of migrating hundreds of miles, they migrated thousands, all across the globe. And they went to certain places at certain times. Rotating on a fifty-year cycle. It was very clear once you saw it. We never had a chance to tell Pym because we only discovered all this just before we were captured. But they should be here now."

"If our theory is right," Richard said quietly.

Which, Gabriel thought, was a rather large *if*.

But he did not voice his doubt. Nor did he question how, even if they did find this lost tribe, they expected that to lead to the revelation of the rest of the prophecy. Did they think the prophecy would be written down in the village library? That the prophet's old tribe would remember it verbatim? He didn't ask because he already knew the answer. The couple didn't know. They were here because they had nowhere else to go. And slim as this hope might be, it was their only one.

"I don't understand," Clare said. "This isn't right."

They had followed the path up around the side of the mountain till they reached a cliff and were now staring out at more desolate red-brown peaks in the distance. The path wound down the face of the mountain away from them.

"In the spice trader's account," Clare said, "he followed the eastern road from the village, the same as we did, but he said there was a bridge to another mountain, and he followed it to the village. Where's the bridge? Where's the village?"

Her voice was tight with panic and frustration.

"Maybe we missed a turn," Richard said. "Or we're on the wrong road."

"But there are no other eastern roads! It's just like the boy said, there's nothing up here!"

As the couple debated, Gabriel glanced back at the path they had come up.

"The trader's account, it is very old?"

"From the fourteenth century," Clare said. "But it was incredibly detailed. Even if the bridge had fallen, there should be some evidence—"

"So it was written before the Separation," Gabriel went on, "before the magical world pulled away. What was clear then would now be hidden."

Without waiting for the couple to respond, he walked back along the path. Sixty yards from the cliff, he found what he was looking for, a watery glimmer in the air. In the dying light, he had walked right past it. He heard Richard and Clare behind him.

"Focus on the shimmer," Gabriel said as he stepped into it, feeling the tingle and the world widening around him, and then he was through, and the air still tasted the same, the sun hung at the same place in the sky, everything was the same but also different, for he was now in the magical world.

He heard Clare gasp, and Richard say, "Whoa." They were

looking, he knew, at the mountain not a hundred yards away, the mountain that had not been there moments before and was connected to the peak on which they stood by a long rope or hemp bridge that hung suspended over a thousand-foot drop.

"This is the bridge in the trader's account," Richard exclaimed. "The village should be just on the other side." He started forward, but Gabriel put out a hand to hold him back.

"What're you doing? We have to hurry! We—"

"We are not alone," Gabriel said.

Four or five large boulders studding the top of the mountain stood between themselves and the bridge, and the couple was silent now, for they could see the shadows disengaging themselves from the boulders and becoming men cloaked in the same hues as the rocks, holding short, curved bows, and with long daggers stuck in their belts.

"They were here the whole time, weren't they?" Richard whispered. "In the magic world. Waiting to see if we would come through."

"Yes."

"Let me talk to them," Clare said. "I'll tell them we're not here to hurt them."

"I doubt they're worried about that," Richard said.

One man, tall and lean with a thick black beard and skin the color of the rocks, stepped forward. He looked at Gabriel, then held out his hand. Gabriel hesitated, then unslung his sword and passed it over, giving the man his knife and pack as well.

Jamming Gabriel's knife in his belt and slipping the pack and sword over his shoulder, the man turned and motioned for them to follow. They fell into a line, Gabriel, Clare, and finally Richard, with the band of men behind, and they made their way to the bridge and then across, the bridge swinging beneath their feet.

The next peak was narrower than the one they had left, and the tall man led them through a passage in the rock, a short tunnel that Gabriel hadn't seen from the other side. A minute later they stepped out and the village lay before them, thirty red-brown houses of compacted mud terraced into the concave face of the mountain. Gabriel could see figures moving about and hear the bleating of goats and the dull clanking of bells.

As they entered the village, women and children came out to watch them pass, all of them dressed in the same long cloaks as the men, and they stared at Gabriel and the couple with large, dark eyes. Gabriel looked up the narrow path between the mud and stone huts and he saw a figure move aside a rug that hung over the doorway of the last hut and step into the path. It was an old man, stooped and bald, and Gabriel was not surprised when the bearded leader of the band stopped before him.

The old man looked more like a tortoise than anyone Gabriel had ever seen, with his skin both wrinkled and yet strangely smooth. He was leaning on a crooked cane, and he peered closely at Gabriel and at the couple.

"Tell him who we are," Richard said.

Clare said something, and the old man nodded, murmuring a reply.

"He says"—Clare's voice was quiet—"that he's been expecting us."

The old man pulled back the blanket and gestured into the

darkness of his house. Richard and Clare exchanged a glance and stepped through. Gabriel moved to follow, but the bearded man barred his way.

Then the old man stepped into the house, dropping the blanket behind him.

The old man led Richard and Clare to the back room and gestured to them to sit on the floor, which was covered with overlapping rugs. He sat facing them, on the other side of a small oil stove, which he quickly and deftly lit, and began heating up a pot of water. The old man had a weathered and leathery skull, heavy-lidded dark eyes, and as he manipulated the stove, his fingers stayed locked together, giving his hands the appearance of flippers. He was adding various things to the pot—herbs, roots, powders—and stirring them with a stick from the floor.

"Ask him," Richard said, "what he meant when he said he was waiting for us."

Clare spoke, then listened to the old man's response and said to her husband, "He says that we must be the parents of the Keepers. That it was foretold we would come."

"Who is he?" Richard asked. "Is he . . . the prophet?"

Clare translated, and the old man made a dismissive noise before responding.

"He says the prophet has been dead for a thousand years. He is merely the one who sits in his place."

"Look"—Richard leaned forward—"not to be rude, it's just that time is kind of an issue. The reason we're here—"

But the old man was already speaking. Clare listened, then translated. "He asks if we wish to hear the prophecy concerning the children and the Books. Is that not the reason we have come?"

Clare responded herself.

The old man shook his head, and Clare said:

"He says he doesn't know the prophecy."

"But—" Richard began.

"He says," Clare went on, "that we must hear it from the prophet."

"But the prophet's dead!" Richard nearly shouted. "He just said so!"

The pot on the stove was now bubbling, and the old man went to a small wooden box against the wall, undid the latch, and opened it. He took out an object bound in cloth, carefully unwrapping it to reveal a cloudy, whitish crystal in roughly the shape of a cube.

He began to speak quickly, and Clare asked several questions, nodding if she understood or frowning if she didn't.

"What is that?" Richard asked.

"He says it is a moment of frozen time."

The old man dropped the cube into the boiling pot and began to stir.

"He says"—Clare was translating as the man spoke—"that if we wish to hear the prophecy, we must hear it from the prophet. We must go back in time."

"But only the *Atlas* can take you through time," Richard said. "Pym told us—"

"He says the cube was a piece of that time long ago. We will take it inside ourselves. It will be a part of us. We'll see and hear as if we were there."

Then the old man took two slender glasses and poured in the dark, steaming, oddly thick liquid. He held them out in shaking hands.

"I'll do it," Richard said to his wife. "Only one of us has to."

The old man seemed to understand, for he clucked his tongue.

"He says we both have to," Clare said. "That is what was foretold, and that is what has been prepared. Both or neither. That we came here seeking the answer, and this is the answer. Will we take it?"

It was dark now, and the temperature was dropping rapidly. Gabriel stood staring at the hut and the man who guarded the doorway. It seemed to Gabriel that he could feel each second ticking by. He had no idea what was happening on Loris, or to Emma in the world of the dead. But if the couple did not emerge soon, he would force his way in.

Then Gabriel noticed a strange thing. Villagers—men, women, and children—were moving up the path toward the top of the mountain. They moved in ones and twos, sometimes whole families. They were going into what looked like a temple of some kind that had been carved into the stone at the mountain's peak, some fifty or so feet above the rest of the village. They were all carrying bundles. Two young boys herded a dozen bleating goats up the path, disappearing as well into the mouth of the temple.

In less time than Gabriel would have guessed possible, the village was empty and silent. It was just him and the tall guard. Then the blanket over the door moved, and the old man emerged.

He looked at Gabriel and said, in English, "You must protect them till they return. All depends on that."

Then the bearded man took the old man's arm, and they headed up the path. Gabriel's pack, knife, and sword had been left on the ground.

Gabriel immediately stepped into the small house, ducking for the low ceiling. He found the couple in the back room, stretched out on the floor, a pair of empty glasses on the ground beside them. Both were breathing, but their pulses were faint. He sniffed at one of the glasses but couldn't identify the smell.

He hurried out to see the old man and his companion entering the temple above.

"Wait!"

Gabriel raced up the hill. As he got close, he saw that the temple was just a columned façade that had been carved into the rock, giving way to a shallow cave. He stepped into the darkness. The cave was only ten feet deep. He was alone; there was no sign of the villagers, the goats, the old man.

They had moved on.

Gabriel stepped out into the chill night air, and as he did, a distant flickering caught his eye. From the steps of the temple, he could see past the rope bridge and across to the mountain they had climbed that afternoon. A line of torches, far down the mountain, was climbing slowly upward. He could not make out the figures, but on some deep, instinctual level, he knew who they were. And he understood the old man's parting words.

Their enemy had found them.

CHAPTER NINETEEN
The Prophecy Revealed

Peering over the side of the mountain, Gabriel saw what he was searching for—a small cave, thirty feet down the face—and he went back to the house and carried first the woman, then the man, up to the edge of the cliff. He tied a rope around each in turn and lowered them down. Then he fixed his rope to a large boulder and climbed down himself.

The cave was just deep enough that Richard and Clare would be invisible from above. The question was, if he himself were killed, would they be able to climb up without a rope? But to leave a rope in place would negate the whole point of their being hidden. He debated the point for a few seconds, then climbed up the cliff and took the rope from the boulder. He would have to make sure he survived.

Before hiding the children's parents, Gabriel had first assured himself that the grass bridge was the only way on or off the mountaintop, and indeed, there were only steep cliffs on all sides. The simplest thing would be to cut the bridge. But that would only strand him and the couple while doing nothing about the enemy, who would, sooner or later, find another way across.

In the end, he sawed through half of the grass cables that held the bridge in place, then hurried over to the other peak and along the path to take up a position that gave him a vantage point on the trail below. He counted twenty-eight torches, and thought he could see more figures that were not holding torches. Perhaps forty in all.

Gabriel had found a bow left behind in the village, as well as a dozen arrows, and he now identified two places higher up the path where he could retreat and continue firing. He settled in to wait, and as he did, he found himself remembering how, over the past decade, he had made yearly visits to whatever orphanage had then housed the children. The first time had been five years after the adventure in Cambridge Falls, and the orphanage was a grand old building on the banks of the Charles River in Boston. From across the street, he'd seen Emma, still an infant, being rocked in her sister's arms. By the second year, Emma had been staggering around with the drunken, fat-legged gait of a toddler. And so it had gone, year after year, orphanage after orphanage. He never stayed long; he was never seen. Over the course of a decade, those ten visits had added up to what? An hour? But however brief, they had given him strength for whatever missions and trials awaited him in the year ahead.

Richard and Clare had never had that. They had not seen their children once during all their years of captivity, and yet they were still willing to go to any length, to take any risk, to ensure their safety.

The old man's admonition to protect the couple had been unnecessary. Gabriel would protect them just as he would have their children.

He heard a shout from below, and a curse, and he looked and saw, in the midst of the group, a bald head rising above the rest, reflecting the glare of the torches.

He notched an arrow on his string and got ready.

Clare opened her eyes and was blinded. As she blinked, letting her eyes adjust, she heard what sounded like the flapping of a tent in the wind. She sensed Richard beside her.

When she could finally see, she caught her breath. She and Richard were on the rug-covered floor of an open-air tent, encamped beside a small oasis in a sea of endless white dunes. More tents dotted the sand. Cloaked figures moved about.

"Richard . . ."

"It's like he said." Her husband's voice was filled with awe. "We've gone back in time. We're in the Sahara. Back when the tribe were desert nomads. But I don't think we're really here. I think this might be a memory—"

He cut himself off. A few feet away, a man was sitting with his eyes closed. He had white hair and a white beard and a face made up almost entirely of wrinkles. He was so quiet and still that he seemed a part of the landscape.

"You think he can hear us?" Richard said.

"No. It's like we're ghosts." Clare knelt before him. "I wonder if he's—"

The old man's eyes snapped open, and Clare fell backward in alarm.

"Clare—"

"I'm fine. But look—"

The old man's eyes were all pupil, but then, slowly, they changed, the pupils shrinking, the whites and irises appearing.

Clare now turned to follow the old man's gaze. A tall figure in a dark cloak and hood was approaching the tent. Clare and Richard both moved back and waited.

The hooded figure entered and sat down before the old man.

"You've come," the old man said.

It was only later that the couple would wonder how it was that although the two men had not been speaking English, or any language Richard and Clare recognized, they had understood every word.

The hooded figure said, "You know why I am here?"

"Yes. But you must say it."

"I wish to know about the Books. Who will find them? When will they be found?"

"I must see your face."

The visitor pushed back his hood. He was a man in middle age with close-cropped dark hair and severe features. But Clare found herself staring at his eyes, which were the most startling emerald green she had ever seen.

With his twelve arrows, Gabriel managed to down eleven Imps and Screechers. His first arrow had been for the bald giant, but somehow—could his hearing be so sharp?—Rourke had dodged out of the way. Gabriel didn't waste any more time on Rourke, but with a new arrow on his string every second, he drew and released, drew and released, while on the slope below, Rourke cursed and struck at the Imps and *morum cadi* and struggled to maintain order.

After firing his last arrow, Gabriel didn't wait to see what would happen next. The trail his attackers were on skirted the edge of the cliff till it reached the bridge and for nearly sixty yards was no more than two feet wide, with a plunge of a thousand feet on one side and a steep rocky slope on the other. Gabriel planted himself in the middle of the trail, drew his sword, and waited.

A Screecher was the first to appear; Gabriel saw its yellow eyes glowing in the darkness, and the creature ripped forth one of its awful cries and charged. Gabriel had chosen a spot where the ground gave way, a fact he hid with his body. He stood utterly still, and when the *morum cadi* was a yard or so from him, he leapt backward, and the Screecher, rushing forward, lost its footing and, with a kick from Gabriel, tumbled off the cliff.

His next attacker was hard on the heels of the first, the next right behind him, with yet another following. Gabriel fought with every ounce of skill and strength and cunning he had, blocking, striking, thrusting, kicking, punching, shoving, cutting down some of his attackers while doing his best to hurl others off the cliff, and all the while he was being pushed backward step by step. Several times, his enemies tried to rush him, but they got jammed up on the path, with one invariably grabbing at another and sending both into the void.

By the time he'd reached the grass bridge, he'd cut their numbers by another thirteen. Then a crossbow bolt whizzed out of the darkness and buried itself in his left shoulder, the same shoulder that had been wounded by the Imp the night before. The impact jerked him back, and a moment later, pain exploded across his chest and neck. He yanked the bolt out and jammed it into the eye of an Imp that was rushing forward—then, seeing Rourke's bald head round the edge of the path, and feeling the throb of the poison in his shoulder, he turned and ran.

When he reached the far side of the bridge, he looked and saw only six—four Screechers and two Imps—rushing across. Rourke had held the others back.

An Imp was nearly to him when Gabriel cut the bridge. The creatures tumbled into space, a few clinging to the bridge till it whiplashed down and struck the side of the mountain. He heard Rourke's laughter from across the chasm.

"Well played, lad! Though seems to me you've treed yourself! How are you expecting to shimmy down from there? Never you fret. We'll be over soon enough!"

But Gabriel had already turned away to begin planning the next stage of the fight.

"That cannot be."

The old seer opened his hands. "It is as it will be. Three children will come. They will find the Books. They are the Keepers."

"And then what?" the green-eyed man sneered. "Speak! What happens when they find the Books?"

The old man closed his eyes again, shaking his head. "The path from there is not yet determined. If the Keepers bring the Books together and no more, then they and the Books will be destroyed."

"But there is another path," the man said, leaning forward. "A way the Books will not be destroyed. The power cannot be lost! What is the other way?"

After a moment, the old man nodded. "I see two paths. In one, the Keepers bring the Books together, and they and the Books are destroyed. In the other, the three become one."

"What do you mean? Three become one?"

"Three Books into one Book. Three Keepers into one Keeper. If this happens, the Final Bonding will occur."

The green-eyed man was silent, his head bowed. Then he looked up and smiled. "Another Keeper. That is what you are saying. A Final Keeper for the Final Bonding. One who can control the power of the Books." He reached into his cloak. "Thank you, old man."

Clare saw the knife and screamed, but only Richard heard her.

They used crossbow bolts, the ends of which were tied with light, strong ropes, and they fired them across the chasm so that the bolts buried themselves in the dirt and rock on the other side. Gabriel tried to leap out and cut the ropes, but Rourke was ready, and more bolts and arrows drove him back.

At that point, there was nothing he could do but wait.

Finally, when there were more than a dozen of the narrow ropes suspended across the chasm, one of the *morum cadi* took hold of the bundle of cables and scuttled across upside down. Once on Gabriel's side, the creature secured the ropes around one of the posts that had held the bridge. At that point, only Rourke and five others, three Screechers and two Imps, remained, but Gabriel's left arm was nearly useless, and he could feel the poison spreading through his body. He knew that if he didn't treat the wound properly, and soon, the poison would find his heart.

Gabriel got lucky when one of the Screechers simply fell off the improvised rope bridge. That left four. Rourke himself started across last of all, the posts on either side bowing under his weight. There was still one Imp on the ropes, but two Screechers and another Imp were already on his side, and Gabriel rushed down upon them, howling. The ground where they fought was rocky and sloped, and Gabriel cut down all three, but the last Imp, leaping off the ropes, slashed him viciously down his back before Gabriel kicked him in the chest and sent him over the cliff.

Gabriel was gasping with pain and using his sword as a cane to steady himself.

"Ah now, lad, I do hate to see you in this sad state."

Gabriel turned to see Rourke stepping over the smoking body of one of the Screechers as he pulled out his long twin knives.

"But you must've always known it would come to this."

Gabriel looked at him for a long moment, then straightened, ignoring the pain in his shoulder and back, and said, "Are we going to talk or fight?"

"Clare—"

She had fallen to her knees beside the old prophet, who was bleeding out on the rugs.

"That can't be all!" she cried. "There has to be something else! Some way to save them!"

Figures had come running when the seer had cried out, but the green-eyed man had already vanished. Three men had laid the old man down, and one was pressing a bundled scarf onto his wound. The old man grabbed at the man, and Richard heard the prophet ordering the man to take their people away, warning that the green-eyed sorcerer would return. They had to run, and keep running.

Then the old seer reached out and grabbed a handful of sand, brought it to his lips and seemed to breathe into it, whispering. He held out his hand.

"They will come. The parents of the Keepers. One day they will come. Give them this. Keep it safe."

He opened his hand, and Richard saw the milky white cube fall into the hand of the other man. The scene before him began to dim.

"Clare—"

But she was leaning toward the dying prophet, sobbing.

"Tell me! Tell me how to save the children!"

Then the old man said, his voice failing, "He did not let me speak the end. . . ."

"Tell us! We're here! Tell us!"

"After the Final Bonding . . ." The man's voice dropped below a whisper, and Richard saw his wife place her ear next to the man's lips, straining to catch the words, her tears falling unfelt upon the old man's face. Then Clare wrenched back, shouting, "No!" and the world vanished before them.

"This is so disappointing."

They were battling along the edge of the cliff. Gabriel was fighting one-handed, and, whether out of sportsmanship or contempt, Rourke was doing the same. Gabriel had attacked with all his remaining strength, but it did no good. He remembered their fight in the fortress and, before that, in the volcano in Antarctica. Somehow, the giant Irishman was stronger and faster than ever, as he blocked or dodged every one of Gabriel's blows with ease.

Gabriel swung his sword in an arc, but Rourke ducked and punched him in his wounded shoulder with the butt of his knife, causing Gabriel to cry out.

"Come now, lad. I scarcely touched you. Don't be going soft on me."

Gabriel lunged again, and Rourke again slipped inside and this time thudded an elbow into Gabriel's face. Gabriel went blind for a moment and stumbled backward over the rocks. He knew that the edge of the cliff was near, but he caught himself in time, even as he felt the emptiness only feet away.

Rourke was walking slowly forward.

"So where are the kiddies' parents? I don't imagine they'll be too hard to flush out. There can't be too many places to hide around here."

Gabriel attacked again, and this time, when Rourke slipped inside his intentionally clumsy attack, Gabriel was ready and ran his shoulder into the man's stomach. Rourke let out a grunt and grabbed Gabriel by the hair and smashed his head against a boulder before tossing him away as one might a cat.

"You know all this is pointless, yes? The children are doomed. It's fate. Stronger than any of us."

Gabriel glanced toward the edge of the cliff. He needed to lure the man closer.

Rourke feinted, feinted again, and then struck with his knife. Gabriel felt the tip slide across his chest and stomach. He staggered back, his hand going to his sliced-open stomach, as if to hold himself together.

But he saw that he was, finally, at the lip of the cliff. He raised his sword feebly, but Rourke struck it away, and the sword went spinning out of his hand into the void. Rourke thrust again, and Gabriel twisted so that the blade only went through his side instead of killing him.

He dropped to his knees. Rourke was above him.

"Your whole life, lad, and it's all been for naught. Just a grand waste."

Gabriel felt himself seized by the neck and lifted so that his feet came off the ground. He was staring into the black pits of Rourke's eyes. Was he right? If Gabriel died now, if the children died, had it all been for nothing?

"Time's up, lad." Rourke drew back his knife.

"You are wrong," Gabriel said, his voice choking under the man's grip.

"What's that?" Rourke asked, pausing. "You say something?"

Gabriel knew there was no way he could make the man understand, even though, in that moment, it was so clear to him that to love someone, and to live your life guided by that love, could never be a waste. Indeed, it was the only life there was.

"Are you smiling? Have you gone daft on me, lad?"

Gabriel repeated, "You are wrong."

Rourke snarled, and his knife drew back again. Then Gabriel thought of his sword, of Granny Peet's gift, and it was not at the bottom of the cliff, but in his hand, warm and solid, and with one thrust he drove the blade through the giant man's chest. It seemed to take Rourke a moment to understand what had happened. Then, almost carefully, he set Gabriel back down on the ground. The stunned expression never left his face, and Gabriel watched the man's eyes as the light went out of them.

"Well now . . . ," Rourke said.

He pitched forward and lay still. With difficulty, Gabriel turned him over, then drew his sword from the man's chest and used it to walk to the top of the hill. He passed out once on the way, but he got to the place where he'd hidden the rope, secured it again to the boulder, then threw the coil over the cliff so that the rope dangled over the mouth of the cave.

He called down, "It is I."

A moment later, the silhouette of Richard's head appeared in the darkness below.

"Thank goodness." The man's voice sounded very small in the empty air. "We didn't want to shout. We only just came to. What happened?"

"Rourke found us."

"Rourke—"

"He is dead. Did you learn the rest of the prophecy?"

"Yes. I mean—I think so. Clare heard it. She . . . hasn't been able to tell me yet."

And Gabriel heard the sound of sobs coming from deeper inside the cave.

"Listen," Richard said. "We'd better come up. Then we can talk about it."

Gabriel sat down at the edge of the cliff to wait. There were bandages and herbs in his pack, but he had no energy or strength to go and get them. He would wait for the couple. He found himself thinking about Emma. For fifteen years, he had traveled the world, and she had been with him every step of the way. Just as she was with him now. He saw the rope go taut, and he heard the scrape of the couple's feet on rock as they began to ascend. Then he looked up at the stars and thought that his heart had never felt so full.

CHAPTER TWENTY
The Prison

Emma tried to keep up, but, her legs being by far the shortest, she invariably fell behind; then there'd be a hard yank on the cord binding her wrists, curses, perhaps a kick, and she'd be dragged forward. She tried whispering to her fellow captives (three men and a woman) to find out where they were being taken, but they only stared at her with the blank expressions of the dead and said nothing.

She told herself she just had to get free, get the book, find the portal back to the world of the living, and then it would all be okay. That was it; she could do it!

But even if she did all that—which, she knew, was a pretty big *if*—the thought of touching the book, of letting all those voices back into her head, filled her with a terrible, throat-clenching panic.

And the book had spoken to her. *Release them*, it had said.

Release who? Did it mean the voices? She'd be happy to. But how? And release them where?

She sucked on her lip, swollen where the man had hit her, and for the hundredth time she wished that Gabriel was there. She'd like to see what he'd do to that guy who'd hit her. He'd kill him— that's what he'd do! Or kill him again, since technically, the guy was already dead. But if he and the fat one were dead—which they had to be, didn't they, if they were down here?—how come they weren't all zombied out like the other dead people?

The small train stopped once so the guards could fill their canteens in a stream, and Emma approached the fat one, the one who had the *Reckoning* jammed into the top of his pants.

"Hey," she said. "What's your name?"

Her thinking was that she would act nice, like she wasn't angry at being made a prisoner, and somehow convince him to return the book. At least then she would have it when she escaped. But on being asked his name, the man simply stared at her, his expression empty, and Emma had the sudden realization that he no more knew his name than did anyone else in the world of the dead, that the two guards might talk and act like living people, but scratch the surface, and it was just that—an act.

As she and the others were pulled onward, Emma's mind continued to spin. If the guards were the same as the rest of the dead, then who or what was controlling them? Was it the Dire Magnus? Neither guard had mentioned him. They also hadn't given any sign that they knew who Emma was. She told herself that as long as she could keep it that way, she had a chance.

Time passed. They trudged on. Then at one point, Emma looked up and gasped.

Their group had come over the ridge she'd seen when she'd climbed the cliff with the *carriadin*, and they were heading down to a wide plain that stretched away to more mountains or hills in the distance. There was not a tree or blade of grass in sight. A stinking gray-green river, thick with sludge, slithered across the plain. Trash littered the landscape. But what drew Emma's attention, and what had caused her to gasp, was a vast shantytown directly ahead of them that was clustered around an enormous circular structure, from the center of which a tower of black smoke—the tower of smoke she had seen from the cliff—rose into the sky.

Emma had no doubt that was their destination.

Soon enough, Emma and the other prisoners were being pulled along the dark, mud-slick passages that twisted between the shacks. The shacks were made from sticks and dried mud, and Emma could see through gaps in the walls to the people moving about inside. As their captors dragged them deeper into the maze, the sky was blotted out by overhanging roofs, and Emma kept close to the back of the woman before her, certain that if she fell she would be dragged by her wrists through the filth. Several times Emma saw what she took to be scrawny gray cats, but when she looked closer, she saw they were rats, giant ones, with long, curving claws and needle-like fangs, and the creatures hissed and spat whenever a person came too near.

Then Emma and the others were yanked to a halt. The sky was still blocked by the ramshackle roofs of the shantytown, but they had come to a sort of indoor arcade or forum. Grim-faced men were moving about, leading bound-together groups of men and women. Half a dozen or so wooden tables had been placed in a line, and at each table sat a man with a notepad and pencil.

Emma's tall captor, the one who'd struck her and stolen Michael's knife, moved off without a word while the one with the hairy stomach—Emma could see the top of the *Reckoning* sticking from the waistband of his pants; she would need to give it a good scrubbing when she got it back—led her and the others to a table where a bald man sat squinting at his notepad and writing.

"You're late," the man said. "How many is that?"

"Five."

"Your quota's ten."

"You try finding that many! Lands are empty. Miles and miles, there ain't a soul. We're gonna run out of the dead soon."

"Ha! He'll just make more then, won't he?"

The bald man looked up, and Emma felt his eyes go over her, with no feeling, before returning to his notepad. She'd worried that someone more in charge would identify her, but apparently she was safe. And as she was thinking this, she glanced over and saw a red-robed figure approaching. It was the same rat-faced man from the beach the day before, and she quickly dropped her head and turned away. As she did, the name that had eluded her, the name Rourke had used for the wizards who served the Dire Magnus, came to her—the *necromati*.

"Hurry up," snapped the rat-faced man. "The master is impatient."

"Yes, sir," the bald man replied. "Going fast as we can."

Emma didn't look up till the red-robed figure had moved off.

"Place is busy," her fat captor said.

"Been working nonstop for days. And all the ones we're still holding are to go tonight. Something big is happening up above.

What's that, then?" The bald man aimed his pencil at the top of the *Reckoning* protruding from the other's pants.

"Just a book. Took it from the girl."

"Give it here."

"It's mine, though."

"Not anymore. Not unless you want me to put down you didn't make quota."

Emma's captor grumbled but pulled the book from his pants. Emma acted without thinking, the brush with the *necromati* having made her panicked and desperate, and reached for the book as the man held it out. For one brief moment, she and the man were both holding it. Even if she'd managed to wrench it away, she had no plan for what to do next, and in any case it didn't matter. The moment her hand touched the book, she felt the magic stir.

And the rest of the world fell away.

In her mind Emma saw an image of an old woman with thick gray hair, sun-spotted skin, and watery blue eyes; her name was Nanny Marge, and she held Emma's hand in her large, soft one, only it was not Emma's hand being held, it was the fat guard's hand, his hand when he'd been a child; and Emma experienced a sudden overpowering love for the old woman; it filled her up—

"Off!"

Emma was shoved hard in the shoulder, lost her grip on the book, and tumbled to the ground. The bald man was standing at the table, red-faced with anger. He seized the book from the dazed guard and jammed it in the pocket of his coat.

"Lock 'em up. Now! And watch that one!" He pointed at Emma.

The guard—with a shock, Emma realized that she now knew his name: it was Harold Barnes; though that was all she knew, that and his love for the old woman—came out of his stupor and pulled Emma to her feet. Emma tried to catch his eye, but the man wouldn't look at her. Dragging on the cord that bound Emma and the others, he led them past the man at the desk and into a dark passageway. Emma stumbled along, trying to make sense of what had just happened. Ever since passing out in Willy's room, back in the land of the giants, she'd known that some of the *Reckoning*'s magic was within her. But this was new. And why had the book shown her that old woman? What did it mean?

Then they came out of the tunnel, and every other thought was driven from her mind.

Traveling through the maze of the shantytown, Emma had lost all sense of direction and progress, and so it was a shock to find herself in the middle of the enormous circular structure she'd seen from across the plain. The thing had an arena-like quality, with its large, open central space. But this was not a place for spectators, at least not willing ones, for the circular building—now that Emma was close to it—revealed itself to be made of hundreds of wooden cages, each the size of a boxcar and stacked on top of one another. And in the cages, Emma could see people.

It was a prison for the dead.

And that wasn't all. For in the center of the open area, not far from where Emma and the others had emerged from the tunnel, was a pit, perhaps fifty feet across and twenty feet deep. There was no fire that Emma could see, but black smoke rose up from the pit as if the bottom was covered in smoldering ash.

Why were the dead being held captive? What happened here? What did the Dire Magnus's minions do to them? The bald man who'd taken the book had said they were all to go tonight, but go where?

She remembered Dr. Pym saying that there was some evil in this land, and she felt as if she'd penetrated to the heart of that evil only to find that she understood even less than before. And did she want to understand? Emma had never been anywhere that felt so utterly hopeless and foul. She wanted just to get the *Reckoning* and escape.

A lattice of scaffolding connected the cages, and with shouts, kicks, and shoves, Harold Barnes drove Emma and the others up a ladder to a cage on the second level. There was a crude metal lock he had to work at for several moments, then there was a *clank* and he jerked open the door, cut the cords that bound their wrists, and pushed them inside. Emma landed hard on her knees and heard the door slam shut.

"Wait!" Emma turned and threw herself against the door. "You saw her! Nanny Marge! You saw her!"

The man stopped on the ladder and looked back, and for one instant his face changed. Quite simply, it came alive. And Emma saw the change and knew for certain then that he'd seen what she had, and what was more, he still remembered.

There was a shout, someone from below calling the man.

"No!" Emma cried. "Don't—"

But Harold Barnes had already hurriedly climbed back down.

Emma stood there, gripping the bars. Okay, she thought, think for a second. When she and Harold Barnes had touched the book at the same time, the magic had opened a window into his life. Then, somehow, either she or the book had given him back his memory; he knew who he was!

Great. And that helped her how, exactly? She was still a prisoner; she still didn't have the book; she still didn't know how to get back to the world of the living.

One thing at a time. She just needed a plan. Emma knew that planning wasn't really her strength, but Michael was always coming up with plans; how hard could it be?

Night was beginning to settle in, but Emma could see that there were maybe twenty people in the cage, including the four she'd arrived with. They were men and women, both young and old, though she, it seemed, was the youngest. Most of the other prisoners were sitting on the floor with their backs against the wooden bars. All of them had the vacant expressions of the dead.

As to the cage itself, the floor and ceiling were solid, but Emma could see through the bars into the open arena and smoking pit in one direction, and in the other, out over the roofs of the shantytown to the plain and mountains in the distance. She could also see into the cages on either side. One was filled with people, while the other appeared to be empty, save for a pile of dirty rags in a corner. Emma walked to that wall and sat down with her back against the bars.

How she wished she had someone to help her! Or just to talk to! Kate, Michael, Gabriel, even Dr. Pym! He should be here helping her instead of running a water taxi for dead people! And it was pointless trying to engage the dead trapped with her. As it was, just being around them depressed her.

If only Gabriel were here! Her mind kept coming back to that one thought. She knew that only the Keeper of the *Reckoning* could pass into the world of the dead, but such was her faith in him, and in his love for her, that some small part of her still clung to the hope that he might somehow find a way.

Stop it, she told herself. It's just you, and you need a plan.

Then a voice behind her, from the cage she'd thought was empty, spoke:

"I wondered how long it would take them to find you."

Emma leapt up and whirled about, staring into the shadows of the other cage. The pile of rags was starting to move, and she watched as the thing dragged itself into the light, revealing twisted and mangled bones, sagging, mottled skin, black nails, and, finally, a pair of blinking, bloodshot, violet eyes.

"But where's the book?" the Countess sneered. "You found it, didn't you? When I first came here, the first time I died, I tried to force the *carriadin* to give it back to me. But they refused! 'Only the Keeper! Only the Keeper!' So where is it, child?"

Emma clung to the bars of the cage. She felt as if she might pass out.

She heard herself answering, "They . . . took it. The men who brought me here."

Emma couldn't stop staring at the Countess's broken body. Was she that way because Willy had stomped on her? It crossed Emma's mind to wonder how someone could look like that and be alive, but then she remembered that the Countess wasn't alive.

"You lost it!" The woman grabbed the bars of her cage as if she intended to rip them free. "You can't have lost it!"

"I couldn't help it! They—"

Emma stopped herself. The witch's head had dropped, her

shoulders were shaking, and she was making little whimpering sounds. She was crying.

"Hey," Emma said quietly, squatting down, "are you all right?"

The Countess looked up; tears streamed down the thick grooves of her face. "Do you have any conception of what I have been through? I died more than two thousand years ago. The dead do not feel the passage of time; I do. I felt every day as I waited for your brother to restore me to life. But I never gave up hope.

"Even forty years ago, when the Dire Magnus himself came to this world and began all this"—she waved her gnarled hand to indicate the prison, the shantytown—"I did not doubt but that I would one day succeed. And then I did. I came back—"

"And Willy squashed you like a bug."

The Countess's already twisted face contorted even more. "Yes. And I was returned to this hell as the warped creature you see. Captured instantly by the Dire Magnus's minions and brought here. But still I clung to hope. Of what? That you would come and retrieve the book. That if nothing else, even if I spent the rest of time trapped in this wretched place, in this wretched body, that you would carry out my revenge and destroy the Dire Magnus. But you lost the book! You failed! Utterly and totally. So no, I am not all right!" And she spat, disgusted, on the floor of her cage.

Emma said nothing for a moment. She had no idea what waiting for something for two thousand years and not getting it might feel like, but she guessed it would feel pretty bad. And after giving the Countess's words the amount of silent consideration they seemed to deserve—Emma accorded them three seconds—she said:

"So how do you remember me? Even Dr. Pym couldn't remember me. How is it you can?"

The Countess stared at her. She seemed exhausted by her tirade and to be debating whether to answer Emma's question or simply retreat to her corner. Finally, she said, "I once wielded the *Reckoning*, girl. Not for long, I grant you, but it left its mark. Death could not touch my memories. Now, leave me alone."

She started to crawl away.

"Hey! Wait!"

"It is over." The witch sounded merely tired now, not even angry. "You've lost your only chance. Our only chance."

"Wait! I don't understand any of this! Just tell me, I get why you can remember me. But those creeps who brought me here. They're not like other dead people either." Emma wasn't quite sure why she was pursuing this point, but she sensed it was important. It was related somehow to the *Reckoning;* and the Countess knew the answer. "They talk and act almost like real people. Evil people, yeah, but—"

"Shut up! Just stop talking!" The Countess shook her head, but it was more in resignation than anything else. "They are but tools of the Dire Magnus. They remember no more of their lives than these fools." She jerked her chin toward the men and women in Emma's cell. "But his power here is very great. He finds weak spirits and forces them to do his bidding. He winds them up like dolls and sets them into motion. The men who brought you here, they may have given a semblance of intention, but they are empty inside."

Emma thought of Harold Barnes and the tall man who'd

captured her, of the bald man at the desk, how they moved with more purpose than the rest of the dead, but there was still a vagueness in their eyes. Everything the Countess said matched Emma's own observations.

Only Harold Barnes had been different after she'd given him the memory of his Nanny Marge; she'd seen it in his face.

"What about those wizard guys in the red robes?"

"The *necromati?*"

"Yeah, I know what they're called," Emma said testily, wishing she had said the name, since she had actually remembered it. "What about them?"

"Their master shares with them some of his power. But in the end, they are no different from the others. Since the beginning of time, only two have ever come to the world of the dead and managed to keep their memories. Myself and the Dire Magnus."

And me too, Emma thought, though she didn't say it.

"So what is this place? Why're all these people locked up? You've gotta tell me that!"

The Countess looked at Emma, and a leering, wolfish grin spread across her face. "Yes, child, I will tell you that." She edged closer to the bars. "You've stumbled onto the Dire Magnus's great secret. The source of his newfound power. And he is stronger now, is he not? In the world above?"

"Yeah. Rourke said this whole war was something he never could've done before."

"And did Pym ever tell you how the Dark One lived as long as he did?"

Emma knew that he had, in the elfish forest at the bottom of the world, after she and Michael had escaped from the volcano.

But Emma had hardly listened; Kate had just returned from the past and died, Gabriel had been hurt, and, well, who could really pay attention to everything the wizard said anyway?

"You don't remember, do you? What a waste. I actually feel bad for Pym, having to deal with such a blockhead."

Emma started to say something along the lines of how funny it had been to watch Willy stomp the Countess like she was an ant, but in an act of self-control that would've surprised anyone who had ever met her, she kept her mouth shut.

"You see," the Countess said, "the universe has been—"

"Blown up and put back together over and over," Emma said. "I remember that part."

"Aren't you a bright penny! Well, long ago, the Dire Magnus reached into those previous versions of the universe and pulled out nine different incarnations of his spirit, his essence, his soul, whatever word you like. And he spread them out across time so that he would be reborn again and again."

"He can do that?" Emma said.

"He has done it, child! Is that not proof enough?"

Emma acknowledged that this was a fair point.

"But the question"—the Countess brought her sagging lips even closer—"is what happens at that moment when one Dire Magnus dies and the next is born?"

"Do you want me to guess?" Emma asked. "'Cause Dr. Pym always asks questions like that but then just answers them himself."

The witch looked annoyed. "A transference. The spirit of the dying Dire Magnus is grafted onto the spirit of the new, along with all the old one's memories and powers. You've met your enemy, have you not? And he seemed to be one being? One person? The truth is that inside him were the spirits of each previous incarnation quilted together into a patchwork soul."

Emma thought about Rafe, the boy Kate had known in the past, who had saved her life and in so doing become the Dire Magnus. According to the Countess, the spirits and memories of each Dire Magnus had basically latched on to his own. No wonder Kate believed Rafe was still alive in there. Maybe he actually was.

The Countess went on, "And one's spirit—pay attention now—is the seat of magic in all of us; its very substance is magic, and so each time he's taken on a new spirit, his own store of magic, his power, has grown."

Emma shook her head. "That doesn't explain how he's so much stronger now. He would've been just as powerful a hundred years ago or whatever. And Dr. Pym—"

"I'm coming to that. So forty years ago, Pym and his companions bested him. Killed him. They thought their battle won. But the Dire Magnus had prepared, burying his memories where death could not touch them. Like me, he intended to return to the living world. . . ."

There was a commotion in the arena; Emma stayed where she was, listening.

"Yet if he did return, he needed power. Power to wage war against the magical world, power to defeat Pym and his allies, power to finally seize control of the Books. Only, where to find it? Especially now that he was trapped in this wasteland? The answer was all around him.

"For it is not merely witches and wizards whose spirits are infused with magic; all beings claim this gift. And the Dark One reasoned that if his power had grown each time he'd taken on the spirit of his former self, then would it not also grow if he consumed the spirits of others? Say, a hundred others! Or a thousand! Or ten thousand! You see, in killing him, Pym sent his enemy to a world of spirits ready-made to be devoured."

"But"—Emma's voice was beginning to shake—"why did he have to wait till he was here? Why couldn't he just eat the spirits of people when they were alive?"

"Think, child: each time he consumed another spirit, it brought with it all the memories of that person's being. And on the scale he intended, he would have had thousands of memories swarming and shouting inside himself."

Emma remembered touching the *Reckoning* and the voices clamoring inside her. She said, "He would've gone crazy."

"Exactly. And in the world of the dead, the spirits have no memories. They are empty vessels."

Emma turned and looked at the listless figures in the cage. Did they know that they were basically food for the Dire Magnus? She hadn't been able to imagine a worse fate than having the memories of the people you'd loved taken from you, to be so awfully, terribly alone, and yet, here was such a fate.

"The fire serves as a portal," the witch said, "for him to call up the souls of the dead."

"Uh-huh." Emma was thinking of how, when Rourke had taken her to the Dire Magnus's tent, she'd seen the boy Rafe kneeling in the fire. She remembered thinking she saw shapes in the flames. Had those been the spirits of the dead?

"I think he made one of those portals for me too. When he tried to bond me with the *Reckoning*, he pulled my spirit out of my body and sent it through a fire. He sent it here."

"He collected the dead for years," the Countess went on, as if Emma had not spoken. "Housed them in this prison. And since he's returned to the world above, he's been using them to feed his power. Of course, soon he will have the Books. Power that dwarfs even this."

Emma was still trying to process all this when the shouts and curses from outside rose sharply. The Countess gave a ghastly smile.

"But see for yourself."

Emma rushed to the front of her cage and peered down. Six or seven guards—Emma looked, but did not see Harold Barnes—were using whips and sticks to herd fifty or so men, women, and children up to, and then over, the edge of the pit.

Then Emma saw three of the red-robed sorcerers, the *necromati*, emerge from a passage under the cells. One of them leaned on a gnarled wooden staff, and Emma felt a shiver of recognition as, in the dying light, she made out an all-white eye in the shadows of the man's face. The figures in the pit were just visible amid the clouds of black smoke, and Emma could hear them choking, see them struggling for air. And although Emma had expected more ceremony, the old white-eyed sorcerer simply gestured with his staff, and flames shot across the bottom of the pit and exploded upward. Emma raised an arm to protect her eyes, and when she looked again, the flames had already died, and there was only a great black cloud billowing into the air. The pit was empty.

"They're gone."

"Not gone," the witch said. "With him. As you will be soon."

"You're gonna tell them, aren't you? You're gonna tell them who I am."

The Countess smiled the same wolfish grin. "And why would

I do that? If I told the *necromati* who you were, they would take you across the plain to the portal to the world above and send you through to their master, carrying the book and yourself like an offering. I did not lie, the last thing I want is for the Dire Magnus to achieve his goal. In this, you and I are together. No, child, I will not tell."

Then she crawled back to the shadows on the far side of her cage and was quiet.

Emma stood there, very still, saying nothing. Something was happening in her mind. It took her a few moments to realize what it was, the experience was so novel, but finally she had to admit that it was a plan taking shape, the pieces slowly fitting together. It was a dangerous plan, incredibly so, and she clenched her fists and willed another, less risky plan to emerge. But there was no other; this was the only way, and if it succeeded, the Dire Magnus would not survive.

But probably, she thought, neither would she.

CHAPTER TWENTY-ONE
Judgment

The cage shook from the impact of footsteps on the ladder, and then the guard's head came into view. It was the tall one, the one who had hit Emma in the mouth and taken Michael's knife, which was there, still tucked in his belt.

Night had fallen, but Emma could see, thanks to the torches burning in the arena, the constant reddish glow from the pit and the dozens of small fires speckled across the dark expanse of the shantytown.

Since early that evening, the grim-faced men who served the Dire Magnus, directed by the *necromati*, had been removing cage after cage of prisoners, and forcing them, men, women, and children, into the pit. Emma had watched it all, horrified. For though she knew they were already dead, and though she had observed many times that existence in the world of the dead would be akin

306

to hell, it sickened her to know they were being consumed by the Dire Magnus.

Not to mention that each spirit that went into the pit made their enemy stronger, and she couldn't think of that without thinking of Kate and Michael and Gabriel in the world above, and what they might be facing.

"What is it?" the tall guard demanded of the Countess. She had been hurling down abuse and curses for several minutes. "Or do I have to shut you up?"

"You're a fool," the Countess hissed. She was on the floor of her cell, as her legs were unable to support her. "Don't you know who this child is?"

This was her cue, and Emma gripped the bars of her cage and shouted, "Shut up! Shut up!"

"She's the one your master is looking for, the living girl. The Keeper of the *Reckoning*. You locked her up with the others! You were going to feed her to the fire! What would your master have done then?"

"She's lying! She's a liar! Don't listen to her!"

The Countess ignored her. "She brought you the *Reckoning* itself and you didn't even realize! She said some fool of a clerk took it! She laughed about what idiots you all are! Ha!"

"Shut up!" Emma wailed. "Please! I—I'll— Just shut up! You promised!"

The tall man stepped across the scaffolding, reached between the bars, and seized Emma's arm. He pressed two fingers against the underside of her wrist. Emma struggled and made protesting noises, but there was no breaking his grip. It seemed she could feel her own pulse pounding against the man's fingertips. Then, still holding her, he took a key off his belt.

"The Dire Magnus must learn what I did!" the Countess shouted. "He must reward me! He must forgive me!"

Emma didn't look at the witch as the man pulled her from the cage and carried her down the ladder. She fought, punching, kicking, scratching, but soon they were on the floor of the arena, engulfed in a scene of chaos: shouts and cries of anger, smoke, heat, people being struck and driven about. Emma guessed there were maybe thirty guards, along with five of the red-robed *necromati*. She'd already spotted the rat-faced, black-haired man she'd seen earlier.

Emma looked but did not see Harold Barnes.

With his hand on her arm, the tall guard dragged her over to the pit, stopping a few feet from the edge. A single red-robed figure stood looking down into the smoke and flames. The tall guard said nothing, and after a moment, the figure turned, still leaning on his gnarled black stick. The old man's one gray eye studied her. But it was his blind white eye that unnerved Emma. She imagined it saw more clearly than the good one, as if it could see into her mind and heart, see her entire plan. Despite the heat from the fire, she shivered.

It will work, she told herself, it has to work.

If it didn't, she had just doomed herself, her brother and sister, everyone.

It had taken some time to coax the Countess out of her dark corner, but Emma had persisted, as there were things only the witch could tell her.

"I mean it—I have a plan!"

"Oh, you have a plan! Oh, we are saved!"

"Shut up! Do you want your stupid revenge or not?"

Finally, the witch had dragged herself back across her cage. "Well?"

"First, you gotta tell me, when I get the book, how do I kill someone? I know you know, you used it to kill all those giants."

The Countess had chuckled. "Yes, I slaughtered those fools. You should have felt the earth buckle when they fell! *Timmmberrr!* He-he-he."

"Yeah, yeah, so how'd you do it?"

"Do you know what a reckoning is, child? The meaning of the word?"

Emma had opened her mouth to reply—she knew this because Michael had told her—but the Countess was too quick.

"A reckoning is a debt. And there is one debt that every living being must eventually pay: death. When you engage the magic of the book and fix your mind upon a person, the *Reckoning* calls that debt due, and the person's spirit is severed from their body and brought to this world. Even the Dire Magnus is not exempt from this."

"What about the voices?"

"What voices?"

"You know, the ones that start screaming when you touch the book."

"I heard no voices."

Emma had studied the other's face. The woman had seemed to be telling the truth. Could it be that despite allowing the Countess to kill the giants, there were things the book revealed only to its Keeper?

Lucky her.

"What is it you intend, girl?"

Emma had hesitated for an instant, then reasoned that if the woman was going to betray her, she could've at any time. There was no point in holding back now.

"According to you, all I have to do to kill the Dire Magnus is call up the magic and think about him. Only first, I've got to get one of those *necromati* guys to give me the book. Well, I know how to do that!"

And she would just put up with the screaming voices. She had to; there was no other option.

The Countess had sneered. "You arrogant little fool. You cannot trick the *necromati* into simply giving you the book!"

"I'm not going to trick them. One of them's going to help me."

And then she'd told the witch about the old white-eyed sorcerer, and how he'd once been a friend and ally of Dr. Pym, and about Harold Barnes and what she'd done to him. Finally, the witch had started nodding, murmuring, "Yes, perhaps it could work. . . ." and had even suggested that *she* call for the jailers, saying it would be less suspicious than Emma calling them herself.

After hearing the guard's report, the old man spoke to the black-haired, rat-faced *necromatus*, who then scurried away across the arena. The white-eyed sorcerer stepped closer, the point of his staff stamping dully in the heat-cracked mud. Emma guessed he was taller than she was, but he was so stooped over, like someone who had spent his life hunched at a desk, that their eyes were level.

As she stood facing him, Emma was aware of another cage's

worth of people being herded toward the pit, and she glanced toward them without thinking. It was like being struck in the chest. One of the figures, his face blank and confused, was Wallace. Emma had met the dwarf just once, during the Christmas party at the mansion in Cambridge Falls—he'd been more Kate's and Michael's friend than hers—but he had given his life trying to rescue her, and now he was being pushed over the edge of the pit, and she could only watch, powerless.

She looked back at the old man and ordered herself not to be weak. The tall guard stood several feet to the side; Emma kept her voice low.

"I know who you are. You used to be Dr. Pym's friend. You helped him fight the Dire Magnus. You've got to remember!"

The old man stared at her, then said, "Your words mean nothing to me."

He waved his staff, and flames exploded from the pit. When Emma was able to look again, Wallace was gone. She felt sick to her stomach, and her plan suddenly seemed childish and flimsy.

It came down to this: Emma knew that when she and Harold Barnes had touched the *Reckoning* together, she'd restored at least some, and perhaps all, of his memories. That had started her thinking: All those voices shouting in the book, what if they were the memories that had been taken from the dead? And if she'd given Harold Barnes his memory back, couldn't she do it again? She just had to manage it so that she and the old sorcerer were both holding the *Reckoning* at the same time. Then she'd restore his memories, he'd realize who he was, and he'd help her kill the Dire Magnus.

The rat-faced *necromatus* was hurrying forward, clutching the book to his chest, the bald clerk trailing behind. There was no more time for doubt. Emma took a step closer to the sorcerer, to be next to him when he received the *Reckoning*.

Then the old man said, "Hold her."

A pair of large, strong hands seized her wrists, pinning them behind her back. Panic swept over her, and she screamed and struggled.

The old sorcerer ignored her and spoke to the *necromati* and guards gathered about. "After all these years, our master will finally possess the Books. But only beings of pure spirit can pass through the fire, and the Master wishes the book and Keeper complete. We will go to the last portal, the one in the mountains across the plain."

He began to give orders. They would leave immediately. The rat-faced *necromatus* would stay and finish herding the dead into the pit.

A voice whispered in Emma's ear, "You saw Nanny Marge?"

She jerked her head around. It was Harold Barnes who held her wrists. He was leaning close, and there was a desperate, searching look in his eyes.

"You really saw her? You saw my Nanny Marge?"

Recovering from her surprise, Emma nodded, and the man, without making a sound, bit his lip as tears welled in his eyes.

"Please," she whispered, "you have to let me go. Please."

And for a moment, it seemed that it was just her and Harold Barnes, alone in the arena. Then he nodded, and his hands opened.

The old man was still giving orders when Emma leapt forward

and grasped his hand, her fingers stretching to touch the hard leather of the book—

Instantly, the magic rose up, filling her, and she was overwhelmed with relief and gratitude—

Then the arena, the fire, the guards, the *necromati*—all fell away.

Emma saw a brilliant blue sea, felt salt air against her skin, and saw a man with a tanned face, thick hands, and a quick smile. She saw him in a boat, teaching a boy, teaching her, how to care for his nets. He was the sorcerer's father, a fisherman, and he was the boy's entire world. And the day he disappeared at sea, Emma felt the hole it left in the boy's life . . . and then she saw a young woman, with dark hair and dark eyes, and felt the old man's—the young man's—love for her . . . and then she saw another boy, the sorcerer's son, with hair like his mother's and his father's gray eyes, and Emma felt how the wound made by the death of his father had finally begun to heal—

Emma was knocked back by the rat-faced *necromatus*. She landed on her side, close to the edge of the pit. A stillness had descended on the arena. The old man's head had dropped forward. He sagged against his staff. Emma was scarcely breathing. She willed the old man to look up. One glance would tell her if he remembered who he was.

Seconds passed. Still, no one moved.

The thought came to her that touching the book, being in the old man's memories, hadn't been anything like how Michael described using the *Chronicle*, how he experienced a person's whole life in an instant. She'd only seen the people the old sorcerer had loved. The same thing that had happened with Harold Barnes.

What if the sorcerer only remembered those three people and not the rest of his life? Her plan was doomed to fail! How could she have been so stupid! Who was she to try and plan anything!

Then the old man raised his head, and everything inside Emma turned to ash. His face was just as blank as before.

He said, "Bring a table. We will perform the Bonding here."

Emma froze. What did that mean? Why would he say that? She lay there, tense, hoping, telling herself it was stupid to hope—

"But," the rat-faced man said, "the Master—"

"Has spoken to me," the old man said. "He needs her power. Once she is bonded to the *Reckoning,* we will throw her into the pit, and her spirit and the magic within it will be consumed by his. Her body will perish in the flames. Now, bring a table."

So she had failed after all. Emma knew she should jump up, snatch away the book, and try to use it before they stopped her. But she couldn't even summon the strength to rise from the ground, so crushing was the weight of her failure. And it would've been pointless anyway. Her enemies would've been on her in an instant.

The rat-faced man rushed off. Then hands, Harold Barnes's again, lifted her to her feet, and the old man, still holding the book, stepped closer. He made a gesture, and Harold Barnes moved away, eager, it seemed, to distance himself.

The sorcerer's face was in front of hers. When he spoke, it was in a whisper only she could hear:

"Child . . ."

And in that instant, Emma saw that he'd remembered who he was.

She was on the verge of letting out a cry of joy when the old man held up his hand, still whispering:

"Quiet. Others are watching. If they suspect what you have done, you are doomed."

Emma glanced past him at the three red-robed sorcerers standing nearby; they were indeed watching closely. With effort, she forced her face into an expression of defiance and struggled to speak through the emotion choking her throat and chest. "You— you really remember? That you're a friend of Dr. Pym and hate the Dire Magnus? He kept you like a slave, you know!"

The old man moved his body to shield her as much as possible and allowed himself a sad smile.

"I remember everything. Pym, our friendship, our fight against the Dark One, even my years being bent to the enemy's will. Though what I remember most is my father, my wife, my son."

And perhaps it was the mention of the old sorcerer's loved ones, the memory of whom was still so fresh in Emma's mind, but the tide of feeling inside her could no longer be denied. She had been scared and alone and exhausted for too long. She finally had an ally, someone to bear part of the burden. Her body began to shake with sobs.

She wiped at her tears, whispering, "I'm sorry, I'm sorry, I'll stop. It's just . . ."

"Have no fear, child. It is reasonable you might cry. The others will not perceive the true cause. But every moment now is crucial."

Emma took several deep, trembling breaths and gathered herself.

"Right . . . so give me the book, and I'll kill him!"

The old man gave a small shake of his head.

"The Dire Magnus is no mere man. If you attempt to kill him and fail, we are finished. You will have only one chance, and you must be able to command the full power of the *Reckoning*. That is why I have to complete the Bonding. The book will then acknowledge you as its Keeper."

"But the Countess killed a bunch of giants, and she wasn't bound to the book! Why do I have to be?!"

It surprised her that he actually intended to complete the Bonding, that it hadn't been simply a ploy to gain time. And it surprised her as well how much the idea scared her. Though the truth was, for days now, whenever she'd thought about the *Reckoning*, she'd felt a shiver of fear. In her typical fashion, she'd done her best to ignore it. But then she'd touched the book, heard all the voices trapped inside, and her fear had grown a hundredfold. What would it mean to be bound to such a thing? What might the book demand of her? Take from her? Emma didn't know, and she didn't want to know.

"The Bonding is necessary because there has never before been a creature like the Dire Magnus. He wears the spirits of his former selves like armor. The book's full force must be brought to bear. You must trust me!"

Emma knew that she had no choice. She gave him a short nod.

Abruptly, the old man leaned on his staff, tears welling in his eyes.

"Forgive me, child. It is the memories. You have given me back those I loved most in life, and I am undone." He reached out and laid a hand on her arm. "I am thankful you judged me worthy." He stopped, looking at her. "What is it?"

For the old man's words, seemingly innocent, had called back something the Countess had said after Emma had first explained her plan. The witch had asked if Emma knew there was a second meaning of the word *reckoning*.

"Yeah. It means a judgment."

"Exactly," the Countess had said, "and there is a legend, whispered through the centuries, that the Keeper of the *Reckoning* will judge the dead. But how? What if, as you seem to believe, some remnant of the dead is stored in the book—their voices, their memories—and it falls to you to separate the just from the unjust, the good from the evil? I do not say your plan will not succeed. But I suspect there is more to mastering the *Reckoning* than you imagine."

At the time, Emma had brushed aside the notion; she'd only been concerned with what could help her kill the Dire Magnus. What did she know, or care, about judging the dead? But the old man had thanked her for judging him worthy! Why? She hadn't done anything. At least, she didn't think so.

The old sorcerer had already moved on, his voice a dry whisper.

"Remember, child, all is lost if the others suspect I am with you. During the Bonding, I must be as brutal as the Dark One himself."

"But what did you mean about judging you worthy?"

His gray eye stared at her, searching. "Pym didn't tell you?"

"Tell me what? He didn't tell me anything!"

"Child"—he gripped her arm fiercely—"you must judge them! That is the task of the Keeper! The Bonding will unite you with the book, but to truly wield its power, you must judge them all! Pym should have told you!"

"But he didn't! What're you—"

That was as far as she got, for just then the rat-faced *necromatus* arrived carrying a short-legged table, and the old sorcerer forced her roughly to the ground.

The table was placed before her. The tall guard stepped behind her and gripped her shoulders. Things were moving fast now, too fast. What did he mean, she had to judge them? Judge who, the dead? How? And why hadn't Dr. Pym told her? Had he not known? Or had he planned to tell her but died before he'd gotten the chance?

The old sorcerer laid the *Reckoning* open on the table, and Emma stared down at the blank page and imagined she saw the words appearing, as they had back in the cave, *Release them*, and imagined too that she could hear the millions of clamoring voices.

You must judge them.

The old man held out his hand, and the tall guard passed him Michael's knife.

"Wait," Emma said, alarmed now. "What're you doing with that?"

"The actual Bonding is simple," the sorcerer said. "Though painful. We must ensure your hand stays on the page."

He gestured, and the tall guard grabbed Emma's wrist and held her hand poised over the book. The old sorcerer gave the knife to the rat-faced *necromatus*, who took it, smiling, and stepped to the table.

"Wait!" The fear was rising fast inside her. "Just—just wait!" She looked at the old sorcerer, but his face was empty, a mask.

The rat-faced man raised the knife. "Yes," he sneered, "scream."

And before Emma could cry out, before she could utter a

word, the guard forced her palm onto the page, and the knife plunged down, through the back of her hand, and pinned it to the book.

Emma scarcely felt the knife going in. Partly, that was because of the sharpness of the blade. But more so, it was because the moment she touched the book, the magic surged through her, and millions of voices, millions of lives, threatened to tear her apart. Second by second, she could feel herself losing touch with who she was, as if she stood on a beach and the sand was disappearing beneath her feet, and there was nothing but emptiness below. . . .

Then, abruptly, she was back, on her knees in the dust of the arena. She had somehow managed to pull her hand off the page, though she'd done so only by sliding it farther up the blade of the knife. She could see the blood dripping down.

Then the rat-faced man struck the pommel of the knife with his fist, driving it deeper into the wood of the table so that the knife's metal guard pinned her hand to the page, and again she felt the magic rising up, and along with it the voices, overwhelming her, drowning her. She tried to push them back, to fight them, but it was too much. She could feel herself breaking apart—

Then—again—she was back, on her knees beside the pit. Acting on simple animal instinct, she'd managed to loosen the knife by jerking her arm back and forth, though doing so had made the gash in her hand even wider.

The rat-faced *necromatus* cursed and lunged forward.

In the moment before he reached her, Emma looked up, searching for the face of the old sorcerer—she didn't care who knew that he was helping her; she needed him to do something, say something to stop this—and she saw, stepping from one of the passageways with Dr. Pym at his side, Gabriel.

She had to be dreaming; it couldn't be Gabriel, the living couldn't enter the world of the dead! But it was him! Which could mean only one thing—that he had somehow found a way in! Wasn't this exactly what she'd hoped and prayed for since she'd arrived in this terrible place? He wasn't dead, she knew that; he couldn't be dead! Gabriel, her friend and protector, had found a way to enter the world of the dead so he could come to her when she needed him most, and seeing him—as the rat-faced man hammered the top of the knife, forcing her hand to the page—Emma's heart filled with love.

The magic rose up, the millions of voices and lives crashed over her, but she held on to her love for Gabriel the way a person falling from a ship might cling to driftwood; she held on to it knowing that she had to, that it was her only safety, and the wave passed and she was still there, still herself; and she found herself thinking of Kate, as if her love for Gabriel had led her naturally to it, and from there, she thought of Michael, and how much she loved him, loved everything about him, and the voices still howled, but the ground below her was solid now and secure, she could stand on it, she knew who she was, and the love she had for those three was the very basis and bedrock of her life.

She opened her eyes and saw the handle of the knife sticking out of the back of her hand, the dark red blood pooling over the page and running onto the table, and the pain didn't matter, and the thronging, shouting voices didn't touch her.

Gabriel and Dr. Pym were still standing at the mouth of the tunnel, not moving any closer. The old white-eyed sorcerer was leaning forward, watching her intently. She sensed motion above her and saw huge black birds landing around the arena.

She understood then why the book had shown her Nanny Marge; understood why it had shown her the old man's father and wife and son, and why both Harold Barnes and the old sorcerer had been judged worthy. She understood how she was to judge all the lives contained in the book.

It was a question she had to ask; she had only to shape it in her mind, and the fate of each life would ride on the answer.

And she thought again of the message the book had given her: *Release them.*

She looked at Gabriel, and he stood there, his eyes dull, not knowing her, and she knew the truth then, the truth she wanted so badly to push away; and she felt his love for her, for it was there in the book, among all those millions of other lives; and she felt how that love had been the cornerstone of his life, and more than anything, more even than killing the Dire Magnus, she wanted him to remember that.

Go, she thought, and the memory flowed out of the book and through her.

And she felt the storm of voices raging, stronger than ever, all clamoring, begging for release.

She heard the rat-faced man shouting:

"Something's happening. We must throw her in the pit! Now!"

The knife was yanked out, but she kept her hand pressed down flat and hard, the blood wet and thick between her hand and the page, and even as the tall guard reached down and seized her wrist, she formed the question in her mind, and somewhere deep inside the book, a key turned in a lock.

The memories poured forth, out of the book, out of her, and though it felt like an eternity, she knew it only took an instant, and then her hand fell away and she collapsed on the ground. She could hear screaming and shouting, the sounds of cages being broken open. She sensed the rat-faced *necromatus* dragging her toward the pit; then something knocked the man down. It was the old white-eyed sorcerer; he was wrestling with the man. She saw the other *necromati* fleeing as the dead broke free from their cages, and many of the guards were now joining the prisoners as the crowd flooded the arena; and Emma realized she was cradling the book in her good hand while the other throbbed and bled, and then Gabriel was there, lifting her into his arms, just as he had so many times before, and Emma wanted to tell him that it was love, that was the standard on which the dead were judged, that was the reckoning, but she didn't say it because she couldn't speak, because the truth she'd realized moments before was that Gabriel hadn't found some secret way into the world of the dead, there was only one way into the world of the dead, one way his memories could've gotten into the book, and she pressed her face against his chest and sobbed.

CHAPTER TWENTY-TWO
Michael's Army

Kate opened her eyes and sat up. Both proved to be mistakes. Pain shot through her skull, and she groaned.

"Easy now, girl. Easy."

She was back on her cot in the tent. It was dark outside, but a small lantern on the floor gave up a dim, yellow light. On Michael's cot, leaning forward and offering her something in his hand, was the burly form of Hugo Algernon.

"Drink this."

"What is it?"

"Whiskey."

"What—"

"Kidding. It's water. You've had fever. Drink."

She did; the water was cool and tasted marvelous.

"Those children on the beach . . ."

"Both fine." He chuckled. "More than you can say for that

Imp you skewered. That was a good one. Like something Clare would've done."

"Clare . . ."

"Your mother. She always had a spark in her."

Kate nodded, but wondered if he was just saying that to make her feel better. As it was, it did make her feel better.

"What about the others? In the attack?"

"All taken care of. There was only a single raider. How's your noodle?"

Kate felt the back of her head. It was still tender from where it had struck the rock, though she knew that wasn't why she'd passed out. "Fine."

"So," Hugo Algernon said, "how much have you told your brother about what's going on?"

Kate looked at him sharply. The lamp on the floor cast shadows across his face, and she couldn't see his eyes. How could he possibly know about Rafe appearing to her?

But he went on, and she realized what he actually meant:

"The boy knows you're having trouble controlling the Atlas. You said as much yourself. Have you told him the rest? What it feels like?"

Kate shrugged. "A little. He feels some of it too."

"But not like you do."

Kate shook her head.

Hugo Algernon grunted. "It'll get worse. For both of you."

"Why? What's happening?"

Kate hadn't forgotten what Rafe had told her in the land of the giants, his warning about the damage the Books were causing, but she found she needed to hear it from someone else.

Hugo Algernon pulled a small bottle from his pocket, un-corked it, and poured some into a cup. The biting, sour smell of spirits filled the tent. He took a sip and grimaced before speaking.

"There're things you need to know. You and your brother. I talked to von Klappen and she agrees."

Kate was surprised to hear him refer to the witch with such apparent lack of venom.

"Yes, yes, I know. She's an insufferable, humorless know-it-all, but she's good at what she does." Hugo Algernon leaned forward. "Did Pym ever caution you about not using the Books unless it was absolutely necessary?"

Kate nodded.

"Ever say why?"

"Not really."

"What do you know about quantum mechanics?"

"Nothing."

"Good. Load of rubbish."

"What's that got—"

"Not a thing. Don't interrupt. First off, you have to under-stand that when it's working right, the universe is this perfectly balanced mechanism. All the pieces fitting together just so. Only, it's fragile. And when Pym and his buddies pulled out the magic that went into the Books, they upset that balance. That's for start-ers." He leaned closer. "But this is where it becomes tricky. Because yes, the Dire Magnus is the enemy, no doubt about it. He gets hold of the Books, the *Reckoning* especially, he'll wreak havoc and probably destroy the entire world. So that's bad, and we should do something about it. But in the end, he's not the real threat."

"Who is?" Kate asked quietly.

Hugo Algernon looked at her. "You are, girl. Your family. See, the magic in the Books is still connected to the magic responsible for all this." He made a gesture to indicate the world outside the tent. "So every time you and your brother, and soon your sister, use the Books, things get more and more out of whack. The reason you passed out is that you're feeling how much harm you're causing. And it's getting worse. The universe is breaking apart at the seams."

"So we'll just stop using the Books!"

"Too late for that."

"But there has to be something we can do!"

He nodded. "There is. The Books have to be destroyed."

"And that would fix it?"

"Yes. The problem is that the Books themselves are pretty much indestructible. I mean, the *Chronicle* was in a pool of lava for a thousand years and it doesn't have a scratch on it."

"But there's a way around that, isn't there?" Kate's voice was no more than a whisper.

The man sat back, poured himself more whiskey, and took a sip. "Yeah. There's a way."

And now it was Kate talking, her mind rushing forward, as it all suddenly made sense, the tearing she'd felt every time she used the *Atlas*, both in the world and inside herself, the true meaning of the prophecy.

"If the magic were in something that could be destroyed—like in a person, like me, or Michael, or Emma—and we were to die, that would do it. That would fix things."

Hugo Algernon nodded. "The magic of the *Atlas* is already in you. If the *Chronicle*'s not inside your brother, it soon will be. And the same for the *Reckoning* once your sister gets it."

"And then we die, and the universe is fixed." Kate felt nauseous from the closed tent, the smell of the man's whiskey. She wanted to get away but she couldn't, not yet. "Then . . . why's the Dire Magnus even matter?"

"I told you, he'll try to control the power. Like turning a nuclear reactor into a nuclear bomb. And he'll be able to, for a while. Even if it means destroying this world to create another. So we have to stop the Dire Magnus. But we also have to destroy the Books."

"You mean you have to kill me and my brother and sister," Kate said coldly.

"I didn't say that. Von Klappen and Chu and I've been talking—"

"I need to find Michael."

And she rushed out of the tent, into the night air, and stopped. She heard Hugo Algernon come out behind her.

"Yeah, I was gonna tell you about that next."

The island was nearly empty. The campfires were out. The encampments, gone. The few soldiers who were still there were busy helping the refugee families load onto ships. And Kate realized that she'd been aware, the whole time she'd been talking to Hugo Algernon, of how quiet it had been outside the tent.

"What happened? Where is everyone?"

"We're moving the families. Just in case that scout ship reported our location to the enemy. But the army's gone to Loris. Left just before sunset."

"But they're outnumbered! It's suicide! Everyone said so."

"Well now." Hugo Algernon scratched his beard. "You've been unconscious a while. That attack sort of pulled everyone together. Made those nitwits remember who the real enemy was. And then King Robbie had this idea—for a dwarf, he's not completely thick—he appointed a new commander, one that was acceptable to all three races. It's mostly a ceremonial position, of course, but soon as word got out, new recruits started pouring in from around the world. Von Klappen and Chu and I must've had a dozen portals going nonstop. From noon to sunset the army doubled, then tripled in size. They've got a chance. Not a big one. But a chance."

Kate turned to face him. "Who's the new commander?"

Hugo Algernon grinned and actually looked sheepish. "Well, imagine there was a human who was also an honorary dwarf and who just so happened to be the boyfriend of an elf princess. If you can, try to see the humor in this. . . ."

Michael stood on the deck of the ship. There was no moon, which was a good thing, but the stars were clustered densely overhead. The air was warm and heavy with salt. He was wearing the chain mail tunic King Robbie had given him, which was remarkably light and supple, and he also had on dwarfish battle leathers, which were thicker and stiffer than he would have liked. A sword and a knife, both given to him by King Robbie, were strapped to his waist. He stared out at the fleet—his fleet—spread across the dark water.

(Michael knew it was silly to think of any of it—the ships, the soldiers—as *his*, that he was commander in name only, but he couldn't help himself.)

As all the ships were sailing at the same speed, they hardly seemed to be moving, but Michael could hear the sluicing of water across the hulls, the snapping of ropes, the creak and whine of wood.

All afternoon, as Kate had lain unconscious in their tent, watched over alternately by him or Hugo Algernon or Magda von Klappen or Wilamena—soldiers had arrived to swell their ranks. The first to arrive had been the fighters from Gabriel's village, two dozen stern-faced, dark-haired men whose presence in the camp had filled Michael with confidence. Then there were dwarves from Lapland, who came with icicles hanging from their beards and axes as long as they were tall; river elves from Thailand, who spoke a language that even the other elves couldn't understand; more elves from the mountains of Morocco, who dressed in long, colorful robes; human fighters from the Badlands. . . .

So many, Michael thought. But would it be enough?

Magda von Klappen stood on the foredeck conversing with Master Chu. She had already had the same conversation with Michael that Hugo Algernon had had with Kate.

"But we still have to deal with the Dire Magnus," Michael had said. "And we still have to rescue Emma."

"Yes. If he gains control of the *Reckoning*, we are all dead anyway."

"And if we beat him, then just me and my sisters have to die."

"We're working on that," the witch had said.

Even now, Michael marveled at his own calmness. It was as if he'd split himself in two. There was Michael Wibberly the head of the army, who knew that the only way of keeping the world safe was to defeat the Dire Magnus. Then there was Michael Wibberly the thirteen-year-old boy, who'd do anything to save his sisters and who felt death and disaster breathing down their necks.

His hand rested on the shape of the *Chronicle* in his bag, and he wondered how much of the magic was in him. How long did they have?

With effort, he pulled his mind back to the present.

He glanced up to the outline of Captain Anton in the crow's nest, the elf peering through the darkness for the first sight of Loris. All about Michael, men and dwarves were quietly checking their kits. He noted how, apart from the usual weapons and equipment, they had all been outfitted with an odd-looking metal apparatus fashioned by dwarf blacksmiths on the island. Michael had examined one of the objects, but could not figure out what it was or what it was intended to do. He'd asked King Robbie, who'd only smiled and said, "Let it be a surprise, lad. For you and for the enemy." Then he added, "Besides, it may not even work."

"Rabbit?"

Wilamena stepped toward him. She was wearing a dress the color of midnight and had a dagger at her waist attached to a silver belt; her hair, which shone faintly in the darkness, was in two thick braids down her back.

"What troubles you? Are you worried about Katherine? She will recover."

"No. I know."

"Then what is it?"

Michael thought of telling her what Magda von Klappen had told him about what the Books were doing to the world, about his and his sisters' deaths being the only way anyone knew of that would fix the damage. Did she already know? No, he decided, she would've said something. Or written a poem about it.

"Nothing. I mean, we've got a plan. We're all going to do our best and—"

Michael felt her hand, cool and soft, take his. He stopped rambling and looked into her eyes. As always happened, he was pulled into a private magical space that belonged solely to the two of them.

He spoke so only she could hear.

"I know this is necessary, that if we're not at the portal when Emma comes through, the Dire Magnus will get the *Reckoning*, and life as we know it will end. But even with all these new soldiers, we could still fail, and . . ." He paused, feeling embarrassed by the chain mail and sword. He wished he was wearing his own clothes. "It'll be my fault. Our fault. Mine and my sisters'. Because everyone here's thinking we can defeat the Dire Magnus. I'm scared we're just going to get them all killed."

The elf princess put her finger under his chin and lifted his face till his eyes met hers again.

"This fight found us. What you and your sisters have done is to give them hope. That is magic in itself."

"But . . . what if we lose?"

"Then we lose. There are things worth dying for. Friendship. Loyalty. Love. And if in fighting for those, this is the last stand of the elves, then so be it."

Michael found himself struggling to hold back tears. "Thank you."

She kissed his cheek. "Now come see what I've brought you."

She led him down the deck to where a large object was covered with black cloth. She drew the fabric away, and at first Michael could make no sense of what he was seeing. It was made of leather, but he found it to be a leather of such softness and suppleness that he thought he was touching silk. Then he realized:

"It's a saddle!"

"Indeed."

"But we don't have any horses!"

"Oh, it's for something much larger than a horse."

"You don't mean—"

"There is no one else whom I trust to protect my Rabbit. We will fight this fight together."

She kissed him again, not his cheek this time, and Michael felt a warmth spreading through his body and sensed he was on the verge of saying something extremely embarrassing when a sound as quiet as the footfall of a cat made them turn.

Captain Anton had leapt down to the deck.

He said, "Something is coming."

Carrying the lantern from her tent, Kate made her way to the beach where she'd killed the Imp. The island was emptying out, the families from Loris almost completely loaded onto the boats. Hugo Algernon had already disappeared, saying he had a matter to see to. "No doubt a fool's errand, but as Pym is not here to do it, I suppose I have to." He'd told her to get on one of the boats transporting the refugees, and she'd promised she would.

But she had something to do first.

She'd discovered when she'd woken that her jacket had been taken from her. Apparently, it had been covered in Imp blood and burned. That was fine. But her mother's locket was also missing. Kate surmised that the chain must've been broken when the Imp had fallen on her. So now she had gone back to the beach alone, in the dark, to find it.

The beach was empty, and the tide had come in a long way. Kate searched carefully, holding the lantern down low, and she found the locket along the water's edge, nestled among the stones. The chain had indeed been broken, but both locket and chain were still there, and Kate lifted them with trembling fingers. She had lost the locket once before, in New York, and Rafe had recovered it and the chain and returned them to her.

She slid the locket and chain into her pocket.

She said, "You're there, aren't you?"

"Yes."

She turned. Rafe stood just behind her. The lantern at her side lit only part of his face; his eyes remained in darkness. She tried to ignore the pounding of her heart.

"You think Michael and the others have a chance?"

He shrugged. "I guess we'll see."

"I had that dream again."

"What dream?"

"When I was in the church. In New York. You were there."

"Did I say anything?"

"No."

"Sometimes a dream is just a dream."

Kate found herself wishing she'd been able to talk to Michael before he'd left with the army. She would've finally told him about Rafe appearing to her. She would've apologized for keeping it secret and would have asked him to forgive her.

She said, "Can we stop pretending?"

For a moment, nothing happened. Then he smiled.

"When did you figure it out?"

And that smile, the confirmation it held, was like a hammer blow. She swallowed and managed to speak.

"Just today. I think . . . I've known for a while, but I didn't want to."

She dropped her gaze to the stones at her feet. She couldn't look at him, for to look at him was to see Rafe, and he wasn't Rafe. Rafe was dead. He had died a hundred years ago, the night he had sacrificed himself so that she could live. The thing next to her was the monster that had killed him. That was what she had to remember.

"Why did you do it? Just to torture me?"

He actually managed to sound hurt. "Of course not."

"So from the beginning, that first time in the Garden, that was . . ."

"It was me, yes."

"But why?! Why appear to me at all?! Why trick me?!"

It was taking all of Kate's will and strength to hold herself together.

"Because I needed you at the fortress, you and your brother. I already had Emma. And if I'd succeeded in bonding her to the *Reckoning*, I could've fulfilled the prophecy and my quest then and there."

"But you didn't! Michael pulled her spirit back, and Dr. Pym, he—"

"Sacrificed himself. It just made things more difficult. And anyway, I'd planned for the chance my first attempt might fail."

"What do you mean?" She glanced up at him and had to bite her lip to keep from crying out. She felt as if she was being ripped in two. She wanted to run to him, hold him. And at the same time, she wanted to kill him. Why did he have to look like Rafe? Why couldn't he look like the murderer he was?!

"It's difficult, I know." He sounded almost sympathetic. "You'll get used to it."

She turned away, her arms tight across her chest, staring across the black water.

"To answer your question: I hadn't waited thousands of years to risk everything on a single chance. I knew there was a possibility you three might escape. And I knew if you did, it would be by using the Atlas. So I took precautions. When I came to you in the Garden on Loris, I placed the image of the giants' land in your mind. I made it so it would be the first thing the Atlas seized on when you tried to escape. From there, I hardly had to do anything. The three of you found the giants' city and the Countess all by yourself. You brought her back to life—as I knew you would—and discovered where the book was hidden."

"How long have you known where it was?"

"A thousand years or so."

"I don't— You couldn't have planned it all!"

"It really wasn't that hard. And now we're almost done." Then he said, "Come to me."

"No."

She felt him step closer, so close he could whisper in her ear.

"You believed I was Rafe because you wanted to believe. I am still him. But so much more. I told your sister, the only fight you'll never win is the one against your own nature. I stopped fighting that battle long ago. I'm who I was always meant to be. A new world is about to be born, Kate. I want you there with me."

Kate could feel the magic of the *Atlas* stirring within her. She could call it up, command it to take her somewhere, anywhere. So what if she wasn't able to control it like she used to, so what if it hurt her. She would be far away from him.

But she couldn't bring herself to do it.

You're weak, she told herself. You're weak and an idiot. And you betrayed the two people you love most in the world.

"Kate . . ."

She shook her head.

"Then I'm sorry about this."

She was still staring across the water when she heard the roaring, and then the screams. She didn't look at him; she just dropped the lantern and ran.

In no time, she was back on top of the cliff, and could see down to the harbor and beyond, to where the families from Loris were escaping, a jagged line of boats stretched across the water.

A pair of waterspouts, giant whirling funnels of wind and water, had sprung up and were tearing toward the line of boats. Kate saw the tip of the first funnel cleave its way through a boat carrying more than thirty people. She heard wood splinter and break, she heard screaming—

"Stop it! Stop it!"

"It's your choice, Kate." He was standing beside her. "Just say the words."

Kate saw the second waterspout heading toward a boat carrying dozens of families. Despite the distance and the darkness, she could see the children aboard; she could hear their terrified voices.

"Yes! Fine! Whatever you want!"

Instantly, the winds died, and the waterspouts sank into the sea. Kate stared at the bay, at the other ships moving to rescue those who had been thrown from the boats, the water now littered with broken bits of wood and the luggage of the refugees, with people.

"But . . . how am I supposed to get to you? I can't control the *Atlas*! It—"

He made a calming noise. "It's okay. I can help."

She felt the tingle as he reached up to touch her temple, just as he had in the Garden, days before. He said, "It's almost over. Now. Come to me."

CHAPTER TWENTY-THREE
Fog and Ice

It was fog. That was what the elf captain had seen, a gray mass in the distance where the island of Loris should have been, and moving toward them at a completely unnatural speed. Before long, Michael was able to see it himself, as the stars along the horizon began to disappear. At King Robbie's order, the soldiers started to prepare themselves while a dwarf with a shielded lantern flashed a complicated staccato to the other ships.

"He's trying to cut us off from each other," the dwarf king explained.

"What can we do about it?" Michael asked.

"Master Chu?"

"Already working on it," the wizard said.

That should have been reassuring, but as far as Michael could see, Master Chu wasn't doing anything but standing there and smiling and fiddling with his beard.

Soon, the first tendrils were reaching over the prow of the ship, long gray snakes of cold, damp air. It was almost like sailing into a dream. Michael watched the other ships vanish, one by one, as their keel continued cutting steadily through the water, propelled by the enchanted wind that Magda von Klappen and Master Chu had summoned. Now and then, there was the muffled sound of a bell or a shout. Otherwise, silence. Michael felt Wilamena take his hand.

On they went, and time too seemed to be lost in the mist. Then the wrinkled dwarf helmsman said, "We must be no more than a thousand yards from Loris, I'd bet my beard."

King Robbie muttered something, a curse, perhaps, then: "Master Chu?"

"Almost there."

To Michael, Master Chu still appeared to be doing nothing but smiling and touching his beard, and he was about to ask why didn't they stop until they got rid of the fog, when Captain Anton stepped in front of Michael and the elf princess, an arrow notched on his bowstring.

"What is it?" King Robbie said, and the words were scarcely out when the elf captain loosed an arrow up into the mist—another instantly on his string—and a swarm of black shapes swept howling down out of the fog, and King Robbie cried, "Cover!" and threw Michael to the deck. Michael's breath was knocked out of him, but he could still see the creatures raking across the ship, tearing at dwarves and men with their claws and disappearing upward into the fog.

"Archers!" King Robbie roared, his ax gripped in his right hand. "Watch the captain! Follow his lead!"

There was movement everywhere now, shields were up, swords and spears at the ready, men and dwarves scoured the mist for any sign of attack.

"There!"

The elf captain shot his arrow into the fog, Michael heard a distinct, muted *thud*, and instantly a whispering hail of arrows followed it upward as the creatures swooped down. Three of the creatures fell clumsily onto the deck, more splashed into the water, wounded or dead, but others made it through the rain of arrows, and all around them dwarves and men were struck down or knocked into the sea. One of the creatures was flopping about on the deck just in front of Michael, an arrow sticking from its chest. The thing was the size of a vulture, with batlike wings, claws as long as Michael's hands, a body that was all leathery skin and bone.

King Robbie swung his ax, and the creature's head leapt from its body. The dwarf king heaved the carcass over the side.

"Princess," King Robbie said, "any help, I'd appreciate it."

Wilamena took the golden bracelet from her pocket and looked at Michael. "Get the saddle." Then she turned and dove over the side, disappearing into the fog-covered water. Michael ran to the saddle and swung it onto his shoulder. It weighed almost nothing. King Robbie bellowed, "They're coming round again!" But just as Michael looked up to see the dark shapes rushing toward them, there was an explosion of gold from the water, a great rippling jet of flame, and Michael saw four of the demon birds fall burning into the sea as the dragon seized another and literally ripped it apart.

"Ha!" King Robbie shouted. "That's the way!"

The dragon hovered next to the ship, and Michael felt, as

he always did in the dragon's presence, a thrilling wildness in his breast, a sense of being desperately, dangerously alive.

"Are you ready, Rabbit?"

"Yes! How do I—"

"The saddle knows what to do. Throw it."

Michael obeyed, and watched as the saddle settled perfectly on the dragon's back, the straps fastening themselves underneath her torso.

"You'll have to leap. I cannot hold to the ship without swamping it."

Michael didn't hesitate, but climbed immediately to the railing. They were still cutting through the water, and Wilamena was flying to keep pace, the beating of her wings taking her up and down, up and down.

"Whoa, there!" King Robbie said, catching sight of Michael. "What're you—"

Michael jumped, landing askew in the saddle, his arms grasping uselessly at the scales of the dragon's neck, and for one terrifying moment, he thought he might tumble into the sea, but then the saddle seemed to grab hold of him and pull him into place, the straps lashing themselves around his legs.

"Never fear, Rabbit. Once on my back, you will not fall!"

Then Michael heard Master Chu clap his hands once— twice—

A powerful gust of wind swept over the sea, almost pushing the ship onto its side. The fog cleared. Silence.

The island of Loris was not six hundred yards distant, the city and harbor lit by hundreds of fires. But between themselves and the island was a solid mass of ships, at least twice as many as the attackers, and each one larger and taller than Michael's ships and bristling with Imps and Screechers and trolls and who knew what else. The sky above was thick with the demonic birds. Their enemy had been waiting for them.

Then, as if on cue, all the Screechers on all the ships let out a single, shattering cry.

"Open your eyes."

Kate felt fingers at her temples. And it was not the tingle of ghostly fingers, but the pressure of real ones, and she looked up into a pair of green eyes. He was leaning over her; she was lying on the floor, a pillow under her head.

"How do you feel?"

"Fine."

He moved back as she sat up. She was in the Rose Citadel. She knew that, though she had never been in this room before. It had a stone floor, a long wooden table, paintings and maps on the walls. There were candles about the room, more hanging from a pair of iron chandeliers, and there were three curtained archways that gave out to a wide balcony, past which she could see the glow of fires. And she could smell smoke and burning metal and tar. There was the shrieking of *morum cadi*, but it sounded far away.

The patched pants and shirt and jacket that he'd worn when he'd appeared to her—Rafe's clothes—were gone, and he was dressed in a long black robe. His dark hair, his slightly crooked nose, his eyes—all that was the same.

She tried not to look at him, and forced herself to stand.

"Has anyone told you what the Books are doing?"

"Yes. They're tearing apart the world; and the only way to stop it is for me and Michael and Emma to die."

"Then lucky for you, I'm the one person who knows how to save you."

She looked at him now, unable not to.

"I'm not lying," he said. "Why would I? I've already got you here."

"Tell me how."

He smiled. "Patience."

Frustrated, Kate turned away, and her eyes fell on a sword that was lying on the table. It was three feet long and sheathed in a beaten leather scabbard, and had a bone handle. She knew she had seen it somewhere before.

He reached over and picked it up. "This belonged to your friend Gabriel. He used it to kill Rourke, which was a blow, I'll confess. Rourke was a faithful servant. Perhaps after I've got the *Chronicle*, I'll bring him back."

"Where's Gabriel now?"

"Dead."

He threw the sword carelessly onto the table. Kate sensed he was telling the truth about Gabriel, and struggled not to show how much it upset her.

"Come here." He took her hand and started to draw her toward the balcony.

"Emma—"

"Not yet. I'll know when she's close. I want to show you something."

Holding his hand caused a shiver to run through Kate's entire body, the same as it had on a street in New York a hundred years ago. And though she hated herself for it, she did not try to pull away.

But this isn't him, she told herself. This isn't Rafe.

He led her to the edge of the balcony, to where they could look out over the city to the harbor and the sea beyond.

The Loris that Kate had first come to, days before, had been calm, peaceful, beautiful. Terraced houses and narrow stone streets, groves of olive and lemon trees, and even at night, the white stone that the city was built from seemed to make everything glow. What she saw now was a hellish version of that city. The houses torn down. Olive and lemon groves burned. The white stone scorched with smoke. The city swarmed with Imps and Screechers and other creatures that Kate couldn't identify, and she could see huge engines of war gathered behind the walls, great boiling vats of tar and oil. And the noise rising up—the shrieking and shouting, the steady and terrible beat of drums—was both deafening and jarring, and it battered at the remnants of her courage.

But that wasn't the worst.

Just past the arms of the harbor, she saw the two fleets, the one massive, the one so much smaller, and the smaller she knew contained Michael and King Robbie and all their friends—

There was no way they could win; they were doomed.

"Please—"

"No, not this time."

"But—"

"It's up to them. If they surrender, I won't harm them. It's their choice."

"But they'll never surrender! King Robbie, the others, you know they won't!"

And he said, "Then they'll die."

For the first few minutes, though Michael told himself the elfish saddle would keep him firmly on the dragon's back and he was in no danger of falling off, he found he could do nothing but hold on and try not to vomit as Wilamena spun and flipped and dove through the air. It was still hours till dawn, but Michael could see, thanks to the showers of flaming arrows, the fires aboard the ships, and the glow from the distant lights of Loris. He could see how the two fleets had moved in among each other, the enemy throwing out chains and hooks to grapple onto King Robbie's ships, pulling in close so that their Imps and Screechers could swarm over the sides. And even with the wind rushing past, he could hear the cries of the *morum cadi*, the horns and drumbeats, the swoosh of arrows, the thud of spears striking wood: none of it escaped him.

And there was something else, apart from the battle raging on the water, that engaged Michael's attention. He'd always—at least since he'd known who the dragon was—been able to detect Wilamena in her. Now, as she ruthlessly tore through and burned and ripped apart the flying creatures of the enemy, she seemed somehow more dragon, and less elf princess, than ever before.

Fortunately, this new viciousness meant that soon enough, the sky was clear. But Michael didn't celebrate. For, looking down, he could see that their side was still greatly outnumbered.

"Go back to the ship!" Michael shouted. "We need to talk to King Robbie."

To his distress, Wilamena flipped backward and dove straight down.

They found the dwarf king's ship trapped by a much larger ship and in the process of being boarded, with Imps and Screechers storming across planks and King Robbie's soldiers struggling to fight them off.

"We have to help them!" Michael cried.

The dragon growled, "How long can you hold your breath?"

"What?"

And Michael just had time to grab hold of his glasses and take a deep gulp of air as the dragon plunged into the water beside the enemy ship. All around them was darkness, and the water was very cold, but Michael could feel the dragon wiggling like a great fish, her tail whipping behind them; then she grasped on to something and, a moment later, there was an explosion of light. By the time he dared to look, he saw the dragon unleashing a concentrated stream of fire into the wooden bottom of the ship. Michael could feel the water heating up around him, then the fire stopped, and the dragon began ripping out the charred planks with her claws, creating a bigger and bigger hole in the bottom of the ship, and Michael pounded against the dragon's back to tell her he had run out of breath, but she kept ripping out planks, making the hole ever bigger, and just as Michael reached the point where he truly knew he couldn't take any more, the dragon let go, thrusting up to the surface.

The air was the sweetest thing Michael had ever tasted.

"Forgive me, Rabbit. I had to make sure the hole was large enough."

"Wa—was it?"

"Look."

And Michael put his dripping glasses on in time to see the enormous ship disappearing below the surface of the sea, the Imps and Screechers jumping into the water, where they were being picked off by Robbie McLaur's archers.

Okay, he thought, one down. Fifty to go.

Then the dragon dove toward the dwarf king's ship. Robbie McLaur was at the rail to meet them.

"That was well done, Princess! We're in your debt—again!"

"But how're you gonna get past their ships?" Michael shouted, looking out at the still-massive fleet that stood between them and the harbor.

The dwarf king smiled, and Michael could see that in his own way, he was loving this.

"We just had to get close enough to shore. Remember the surprise." He raised his shield, and a crossbow bolt thudded into it. "The fact is, dwarves fight better with something solid under their feet." Then he turned to where Magda von Klappen stood with Master Chu and shouted:

"You ready?"

"We are!" Magda von Klappen snapped. "Though this is complex and—"

"Right! Get a move on!" And Michael saw the dwarf king signal a trumpeter, and four short blasts sounded through the din. There followed more shouts and bursts of activity on all their ships, and Michael could see the human and dwarfish soldiers doing something to their boots.

"What's going on?" Michael asked. "What's happening?"

For already he felt the temperature dropping sharply, and the dragon said:

"Look at the water."

Michael glanced down and saw ice forming across the surface of the sea, spreading at an incredible speed as the black water turned white and hard, and all the ships were held fast. Then wooden ramps and iron poles shot down out of their ships, biting into the ice so that the ships were held upright, and Michael saw dwarves and men running down the ramps, and he waited for them to hit the ice and slip, but they didn't. And he saw that each one had affixed a kind of sharp-toothed metal bracket to the bottoms of their feet—and Michael recalled all the dwarfish smiths on the island so hard at work—and the soldiers' feet gripped the ice, and this was happening all over, their boats held in place while their armies poured down onto the ice. He noticed that the elves did not wear the crampons, and at first he thought they must not like how they looked, but then he saw that they didn't need them, the elves ran lightly and surely across the ice.

The enemies' ships, meanwhile, were sprawled on their sides, many of the Imps and Screechers trapped within, and the ones who could scramble out were slipping and falling and no match for the sure-footed dwarves and elves and humans.

In a moment, the tide of the battle had turned.

There was another blast from the horns, and Michael heard the dwarf king's voice, booming, "To the wall! To the wall!"

"Shall we help them?" the dragon purred.

"Yes," Michael said. And he felt a new strength rising inside him.

The dragon tore over the now-chaotic enemy, scattering them

further while King Robbie and the army raced into the rocky arms of the harbor.

Before them, the white walls of Loris rose up, and Michael could see the ramparts bristling with figures, and as Michael's army charged toward shore, arrows rained down from above. Wilamena swerved upward, and Michael could hear the steel tips clattering off her mailed stomach.

The dragon checked her climb, just out of bowshot, and Michael, his heart hammering, looked down and saw the army—*his* army—gathering on the strip of beach before the walls of the city, and he knew that King Robbie would be forming them into units, but the crampons that had helped them cross the ice were now hindering them—

"We have to do something," Michael shouted. "We have to—"

"We have our own problems, Rabbit."

Following the dragon's gaze, Michael looked up, past the town, and saw a shape rising out of the Citadel. His heart skipped a beat. Then another shape rose up. And another.

"Oh no," Michael breathed.

The three dragons wheeled about in the air, unleashed jets of flame, and dove directly at them.

For a moment, seeing the ice spread across the harbor, and watching the dwarves, elves, and humans race toward the city—seeing the distant flash of gold she knew was Wilamena—Kate had felt a spark of hope.

But when she glanced at Rafe, he was smiling, and she took in the size of the army massing behind the walls, and then the three dragons rose up into the air, and Kate whirled on him, tears lashing her eyes, wild with fear and anger.

"Why did you bring me here? Just to watch all my friends die?! To watch you murder them?!"

In a flash, his hand was around her neck and he was leaning forward, his voice a passionate hiss:

"I brought you here because I need you. Don't you see that? I need you to keep me human. I told you I know myself and I do. Without you, I'm only the monster! I'm only that!" He swung his arm toward the battle, and Kate understood that it was not hatred fueling him, but desperation. "That's not the world I want! You believed I was still alive in your enemy. Believe in me now. All this will be over. We'll be together!"

"You deserve to die!"

The words sprang out of her, surprising both of them. His hand relaxed. Kate choked back sobs, but she kept her eyes fixed on his.

"Henrietta Burke told me to love you. She said that would make all the difference. But she didn't have to tell me, I already did love you! And I kept thinking, all this time, that Rafe was in there somewhere, that he'd come out if I just believed in him."

"And now what do you think?" His voice was suddenly, eerily cold.

"I don't know if you're still Rafe or not, if he's in there or not, but you need to die."

He pulled her closer; she could feel his breath against her face. "And will you be the one to kill me, Kate? Can you?"

Kate stared at him, wondering the same thing.

Then, without warning, he cried out and fell to his knees.

On instinct, Kate dropped beside him.

He gasped, "How . . ."

Unable to stop herself, Kate asked, "What is it? What happened?"

"She . . . gave them . . . back their memories."

"What . . ."

"Your sister—I can't hold—"

He let out another cry of pain, and then light began streaming out of him. Kate stumbled backward, blinking at the explosion of brightness, and the light rose up from him in a great rush, higher and higher, till it disappeared into the night.

Kate stared in wonder; this was something Emma had done.

She heard a crashing and looked out. A huge part of the city wall had collapsed, and it seemed to her that some power or force had gone out of the hordes of Imps and Screechers and trolls; they looked disorganized, lost.

She glanced once more at Rafe, the light still streaming out of him, his eyes shut tight. Then she turned and ran.

Emma was coming.

CHAPTER TWENTY-FOUR
The Plunge

The prison was being dismantled, the cages smashed and tossed into the pit. A massive bonfire now raged there, throwing its flames high into the sky. For a while, pandemonium had reigned as the prisoners had clambered down the rickety scaffolding to the ground. Now the arena had mostly emptied out, and things were calmer.

During the most chaotic moments, when the arena had been thronged by freed men, women, and children, Emma had clung to Gabriel's side, clutching his large, rough hand in her good one (*How was it that he could be dead? He was so real and solid*), while she held her other hand tight against her chest and above her heart to minimize the throbbing. The first thing Gabriel had done had been to bandage her wound, kneeling before her and wrapping a strip of cloth tightly around and around her hand. It had helped stem the bleeding, though dark red irises had appeared on both the front and back of the dressing.

But Emma scarcely noticed the blood, or felt the throbbing.

Her attention, when she wasn't thinking about Gabriel and how she was going to save him, how she would correct the terrible mistake of his presence here—that's what it was, a mistake—had been drawn by the liberated host of the dead.

Since her arrival in that world, she had grown almost used to the blank expressions, the dull emptiness of people's eyes, their listlessness and silence—perhaps the silence and hush most of all. And so it had been dizzying when a thousand people had all started speaking at once, calling to one another, crying, shouting, laughing even.

And that was just the beginning.

Emma had watched a child reaching for a woman and the woman lifting him in her arms.

She'd watched two old men, hugging each other and sobbing.

She'd watched groups of people all talking at once, all trying to make sense of what had happened, all telling their stories.

Everywhere, she'd seen men and women, young and old, comforting each other with touches, with words.

It had seemed, from what she could overhear, that they were like people waking from a long sleep. Again and again, Emma heard, "It was like I was dreaming. . . ." To her surprise, no one railed against the fact of being dead, and it was not long before she heard people saying that they were going off to find their loved ones. They seemed to believe this was possible, that they and those they'd loved in life could somehow find each other in the vastness of the world of the dead. And perhaps they could, perhaps they would be drawn together by some strange magnetism. Emma was aware that, just days before, she would have scoffed at the idea, but now she thought, *Why not?*

Slowly, the crowd had drifted out through the passages and avenues that had been created in the torn-down prison and vanished into the night.

And the thing that Emma kept reminding herself of was that this was happening all over, that millions were waking up, an entire world.

No, she corrected herself, not an entire world.

A few figures stood idly about the arena, gazing at the ground, all of them wearing the familiar, vacant expressions of the dead. Of these, some had served the Dire Magnus, like the black-haired, rat-faced *necromatus* who stood at the edge of the pit, staring dully at the fire; he seemed to be almost daring Emma to go and push him in, but she wouldn't; she was better than that, though he deserved it, he really did. And there were guards as well—though, obviously, not Harold Barnes, who'd already gone off to find his Nanny Marge, saying, "She'll be worried sick about me."

The others, the former prisoners whose memories had not been restored, Emma could not help but feel pity for. But it was what it was. She had made the judgment the book had required, and the judgment stood. And now the *Reckoning* belonged to her.

She held the book, tucked between her elbow and chest, as her hand throbbed with each beat of her heart.

Dr. Pym had assured her that those who'd been sent into the fire, the ones the Dire Magnus had devoured, would already be returning to the world of the dead.

"Once their memories were restored," the wizard had said, "the Dire Magnus will not have been able to hold them. They will return here, and thanks to you, most will remember who they are. I suspect he has released even those who did not have their memories returned. In the moment, he will not have been able to pick and choose. You have dealt him a grave blow."

As evidence, he'd pointed to the red-robed sorcerers and former guards wandering about.

"Their master has deserted them. Now they have nothing. No memory of themselves. No connection to his power. They are lost."

Emma had merely nodded and said nothing. Even then, her mind had already been moving on, thinking, planning, discarding everything that was not related to one goal: how she was going to save Gabriel.

In those first minutes after his arrival, when the prisoners were escaping from their cages and she had found herself in Gabriel's arms and realized what his presence in this world must mean, she had been sobbing so furiously that she'd been unable to hear or see much of anything. He had held her and made reassuring noises as one might to a small child, finally saying:

"I must bandage your wound."

By then she'd gotten blood all over his neck and chest and arms, but he paid that no mind and knelt beside her, ripping a long strip from his cloak and wrapping it about her hand. Calmly, as if this were just another meeting between them, he'd begun to tell her about finding her parents, how he and Richard and Clare had gone searching for the prophecy as a means of saving her and her brother and sister. It had been loud in the arena, with the shouts of the freed prisoners and the crashing of the cages being destroyed, but Emma had heard every word he'd said, his voice anchoring her, as his love had anchored her during the Bonding, and her sobbing had subsided.

She had even asked questions, some about their parents—how they'd looked, what they'd said, had they mentioned her—and some about Michael and Kate, which he couldn't answer, as he had not seen them since he'd sent them back to Loris. The one thing she didn't ask, and he didn't offer, was how he'd died.

And all the time, her mind was racing forward.

Dr. Pym had moved off to one side, speaking to the old white-eyed sorcerer and one of the *carriadin*. It might have been the one that had led Emma up the cliff earlier; she couldn't tell them apart. The other *carriadin*, perhaps a dozen in all, were systematically destroying the prison, tearing it down level by level.

Emma had asked the wizard what had led him and Gabriel to show up at the prison when they had, and Dr. Pym had replied that just as he'd felt compelled to guide Emma to the book, so he'd felt compelled to bring Gabriel here. He couldn't explain it further, besides to nod toward several of the *carriadin*, saying, "I suspect they had something to do with it. This is their world, after all."

Now Dr. Pym approached to say that it was time to go.

"We must return you to the world above, and the portal is some distance away."

"Uh-huh," Emma said, clutching Gabriel's hand more tightly than ever. "I've been thinking. As soon as I kill the Dire Magnus, I'll get Michael to use the *Chronicle* to bring Gabriel back. You too," she said to Dr. Pym, "though I'm not totally sure you still have a body. We'll have to, you know, work on that."

She nodded several times after she said this, as if to emphasize that Gabriel's returning to life was to be an accepted fact, and she failed utterly to notice the look that passed between Gabriel and the wizard.

Then the old gray-haired, white-eyed sorcerer stepped forward, leaning heavily on his staff. He seemed more exhausted, somehow even older, than before.

"I am sorry about your hand."

"Don't be. You had to do it."

"Still." And he touched, lightly, her wounded hand. "Forgive me. And thank you."

Emma hugged him once, fiercely, then let him go.

The last thing that happened before they left that place was that one of the *carriadin* landed near them, having half flown, half jumped from a cage above, and it was holding the Countess in its arms. The witch's face turned toward Emma and the others, and in an instant, Emma saw that the woman's memories were gone.

"What happened to her?"

"When you bonded with the book," Dr. Pym said, "the last remnants of the magic were taken from her. The same thing happened to me when Michael became Keeper of the *Chronicle*. The Book of Life kept me alive for thousands of years, but after he became Keeper, even had I not been killed, I would have lived out whatever days were allowed me and then died."

The Countess's violet eyes were dull and dimmed, and Emma watched as the bird creature carried her from the arena. Emma felt a knife edge of hatred for the Countess that would never go away—the witch had done too much to try and hurt her and her brother and sister—but in the end, the woman had helped her, and Emma would remember that too.

"Now," Dr. Pym said, "it's time."

Emma sensed movement behind her and felt rough hands under her arms; she was lifted off her feet, and her hand ripped from Gabriel's. In moments, she was high in the night sky, looking down at the prison and the bonfire below. She let out an involuntary "*Whaa—hey!*" and looked up at the *carriadin* holding her.

"Stop! What're you—"

She heard the voice in her mind:

Be calm, Emma Wibberly. You are safe.

And she felt herself, in fact, becoming calm, and she peered down, the wind whipping past, and saw two more dark shapes, the great wings silhouetted against the bonfire, and she knew, without being able to make them out, that Gabriel and Dr. Pym were being carried upward as well.

The *carriadin* flew away from the prison and the shantytown and out across the dark, empty plain toward the mountains in the distance. The air was cold, but clean, and after the smoke and reek of the prison, it came as a relief. Emma was reminded of flying on Wilamena's back, when the elf princess had been in the form of a dragon; there was the same rise and fall with each beat of the creature's wings, the difference being that this time Emma's legs and feet dangled over nothingness, and she was filled with equal parts excitement and terror.

Soon, the mountains were surging up out of the plain, and Emma was looking down at the thickly nestled peaks and saw, winding through them, the long, silvery band of a river. Then the *carriadin* banked sharply, going into a steep, spiraling dive, and Emma clutched the *Reckoning* against her chest as the wind roared past and the jagged peaks rushed toward them, and they were coming in too fast, there was no way they could slow down in time, but at the last moment, the *carriadin* turned upward, suspending its momentum to hang in the air, then beat its wings twice to land and set Emma gently on the ground.

Her heart was pounding wildly, and she stood there as if not quite trusting the earth beneath her feet. They were on a rocky outcropping beside the river, just before it plunged over a cliff. The roar of the waterfall filled the air, but Emma heard the thick, muscular rustle of feathers and turned to see the *carriadin* launching itself back into the sky. She thought of shouting a thank-you, but already the creature was gone, into the night.

Emma crept out as far as she could, to where the river plunged over the cliff, and stood there, letting herself be soaked by the spray blowing back off the water, peering down to where the river disappeared into mist and darkness. The only other waterfall she knew was the one in Cambridge Falls, which she had thought enormous. She guessed that this one was at least twice that size, and doubted she could have seen to the bottom even in the daytime. But why were they here? Where was the portal?

She heard the rustle of wings, and she turned to see Gabriel landing, sure-footed, on the ledge, his *carriadin* not even stopping, but continuing past, over her head and away. And even though Emma had only left Gabriel minutes before, she ran to him and hugged him, and he, again, folded her in his arms.

"It'll be okay," she said. "I'll make it okay."

Then she stepped away, wiping her eyes, as the wizard landed, the *carriadin* who'd brought him also hardly stopping before climbing into the sky.

"Well," Dr. Pym said, smiling like his old self, "here we are."

"Here we are where?" Emma demanded. "Where's the portal?"

The last portal she had gone through had been a tunnel under a spider's nest. Obviously, there was nothing like that around here.

Still, what the wizard said next surprised her.

"Over the waterfall. About halfway down."

"What?! How'm I supposed to get there? You gotta call back those bird things!"

"That will not be necessary; I have a plan. But first, now that we three are alone, I must know how exactly you returned the memories of the dead."

Emma didn't respond right away. She knew that what she'd done, she'd had to do, and she knew too that she had made the right decision, but it was still hard to talk about.

"There're two different meanings to the word *reckoning*." She did not try to speak over the roar of the falls, sensing that Gabriel and the wizard could hear. "One's like something you owe. Like we all owe a death. That's how the book kills people. But the other meaning is judgment. And when people died, their memories were stored in the book. Waiting for someone to judge them. Waiting for me. You probably knew that, didn't you?"

The wizard nodded.

"You could've told me."

"I foolishly thought there would be time. And then there wasn't. I am sorry."

"It's okay."

She couldn't be mad at him now, not after everything. And she had figured it out, hadn't she? With almost no help from anyone. The more she reflected on it, the more Emma felt a kind of pride in what she'd done, and it was not the same pride that she'd felt in the cave, when she'd first come upon the book. In that case, she'd done something difficult and dangerous and been brave and strong. But to do what the *Reckoning* had asked of her, she'd had to accept the responsibility that came with deciding whose memories would be restored to them and whose would not.

Even now, Emma could feel the weight of the decision on her shoulders, and a part of her wondered if this was what Kate had felt for the past ten years, knowing that she was responsible for her and Michael.

"Only, like, how do you judge everyone who's ever been alive? There're so many people and they're all so different. And who was I to judge? I mean, really. But then I saw Gabriel, and it made me feel so good and strong, and it was so clear that that was the best part of me, that I loved him, and that I loved Michael and Kate, and even you, though you kinda lied to us. And so that was the question I made the book ask:

"'When you were alive, did you ever love someone?'"

She had been afraid that when she said it out loud, it would sound silly, this one question that she, a twelve-year-old, had come up with to decide the fates of everyone who'd ever lived. But it didn't; it sounded right.

When you were alive, did you ever love someone?

It didn't matter if you'd been loved in return, or if the love had foundered and died. Had you ever given love? If the answer was yes, your memory flowed back to you. But if you hadn't, or if you'd only loved yourself, or money, or power, or objects, or nothing, then you remained as empty as you'd been in life.

And the book itself had given her clues. Like when she'd touched it the same time as Harold Barnes and seen his Nanny

Marge. Or when she'd seen the old sorcerer's father and wife and son. The book had been telling her, this is what matters, this is what you must look for, and finally, she had listened.

Release them, the book had said. And she had.

"It's like, when I first got here, I thought this place was a hell. You're the one who told me it could be a paradise. It turns out we were both right. It could be either. It depends on who you are. Because the world of the dead shouldn't just be a place where you wait around like some kind of houseplant; it should matter what you did when you were alive. And if you spent your life living only for yourself, then yeah, maybe this should be a hell. But if you ever forgot yourself enough to love another person, then you should be able to remember that."

"And there is no heaven or hell but of our own making." The wizard's eyes glistened, though whether from the mist or his own tears, Emma couldn't say. "Emma Wibberly, all the hopes I had for you, all the faith I placed in your wisdom and bravery, you have exceeded and repaid. In one stroke, you created a new foundation for both life and death. And that foundation is love. I have never been more proud."

He placed his hand, trembling with emotion, on her shoulder, and there was nothing Emma could do to stop the tears from tumbling down her cheeks.

"Now it is time you returned to the world above. I do not know what is transpiring there, but the Dire Magnus certainly knows you have the book. Every moment counts."

Emma gripped the *Reckoning* even more tightly, sniffled twice, and found her voice. "Yeah, like I said, as soon as the Dire Magnus is dead, I'll get Michael to bring you back—"

"You will not bring me back," the wizard said.

"But maybe there's a way! Don't give up just because you don't have a body. I'll bet Michael can build something. Maybe a robot or something, I don't know—"

"I was alive for thousands of years. I stayed alive for one purpose. To have my great mistake in helping to create the Books rectified. To see them finally destroyed—"

"What?! What're you talking about?!"

The wizard looked down at her. "The Books must be destroyed. That is the only way this all ends."

"But—but we need the Books to kill the Dire Magnus!"

"Yes. And once the enemy is no more, the Books must be destroyed! Their very existence upsets the balance we depend upon. The bonds that hold the universe together are being ripped apart. To fail to destroy them would spell the end of everything."

Emma felt herself relax. For a moment, she'd thought the wizard had actually gone crazy. But as long as she got to kill the Dire Magnus—and Michael was able to bring Gabriel back—she didn't really care what happened to the Books afterward. And though she still wanted to argue with the wizard that he was being stupid, that he should let Michael bring him back as well, she could understand what he was feeling. He'd done what he had to.

"We are close to the end," the wizard said. "Soon, I will rest. And because of your actions, I will do so with the memory of you and your brother and sister."

Then Dr. Pym bent down, and Emma, knowing it was the last time, hugged him with all her might.

The wizard released her and stepped back, and Gabriel knelt before her.

"You must find your parents," he said. "They will know the end of the prophecy, the secret to how you and your brother and sister will survive. They were not able to tell me, but our plan was always to go to Loris. They should be there by now."

Emma nodded. "And I'll see you soon, okay?"

Gabriel took her good hand in his and opened his mouth to speak, but she could sense what he was going to say.

"No! Don't tell me you're staying too! I'll find out what my parents know and I'll kill the Dire Magnus and Michael will bring you back! He can do it! He brought back Kate! He brought back the stupid Countess! He can do it!"

Gabriel waited for her to be silent. Then he said, "There is an order to life and death. We have altered it to meet our own needs and desires, and the universe has paid the price. The damage must end here."

"So we'll bring you back and that'll be it! Then we'll destroy the Books!"

Gabriel shook his head. "It is too late."

"But—"

"Listen to me—all I have done since I met you, I would do again. I regret nothing. But if you have your brother bring me back, then everything, every sacrifice I have made, will be meaningless. Your destiny is to restore order and peace. You must let me stay."

Emma was gripping his hand as hard as she could. He was wrong; she knew he was wrong; she just had to convince him!

He lifted her chin so her eyes, blurry with tears, met his.

"Remember, no matter the distance between us, you will always be with me."

The sobs broke from her chest, and Emma threw her arms

around his neck. He was wrong! He was wrong! She knew he was wrong! And yet, even as she thought that, a voice inside her, a voice that hadn't even existed just days before, told her that he was right, that the order of the universe was that people died, and you lost them. Today she would say goodbye to Dr. Pym and Gabriel. One day, years and years from now, she would lose Kate and Michael or they would lose her.

Death was the reckoning all had to pay.

But the love you gave was yours. That, you got to keep.

And even as her heart broke, she could feel her love for Gabriel like a flame burning inside her.

"She must go," Dr. Pym said. "Now."

Still clutching him around the neck and sobbing, Emma whispered, "I love you."

And he whispered back, "And I, you."

Then Dr. Pym took her hand and led her to the edge of the cliff. She drew her arm across her eyes to wipe away the tears. She could see out over the mountains to the endless space open before them. Gabriel stepped to her other side. She took several deep, shaking breaths. She didn't look at him. It was enough to know that he was there.

"So . . . how do we get to the portal? Can you fly me there or something?"

"Not exactly," the wizard said. "Hold the book tightly."

"What—"

"I am sorry about this."

And then he pushed her off the cliff.

Of the three dragons diving toward them over the roofs of the city, all were black and two were roughly the size of Wilamena, while the third was half again as large.

"I'm going to put you down with King Robbie."

"No!"

"It's too dangerous."

"It's just as dangerous down there! I'm not leaving you!"

"Very well, Rabbit."

And Wilamena drove herself forward, aiming them directly at the trio of dragons.

Michael shouted into the wind, "Are you sure this is the best course of action?"

But the golden dragon only beat her wings harder. As they passed over the city gates, Michael glanced down and saw King Robbie and the army of elves and men and dwarves as they began to lay siege to the walls. King Robbie had already erected bulwarks to protect the fighters from the arrows and spears and boiling tar being poured down from above, while behind them the ice was cracking as the last of their soldiers reached the shore.

Then the three dragons were upon them. Wilamena unleashed a jet of flame, and the trio spiraled out of the way as the flames licked at their wings.

"Why didn't they try to burn us?"

"Because of you. You are too precious. That is the only advantage we—"

Wilamena shrieked in pain and lurched to the side. One of the smaller black dragons had spun about and sliced her belly with its claws. The dragon grappled with them, its jaws snapping at Wilamena, who was biting back just as fiercely. Michael, in desperation, had drawn his sword, but there was nothing he could do. Then he heard a shriek behind him and whipped about to see the second of the smaller dragons coming directly for them.

"Wilamena!"

He didn't know if his voice would carry over the shrieking and hissing, but the golden dragon thrust herself away and dove. She banked across the top of the wall, beating her wings furiously, but Michael could see the two black dragons close behind.

"Where's the other? Where's the third?"

But Wilamena didn't respond.

In seconds, they were away from the city, out over the cliffs, and all was strangely silent and dark. Wilamena flew lower, skimming the water, and Michael could feel the spray cool and wet against his face as the sea threw itself against the rocks.

"There," Wilamena growled.

Before them, the cliffs curved, and in the rock was a kind of natural archway.

"I don't understand. What're you—"

But Wilamena was already through the archway and banking to follow the curve of the island. The moment she was out of sight of the other dragons, she climbed hard, looping back as she gained altitude, and Michael looked down and saw the other two dragons heading into the archway, the first one already through, and then he and Wilamena were plunging straight down, and this time she didn't have to tell him. Michael put a hand to his glasses and took a deep breath.

She slammed into the back of the second dragon, driving it underwater, forcing it down to the rocky floor of the sea, and it was impossible to see anything with the darkness and the thunder of bubbles, and Michael's lungs were soon screaming for air. He was aware of a great ripping and tearing, a terrible violence happening very close by; then Wilamena launched herself upward, breaking the surface of the water, and Michael took deep, gulping breaths, and he looked to see Wilamena throwing aside a pair of huge, bat-like wings.

Then the first dragon was on them.

This time, amazingly, it was Michael who helped.

His sword was still drawn, and he turned with it raised, and, thanks to the sharpness of the dwarfish steel and the force of its dive, the other dragon impaled itself on the point.

Michael felt as if his arm had been wrenched from his body and he cried out and let go of the handle, leaving the sword embedded in the dragon. The two-and-a-half-foot sword was not long enough to kill the creature, but the beast fell away, shrieking.

The wind was now whipping all around them, and clouds gathered overhead. A shard of lightning broke across the sky, and Michael saw what looked like a large cave, high up the cliff.

"There!"

A moment later, they were flying full tilt into a deep, wide cave in the side of the island.

"Do you know where this goes?" Michael asked.

"No."

Michael said no more, but he glanced back to see the other dragon entering the cave behind them.

"But there must be someone who can take us! Please! We—"

"Maybe you didn't hear so good," said the boat owner, whose face was the shape and texture of a paper bag that had been left in the rain. "Loris belongs to the Dire Magnus now. He's the baddest of the bad. And it ain't just him. Monsters. Trolls. Whole island's overrun."

"Worse than that," said a sailor at the next table. "I was talking with Giuseppe. He saw a fleet heading toward Loris. Warships and the like. Gonna be a heavy squall. Better steer clear."

"Exactly," the first man said. "Forget about Loris. Drop anchor here."

"You don't understand!" Clare was frantic. "Our children are there!"

But the men in the tavern were through talking and turned away from the couple.

Angry and frustrated, Richard and Clare walked out into the night air. They had arrived here, in San Marco, an island at the edge of the Archipelago, perhaps an hour before, flown by Gabriel's friend, the old pilot. The pilot would've taken them farther, but there was nowhere to land on Loris, which meant the couple needed a boat. For that, the pilot had directed them to the tavern where the boat captains congregated. Then he'd left, intending to retrieve Gabriel's body from the village on the Arabian Peninsula. There had been no way for Richard and Clare to carry his body across the ropes that Rourke had strung over the chasm; indeed, they'd barely made it across themselves. Still, the decision to leave Gabriel's body behind had been heartrending, all the more so because of his sacrifice.

But the time to reflect on that, and mourn his loss, would come later.

"What're we going to do?" Richard said as he and his wife stood outside the tavern.

"Maybe we could steal a boat."

There was a sound behind them, and they turned to see that the waitress had followed them out. She was a thick-shouldered woman in her fifties.

"You say your children are in danger? That's why you want to get to Loris?"

"Yes," Clare said. "Can you help us?"

"There were two fellas trying to get there a while ago. No one would take them either, so they ended up buying a boat." She looked toward the harbor. "The jetty there. Fourth berth. You can just see 'em. Careful, though. They seemed a bit strange."

Richard and Clare thanked her and hurried down to the water. They found a small boat, not more than twenty feet long, with a rickety-looking motor that a pair of extremely old men were arguing about how to start.

"I thought you said you knew how to do this. The battle'll be over by the time we get there."

"Well, if it is, I promise I'll clobber you on the head with a club. Can't have you missing all the carnage."

"I'm gonna take a nap. Wake me when the motor starts or the world ends, whichever comes first."

"Excuse us," Clare said. "Are you going to Loris?"

The two old men stopped what they were doing and looked up. Richard would have guessed they were both a hundred years old if they were a day. And there was also something about them that made him think instantly, *Wizards*.

Neither old man spoke; they just went on staring at the couple.

"I'm afraid we can't pay you," Richard said. "At least not right now. But we really need to get there. And yes, we know about the battle."

One of the old men nudged the other. "You thinking what I'm thinking?"

"That I'm a handsome devil?"

"No."

"That she looks exactly like you know who."

"Yep."

"Spitting image."

"Spitting image."

Richard realized that they were looking at his wife.

Then, all by itself, the engine roared to life. The two old men let out yelps of joy.

"Get in! Get in!" cried one of them. "No point standing around! The battle ain't gonna go on forever!"

"That's right," cried the other as the couple climbed down the ladder and into the boat. "That's unless you're thinking of opening a shop, the Standing-Around-on-the-Dock-While-We-Save-the-World Shop."

"Let me introduce myself," said the first old man after they'd cast off the ropes and were speeding out of the harbor. "My name is Beetles; this is my butler, Jake."

"You're bleeding."

"I'm fine."

"No, you're not; you're bleeding."

The second black dragon was dead. Wilamena had lain in wait for it past a bend in the cavern, clinging to the ceiling till it was right below her; then she'd fallen on it, the same as she had with the other dragon. This time, though, the dragon had been prepared, and the fighting had been savage. Michael had found it the more frightening for being difficult to follow in the darkness, though it was illuminated now and then by blasts of fire from both dragons.

Michael had felt useless, and even more than useless, an encumbrance, for in trying to protect him, Wilamena was leaving herself more open than she should. Finally, he'd taken his knife and sliced the straps that held him in the saddle and leapt off, bouncing and rolling down the rocky wall, and it was a testament to his dwarfish armor that he hadn't broken every bone in his body.

Once at the bottom, he'd turned over, groaning, just in time to see an enormous shape falling toward him. He'd barely managed to roll out of the way as it had landed with an earthshaking crash. The shape had come down so fast and the cave was so dark that he hadn't been able to tell which dragon it was. Then he'd looked and seen the black scales. He'd waited, hardly daring to breathe, but it hadn't moved.

Finally, he'd ventured, "Wilamena?"

A long, terrible moment. Then, from the darkness above: "Yes, Rabbit. I'm alive."

Michael had watched her moving down the cave wall, slow and careful, clearly favoring her right side. Then she'd tried to glide the rest of the way, and he'd seen that her wing was injured as well. She'd landed heavily beside him. Up close, and with the glow coming off her golden scales, he'd seen wounds crisscrossing her body.

"Come. We will fly back to the city."

At first, Michael thought she was not going to be able to fly at all, but she found her balance, pumping harder with her left wing, and soon he saw flashes of lightning that told him they were nearing the cave mouth.

"You should not have leapt off like that."

"I had to; you were getting hurt trying to protect me."

She said nothing, but he heard, and felt, her deep, rumbling purr.

Then they emerged from the cave into the open air, and the largest of the black dragons fell on them from above. Michael saw the movement from the corner of his eye, but by the time he yelled a warning, one of the dragon's talons had ripped a gash, the deepest yet, in Wilamena's side. The dragon's dive took it past them, and Wilamena jerked herself in the direction of the city. She beat her wings frantically, but she could muster no real speed, and when Michael turned, he saw the black dragon circling above them.

"It's not attacking!"

"It knows I'm as good as dead. It's savoring the victory."

Suddenly, Michael felt a searing pain, and he looked down to see that fresh blood, bubbling up from the wound the dragon had given Wilamena, was scalding his leg. He reached into his bag and gripped the *Chronicle*, then laid his body flat, placing his hand directly on the gash. The dragon's blood burned his skin, but he kept his hand where it was. For one fleeting instant, he thought of Magda von Klappen warning him not to use the *Chronicle*; then he closed his eyes and called the magic forth.

For the second time, Michael shared the elf princess's life, her joy in the living world, the way she could feel the hush of moonlight across her skin, or remember, perfectly, a birdsong she'd heard a hundred years before, and as he shared her memories, he learned that she had transformed herself into the dragon too often and for too long, that Pym had warned her when he'd refashioned the bracelet, telling her that if she wasn't careful, she would find herself trapped forever as the dragon, but she had taken the risk, and kept taking it, for Michael's sake.

Then came a tearing deep inside him, and Michael cried out and collapsed against the dragon's back.

"Rabbit!"

Gasping, Michael couldn't bring himself to respond. But he thought of Kate collapsing on the beach after using the *Atlas* to stop time, and told himself that whatever damage he'd done to himself, or to the world, Wilamena had been hurt, and he'd had no choice.

Then there was a scream behind them, and the black dragon attacked.

"Hold on, Rabbit."

Wilamena dove hard for the island, and Michael, even in his

pain and confusion, noted that she still flew unevenly, swerving about as if she had no control. He saw the ground rushing up and scrambled to grip the saddle as Wilamena crashed face-first into the beach. He went flying head over heels, but landed unharmed on the sand. When he finally had managed to stand and his vision righted itself, he turned to see the black dragon crowing over his foe, letting out long triumphant roars as Wilamena cringed before it. Wilamena herself was covered with blood and sand and favoring the side that had been wounded. Her left wing lay crumpled beneath her. Michael didn't understand; why hadn't the *Chronicle* worked? Why wasn't she healed?

Then the black dragon threw back its head to let out a belt of flame, and Wilamena leapt upward, snapping her jaws tight around the other's neck. The jet of flame was cut off. But the black dragon was bigger and stronger, and it fought back, clawing at Wilamena's chest and torso, sending cascades of golden scales shimmering into the darkness. Only Wilamena refused to let go. With her jaws locked tight, she yanked this way and that, till with one great, vicious, twisting wrench, she ripped the other dragon's head clean off. The black dragon stood for a moment, blood and fire shooting from its neck, then fell over on the sand.

The golden dragon let out a thunderous roar and shot flame hundreds of feet into the sky. For Michael, it had been like watching dinosaurs battle, creatures from some savage, primeval past, and Wilamena was one of them.

She walked toward Michael, limping slightly.

"You tricked him. You made him think you were still wounded."

"Yes. But you used the *Chronicle* when you should not have. I felt it."

"It doesn't matter." Though the truth was, Michael sensed that something inside him had been broken, something beyond even the *Chronicle*'s power to fix. His hand trembling, he pulled the red book from his bag and leafed through the pages.

"It's just a book now. The magic's all in me."

He said it woodenly, both knowing and not knowing what it meant. Then he opened his hand and let the book drop onto the sand; he didn't need it anymore.

"You saved me," the dragon said. "But at great cost to yourself."

"I'd do it again."

The dragon lunged forward, seizing him by the collar of his tunic and lifting him, like a mother cat might a kitten, then depositing him on her back.

"Come."

In less than a minute, they were over the city. Michael saw that several large holes had been blasted along the walls, and the fighting there was close and intense as their army surged forward. The golden dragon landed on the beach, where there seemed to be a command area of sorts. As Michael leapt down, King Robbie rushed up and hugged him.

"You're alive! I was worried when I saw those three worms—no offense, Princess! But now you're back! And just in time! You see we knocked a few holes in the city wall—buggers didn't know I'd mined it before we abandoned the island! We'll break through their line soon enough and rush the Citadel. We may just do this after all!"

Michael looked at Wilamena. "Take off the bracelet."

"What?"

"Take off the bracelet."

"Don't be foolish. You need me."

"I know what it's doing to you. If you wear it much longer, you won't be able to turn back. Take it off."

Michael waited, not entirely sure how this was going to go.

Then, after what seemed a very, very long moment, the dragon bent her head and flicked the clasp on the bracelet. Instantly, the giant lizard began to shrink, the wings vanishing, the great scaly arms transforming into slender, delicate limbs, the blood-red eyes turning the blue that Michael had always remembered but could never describe, and Wilamena collapsed against him.

Without Michael's having said a word, a pair of elves appeared at his side.

"She's wounded," he told them. "You have to get her to a doctor."

After the elves had carried her away, Michael picked up the bracelet, which had shrunk as well to human size, and placed it on a stone. He turned to King Robbie; he was working hard to stay on his feet and keep his voice steady. "Can I borrow your ax?"

The dwarf king handed it over; Michael dropped it.

"I can get you a lighter—"

But Michael, using both hands, lifted up the ax as high as he could, then let it fall, cutting the bracelet in half.

"Hope you know what you're doing," the dwarf king said. "Having a dragon around is awful helpful."

"I know—" Michael began, and he tried to hand the ax back to King Robbie but dropped it again, and almost fell himself, stumbling against the dwarf.

"Hold on, lad. What's wrong? Are you wounded?"

Before Michael could respond, there was a sound that drew

the attention of everyone on the beach, and they turned to see the dark water of the bay beginning to churn and boil as an enormous—Michael didn't know what it was, a *something*—rose out of the sea.

"What . . . what is that?"

"No idea," Robbie McLaur said. "But I have a feeling this is one of those times you'd want a dragon on your side."

Running through the Rose Citadel, Kate had expected at every turn to find the Dire Magnus—Rafe—waiting for her. But she hadn't. And somehow, despite the way her mind had been spinning with questions—*What had Emma done? Was she hurt? Was she really coming?*—she'd been aware enough to avoid the troops of Imps and Screechers stomping through the halls.

And she had been racing along for some time, with no direction in mind save down, when she'd exploded out of a doorway and into the Garden, crashing through branches as lightning broke across the sky.

She'd stumbled forward blindly and abruptly come out into the clearing, and there before her were the tree and the pool.

She'd stopped.

Half the tree's branches had snapped off and lay about the clearing. Dead leaves littered the ground; they covered the surface of the pool. There'd been more lightning, and she'd felt the rippling shock of thunder.

It had occurred to Kate that no one had told her where to go; she'd simply known. But where was the portal? Where was Emma going to come from? She screamed her sister's name again and again, even as the sound of her voice was swallowed by the storm. At one point, she glanced back the way she had come, into the darkness of the Garden, half expecting to see Rafe stepping from the gloom, and it was then she heard something behind her, a splash, the sound of someone gasping for air, and she turned to see Emma pulling herself out of the leaf-clogged pool. For a moment, Kate forgot everything else—the Books, the battle, Rafe—and rushed forward, clutching her sister to her breast and sobbing.

"Emma! Emma! I thought we lost you! I didn't know—"

Emma dropped to her knees, hacking up water.

"Are you okay? Emma?!"

"I can't . . . I can't believe he pushed me!"

"Who pushed you? And what happened to your hand? Oh, Emma!"

Emma shook her head. "It's all right. I'm . . . I'm okay."

Kate stared at her. Perhaps it was because she was sopping wet, but Emma had never seemed so small and thin and tired, as if she had not eaten or slept in days.

Emma looked up and met her sister's eyes. "Gabriel's dead."

"I know. I'm so sorry. But how did you find out?"

"It doesn't matter." She stood slowly, shakily, still holding Kate's arm.

"Wait—you have to tell me what happened. You did something, didn't you? Ra—the Dire Magnus, something happened to him. It was like this light was streaming out of him."

"I gave the dead back their memories. He couldn't hold on to them." Then Emma said, "I've got the book."

And Kate saw that Emma's bandaged hand, which she had kept pressed against her chest, clutched a small black book.

"Good."

Both Kate and Emma turned to see the figure stepping from the shadows.

Rafe said, "Then we can finish this."

Robbie McLaur shouted, and thirty archers ran from the wall to take up positions along the beach and begin shooting arrows at the monster.

The creature had a huge, rounded back covered with barnacles and seaweed and black sludge. Along its sides there were a dozen long tentacles waving through the air. The creature was still rising out of the water, and Michael saw a pair of glowing eyes, each as large as he was tall, and then its great mouth was revealed, with rows of teeth furrowing back into its throat.

"It's a kraken."

Michael turned and saw Wilamena's father, the elf king, beside him.

"But it can't come up here, right?" Michael said. "It can't come up on land."

In answer, the creature stepped forward on legs as thick as tree trunks, and its tentacles began snaking out and snatching up soldiers and either throwing them into its mouth, bashing them against rocks, or tossing them far out to sea.

Michael ducked as a tentacle swung toward him, and he felt the *whoosh* as it passed overhead. But his escape was short-lived, for the tentacle whipped back, wrapping about Michael's body and pinning his arms to his sides. He was lifted into the air, high over the beach, and he struggled to reach his knife, but the tentacle held him fast. Then it was carrying him toward the gaping, razor-fanged mouth, and just as he was about to scream, Michael saw a shimmering off to his right, almost lost in the darkness and the rain, and something incredibly large came charging toward him. There was a heavy, wet *thud*, and he was dropped.

Michael fell, and fell, and then—

"You okay, Toadlip?"

Michael found himself staring into the enormous, grinning face of Willy the giant. He had caught Michael in midair.

"How . . . how'd you get here?"

"Come through the portal, of course."

He hooked his thumb, and Michael saw that a portal had been created just beyond the mouth of the harbor—that was the shimmer he'd seen, and one giant after another was stepping out of it. They were wearing armor and carrying clubs and maces, and they were now, as a group, pounding away at the kraken, which was keening and shrieking and doing its best to crawl back into the water.

"Your friend, the hairy, rude one, told us you needed help."

"Who?"

"Who'd you think?" barked a voice, and Michael saw Hugo Algernon clinging to the giant's shoulder. "I heard your story and thought having some a' these great lumbering clods around would be useful! Magda von Strudel-Brain said I couldn't make a portal big enough! Looks like I was right and she was wrong! As usual—"

And then he tumbled forward. But Willy caught him, then bent down and placed both Michael and the unconscious Hugo Algernon on the beach beside a stunned-looking Robbie McLaur and the elf king.

"He tuckered himself out bringing us here," Willy said.

Then he noticed the elf and dwarf staring up at him. **"How do? You all friends of the little wee children?"**

Both King Robbie and the elf nodded silently.

"Right, so we'll just sort out this sea slug, then we'll help you with your whole battle thingy. Perhaps we could throw some boulders at those monster-looking fellows. We do like throwing boulders."

"Throwing boulders," King Robbie said hoarsely, "would be fine."

The giant then bent toward Michael and did the thing where he made an attempt to lower his voice, though the volume still boomed. **"You notice the armor? It's King Davey's; I had it polished up. It fits nice, don't you think?"**

It seemed to Michael that the armor was several sizes too large, but he said, "It looks great."

"Thanks. Okay, now I'm gonna go hammer that big fish beasty."

And he strode off through the harbor, sending up great plumes of water with each step. King Robbie put his hand on Michael's shoulder.

"Lad, you know how to make the right friends, I'll give you that."

Before Michael could respond, he heard voices shouting his name, and he turned and saw two figures running toward him along the beach. As they came closer, Michael saw they were a man and a woman.

Then he saw their faces, and he felt something break loose inside his chest.

And he was still watching when there was a hiss of arrows,

and both figures jerked about and fell onto the stones. Even from where he was, Michael could see the feathered shafts studding their bodies.

"Congratulations."

Rafe walked toward Kate and Emma. He was carrying a long, unsheathed sword, Gabriel's sword, loosely in one hand. The rain came down in thick sheets. Above them, the branches of the tree swayed and creaked in the wind. It was a storm in which the very screws and bolts that held the world together seemed to be coming undone.

"You gave the dead back their memories. I never thought you'd manage it."

"Emma," Kate said, "take my hand."

"No." Emma held the *Reckoning* tight against her chest. She felt anger, pain, the memory of Gabriel, all roiling inside her. And here was the reason she'd suffered everything she'd suffered; she was going to make him pay. "Not before I kill him."

Rafe smiled, planting the sword in the wet ground. "You can't kill me. You do, and you and your brother and sister are doomed."

This threw Emma, but she managed to spit back, "What're you talking about?!"

"Ask your sister."

"It's the Books," Kate said. "They're tearing apart the world. They have to be destroyed—"

"I know! Dr. Pym told me!"

"And the only way that happens," Kate said, "is if the magic is in us and we die."

"Which means," the boy went on, "that if you kill me, then

all those people you think of as your friends, they'll come after you next. They won't want to, they'll hate themselves for it, but what are the lives of three children weighed against the entire world?"

Emma could scarcely speak. "That's—that's not right!"

Rafe let out a short, bitter laugh. "And what does that matter? It will happen. But I can save you. You and your brother and sister. The magic coursing through each of you is a death sentence. I can take it away." He shrugged. "Or you can kill me."

Emma saw it all then, the way everything had narrowed to this one moment; and her and Kate's and Michael's lives would hang on what she did next.

She could hear the tree's branches creaking and groaning above her. The rain stung her cheeks. She wished more than anything for her mother and father to appear with the answer that would magically save them. Hadn't that been the point of their finding out the end of the prophecy? The point of Gabriel dying? Why weren't they here when it really, finally mattered?!

But the thought only lasted a second. Maybe their parents had gotten delayed or been captured or killed—the fact was, they'd been gone for ten years. And for ten years, she and Kate and Michael had been saving themselves. Why should it be any different now?

"Emma," Kate said, "let's go. Please. We'll find some way out of this!"

Emma knew that if it had been possible, her sister would have gladly sacrificed herself so that she and Michael might live, but that wasn't an option.

The boy watched her, waiting.

She said, "How?"

"Emma! No! You don't know what he'll do!"

Emma whirled on her sister. "There's no more time! You can't see it, but I can! It's hanging over you!"

"What do you mean? What's hanging over me?"

"Death," Rafe said. "The *Reckoning* lets her see it."

And so it was: from the instant Emma had climbed out of the pool, she'd seen the shadow over her sister, a shadow darker even than the night, and so close—it was almost touching her.

"I'm sorry, Kate. I can't lose you and Michael. I won't." She said to the boy, "Tell me how."

He smiled. "Please. You know how."

And Emma realized it was true.

"You'll take on our spirits. Just like you took on the spirits of the dead. It'll give you the power."

"This is the end of the prophecy. Three shall become one. Three Books in one. Three Keepers in one. Once the power of all three Books is concentrated in me, the Final Bonding will occur. The magic will transfer to me. I am the Final Keeper."

"And what about us? What happens to our spirits?"

"I'll release them once the Bonding is complete. Just as I released the spirits of the dead when you returned their memories. You really think I want you jabbering in my head for the rest of eternity?"

Emma hesitated; she could see the boy becoming impatient.

"There's something you're not telling us! There must be something—"

He waved his hand, annoyed. "There's a great deal I'm not

telling you. You know what you need to know. What's your answer? Do you kill me, and in doing so doom yourself and your brother and sister? Or do you save your family?"

"Emma, please! Don't do this!"

Kate moved closer, and for one moment, Emma was blocked from the boy's view. She looked at Kate, willing a lifetime of love and gratitude into her eyes, sending her sister the message that though she had cared for and protected them all for so long, now it was her turn.

She mouthed, *Trust me*.

The rain lashed down, the wind howled.

Kate gave a small, imperceptible nod.

Emma looked past her sister. She said simply, "Do it."

Michael's father had been struck by two arrows, his mother by one. The elf king carried his mother while King Robbie lifted his father—though his father was almost twice the dwarf's size, King Robbie showed no sign of strain—and they raced down the beach to one of the fortified shelters while Michael ran behind and arrows skittered off the rocks around them.

Michael was shaking. He felt stripped of everything he had been just moments before: Keeper of the *Chronicle*, leader of the army, commander of dragons and giants; he was suddenly only a young boy, trembling and uncertain.

By the time he arrived at the shelter, his parents had both been laid on cots, his father's eyes were closed, and his breath was fast and shallow. An old bald man was leaning over him while another man, equally bald, equally old, examined the arrow protruding from his mother's side.

And his mother reached toward him. "Michael . . ."

It was such a simple thing, hearing his name spoken by his mother, but it answered a need at the core of Michael's being, a need that had gone unanswered for so long that he felt his heart swell and break in the same moment.

The shelter was a lean-to that was open to the harbor and lit by lanterns strung from the top beam. There were some two dozen cots where the other wounded had been laid. The rain blew in, drenching both the wounded and those tending to them, while the air was charged with the sounds of battle and the fury of the storm overhead.

Michael dropped to his knees in the space between his parents' cots and grasped his mother's outstretched hand.

"I can heal you!" His voice shook with sobs. "I can—!"

He began to reach for the *Chronicle*, remembering only then that he no longer had the book, that he no longer needed it; the magic was in him. The old men were muttering as they snapped the feathered shafts protruding from his parents' bodies, their hands moving with surprising speed and steadiness as they drew out the tips of the arrows and placed bandages on the wounds.

"Wait," his mother said, gasping from the pain. "There's something you need to know. . . ."

His father groaned, and Michael turned to see him, his eyes still closed, wincing as the old man removed the second arrow.

"Michael." His mother clenched his hand, bringing him back. "He can't die."

"He won't! I won't let him! I can heal you!"

"No! I mean the Dire Magnus. He can't die."

"But—I don't understand! What're you talking about?"

Her voice was growing weaker. "Not until . . . the Final Bonding . . . only then . . . That's the only way. . . ."

Her eyes closed, and before Michael could shout or react, the old man leaning over her said, "I made her sleep. She needs to rest."

"I can heal her!" Michael sputtered. "I can heal them both!"

"There's no need," the other old man said. "They will both survive."

"No!" He was insistent! He felt that this was why he'd found the *Chronicle* to begin with, to do this one thing, to save his parents. "I'm going to heal them!"

But as he took his father's hand and reached for the magic, he sensed something happening to him. It was almost as if he were being pressed on all sides by some invisible force, tighter and tighter, and then he gasped as a thing he'd never known existed, but now realized had always been a part of him, was taken away.

"What the . . . ," he heard King Robbie say.

And Michael looked and saw something shimmering in the air before him, and then it rose up, vanishing through the roof of the shelter.

"Beetles . . . ," said the old man beside him, "was that . . ."

"Yes," replied the other, "it was his spirit."

But Michael scarcely heard them; for he'd realized something else.

"The magic," he said, still gripping the hands of his mother and father, "it's gone. . . ."

Emma stood there, clutching the *Reckoning*, staring at the boy as he looked skyward, his arms outstretched as if he were beseeching the storm. Emma had already watched as Kate collapsed into the drifts of sodden leaves, and a shimmering had passed from her to the boy. Emma knew what having your spirit pulled from you felt like, and she would have done anything to spare her sister the pain; but there was nothing for it, and she watched as a shimmering she knew was Michael's spirit floated down into the clearing.

There was a kind of glow too around the boy, as if the energy and magic he'd absorbed was pulsing at the limits of his skin. She imagined that behind the boy's face she saw a skull's head, staring out, and she wondered if it was the *Reckoning* that allowed her to see that, or if she was just imagining it.

"Life and time," he said as Michael's spirit disappeared into him, and the glow around him became brighter. "And now, death. The Bonding is nearly complete."

"No," Emma said, opening the book so that raindrops splattered against the pages. "This is when you die."

He stepped closer, and Emma felt a familiar thickening of the air around her.

She went on, her voice trembling but determined: "And because the *Chronicle* and the *Atlas* are in you, they'll be destroyed too. Kate's and Michael's spirits will go back to their bodies, and this whole thing will be over."

"What about you?" the boy said. "The *Reckoning*'s power will still be in you. Your friends, the people you trust, they'll hunt you down."

"Maybe," Emma said. "But that's my problem."

For who was to say that Hugo Algernon or some other witch or wizard wouldn't find some way to destroy the *Reckoning* without killing her? Or maybe her parents would finally arrive with the secret that solved everything.

But it didn't really matter. What mattered was that the moment the Dire Magnus was dead and the *Atlas* and the *Chronicle* destroyed, Kate and Michael would be safe. They would get to live their lives. Be reunited with their mother and father. And if it turned out there was no way to destroy the *Reckoning* without her dying, at least Emma knew that Gabriel would be waiting for her in the next world.

She placed her hand on the book, the power rose up through her, filling her, and she saw the look in the boy's face, the understanding, and she imagined she could see the shimmering spirits of each Dire Magnus clustered around him.

Then, as she reached toward him with her mind, the words of the old white-eyed sorcerer, spoken in the world of the dead, returned. "He wears the spirits of his former selves like armor." Suddenly, Emma could see in a way she never had before, and in place of the physical boy, she saw a throbbing, glowing mass. It was the spirits of each of his former selves, grafted one onto the other. She could feel the different voices, the different selves, of each Dire Magnus; she could sense too the spirits of Michael and Kate, and how they had been sucked into that terrible, cancerous mass.

Emma felt the air around her becoming more and more solid, trying to press her spirit from her as it had in the fortress days before. She was running out of time.

She reached out with her mind, fixing upon one of those former selves, and stripped it away from the others. It was like peeling tar off tar; the spirit fought to stay connected. And as she pulled it free, the life of a Dire Magnus who had existed hundreds of years before passed through her and through the book, and there were no memories of love. It was an empty, cold, hungry thing, and Emma held the spirit for a moment in her mind, then cast it into the world of the dead.

She went quickly then, scarcely feeling the force pressing against her from the outside, pulling the spirit of each Dire Magnus away from the mass. Some of them fought harder than others, but none had a single memory of love. And Emma could hear, as if from a great distance, the boy screaming for her to stop, vowing to kill her, but she paid him no mind, holding each spirit for a moment, then casting it into the world of the dead. And the magic was still filling her, pulsing through her, and Emma realized how terrified she'd been for so long, and how in the end there was nothing to fear, that the only thing you could control was the love you gave or withheld, and that was all that mattered; and finally there was only Rafe's spirit and one other, which clung like a spider to his own, and she knew it was the first Dire Magnus, the one who had set it all in motion, and she reached out toward it, but as she did, the magic rose up, stronger than ever, and something inside Emma was torn apart.

Kate lay without moving, having woken to the sound of Emma's voice. She knew her spirit had been taken from her and that the magic of the *Atlas* was gone. She knew because she had never felt so empty and desolate and weak. Finally, calling upon all her strength, she had managed to open her eyes and see Emma place her hand on the book and the Dire Magnus fall to his knees.

Then Emma cried out and collapsed.

For a time, nothing happened. Then she watched as the boy, their enemy—she couldn't see his face—slowly pushed himself up and walked to where Emma lay. He seemed to be moving stiffly, as if in pain. Emma had fallen forward, on top of the book, and he rolled her over and picked it up.

Then he knelt, holding his hand just above her body, and after a moment, Kate saw a shimmering rise out of her sister and begin to pass into him.

She was on her feet before she knew it, seizing the sword still planted in the ground, and racing toward the dark figure crouched over her sister. Unlike with the Imp on the beach, her hand did not tremble. There was no hesitation. The sound of the rain muffled her footsteps, but perhaps he sensed her approach, for he rose and turned just as Kate reached him, having time only to hold out his hand, for her to meet his eyes, and hear him say—

"Kate—"

—and she drove the sword through his chest.

CHAPTER TWENTY-SIX
A Promise Kept, a Promise Made

Michael stood on the jetty, waving at the ship that was carrying away the last of the expanded army, in this case a clan of burly Bavarian cave dwarves, several of whom, Michael had noticed, had thick green moss growing from their beards.

Well, that's it, Michael thought. So much for my military career.

It had not taken the army long to disperse; it had only been a day since the battle had ended, a day since the Dire Magnus's forces had scattered and been destroyed, and already all the various factions and clans and races had drifted away, and the first of Loris's displaced families had begun to return. Even now, boats laden with homeward-bound refugees were maneuvering past the two giants who stood waist-deep in the harbor, clearing away the ships that had been sunk during the battle.

Behind him, King Robbie's dwarves were busy rebuilding the

blasted-out sections of the city wall. The dwarves were providing their work and masonry expertise free of charge, which Michael thought was very generous of them, though he'd privately cautioned King Robbie that if you simply gave away high-quality craftsmanship, people would start to take it for granted. "Well, lad," the dwarf king had said, "I think this time we'll let that pass."

Fair enough, Michael thought, I warned him.

Michael knew too that Wilamena, having been returned to perfect, glowing health by a team of elfish physicians, was going around the damaged city on a personal "beautification program," which basically entailed her walking around and smiling at people.

The air was warm, and Michael took a deep breath, grateful that the towers of black smoke from the fires that morning, when the army had incinerated the bodies of the dead Imps and trolls (apparently necessary for public health reasons), had been carried away by the sea breeze.

A new day. People were getting on with their lives.

It was probably good, Michael thought, that so few of them were aware of the truth.

"Michael!"

He turned, knowing whom he would see coming down the jetty. But it made no difference; the earth still seemed to shift under his feet. It was the same every time he saw his father, or his mother, for that matter. Like Wilamena, they were both fully recovered from their wounds—the two old wizards, Jake and Beetles, despite spending most of their time insulting each other, had turned out to be remarkably capable healers. But it wasn't his parents' magically restored health that so unmoored Michael; it was the simple fact that they were here with them, that this was real and not a dream.

"She's awake," his father said. "Emma's awake."

Emma had woken to find herself in a bed with cool, clean sheets, in a light-filled room, and her first realization had been that she was alive, and the way she had known this was that her entire body was one giant, aching bruise.

So that was the first thing. The second realization was that someone was sleeping in the chair beside her bed, and she'd almost said Kate's name before she saw that the person was not, in fact, her sister. Not unless Kate had suddenly aged twenty-five years.

This had led to her third realization, of who the woman in the chair had to be.

Then her mother had opened her eyes.

Throughout her childhood, Emma had imagined, just as Kate and Michael had imagined, what the reunion with their parents would be like. As Emma had had no memory of her parents, her mother and father had always presented themselves as generic, loving blobs. But she'd imagined what they would say. The various gifts they would bring. How she would wring from them the promise of a dog. There were a million different scenarios, most involving cake, tears, and a mountain of presents.

In the end, what happened was that she and her mother had simply lunged for each other at the same moment, sobbing. And then her mother called, "Richard!" and her father ran in from the balcony and joined the hugging. After a few moments, and after all the expected exclamations and queries—"It's really you!" "We were so worried!" "Are you sure you're okay?"—and her mother explaining how Jake and someone else (Bug? Was that right?), a pair of old wizards they'd befriended, had fixed the wound in her hand—there were only faint, matching scars on Emma's palm and the back of her hand as evidence—her father had kissed her and hurried out to find Michael.

Alone with her mother—who continued to alternate between hugging Emma and holding her back to look at her—Emma had finally been able to register the fact that the magic of the *Reckoning* was gone. On some level, she'd known it the moment she'd woken, but the appearance of her mother and father had pushed the knowledge to the edges of her mind. Only, something about it didn't make sense. But before Emma could put her finger on what that something was, her father returned with Michael.

Emma was sitting there, letting her mother hold her hand, and she almost laughed, seeing her father and brother together, they looked so much alike.

"Michael!" she cried, and ran and threw her arms around his neck. "Look! It's . . ." And though she couldn't quite say "Mom and Dad," he understood.

"But where's Kate?" she asked. "Why isn't she here?"

Emma saw Michael glance at their mother, who shook her head.

"You'd better sit down," Michael said. "I can tell you the whole story."

Michael began at the moment of their parents' appearance on the beach, saying how he'd seen them both struck down by arrows. They'd been carried to the convalescent tent, and Michael explained how he'd followed them there and had been about to use the *Chronicle*'s magic to heal them, only before he could, both his spirit and the magic were taken from him.

"I know," Emma said. "I mean, I know why."

"You do? That's great. I was hoping you would."

"But tell your side first."

So he went on, saying how he was there in the tent, their parents both unconscious, and how everyone, King Robbie, King Bernard, everyone was yelling and arguing about what to do, when he'd felt his spirit return.

"It was like I was all empty and cold inside; I'd never felt so awful. And then, I don't know, I was filled almost with light or something."

"Yeah," Emma said. "I know that feeling."

And there'd been a great cry from near the city wall, and King Robbie had shouted that all the Imps and trolls were fleeing, while the *morum cadi* were simply dissolving where they stood, as if the power that had fed them was cut off. And Michael said he had known, instantly, that Emma was back. Michael had left their mother and father with Jake and Beetles and told King Robbie that he had to get to the Citadel, and the dwarf king had shouted for guards and they had joined the army that was streaming through the hole in the city wall, the Dire Magnus's army evaporating before them, and Haraald and Captain Anton had been at his side as well, and together, they had run from the harbor all the way to the Rose Citadel, and they hadn't stopped running until they'd reached the center of the Garden.

"And that was where we found you. Just lying there, unconscious."

"Can you tell us what happened, honey?" Clare said. "Or are you hungry? Do you need to eat something first?"

"I'm okay. But didn't Kate already tell you everything?"

"We'd like to hear it from you," Richard said.

"Sure," Emma said, though she was now wishing she'd asked for a cheeseburger or something; she was starving. "I probably can tell it pretty good, leave out the boring bits. But when did you get here?"

"It's a long story," her mother said. "Gabriel found us. He told us where you were. But he—this will be hard to hear—"

"He's dead," Emma said quietly. "I know."

"He died defending us," her father said, "while we were hunting down the end of the prophecy."

"That's what we were bringing here," Clare said. "Pym thought it was the secret to saving your lives."

"But we didn't need it! We did it on our own! We killed the Dire Magnus!" Emma paused, struggling to recall exactly what had happened in the Garden. "I mean—it's over, right? The *Reckoning* isn't in me anymore! Is the *Chronicle* in you?"

Michael shook his head. "No."

"Without a doubt, what you all did was incredible," her father said. "But we're still putting together the pieces. We need to hear your story. From the beginning."

Emma gave in; she didn't want to fight. Indeed, she didn't think she wanted to fight ever again, and she started telling them how she had returned from the world of the dead, carrying the *Reckoning* with her—

"What was it like?" Michael said. "The world of the dead?"

Emma opened her mouth to answer, to tell him about the walkers, about Dr. Pym, about the *carriadin* and the cave in the cliff, how the Dire Magnus had been consuming the souls of the dead, about Gabriel, and found she couldn't. She wasn't ready.

"It's okay," their mother said. "Just tell the parts you can."

So Emma told about finding Kate in the Garden, and how the boy, the Dire Magnus, had come upon them, and he'd offered her a chance to save her and her brother's and sister's lives by taking on their spirits, and she'd agreed, but once he'd taken Kate's and Michael's—

"That's what I felt," Michael said. "That's what happened."

—she had tried to kill him with the *Reckoning*, which she guessed made her kind of a liar, but you're allowed to lie to totally evil people, right? And she'd started peeling away the spirits from all the other incarnations of the Dire Magnus and sending them back to the world of the dead, and then . . .

"What?" Michael prompted.

"I don't know; it all went black. But I must've killed him. I mean, we won the battle. And now everything's fine!"

"Not exactly," her mother said. "You see, the Books—"

"Were tearing apart the world! But we destroyed them! I destroyed them! They were in him, and I—"

Emma fell silent. It had occurred to her why the magic of the *Reckoning* being gone didn't make sense. While it was logical that Michael wouldn't have the *Chronicle*, as both it and the *Atlas* had been transferred to the Dire Magnus, the *Reckoning* had stayed in her. She'd held on to her spirit. So what had happened? Where had the magic gone?

"That's the thing," her father said. "It seems that whatever the Books were doing, it's just gotten worse. I hate telling you this after everything you've done, but Hugo Algernon, Magda von Klappen, all the magicians assure us it's so. They feel the tearing in a way that we don't."

"You can see the effects," Michael said. "Down by the water, there've been dead fish washing up all morning. Dozens of them. People think it's because of the battle, but Dr. Algernon said it's the Books."

"But I killed the Dire Magnus!" Emma cried, clinging to the idea that this should've somehow fixed everything, even though it didn't explain what had happened to the *Reckoning*. "I know I did! I killed him!"

"Well," Richard said slowly, "we're not completely sure he is dead."

"What're you talking about?"

"He's gone," Michael said. "Vanished."

Emma stood up. She had a terrible, awful, sick feeling. "Where's Kate? I want to see her now. Where is she?"

"Emma"—her mother took her hand—"when Michael found you in the Garden, you were alone. Kate and the Dire Magnus, they're both missing."

Kate knelt beside the stream and tilted the bucket till it was full, the gurgling of the water the only sound to be heard on the mountainside. Then she leaned down and drank, mouthful after mouthful of cold, clean water. When she was done, she stood and looked out over the mountains. The sun was setting. Soon, it would be dark, and much colder; she would make a fire. She hadn't during the day for fear that someone might see the smoke.

Kate searched the sky, but there were no birds to be seen.

As she walked back along the path, she wondered again why she had chosen this place of all places. But there had been so little time to decide. Everything had happened so fast. She kept replaying the scene in her mind. . . .

Sword in hand, she had been charging forward when Rafe had turned, and then the tip of the sword had been at his chest, her momentum carrying her relentlessly onward, the blade so sharp there'd been almost no resistance. He'd staggered back, collapsing against the tree. Instantly, all her anger had melted away. She'd screamed his name, the sword dropping to the ground, and rushed to his side, pressing her hands against the wound in his chest, sobbing—

And she'd seen a shimmering rise from his body and she saw and felt it pass into her, filling her up, warming her, and she knew it was her own spirit returning, that it was returning because Rafe was dying, and she'd watched two more shapes rise from his body and one drift toward Emma and another—Michael's spirit, it had to be—rise up out of the Garden, vanishing into the darkness.

"Please," she'd begged, "please don't die."

And then she'd seen another shimmering form, and there had been something about it, some emanating malice, that had made Kate shrink back in revulsion and fear, and then it too rose up and was gone.

And Kate had still been staring after it when she'd felt a hand touch her own.

"Kate . . ."

He'd sat up, getting slowly to his feet, and she'd risen as well, too stunned to speak, and they'd stood there, she looking at him, he at her, the rain drenching them, and she'd known, with every fiber of her being, that it was him, only him, and then he'd stepped forward and kissed her.

He'd said, "I've waited a hundred years for that kiss."

"Rafe . . . how . . ."

"Your sister stripped away the spirits of each Dire Magnus that came before me. All save the first one. He wouldn't let go. Till you stabbed me through the heart. I should've died, only the *Chronicle* wouldn't let me. It had bonded with my spirit. But he couldn't hold on. His spirit was pulled into the world of the dead. It's over."

Then he'd looked off, as if seeing beyond the confines of the Garden and Citadel. "Your parents are here. They're in the harbor with Michael."

"Are they okay?"

"Yes."

"What is it?" For there was a strange expression on his face.

"Your parents discovered something and told your brother. I learned about it when I took on his spirit. I wouldn't have known otherwise. Though it makes sense."

"Tell me."

"Not now." His eyes were closed. "It's amazing, the power of the magic, the sweep and depth of it. And it's all in me. Even this"—he'd held up the small black book—"is just a book." Then he'd lowered it, saying, "Your friends are near. I have to go."

"But it's over!"

"The others won't trust me. They don't . . ."

He hadn't said it, but she'd known what he'd meant: they didn't love him.

"I'm coming with you."

"No."

"Yes. I'm coming with you."

"Kate—"

She'd glanced at Emma on the ground, still unconscious. "Is she okay?"

"Yes. So's your brother. He and the others will be here any moment."

She'd stepped closer. "I believed in you when no one else did. You owe me this."

He'd stared at her then as the rain sheeted down. Finally he'd nodded and taken her hand. "Think of somewhere safe."

And the ground had disappeared beneath her feet.

Kate found Rafe sitting on a bench in front of the cabin, gazing out over the valley. He had on a set of well-worn clothes he'd found in the cabin, and as she approached, he rose, took the bucket from her, and placed it on the ground.

"It really is beautiful here. I'm glad you chose this place."

Then he took her hand and drew her down beside him.

When Rafe had told her to think of somewhere safe, she'd known he'd meant somewhere they could hide, and the first place that had come to mind had been Gabriel's cabin, outside of Cambridge Falls. Perhaps she'd thought of it because of Gabriel's sword, lying in the clearing under the tree. But whatever the reason, the cabin turned out to be the perfect choice—alone on the mountainside, with no one nearby to disturb them. At least, she hoped that was the case. They'd found the cabin well-provisioned, making Kate suspect that it was now used by people from Gabriel's village. So far, though, no one had stopped by.

They had arrived just after dawn, one moment standing in the darkness and storm in the Garden on Loris, the next here, the sun rising over the mountains, the air cool and still and heavy with mist. Then the release that had been building for days had finally come, and Kate had collapsed against him, sobbing. He'd half led, half carried her into the cabin, and they'd lain together on the bed where she'd slept with Michael and Emma years before, and he'd held her as she cried. Neither of them had spoken, content just to lie there, long after her tears had stopped.

It had been midday when they'd finally risen, impelled by hunger and thirst, and they'd found food in the cabin, and Kate had made her first trip to the stream. Alone, she had allowed herself to think about her brother and sister, about her parents, to wonder if they were okay—Rafe had promised they were—and to hope that they weren't worrying about her, though she knew they must be.

Neither had yet mentioned the future, as if by not doing so, the future wouldn't exist, and there would only ever be this present. They had spent the day wandering together in the woods, never straying far from the cabin. Kate had imagined they looked like any normal boy and girl, and there were moments, like now, sitting beside him, his hand solid and warm in hers, that she could almost convince herself that was true.

If only it hadn't been for the birds.

She and Rafe had been returning to the cabin when they'd

heard a great rushing that had grown louder and louder. They had climbed a large rock in a clearing and looked out over the trees to see a dark curtain being drawn across the sky. As the massive flock had come overhead, the sun had been blotted out, and all around them, birds had launched themselves out of the trees to join the migration.

It had taken more than an hour for the flock to pass, but even that had only been the beginning. All afternoon, they had watched animals—bears and deer and foxes and raccoons—moving through the forest in the same direction as the birds, as if heeding some silent alarm.

Kate knew what it meant, and knew Rafe knew, but neither spoke of it.

We're together now, she told herself. That's all that matters.

After the sun had set, the temperature dropped quickly, and she and Rafe rose from the bench and went inside. Rafe lit the fire, and together they made a stew out of the carrots and onions and salted meat they'd found in the cabin's hutch, adding in sliced bits of ginger and sprigs of parsley from jars in the cupboard. While it cooked, Rafe asked her to tell the story of the first time she and Michael and Emma had come to Cambridge Falls, and she told about leaving Baltimore on the train, arriving at the house, finding the *Atlas*, being captured by the Countess, escaping, fleeing from the wolves, how Gabriel had saved them and brought them here through the rain. . . .

She stopped and looked at him.

"You must already know all this."

"I like hearing you tell it."

They ate sitting on the hearth, shifting as the heat from the fire became too great. When she finished the story, she was silent for a moment, then looked at him, the shadows and light moving over his face.

"Can I ask you something?"

"Of course."

"What was it like?"

She didn't explain what she meant, but he understood.

"It was like I was pushed down deep inside myself. Like I was watching the world through someone else's eyes."

"Like you were a puppet."

He shook his head. "No. I mean, partly, yes. But I was also the Dire Magnus. It's important you know that. Those other voices in my head, they urged me to do things, pushed me, but they played on things that had always been there: anger, bitterness, hunger for power and revenge. All that was in me already."

Kate looked down for a long moment, and when she lifted her gaze, her eyes glistened in the firelight. "But love too. That was in you."

He nodded. "Yes. That too."

He set his bowl on the hearth and leaned toward her. "I can't stay much longer."

She shook her head, not so much arguing as refusing to listen, as if by talking about what was coming, he had broken some compact between them.

He took her hand. "You know what the Books are doing. The fact that the magic is in me instead of in you and your brother and sister hasn't changed what's happening to the world. You saw the birds. The animals. They sense it too. Things are coming apart."

"Hugo Algernon said that maybe there's a way—"

"There isn't. Remember I said that your parents had found out the end of the prophecy?"

Kate looked up; she couldn't help herself.

"I told you in the Garden, I learned about it when I took on Michael's spirit. The prophecy says that three will become one. Three Books in one; three Keepers in one. And it says the Final Keeper must die to heal the world. Otherwise . . ."

"Otherwise what?!" Kate said furiously. "The world's going to end?! I don't believe it! And I don't care! It's not fair! Not after everything!" She stood, flinging her bowl across the cabin. "I don't care! I can't—I can't . . ."

But she couldn't even finish her statement.

Kate let him hold her then, and time passed. All day, she'd tried not to think about the power of the Books being inside him, and how that included the power of the *Reckoning*. Did that mean all he had to do was wish himself dead, simply think it, and it would be so? She hated the idea of him having that power.

"Kate . . ."

She sat up, turning to face him. He was staring at her intently.

"Do you understand what Emma did in the world of the dead?"

"She . . . gave the dead back their memories."

"But do you understand what that means? Now, when someone dies, they carry with them all the love they had in life. Forever. It's a great, great thing."

"Why're you telling me this?"

"Because it's important you know it. What happened to your locket?"

"The chain broke. But—"

"Show me."

She paused just a second, then reached into her pocket and pulled out the locket and chain. Rafe pressed the broken links between his fingers, and when he opened them, the chain was whole again. He slipped it over her head, and she felt the familiar weight settle on her chest.

"Do something for me," he said.

"Anything."

"That locket, it always made you think of your mother, the promise you made?"

"Yes."

"And you kept your promise. Your brother and sister are safe with your parents. So maybe now, when you wear it, you can think of me."

Kate turned away. Tears ran down her cheeks and fell into her lap.

He took her hand. "Promise me."

And she nodded and said, quietly, "Yes, I promise." Then she gripped his hand with all her strength and looked at him, her vision blurry with tears. "Isn't there anything I can do? There has to be something!"

"There is," he said. "You can live."

All day, there had not been a cloud in the sky, and so when the storm came, it came without warning. Rain beat against the side of the cabin, the windows and doors shuddered in the gale, the wind screamed down the chimney and scattered ashes across the room. It had seemed to Kate that this was the same storm that had been over Loris the night before, that the storm had somehow followed them here.

She'd resolved not to fall asleep; she would stay awake as long as she had to, she would not lose a single moment, and she wondered later if Rafe had done something to make her sleep, or if the days of struggle and strain had finally caught up to her. She had a vague memory of being carried to bed.

When she woke, the cabin was filled with sunlight, the storm had ended, and all was still and peaceful. She looked at Rafe beside her, then rose and walked outside, glancing on her way at the black leather book on the table.

She sat down on the bench. The morning was cool, and she closed her eyes and listened to the birds, all across the mountainside, calling the new day.

It had been his choice in the end; the power had been his, and he'd used it to save them all, to save her. She tried to keep that thought in mind.

But inside her was an emptiness she had never imagined possible.

She was not surprised when, a while later, she heard noises and looked to see Michael and Emma emerging from the trees. She stayed where she was, waiting till they got to the cabin and she could take them inside and show them where Rafe's body lay.

Kate chose to bury Rafe close by the cabin, in sight of the bench where they had sat on that last day and watched the sun sink below the mountains.

And she stayed with him all night in Gabriel's village while Granny Peet prepared his body for burial, cleaning his hands and face, combing his hair, whispering blessings. It had been Granny Peet, of course, who had sensed her and Rafe's presence at the cabin and spread the word that had drawn the others. In the end, Kate was glad that she was not alone, and Emma, Michael, her mother and father, they all took turns sitting with her throughout the night. In the morning, with the help of Robbie McLaur and his dwarves, they carried Rafe back up the mountain to where the grave had already been dug. The only ones in attendance were Kate and her family, Granny Peet, Hugo Algernon, King Robbie and his dwarves, and Princess Wilamena, who was dressed almost demurely in black silk.

Once he was laid in his coffin, Kate placed the *Reckoning* on Rafe's chest, beneath his folded hands. Then she stepped back as the lid was settled into place and the nails hammered home. With her mother and Emma beside her, she watched as the coffin was lowered into the ground.

They spent that night as well in Gabriel's village, eating dinner in the tribe's main building. Michael knew many of the men to nod to, having fought alongside them during the battle. They slept—though Kate did not sleep—in a cabin given over to their family, and though no one said anything directly, it felt strange to Kate, and she knew it must've been strange for Michael and Emma, to be spending the night under the same roof as two adults they scarcely knew, even if they were their mother and father. But her mother seemed to sense it, for as she kissed her good night, she whispered:

"I'm sorry about this. It will get better."

"What will?" Kate asked.

"Everything."

The next day, Hugo Algernon left, as did Wilamena, though she promised to return as soon as possible, and so there was only Kate, her family, Granny Peet, and King Robbie, who came dressed in his finest armor, and a few attendant dwarves when they climbed the mountain to bury Gabriel in the grave that had been dug alongside Rafe's.

Gabriel's body had been recovered from the village on the Arabian Peninsula, and Emma placed his sword, brought from the

Garden on Loris, in the coffin beside him. After the coffin was lowered into the ground, Granny Peet asked Emma if there was anything she wanted to say.

"No," Emma said, "I already told him."

And King Robbie himself filled in the grave, and it was done.

Their parents and Granny Peet and the dwarf king all moved off, and Kate stood with her brother and sister beside the pair of fresh graves, and though none of them spoke, Kate thought—and she imagined Michael and Emma thinking the same—of how both Gabriel and Rafe had died for them, and that was a thing impossible to repay.

That afternoon, after saying goodbye to Granny Peet and thanking her for everything, they followed Robbie McLaur over the mountains to the house in Cambridge Falls, the house where they had first found the *Atlas*, where they had met Dr. Pym. It was perhaps a strange place to return to, but none of them, neither the children nor their parents, were quite ready to reenter the real world.

Once in sight of the house, the dwarf king said his farewells, hugging each of the children and kissing them on both cheeks, assuring them they would always be welcome in his kingdom and inviting them to return as often as they liked and more often still. Then, shaking hands with their father and bowing to their mother, he walked off into the woods and was swallowed by the gathering dark.

Kate, Emma, Michael, and their parents walked on to the house, where they found Abraham, the old caretaker, and Miss Sallow, the cook, waiting for them on the front steps. After having been hugged and exclaimed over by Abraham and nodded curtly to by Miss Sallow, who had to rub her eyes with her apron because "the blasted stove's so smoky," though she was outside at the time and nowhere near the stove, the children and their parents were brought inside, where they found a hot and bountiful dinner already waiting.

It was the first time they had felt truly alone as a family, and as such, it was a vision of the future. Their parents talked nervously throughout the meal, as if trying to fill the silences, but in truth, the children hardly noticed the awkwardness. Being in the house and eating Miss Sallow's food, they had realized how utterly, deeply, bone-crushingly tired they were. They found they could hardly chew, and soon they were being led upstairs, almost dropping with fatigue, to their old room, which Abraham had made up hours before.

The children and their parents stayed in the house for more than two weeks, eating, resting, and getting used to the idea of being a family. At first, it was strange for Kate to no longer be the one responsible for her brother's and sister's safety and well-being; but she couldn't deny that every day she felt lighter, as if she'd set aside a little more of the weight she'd carried for ten years. She sensed, however, that the day would come when she would miss the weight and wish it back.

Beyond that, those first days were trying for everyone. For as much as the children had yearned to be reunited with their parents, and as much as Richard and Clare had yearned for and missed Kate and Michael and Emma, no one could pretend that the years apart had never happened. They had to get to know each other, and that would take time.

It was easier at meals, which Kate partly attributed to Miss

Sallow's cooking, which was as mouthwateringly delicious and nourishing as always, so much so that Kate wondered if the woman wasn't just a little bit of a witch. But they couldn't always be at meals, and after all the years of looking forward to being together, it was hard when things weren't immediately perfect.

"It's okay," Clare assured Kate. Not surprisingly, Kate and her mother found their footing first, and soon the two of them were taking walks in the woods around the house. "Your father and I understand. It's going to take time."

It was on one of their walks that Clare told Kate how this was not her and Richard's first visit to Cambridge Falls. They had been there once before.

"It was just after your adventure here, though before any of you were born. Stanislaus had told us who you were destined to be, what you would do. Imagine not having any children, and then hearing that you're going to have three, and they're going to be at the heart of this ancient prophecy. We talked him into bringing us here. And we saw them, all the children you'd saved. We were so proud of you, and you hadn't even been born yet. That day, Richard and I both knew that whatever life had in store for you, we had to trust that you would be strong, you would stand by each other, and you would survive. And you have."

It was also during one of their walks that her mother pointed out the locket Kate was wearing, the one she'd given her the night they'd been separated.

"You held on to it all this time."

"Yes."

"I'm glad. I've always imagined you wearing it."

"I'm going to keep wearing it," Kate said, and her hand went to it, clutching it, as if her heart lived not in her chest, but in the small, golden chamber.

And if her mother sensed there was something Kate wasn't telling her, she let it be.

Soon enough too, Michael and their father had begun to find their way toward each other. It started when Michael apologized about losing his *Dwarf Omnibus*, and his father had told him not to worry; in fact, he'd heard that G. G. Greenleaf had put out a new edition, and Robbie McLaur had promised to send him one, and he and Michael could read it together. From there, they seemed to be talking about dwarves whenever Kate saw them, and their comfort with each other, their sense of being two kindred souls, only increased. Though once, Kate heard Michael admonishing his father, telling him, "Well, the truth is that elves aren't silly at all. It's a common enough misconception, but you should try and get past it. It's very small-minded."

Then one day, in the middle of the second week, Kate saw Michael entering the house and his eyes were red and swollen.

She asked if something had happened.

"Oh," he said, pulling out his handkerchief and blowing his nose with a loud honk, while making an offhand comment about summer allergies (though it was nearly autumn), "Wilamena was just here. She couldn't stay. Her people are looking for a new home. Now that the *Chronicle*'s gone, their valley in Antarctica has frozen over, and with the portal to the world of the dead closed, there's kind of no reason to be there. They're thinking about moving to the magical quarter of Paris, but apparently, it's really expensive."

"Uh-huh."

"And we decided, you know, after talking it over, that we

would just be friends. I mean, I'm probably going to be really busy with school soon, and it turns out her dad's retiring as king, something about the stress being bad for his hair, so she'll have to take over. . . . It was a mutual decision, of course."

"I guess it's for the best," Kate said. But she hugged him tightly, and he let her, while muttering something about wartime romances burning brightly but not long.

It was Emma who had the hardest time with their parents. Following that first morning after the battle, when Emma had seen her mother and hugged her and cried, she had pulled back. It was almost, Kate thought, as if Emma wasn't convinced that her parents were there to stay, as if she thought that she and Kate and Michael might wake up one day and find their parents gone, and the three of them on their way to the next orphanage. She even avoided calling them *Mom* and *Dad*, referring to them instead, when she was alone with Kate and Michael, as *Him* and *Her*.

Her mother insisted that she and their father understood. "It'll take time; that's all. We've just got to prove to her we're not going anywhere."

They were more concerned about what else might be weighing on Emma, the ordeals and trials she had gone through, which she refused to discuss.

"We're not saying she has to open up to us," Richard said. "It could be to you or Michael. It would just help her to talk."

But Kate, who knew her sister, insisted that no one pressure her. "She's been through a lot. She lost her best friend. She'll tell her story when she's ready."

The truth was, Kate herself was worried. Every day, she waited for Emma to come to her, to tell her all that had happened, and every night they went to bed, and Emma turned her back to Kate and curled away, as if closing herself around her grief.

Then, a few days after Wilamena's visit, as they were all sitting down to dinner, their mother set aside her knife and fork, reached for their father's hand, and said:

"It's been wonderful being here. Abraham and Miss Sallow have been very kind—"

"Well," Richard said, "Abraham has."

Clare gave their father a look, then went on. "But we've been talking, and maybe it's time we thought about going home."

"Home," Emma said. "Home, like where?"

"Home," their father said. "Our home. Your home."

Kate wondered what reaction their parents had expected. Probably not total, stunned silence. But the fact was neither Emma nor even Michael—they'd both been too young—had ever really thought of themselves as having a home. Their only memories of the places they'd lived had been years of being bounced from one orphanage to another. And the news that they did have a home waiting for them, and they would be returning to it soon, was almost too large and strange a concept to process.

"Okay," Kate said, answering for all of them.

"Yeah," Michael said.

Emma said nothing. But the next morning, she woke Kate up and said she wanted to go back to Gabriel's cabin, just the three of them, to say goodbye.

When asked, Abraham said he knew the way and could draw them a map, which was fortunate, as none of the children had paid much attention when walking with King Robbie. Abraham also said that if they left after breakfast, they could be back before dark, and Miss Sallow agreed to pack them lunch, though she said that on such short notice there was no way she could prepare foie gras pastries or truffle galettes, so their Highnesses might as well chop off her head now, shoot fireworks at it, and be done.

"Whatever you make will be fine," Kate told her.

"You're sure this is okay? I mean, it's safe?" their mother asked when Kate explained their plans. But she immediately corrected herself. "What am I saying? Everything you all have been through—you can take a walk in the woods alone. Just, now that we have you back, I guess I'm feeling protective."

"We'll be fine," Kate said.

So the following day, after a breakfast of poached eggs, lemon curd pancakes, bacon as thick as sausage, and crispy, buttery potatoes, and after Michael rechecked his map several times with Abraham and double- and triple-checked his equipment (which was more suited to a three-week journey than a daylong hike), they set off.

As soon as they began walking—it was a cool, early-fall morning, the air was clean, the pine needles and earth slightly damp from a drizzle the night before—Kate knew that this was a good thing they were doing, that it was important and necessary, to be out and alone, the three of them, in the place where it all began. And more than that, it was just good to be tramping through the forest; magic or not, Kate could feel something working on her, on all of them.

The children walked in silence, and there was no sound but the calls and whistles of birds, the skittering of squirrels along branches, and the muffled thuds of their own feet. Michael diligently made corrections to the map that Abraham had drawn so that he could show the caretaker his mistakes when they returned. "He'll appreciate it," he assured his sisters. After walking for an hour, they stopped on a ledge that looked out over the mountains. They'd gotten hot and stuffed their sweaters into their packs, and they sat there in the sun, drinking water and eating apples.

And it was then that Emma began telling her story.

She began simply, with no preamble or warning, describing what it had been like to arrive in the world of the dead—the hours, or what had felt like hours, of hiking through the mist, her coming upon the walkers. She told them how she'd met Dr. Pym but he hadn't remembered her, how they'd traveled across a sea and then through the burning, wasted landscape; she told about the *carriadin* and how they'd guarded the book for thousands of years, and how the first time she'd touched it she'd been overwhelmed by the voices of the dead. She told about being a prisoner and discovering how the Dire Magnus had been consuming the souls of the dead, about encountering the Countess, her body twisted and mangled, and how the witch had helped her; she told how the *necromatus* had pinned her hand onto the book with Michael's knife, bonding her spirit to the magic—

(Kate and Michael both noticed her unconsciously rubbing the scar on her palm as she said this.)

—and she told them about Gabriel appearing and how it had saved her, how she'd given the dead back their memories with the question she'd posed and how that question would judge the dead from now till the end of time. She told them how she and Gabriel and Dr. Pym had gone to the last portal, and how both of them had chosen to stay in that world rather than let Michael bring them back, and how she'd said goodbye to Gabriel, standing there on the cliff, and how he'd promised that he would never forget her.

"Anyway," she said, after she had been silent for a moment, "that's what happened. And now he's gone."

When Kate reached for her sister's hand, Emma didn't pull away.

Then Michael said, "So the dead will remember us? Dr. Pym and Wallace and Gabriel, they'll remember us?"

"Yes," Emma said.

Kate felt her heart tighten in her chest, and her hand went to her locket. She saw Emma looking up at her.

"I'm okay." Then she said, "We all are, aren't we?"

And Emma, squeezing her sister's hand, said, "Yes, we are."

Then they lifted their packs and continued on.

The sun was not quite at the top of the sky when they came around a bend in the path, and there, tucked into the shoulder of the mountain, was Gabriel's cabin. They ate on the small bench beside the front door, and though Miss Sallow's lunch was no doubt exquisite, afterward none of them could quite remember what it had been. Then they walked over to the two markers, and already the ground had been tamped down and trodden on by animals and looked little different from the rest of the mountainside, which was as it should be, the children felt.

Kate and Michael left Emma alone to say goodbye to Gabriel, while they went and loaded their packs. Emma came back several minutes later, wiping her eyes, and, knowing it was her turn, Kate walked over to the graves. She stared down at the patch of earth that held Rafe's body while her fingers worried the golden locket. She tried to think of what to say, but none of it sounded right. Finally, she knelt, placed her hand on the still-damp ground, whispered, "I love you," and walked away.

Michael and Emma had already shouldered their packs, and Michael glanced at her, questioning, and she nodded, not yet trusting herself to speak.

"We'd better get going," Emma said. "Mom and Dad will worry if we're not back by dark."

Kate and her brother both stopped what they were doing and looked at her. Emma smiled awkwardly.

"I know. Feels weird calling them that. And weird knowing that there're people out there who worry about you. But I guess it's good." She was silent then, and Kate and Michael waited, knowing she wasn't done.

Finally, she said, "I thought giving the dead back their memories would make everything better. But really, it doesn't change anything. At least not while you're alive. The people you love are still going to die. You're still going to lose them."

Kate watched Emma closely, seeing shades of the sister she'd known, brave, reckless, thoughtless, and this new person who'd grown up in her place, who was working through what she was feeling, piece by piece.

"Then I realized, maybe that's okay, maybe it's even okay loving someone knowing it's going to end, that either you're going to die or they're going to die, or you'll move away and never see them again, because that's what it means to be alive. That's the whole point of life. To love someone." And she looked up at her brother and sister, her eyes wide and shining with tears. "Don't you think?"

And Kate took her hand and said, "Yes. I do."

The End

ACKNOWLEDGMENTS

The Books of Beginning would not have been written without the support, generosity, and intelligence of literally hordes of people. In particular, I would like to thank:

The friends who listened to me talk about the books over the years, read drafts, gave feedback, and did not strangle me, specifically, Kimberly Cutter, Bob DeLaurentis, Nate DiMeo, Leila Gerstein, J. J. Philbin, and Derek Simonds.

Everyone at Random House who has gotten behind this series to such an amazing degree that I frequently think they must have me confused with some other writer and are simply too polite to correct the mistake: Markus Dohle, for his boundless enthusiasm; Chip Gibson, who is everything a writer hopes for in a publisher, but funnier; Barbara Marcus, who had the impossible job of taking over from Chip and then did the impossible; John Adamo, Rachel Feld, and Sonia Nash, for their inspired marketing of the books; Joan DeMayo and her team, who barnstormed the country on the novels' behalf; Felicia Frazier, who helped carry *The Black Reckoning* into the world; Isabel Warren-Lynch and the art department, for putting so much effort and creativity into making such beautiful books; Grady McFerrin and Nicolas Delort, for their intricate, exquisite drawings; Jon Foster, for his gorgeous and evocative covers; in the publicity department, Dominique Cimina, Noreen Herits, and especially Casey Lloyd, the books' indefatigable champion, who came with me on tour and listened to me give the same spiel again and again and always laughed at my jokes; Adrienne Waintraub and Tracy Lerner, who did the essential job of putting the books in the hands of teachers and librarians; Kelly Delaney, for reading these books countless times and always with fresh eyes; Tim Terhune, in production; and finally, Artie Bennett, Janet Renard, Nancy Elgin, Amy Schroeder, and Karen Taschek, for their diligent copyediting, which taught me how much I still have to learn about the English language and whose work made the books better than they had any right to be.

At Writers House: Cecilia de la Campa and Angharad Kowal, for their help with the foreign sales of the books; and Katie Zanecchia and Joe Volpe, for their good cheer and hard work over the years.

Kassie Evashevski, Julien Thuan, and Matt Rice at UTA, for their great enthusiasm and—still ongoing—support.

Karl Austen, who keeps me out of trouble.

Philip Pullman. Honestly, never met the man, but I wouldn't have written these books if it hadn't been for him. So, wherever you are, Mr. Pullman, thank you.

The many foreign publishers who believed in these books and carried them away to far-off lands to readers I could never have imagined I would reach. Indeed, I wish it were possible for me to name and thank everyone at all the different publishing houses who got behind these books with such passion. Whatever trust I gave them, they repaid—both collectively and as individuals—many times over.

And, lastly, my greatest debts.

Nancy Hinkel and Judith Haut. As much as anything, I'm grateful for the people these books have brought into my life, and Nancy and Judith, completely separate from their tireless support during the writing of this trilogy, long ago crossed the line from being publishers to being friends. They're stuck with me now. Ha.

My agent, Simon Lipskar. There are a handful of people who I can absolutely say have changed my life, and he is one. Whatever notice the books received was due to his early championing. He put himself on the line, and I owe him more than I can say.

My editor, Michelle Frey. There is no amount of praise or thanks I could heap upon her head that would do justice to all she's done. Over the past four years, she has never once flagged in her efforts to make these books as good as they could be or ceased to impress me with her insights into story and character, her patience, and her faith. She made me into a better writer, and these books are what they are because of her.

Finally, my family: my sisters, who taught me how siblings can squabble twenty-three hours a day and still love each other; my parents, for their endless encouragement and stubborn refusal to tell a child that being a writer was an unsound life plan; my sons, Dashiell and Turner, who have made my world a bigger place; and Arianne, my wife, first reader, and best friend, for everything, thank you.